FOR THE LOVE OF A CHILD

"Is revenge as sweet as you'd thought?" she asked bitterly.

"No," he said, his mouth slanted upward in self-mockery. "For three years I sustained my fury against you, only to find that things are not quite what I'd thought them to be. You gave Gideon a home when he needed one. You loved him."

"I still love him. I will always love him."

He looked at her finally, his eyes dark with a demand that held her gaze to his.

"I don't want to frighten Gideon. I do want what's best for him." He paused, and an ironic smile twisted his lips. "Perhaps I've decided that he needs a mother more than he needs a father." Hawk's gaze slid back to the clump of trees at the side of the road. "I just want to see him."

Jane willed him to look at her, so she could see the truth or lie in those changeable eyes. But he kept his gaze averted, as if not wanting to see the answer on her face. "If you intend to leave him," she challenged, "why not just go?"

Jane closed her eyes again, hoping that shutting out the sight of Hawk's face might help her think. She didn't dare believe him. He was a traitor and a criminal. For three long years he had plotted to retrieve his son. . . . Too much about Matthew Hawkins, ex–Lord Chester, didn't make sense. A callous criminal, he had cared for her with the gentleness of a . . . a—she shied away from *lover* and substituted *husband* instead. . . .

CACTUS BLOSSOM

HALFWAY TO PARADISE

EMILY BRADSHAW

A DELL BOOK

Published by
Dell Publishing
a division of
Bantam Doubleday Dell Publishing Group, Inc.
1540 Broadway
New York, New York 10036

ISBN: 0-440-21299-5

Printed in the United States of America

Published simultaneously in Canada

October 1993

10 9 8 7 6 5 4 3 2 1

RAD

1

May 1655, London

"It is wicked to buy a child!" Margaret Stratford snapped.

Jane Stratford Alexander winced at her grandmother's tone, but her face retained its cool composure. "My mind is quite made up, Grandmother. I do respect your opinion, but in this case I must follow my own heart."

"Better to follow your reason than your heart," Margaret advised sourly.

Jane sighed and resumed pacing the length of Margaret's bedchamber. Her steps were graceful and measured. Her plain brown wool overskirt, hitched back and fastened to reveal an unadorned taffeta underskirt of the same shade, swished sedately around her ankles. Her fingers moved restlessly, pressing together as if in prayer, then lacing and unlacing uneasily.

"You'll regret this!" Margaret growled. "Those wicked servants! Seeking to sell their master's brat! And Charity! Our own housekeeper! You should have dismissed that girl the moment she came to you with such an evil scheme! To bring a royalist brat into a good Puritan household! What madness! The father is a debauched, traitorous sinner, and the child will be of the same stamp."

Jane paced the bare floorboards from the bed to the wardrobe and back before she answered. Her black-garbed grandmother glared at her like a judgmental archangel from her seat in the room's one straight-backed wooden chair. No cushions or upholstery for Margaret Stratford. Her spine was as rigid as the back of the chair. The lines of her face were set in obdurate righteous certainty.

"You haven't enough knowledge of Lord Chester to judge him so," Jane stated calmly.

"Was he not condemned for treason, for rising up and breaking our precious peace in favor of that son of Satan, Charles Stuart?"

With a hint of a smile Jane shook her head. "You cannot condemn the child because of his father's politics. He is but five years old—almost a blank tablet, a piece of unformed clay waiting to be molded."

"Will you stop that pacing, girl! You are making my old head spin with all that back and forth!" Margaret fixed her granddaughter with a shrewd look as Jane obediently stopped and tried to contain her restlessness in one spot. "You know that however you mold the child, he still will not be *your* son."

Jane looked down at the floor.

Margaret's voice softened just a bit. "In all other things you are such a good girl, Jane. Why can't you accept God's decree that you are not to be a mother? Three years ago He took your son from you and left you barren—a punishment for some wickedness in your youth, no doubt. As a God-fearing Christian you must meekly accept His judgment, not fight against it."

"My son died of pneumonia, not God's decree," Jane asserted in a level voice. "And it was his difficult birth that left me barren, not the Lord's judgment. God would not be so cruel."

"There is no cruelty about it!" Margaret declared with certainty. "We bring our punishments down upon ourselves."

"Then perhaps we make our own good fortune as well. And this child is my good fortune."

"Pah!"

Jane took a deep breath. She had come to her grandmother's chamber seeking comfort. She should have known that she would receive recriminations instead of solace. But Margaret's vitriol had calmed rather than upset her. The old lady's scoffings and condemnations only served to remind Jane of all the good reasons for her to take this unfortunate child. In defending against her grandmother's scorn she defended also against her own doubts. Her hands stopped their nervous wringing as she gathered her usual cool demeanor about her like a soft cloak.

"This thing that we do is not evil, Grandmother," Jane concluded softly. "Rather it is a good deed."

"Pah! There's no *we* about this! Leave me out of it! If your good husband were here right now, he would set you back on the right path, you can be sure of that!"

"But he's not," Jane said with a sad little smile. "And I must find my own way." She silently repeated her oft-said prayer that Colonel Thaddeus Alexander was safely in heaven with the infant son he'd never been privileged to see in life. Her husband had been killed fighting the Scots before little Joshua was even born.

A loud rap upon the chamber door interrupted Margaret's skeptical harrumph.

"Yes!" the old lady snapped. "What is it?"

The door opened and in walked plump little Charity,

their housekeeper. She ignored Margaret's glare, immune through long familiarity, and announced the arrival of visitors.

"They're in the parlor, mistress," she said to Jane.

If the girl's smirk was a bit self-satisfied, Jane readily forgave her, for Charity had given her this second chance at motherhood. Servant gossip at the market had brought Charity the information that the traitorous Lord Chester, having been stripped of property and titles and condemned to slavery in the Caribbean colonies, had a son who was now without inheritance or support. The faithful servants of the unfortunate condemned man were searching out a home for the youngster—for a small pittance of a fee. The fee, Jane discovered when she investigated, was not so small. But she would have given more, if necessary, to have a child once again.

Of course, such dealing with children was flagrantly illegal. But when Charity had brought her the news that the child needed a home, Jane had tossed caution aside. Some things were beyond man's law, and she couldn't but think that in some way God had sent this youngster in recompense for the son who had died.

"Tell our guests . . ." Jane bit her lip as a new fit of nervousness made her voice tremble. "Tell our guests that I'll be right down."

"Evil creature!" Margaret muttered as the housekeeper closed the door behind her. "She shows no respect to God or her betters. You should either dismiss her or see to the improvement of her soul."

"Charity is a good woman at heart." Jane moved to the window and looked at her reflection in the glass. Her grandmother would tolerate no mirrors in the house—they were mere tools of vanity. The windowpane was a poor substitute.

"A good woman, indeed!" Margaret scoffed. "Is it innocence or merely witlessness that makes you not see the evil in others, Jane?" She snorted in disgust. "Just as you cannot comprehend the evil of the deed you are about to do!"

Jane refused to let her grandmother's barbs deflate the bubble of happiness that swelled her heart. She tucked back an errant lock of pale blond hair that had escaped her linen coif. Even in the distorted windowpane reflection she could see the sparkle of her gray eyes and the high color of her cheeks. She looked happier and younger than a twenty-two-year-old widow ought.

In an abundance of exhilaration, Jane stooped to give Margaret a kiss on her seamed cheek before she left the room. "Everything will be all right, Grandmother. Wait and see."

"Fool!" Margaret spat out as Jane quietly closed the door behind her.

The boy was big for his age, Jane mused. Still, he seemed swallowed by the dusky gloom of the parlor—a room Jane almost never used. The child's bright clothing was similar to what a well-dressed gentleman of fashion might wear. His loose-sleeved maroon velvet doublet ended above his waistline to reveal the richness of a silk, lace-cuffed shirt beneath. Wide breeches, the same rich fabric as the doublet, were fastened at his knees with beribboned garters. A stiff standing collar nudged his small chin and pushed aside the black curls that reached to his shoulders. All in all, his costume was a miniature of adult high-fashion wear, and it stood out in Jane's drab parlor like a beacon on a gloomy night.

Standing beside the boy was a ponderous woman of middle years who held the child's hand in hers. In her other hand she carried a satchel. Jane assumed she was the boy's nurse, but her richly embroidered silk gown more befitted a fashionable lady than a servant.

"Good afternoon," Jane said in quiet greeting.

The boy's grip tightened on the woman's hand.

"Good day." The woman's tone was chilly. Her eyes swept contemptuously over Jane's plain gown with its décolletage—modest in itself—completely covered by a white linen gorget fastened at the neck without even the decoration of a broach or pin. "You are the Widow Alexander?"

"Yes," Jane answered. "And you are?"

"I am . . . the boy's nurse."

Jane didn't blame the woman for not wanting to give her name. She decided not to press her. "You received what I sent?"

The nurse nodded a curt affirmative. Jane had insisted on sending the "pittance of a fee" before the boy was brought, in spite of the danger of being cheated. To have the child witness the exchange of money for his guardianship would be unthinkable.

"I am an honest woman," the nurse declared. "I keep my bargains. Another might've bolted, and you'd not have seen hide nor hair of the boy. But I'm one who sticks to her word."

Jane smiled patiently. "So I see. Won't you sit down?"

"It's a fine house you have here," the woman commented as she set down the satchel and plumped her hefty body into Colonel Alexander's favorite chair beside the fireplace, which was as cold as the rest of the parlor. The child followed her. As the nurse let go of the boy's hand he clutched at her skirt. "Is the house yours?" she asked.

"It was my husband's," Jane answered. "When he died, the Lord Protector Cromwell gave it to me outright—in gratitude for my husband's faithful service in the army. He sees that we are provided for."

The woman's lip curled subtly at the mention of Cromwell's name. "If I didn't think the boy would be provided for, I wouldn't let you have him no matter how much you offered."

"Of course not," Jane agreed.

"I am not a heartless jade, or the sort in Southwark that sells children for evil purposes."

"I wouldn't think it."

"The boy is like my own son, and it breaks my heart to let him go. I've had the care of him since his lady mother died from a bad stomach when the lad were but two."

"This must be very hard for you," Jane said sympathetically, though the woman's eyes, she thought, gleamed with more avarice than with pain.

"I must do what's best for the child," the nurse said with a sniff. "His father won't be coming back, poor soul. No man comes back from those wretched colonies in the West Indies. Who's to pay for the boy's keep, or pay off the staff who've served so well all these years? We must fend for ourselves, now that the poor earl is gone."

The nurse's lament was beginning to try Jane's patience. From the richness of the woman's attire, Jane concluded that the nurse, at least, had done quite well in fending for herself, probably with the money she had gotten from Jane for the boy.

"I think we should conclude this as quickly as possible," Jane suggested. "For the child's sake."

The poor boy looked more frightened by the moment, regarding Jane through eyes that were wide and glistening with bravely unshed tears. His face was pale as a milky opal set against the jeweled colors of his clothing. His small mouth, still the sweet cupid's bow of childhood, alternately pressed tight with defiance and trembled with a fear that tugged at Jane's heart. What the child must have suffered these last weeks since his father's arrest and trial!

"Well," the nurse said with a sigh, "I suppose you'll give the boy better than he could've expected elsewhere." She rose ponderously from the chair and picked up the satchel at her side. "I've brought a few of his things. And several of his father's books. The earl worked with the boy on his reading every evening. I thought the child would like to have a book or two from the library. The holier-than-thous who've come to inventory the earl's property will just throw them in the fire." She stuck out her chin belligerently, as if daring Jane to take offense. "Will you let the lad keep them?"

Jane opened the satchel. The child's stolen inheritance from his father consisted of three volumes of Shakespeare, one each of Jonson and Marlowe, a treatise on mathematics—written in French—and a Bible. Strange that such a man as the traitorous earl should have a Bible, and one that was every bit as worn as the other volumes.

What kind of man was the Earl of Chester? Did he ache at losing his son? Did it hurt him more to lose his child than his freedom and, most probably, his life?

Jane remembered how she had felt when her son died. She had not wanted to live, the pain was so great. How much worse the earl must feel, torn from his son's side, not knowing the boy's fate. At least she had the comfort of knowing her Joshua was safe in God's arms.

"I'll let him keep them," Jane promised.

The nurse's face softened a bit. "It's a relief, Mistress

Alexander, that you're not as narrow as some others. The earl used to say, he did, that the evil wasn't in the books, it was in the minds of them what reads them. He said it'd do most Puritans a world of good to spend an evening or two at a play. Not that I can read, and I never saw a play even before Cromwell and his likes closed all the playhouses, but I've a notion Lord Chester was right. He usually was, poor man."

"I'm sure he was a fine man," Jane said, though she wasn't sure at all. "I'll take good care of his son."

"See that you do, mistress." The nurse pulled her young charge from behind her skirt. As gently as possible she drew him forward and placed his moist little hand in Jane's. "This is your home now, Master Gideon. You be a good boy for Mistress Alexander, and she'll treat you right."

The boy looked up at Jane in wide-eyed bewilderment but didn't try to withdraw his hand.

"I'll be going now."

Neither the boy nor the woman who held his hand noticed as the nurse left the parlor, crossed the entrance hall, and let herself out the front door. Not until a loud harrumph sounded from the staircase did Jane's loving gaze leave the child's face. She turned at the harsh noise and saw her grandmother standing in a regal pose halfway down the staircase.

"His name is Gideon," Jane said happily.

"His name is Trouble!" Margaret replied.

Four days later Jane stood in the entry of her house and fastened a chaperon under her chin. The linen hood concealed the close-fitting coif that hid her hair. It also sheltered much of her face from casual view, making her feel a little safer in the mission she was about to undertake—not much safer, but a little. The rest of her costume, also, Jane had chosen to boost her confidence, discarding her sober browns and grays for an un-Puritan-like gown of dark green moiré that her husband had given her during the first year of their marriage. Colonel Alexander had been strict in his religion, but he occasionally had indulged his eye for beauty. The gown was modest enough, with a stiffly boned bodice, deep vee waistline, and full skirt pulled back to reveal an underskirt decorated with a demure ruffle of lace. A hint of lace also peeked from under elbow-length sleeves and at the top edge of the chemise that gathered above the chaste décolletage. A plain stomacher in contrasting lighter green completed the costume.

All in all the gown was very conservative, though grander than her usual mode of dress. It made Jane feel like someone to be reckoned with, someone not lightly to be gainsaid. Right at this moment she needed every morale boost possible.

Margaret, dressed as usual in severe black wool with a starched coif hiding the thin strands of her hair, came out from the parlor into the entrance hall. She folded her arms across her chest. "The Devil has gotten into your brain, girl. This is indecent madness, and you'll be heartily sorry you didn't listen to me."

Jane sighed and flicked a speck of lint from her cloak. "You're probably right, Grandmother. But I'd never forgive myself if I didn't take this chance to ease a condemned man's lot."

"The condemned are damned through their own foul deeds. They deserve no easing of their just punishment."

Jane merely shook her head, unwilling to argue further. She had learned long ago that debates with her grandmother were useless. Margaret always won, by virtue of determination if not logic. "Giddy is napping in the nursery," she said. "If he wakes, have Charity take him out to the carriage house to see the new puppies that Todd's hound birthed last week. When I return, I'll take him to be fitted for a new suit of clothes."

Margaret's sniff plainly conveyed the old lady's doubt of Jane's safe return.

As much as she dreaded her errand, Jane was glad to leave Margaret's frowns behind her. She seated herself in her waiting coach and signaled Todd, who served the household as both gardener and groom, that she was ready. As they jounced along the muddy streets, she ducked her head and held a scented handkerchief to her nose. Her house on Great Queen Street was in the West End, away from the worst of London's odors. Westerly breezes usually carried the stench to the east. But the nearer one drew to the City, the worse the smell.

They turned onto Fleet Street and headed east. Ahead Jane could see the City wall and the prominences of old St. Paul's Cathedral. Her nerves drew ever tighter as they neared her destination. Jane had spent hours trying to talk herself out of this loathsome chore, but the fate of Matthew Hawkins, Earl of Chester, weighed too heavily upon her conscience for her to deny her duty. She remembered too well the desolation of losing her own son. The traitorous Lord Chester no doubt deserved his sentence, but must he suffer also a desperate anxiety on behalf of his child? Christian duty demanded she find the courage to tell the condemned man of his son's happy fate. Even a scoundrel deserved a touch of mercy now and then.

The coach clattered across the bridge that spanned the narrow Fleet River. Just ahead loomed the old city wall, twenty vertical feet of rough Kentish ragstone. Fleet Street continued on through Ludgate into the City itself, but Todd clucked to the team and turned the horses to the left, where Fleet Prison stood between the wall and the river.

The horses slowed to a halt. The coach lurched as Todd clambered down from the box to open the door. "Mistress?" he inquired, his voice rough with concern as he handed her out.

Jane smiled reassuringly. "I'll be quite all right, Todd. You needn't come."

"I'll come, mistress. I wouldn't let ye go into that place alone."

For a moment Jane simply stood, wondering where she would find the courage to proceed. The building before them was old and seemed to stink of evil as well as other more tangible things that Jane didn't want to think about. Certainly not the worst of the City's prisons, Fleet traditionally housed scoundrels, traitors, and other poor wretches who were sent here by monarch's decree. Oliver Cromwell was not a monarch—at least not in name—but he had given the prison as much business as any crowned head who had preceded him.

" 'Ave ye changed your mind, mistress?" Todd asked in a hopeful voice.

"No," Jane said. "I just need a moment to . . . gather my wits."

A uniformed sentinel guarded the one iron door that pierced the blank and forbidding facade of the prison. He regarded them curiously.

Jane ventured a smile at her servant. "I suppose to progress we must go forward."

The guard at the entrance was unsympathetic to the reasons for Jane's visit but listened well enough to the coins

Todd slipped into his hand. Inside, the gaoler was persuaded to cooperate by a slightly larger amount. Jane wasn't surprised. Her husband had once told her that among the worldly gold was a shout where virtue and reason were but a mere whisper. She had thought the statement cynical; now she saw it was merely the truth.

The gaoler led them deep into the bowels of the prison, down damp, poorly lit passages that reeked of sewage and fetid decay. Jane pressed her handkerchief against her nose and mouth, wishing she had troubled to devise a veil of some sort for this venture. She wanted to hide from the filth and wretchedness that assailed her at every turn. The thought of being confined in such a place was too horrible to contemplate. The rebels who had staged April's uprising had been here for over a fortnight waiting to be transported to Barbados and sold as slaves. Jane thought they must envy their comrades who had been condemned to hang. Surely slavery, even death, would be preferable to lingering misery in this hell on earth.

The gaoler motioned Jane into a narrow passageway. On either side were doors of impenetrable iron broken only by narrow barred slits.

"This 'ere's the 'Ole," he informed her. "Yer man didn't 'ave the garnish to pay 'is way up to better lodgin's."

"He isn't *her* man, you rogue." Todd leapt readily to the defense of Jane's honor.

Jane turned her face away from the gaoler and pressed the handkerchief even more tightly against her face.

"Don't ye be wastin' yer sweet sympathy on these dogs, milady. From what I 'ear, once they get to where they're 'eaded, they'll wish they was back at the good ol' Fleet. Eh?" He beat on the iron door of one of the cells with his fist, setting up a pounding that echoed through the dank passage. "Roust yerselves, ye swine."

As the gaoler raised his lantern to light the interior of the cell, Jane glanced through the slit in the door. The cell was small and crowded. Prisoners leaned against the walls, which appeared moist and, in places, green and black with fungus. Others squatted or lay on the bare stone floor, crowded together like wretched livestock. All were thin and filthy, their hair matted, faces bearded, clothing tattered and caked with filth. Several had obvious running sores. One coughed without ceasing, his beard and shirt spattered with flecks of blood. A few faces turned toward the door at the guard's pounding. The eyes in those faces were dull and without hope, squinting against the unaccustomed light of the lantern. Jane felt as though she were gazing through a window into hell. The Hole was aptly named.

The gaoler rapped on the door again. " 'Awkins! Yer lordship!" he called scornfully. "Ye've got a visitor."

A man propped against a wall of the cell pushed himself off and slowly made his way through the clot of his fellow prisoners. Thin and filthy as the rest of the cell's inhabitants, he certainly looked like no earl Jane had ever seen.

" 'Ere 'e is, milady. Say yer piece quicklike. I ain't got all day to spend down 'ere."

Jane hesitated, then gathered her courage. "Lord Chester," she said in a soft, clear voice, though it was not strictly proper to address the man by a title of which he had been stripped. "My name is Mistress Jane Alexander. I am the widow of Colonel Thaddeus Alexander."

Disinterested eyes looked at her out of a haggard face. Black hair hung in lank, dirty strands to the man's shoulders. His mouth, too wide by far on his gaunt features, curved up contemptuously. Jane saw no resemblance to Gideon. No resemblance at all. The earl's stance, his smile, the set of shoulders that seemed too broad for the thin body—all combined to give him an insolent air in spite of his wretched circumstances.

That the earl appeared to be an unrepentant rogue did not change her duty. As a father he deserved to know that his son was well and cared for.

"Lord Chester," she repeated. "I bring news of your son Gideon."

The man's expression changed in a flash. All signs of insolence fell before a wave of concern that tightened his features into a mask of pain. "Where is my son?" he rasped.

"He's well." Jane felt a twinge of sympathy. "He's well and happy in my home. His nurse . . ." She hedged a bit. "His nurse knew that I lost my own son three years ago, and she offered me the chance to make a home for Gideon, since you could no longer provide one. I thought you should know that he is safe and loved. I assure you that I'll bring him up with the same care I would have given my own child."

Hawkins stared at her in a way that made her want to shiver. His eyes had snapped from lackluster hazel to a cold greenish gray. When he finally spoke, his voice was bitter. "The widow of an army officer. You're a Puritan."

"Yes, I am."

He grimaced. "My son to be brought up a Puritan? Now there's an evil twist of fate!"

Jane was disappointed that he couldn't think of his son's welfare before his own misfortunes. "It's not so grim a fate," she told him gently, and smiled as she thought of the boy. Already she loved Gideon. He brightened her barren days with light and filled her soul with a gladness she'd never thought to know again when her little Joshua died. "Gideon will be raised to love God, to use his mind as a tool of logic, to control his base instincts, and to be a responsible member of God's community of children. He'll be cherished as much as any child in the world."

Hawkins turned his head aside and spat. From the expression on his face Jane guessed that she was lucky he hadn't sent the spittle her way.

"You mean he'll be raised as a drab and joyless bigot who spends half his waking hours lamenting his own sins and the other half accusing others of sins he would like to commit."

Jane tried to be generous. "I think you speak from ignorance, Lord Chester."

"Do I now?" Cold green eyes fastened on her face as if they would analyze her every feature. "If you wish to perform a good work, Mistress Jane Alexander, then send the boy to my cousin Ormonde Desmain in France. He is my closest relative, and by rights he should have the raising of my son. Do that and you will have won the gratitude of a condemned man."

"I am not seeking your gratitude," Jane replied. "I want what is best for Gideon."

She also wanted what was best for herself, Jane had to admit. Even after just four days she could not give the child up, especially to a family in France, that nest of debauchery, who would no doubt raise him as a idolatrous papist. Unthinkable.

"Gideon will receive the very best that I can provide," she assured the earl. "I will cherish him above all else."

Hawkins's face twisted. "You deliver the final cruelty. Puritans are nothing if not thorough when they mete out punishment." He grabbed one of the bars in the window slit, his knuckles whitening, as though he would rip the door asunder to get to her. "First you take my property, my title, my freedom, condemn me to sweat out my life under an intolerable sun and an overseer's lash. And now you take my son to corrupt him into the very thing that struck his father down. *You* are the cruelest of all."

Jane retreated a step. "I did not come here as a cruelty." The menace emanating from the condemned man was a palpable force that seemed to press her back. She should have known better than to try to ease the lot of such a rogue.

Fighting to maintain her composure under the wretched criminal's stare, she turned away and spoke to the gaoler. "You said Lord Chester didn't have the money to buy his way to better quarters? Is such a thing possible in prison?"

The gaoler grinned. "Yes, m'lady. The court took all his property and his cash too, so's 'e 'as nuthin' left. But if 'e 'ad a bit, 'e could move up to the Knights' Ward, which isn't a palace, but it's better than this pit. A good bit o' coin would get 'im to the Master's Side, where 'e'd get a cell to 'imself and a bit o' wine to ease his stay."

Jane motioned to Todd, who handed her a purse. She counted out a goodly sum. "Would this be enough to get Lord Chester a cell in the Master's Side?"

The gaoler's eyes seemed to glow with the reflection of the coins in her hand. "It'd get 'im a cell, all right. No meals, but a cell."

Jane emptied the purse of its contents. "Enough for meals?"

"Aye." The gaoler nodded his head. "That'll fix 'im up."

"Then please transfer Lord Chester immediately. I will have a clean suit of clothes sent from his house and some good bread and wine to supplement his meals. Is that satisfactory?"

"Yer an angel, m'lady."

Without looking back at the prisoner, who still stood at the slit in the door, Jane summoned Todd and turned to leave.

"Puritan bitch!"

Jane flinched at the sound of Hawkins's fist hitting the door. She could feel his fury, feel it beating at her in hot waves that pulsed and swelled in the narrow dark passage between the cells. His bitter gaze seemed to burn a hole in her back as she moved away with what dignity she could muster—enough dignity, she hoped, to conceal the fact that she was not so much withdrawing as fleeing.

2

The relative luxury of more comfortable prison accommodations only added fuel to the hatred and resentment that ate at Matthew Hawkins's gut. Jane Alexander's charity grated on his pride. The bitch heaped humiliation upon injury, all the time flaunting an angelic countenance that could fool a saint. Hawkins had almost shouted an obscene suggestion about what she could do with her damned coins, but he wasn't quite that much of a fool. A clean bed —or at least a cleaner bed than where he had slept for these last miserable days—was too much of a temptation. The raw ache in his belly and the itching of filth on his body shouted down his pride. At least in the Master's Side he was given decent food and a chance to wash, though *given,* Hawkins bitterly reminded himself, was the wrong term. He was given nothing. Mistress Jane Alexander had bought it for him. Did she think that was the price of his son?

Hawkins spent a week in the Master's Side of Fleet Prison before the guards released him from his cell, manacled him to a fellow prisoner, and herded him with the other rebels into a cart that would convey them to the docks at Billingsgate, where a ship waited to transport them to Barbados. He didn't dwell on his gloomy future as the cart rumbled its way toward the docks. The present was pain enough. Every turn of the cart's wheels took him farther from what he loved most in the world—his son. He could tolerate losing everything else, but losing Gideon was torture past enduring.

The afternoon was well progressed, the streets crowded. Passersby shouted at the rebels as they bounced down the street. Some yelled obscenities, others encouragement. Occasionally the hecklers threw more than words as vegetables, mud, and dung flew toward the cart.

"There goes your clean suit of clothes." Sir Thomas Waltham grinned at Hawkins as a clod of mud hit its target.

Waltham looked even worse than he had when he'd stumbled into Hawkins's house on St. Martin's Lane almost a month ago. In the nine years that Hawkins had known Sir Thomas, he'd never seen him cowed to the point where he couldn't crack a joke even in the most unappropriate moments.

"Those yokels are doing us a favor," Waltham quipped. "They plaster us with offal that'll provide another layer's warmth during those cold nights at sea."

"You should be well set, then," Hawkins replied in the same vein.

"Aye. That I am. I'm wearing a veritable suit of armor made from filth." Waltham sobered. "Seriously, my friend. What can I say about this whole mess? I'm most dreadfully sorry. If I'd been thinking straight on the night of our little skirmish, I never would have involved you in this. I should have known that the army would ferret me out eventually and drag you to the gallows along with me."

"It's not to the gallows we're headed."

"Might as well be."

Hawkins's manacles clanked as he put a hand on his

friend's shoulder. "I knew what the chances were when I let you in, Thomas. Don't be troubling yourself about it."

Waltham grimaced. "I still find it hard to believe that the damned Roundheads are shipping you out with the rest of us sinners—all for the heinous crime of letting an injured friend into your house. Damn! I told them you had nothing to do with the trouble!" He sounded more upset at being judged a liar than a traitor.

"Giving a mere cup of water to a rebel is enough to condemn a man these days." Hawkins's face tightened into a mask of contempt. "Cromwell and his Puritan crew have little care of whose lives and freedom they take."

Indeed, Hawkins was surprised that freedom, title, and property were all that he'd forfeited. Being a cousin to the House of Stuart, even through an illegitimate line, should have guaranteed his hanging. Perhaps the Caribbean colonies needed slaves more than Cromwell needed corpses. Not that being spared the gallows was a mercy. Slavery in the cane fields of Barbados was simply a slower, more miserable death than the relatively quick end provided by the rope.

Waltham shouted a curse at a young apprentice who was pelting the cart's passengers with a handful of horse droppings. The lad returned the curse with vigor until another boy—apprentice in a rival guild, Hawkins guessed from his costume—targeted the dung thrower with a clod of mud. The two of them promptly forgot the cart and went brawling down the street. Waltham sighed wearily and leaned back against the cart's rail.

"What must the King be thinking?" he wondered aloud. "He was waiting on the isle of Middleburg, you know, ready for a triumphal entrance into England after our work was done. And now—defeated once again. How does he feel seeing his loyal supporters struck down so cruelly?"

"Kings rarely give much thought to the followers who are sacrificed in their causes. I think I've explained that fact to you once or twice before."

Waltham smiled. "And I still choose to disbelieve you, my cynical friend."

"Not cynical," Hawkins corrected. "Realistic."

Or was it realistic? Hawkins wondered. Perhaps his attitude toward the world was a selfish and arrogant conceit designed to let him follow his own inclinations and feel righteous about it. By all rights his life—a quiet life devoted to study, art, and the peaceful pursuit of riches in the wool trade—should never have led to his being in this cart, one of a noisome crowd of prisoners headed for misery, slavery, and death. But here he was.

Hawkins had always made it a point to shun politics, a policy which should have kept him out of trouble if the world had any justice in it at all. He remembered how greatly he had displeased his father when last they'd met five years ago. The late earl, a diplomat for King James and then later for the unfortunate King Charles, had centered his world on the political maneuverings of the King and Parliament. Being a bastard offspring of James had naturally placed him in the camp of the beleaguered throne. When Hawkins last saw his father, the old earl was lamenting the state of an England torn between King and Parliament. Matthew had knowingly provoked him, stating that he cared for neither King nor Parliament nor Cromwell. Politics, he had continued, was the worst plague that had ever bedeviled mankind, killing more people than any pestilence in history.

The old earl had not understood. "You're a better man

with a sword than most!" he had declared. "Why not put the talent to some use fighting for your king and family instead of wasting your time reading and painting and acting like a goddamned common merchant!" Hawkins's father had been very conscious of his aristocracy, even though it had come from the wrong side of the blanket.

They had parted on less than amiable terms. Hawkins had never seen his father again. The old man had taken refuge in France with Charles's widowed queen, Henrietta Maria. He died there shortly after his arrival.

The old earl had been right, Hawkins thought. What had it profited Hawkins to hold himself so arrogantly above the fray? He was condemned in a travesty of justice, his titles, estates, and merchant holdings—the real source of his wealth—confiscated by that bastard Cromwell, his future the horror of slavery and the hope of a quick death. Worst of all, his son, the only worthwhile thing he'd left to the world, was stolen away to be raised as the very thing he despised most—a Puritan.

Hawkins recalled the face of the woman who had come to the prison to gloat over Gideon's fate. He would never forget it, that face—the clear gray eyes, even white teeth, pale ivory skin touched by the delicate colors of youth. He even remembered the dimples in each cheek and the fact that her nose, otherwise fine and straight, turned up just a bit on the end. A hint of light blond hair had peeked from under her coif and covering chaperon.

Jane Alexander was beautiful, Hawkins admitted, but the beauty stopped at her face. What kind of a woman would deny a child his rightful family and snatch him to the very bosom of the monster that had struck down his father? Hawkins squeezed the rail of the cart, the knuckles on his hands growing white, as he thought of a Puritan in possession of Gideon's mind, in control of his future. If by some miracle he ever saw Mistress Alexander again with his hands unfettered and his body unchained . . .

He left the threat hanging in his mind, for just at that moment the prisoner who shared Hawkins's chains jerked him from his thoughts—jerked, literally, for the man's limbs had started to flail about in a most unnatural manner. Strange guttural sounds issued from his throat.

"What's the matter with him?" Waltham asked.

Other eyes in the cart shifted their way as Hawkins's partner in chains trembled and rolled his eyes up into his head. For a moment the man was deathly still, then he wrenched himself upright like a puppet yanked by a string. Suddenly, in a great heaving spasm he launched himself backward over the cart's rail.

"Hold up there!" one of the cart's two guards shouted to the driver. "Prisoner trying to escape!"

"He's not trying to escape, you dunderhead!" Waltham shouted. "He's having a fit!"

The sick prisoner flopped like a landed fish as he was towed alongside the cart by the manacles that tied him to Hawkins. Hawkins, trapped against the side of the cart with his arm dragged over the rail, felt as if his shoulder was being pulled from its socket.

Finally the driver slowed his horses to a halt. The guards leapt off. One started beating the man on the ground with a club while the other grasped Hawkins's arm.

"Here, you rogue! Get off there." The guard dragged Hawkins over the rail. The manacles clanked as he hit the mud. Next to him the sick man twitched, contorted, twisted, and shook in obscene violence. His eyes were wide open, but only the whites were visible. Foamy saliva dribbled from his mouth.

The guard raised his club again, his face grim with disgust. A gathering crowd of spectators from the street and neighboring shops shouted encouragement. Even the prisoners in the cart cheered the guard on.

"He's got a demon!" one spectator shouted.

"He's mad!" ventured another.

"The Devil's shakin' 'im for 'is sins!" an old woman cried.

The guard's club fell again and again. Hawkins was dragged along as the poor man flopped and jerked even more violently. The foam that flecked the sick man's face turned crimson, flaring like fire against the pallor of his skin. Both guards started to laugh. Their brutality lit a fuse in Hawkins's mind. The fuse burned swiftly into an explosion of fury. He launched himself at the guard with the club.

"Stop it, you fool! You're killing him!" Hawkins grabbed the guard's wrist with one hand while his other hand clawed for possession of the club.

The second guard leapt to the aid of his fellow. He pried Hawkins away and held him fast while his comrade wielded the club in retribution. Hawkins heard onlookers from the crowd cheer. The sounds of their raucous approval echoed through his head with the pounding of his heart, or was that the rhythm of the club drumming his skull? He couldn't tell. A wave of blackness flooded his senses.

Contemptuously released, Hawkins collapsed into the mud, his nose and mouth spewing blood, while the guards turned their attention to their original victim.

"Leave off, Bledsoe," the second guard advised the first. "This one's dead." He prodded the sick prisoner with his boot. The man's fit had ceased. He was still and limp as a discarded rag doll.

Hawkins lay in the mud listening to their conversation. The ringing in his head faded as senses slowly returned. He almost envied the dead man.

"Let's get these manacles off," Bledsoe said. "We'll have to take the body back to the prison to prove the rogue didn't escape."

"Let the ship take him," the other suggested.

"Spitler, you shitbrain! That ship ain't gonna set sail with no corpse on board. They'll have those in the hold soon enough without starting out with one."

"Aye," Spitler agreed reluctantly.

Hawkins's arm was jerked up as the guard pulled on the chain and inserted the key into the manacles. As the body on the other side of the chains was released, his hand dropped back down, splatting into the mud. Now he was chained only to himself.

The thought took a moment to swim through Hawkins's reeling senses and penetrate his brain. On the other side of his chains was only air. He could run. The guards would probably catch him and club him down, but what did he have to lose? Was life so precious now that what little was left to him couldn't be risked?

The guards paid him no mind as he lay there. No doubt they thought him close to being a corpse himself. Hawkins took advantage of their inattention to inhale several deep breaths. Then he shot up from the stinking slime of the street, charged through the milling crowd, and sprinted down Thames Street back the way the cart had come. The crowd shouted with delight. Several of the onlookers joined the guards in pursuit.

Hawkins's strength wasn't what it once had been. The guards caught him in under a minute. He turned around and faced them, swinging his wrist chain in a deadly arc.

The chain connected with Bledsoe, wrapping around his bony neck. Hawkins jerked. His victim uttered a strangled cry almost as loud as the sound of his neck cracking. The fickle crowd of onlookers cheered. Bledsoe went limp, and Hawkins felt a surge of black satisfaction, elated and sickened at the same time.

While Spitler stared at his downed mate, Hawkins fled. A hue and cry followed him. He turned briefly to see that his fellow prisoners had overwhelmed the driver and were also sprinting for freedom in all directions, two by two in manacled pairs. The one remaining guard shouted hysterically. People poured out of workshops and warehouses along the street, adding chaos to confusion.

Hawkins ran until his lungs were bursting and his legs trembled with strain. He saw no signs of pursuit, but with his chains and his bloody clothing, he attracted too much attention. The army would be out searching, and they would find him easily if he didn't go to ground like a fox pursued by hounds. People on the street looked at him with a mixture of horror and curiosity. They would be quick enough to point him out to the authorities.

Rapidly he took his bearings. He was still on Thames Street, near the docks at Queenhithe. Staying on the main thoroughfares was suicide, and Hawkins had decided that he wanted to live, in spite of everything. He ran again, this time with purpose. A narrow alley provided dark passageway between two warehouses. Ironically, one of the warehouses belonged to Hawkins, or had up until several weeks ago. He'd used it to store his outgoing shipments of raw wool. How circumstances had changed!

Hawkins slowed to a walk and caught his breath. Gradually he made his way through the maze of filthy alleys, doubling back and detouring, but always working his way east toward London Bridge. He had a plan of sorts, but he didn't dare make his move until dark.

Finally he found a lane so narrow, so rank that he doubted the army knew of its existence. Here he squatted down in the shadows with his back against a wall. He tried not to think about the slime oozing from under his boots or the odors assaulting his nostrils. Trash, litter, and offal were everywhere. A butcher had evidently been using the alley to dump his maggoty leavings. As Hawkins grew still and relaxed, rats peered at him from under heaps of refuse and litter. His stomach rose, but he stayed, reminding himself that rats were more welcome denizens of London than he was at this moment.

Finally, the shadows merged and daylight dimmed. A thick fog settled upon the City, deepening the gloom of night. Hawkins stiffly rose and followed a tortuous path from alley to alley, slowly but steadily moving east. He felt every inch a creature of the night, clinging to shadows, jumping at any hint of sound. In the shadow of the bridge's gate tower he paused and wiped the dried blood from his face with a corner of his shirt. This part of his journey held the greatest risk. Only a single narrow lane passed through the houses and workshops that crowded one another on the bridge. The lane was dimly lit at best, and in most spots not lit at all. That would help, but if he was discovered he would have no place to run, no side alleys in which to hide.

Hawkins straightened his clothes, wiped his face, hid the chain under his filthy doublet as best he could, then walked boldly up to the gate tower and climbed the steps onto the bridge. No one challenged him. The fog was thicker here than in the City. He couldn't see five feet ahead of him. Whichever saint—or imp of hell—looked after fugitives must have arranged this night just for him. He stayed in shadows and avoided pools of light that spilled from the windows of houses. Most of the shops were dark. Foot traffic was light, seen only as vague outlines in the mist.

That the army had posted no patrol on the bridge seemed incredible to Hawkins, unless in the confusion of mass escape the guard failed to notice that ex-Lord Chester had not been retrieved. Hawkins wondered if any of his fellow prisoners had succeeded in their bid for freedom, Waltham in particular. What he would give to be with Waltham as he had been five months ago on a January night in the house on St. Martin's Lane, sipping a small drop of liquor and philosophizing as the night grew old. Giddy had been upstairs, safely asleep in his bed. Now all that was gone—the house, the liquor, friendship—and Gideon.

Hawkins walked on, so near his goal that he almost allowed himself to hope. In the fog, London Bridge seemed unnaturally quiet. The usual raucous cry of the Thames watermen—"Oars! Oars!"—had ended at nightfall. Only the roar of the river rushing through the bridge's narrow arches broke the silence, and even that sound was muffled by the fog. Hawkins could not even hear his own footfalls on the wet paving stone.

Ahead he could see the dim lights of Southwark, for centuries the refuge for both London's seediest and noblest entertainments. Here cutpurses and pickpockets rubbed elbows with whores, actors, singers, murderers, and confidence tricksters. Bearbaiting, cockfighting, and stews competed with Shakespeare, Jonson, and Marlowe to provide entertainment. The Puritans had shut down the theatres and outlawed bearbaiting and cockfighting, but they couldn't change the essential nature of the district. The Church and Cromwell might think they ruled in Southwark, but the denizens of London's underworld knew better.

Hawkins breathed a quiet sigh of relief when he finally stepped onto the south bank of the Thames. He didn't have a specific plan, only a vague hope that he could fade into the dubious society of Southwark until he could somehow arrange passage to France—for himself and his son. Hawkins was determined that he wouldn't leave Gideon behind. He might as well contemplate leaving his heart behind.

Finding a way to escape England would take some creative thinking. He had no money, no identity, and his only possessions were the bloody clothes on his back. One slip could land him on the gallows or chained in the hold of a ship bound for Barbados. No reasonable man would take odds on his chances of surviving. The time had come, Hawkins mused, to cease being a reasonable man.

Hawkins was quick to take to the alleys once again. High Street, the thoroughfare that led through Southwark from the bridge, passed St. Thomas's Hospital and Marshalsea Prison, both bulwarks of authority that he wished to avoid. The alleys here were every bit as squalid as those in the City. Hawkins veered west toward the theatre district. He had frequented the Rose and the Globe before the Puritans shut them down. If one of the buildings was not too securely boarded, it might provide him with a dry and reasonably clean place to sleep. Tomorrow he would worry about food and water. Good fortune had attended him so far this day. He tried to have faith that it would continue.

Halfway to the Globe Theatre his luck suddenly ran out. Hawkins was new to being a fugitive. He didn't yet realize that a rat trapped in a hole had to defend himself from other rats as well as the ratters—a lesson he was about to learn.

The lane where he walked threaded its way between several taverns and stews, all of which were noisily going about their business of breaking the law. In the doorways of the stews lounged women in various states of undress. A whore sitting on the steps of one of the houses fixed Hawkins with an avaricious eye. She smoked a pipe and wore only a robe of the sheerest imaginable material. As Hawkins passed she smiled, thrust out her ample breasts and opened her legs to show her other assets, none of which distracted sufficiently from her mouthful of rotten teeth. Hawkins shook his head in polite negative and walked on by. She frowned after him and signaled with a hand. Three men moved from the shadows at her command.

Hawkins disliked the increasing activity along the lane he traveled. A darker, narrower alley veered to the left ahead. He turned into it and traveled a hundred feet before he heard his pursuers. He stopped and turned, too late. They sprang, a silent pack of jackals leaping for the kill.

Hawkins's strength was depleted by weeks of imprisonment, but even at his strongest he couldn't have fought off the three men who attacked him. They used fists like clubs and feet like cudgels. Hammerlike blows rained down upon his head and face, which had already suffered one clubbing that day. Boots struck his shins and knees shot upward into his groin. The world exploded in violence and pain.

He fought back the best he could, landing a blow on a face here, sinking his fist into a hard abdomen there. The effort was useless. Within painful seconds the thugs pushed him up against a wall. Two held him fast while the third turned out his pockets and pawed his body, searching for hidden purses. All they found was the chain that was still fastened to one of his wrists. "He ain't got a thing!" one whispered hoarsely.

" 'E's gotta!" another declared. "Look at 'im! 'E's a gentry cove!"

"With a chain on 'is wrist and blood all over 'is clothes? You stupid ass!"

"Shit!" The man who had searched him slammed a fist into Hawkins's stomach. Hawkins grunted and felt blood rise into his mouth.

"Useless bastard!" One of the thugs holding him grabbed Hawkins's hair and slammed his head back against the wall. Lights exploded before his eyes, and for a moment he seemed to float. Then an even sharper pain brought him unpleasantly back to his senses. He gasped, unable to contain the agony. Out of the corner of his eye he spied a knife in the hand of one of his attackers. The blade glistened with blood. A darkness that had nothing to do with the night began to wash over his mind.

" 'E's dead," a voice said, strangely muffled.

Even the pain was fuzzy. Hawkins could hear his own heartbeat pounding in his head, blocking out all other sound and feeling. He floated, sinking into a dark vortex, until the blackness was complete.

Ned Crow's mouth stretched into a wide, gap-toothed grin as he stepped out of the Red Rose. This night had been a rare good one, with two of the stew's best whores vying to do him pleasure. Of course, Ned knew they weren't crawling all over him for his good looks. Not that his looks were that bad, mind you, even considering his ear. His wiry body and swarthy face had charmed females the world over when he was a tar in the merchant fleet, and he still had the touch with the ladies. No doubt about that, even though he knew the part of him most interesting to the Rose's ladies was the coin in his pocket. Ned didn't care. Pleasure was pleasure, no matter how it came to a man.

He stepped down onto the street and grinned at Struttin' Sal, who smoked her pipe on the stoop. Sal gave him a wink and a grin full of blackened teeth.

"Not tonight, me love. Yer crewmates done wrung me out."

"Ye didn't save some fer me?"

"Next time, beauty." A man had to be careful of ol' Sal. She was a good whore, gave a man a ride he wouldn't soon forget. But with Sal a fellow was likely to end up paying for his ride with more than he'd bargained for, and if Sal couldn't get in a man's pockets, she had cronies who'd do the job for her—and more besides.

Ned sauntered down the lane and turned up the alley toward his lodgings. He was still drifting in a pleasant cloud of satisfaction when something got in the way of his feet. He tripped and sprang away, suddenly alert.

" 'Ere now! What's this?"

He nudged the obstacle with the toe of his boot. It was soft and yielding, heavy, inert: a body.

" 'Ere's a cove 'oo got more than 'e bargained for," Ned mused aloud. He ran a practiced hand over the body to discover if the attackers had left anything of worth behind. The fellow stirred and groaned.

Ned raised a brow. "Alive, are ye? Sloppy work, this." From the material of the man's clothing Ned guessed he was quality. But something was not quite right. He grabbed the body's ankles and dragged it into a dim pool of light from a window. A heavy chain caught his eye. It was attached to the fellow's wrist and trailed across his chest into the mud of the alley.

"Now 'ere's a thing of interest," Ned commented. "A fellow in satin and chains. I'd wager ye've an interestin' tale to tell." He pulled aside the doublet. It was sticky with blood, and the wounds were still oozing. "Likely you're gonna die, me friend. But maybe not. Yer a tough-looking cove, for all yer satin and ribbon loops."

Ned hoisted the body over his shoulder and was promptly thankful he didn't have to carry it far. The fellow was big. No voice cried out at the rough handling. Passed out or dead, Ned thought. Just as well, either way. But if the fellow managed to stay alive, Moll Cutpurse might find some use for him. She had a soft heart for anyone with an interesting story to tell, though she might rob him blind while she was listening to his tale. This gentry cove didn't have much left to rob, but he might be entertaining just the same.

3

December 1658, London

Matthew Hawkins, Ned Crow, and One-Eye Carey strolled casually down the great arched nave of St. Paul's Cathedral. The cathedral, largest building in the land, was more of a market fair than a holy place of worship. The nave in particular—St. Paul's Walk, it was called—was the site of wrestling matches, ninepins tournaments, merchant booths, and even less holy entertainments such as robbery, murder, and adultery.

The trio that strolled the Walk this afternoon was after no such spectacular fare, though. They merely had an eye out for a cony—some poor gull in from the country who might be easy prey for their wits, and thus quickly separated from his money. There were plenty of candidates to choose from. This being an unusually fine December afternoon, the Walk was crowded with gentlemen taking the air, apprentices dodging their duties, merchants hawking their wares, country bumpkins gaping at the sights, as well as a goodly sprinkling of whores, cutpurses and pickpockets (nips and foists, Hawkins had learned they were called by their fellows in the thieving business), and other less savory characters.

Hawkins, Crow, and Carey blended well with the divergent crowd. Tall, lean, and swarthy, "the Hawk," as he was known by his comrades, had a face that would have earned him the appellation even without the encouragement of his surname. A faint scar slashed one cheek, giving him a dangerous look. His short-clipped, thick, wavy hair matched in color the midnight black of his apparel—an unpretentious belted cossack coat, breeches gartered at the knee, and fine woolen hose. Only his bib-style collar, a contrasting snowy white against the swarthiness of his skin, relieved the darkness of his figure. The fashion was Puritan, but something in the wicked arch of his brows, the tilt of his wide mouth, and the wariness in his hazel eyes was very un-Puritan-like.

The other two members of the trio were easier to place into their niche in society. Ned Crow—short, wiry, swarthy as the Hawk, with hair just as black, had a mutilated ear that testified to his profession. The cartilage of that appendage had been burned through as punishment for being caught by the constables in a cony-catching operation. One-Eye Carey also had his mark of distinction, having lost an eye brawling in a Southwark stew. Fighting over whores was one of the things that One-Eye did best. He was also a fair *charm* and *flick*—picklock and thief—and a master at the art of cutting purses.

Out in the churchyard, someone delivered a rousing sermon from Paul's Cross. The octagonal wooden pulpit with its ornamental cross was a favorite spot for zealots to harangue the public. The sound of the preacher's voice could be heard even above the noise of the crowd in the nave.

" 'E's a loud one," Ned complained of the preacher.

"Just saving a few souls." Hawk smiled cynically. "There's a few here that no doubt could use some saving."

One-Eye merely grunted, his favorite form of expression.

"Not me," Ned declared. "Ain't no one savin' my soul. 'Eaven's gonna be a right dull spot with all those damned Puritans clutterin' up the scenery, tellin' everybody what to do and what to think. 'Ell's the place fer me."

Hawk lifted one wickedly arched black brow. "Perhaps there won't be as many Puritans in heaven as you think— or as many as they think, at least."

Ned dug his elbow into Hawk's ribs. "Take a look at that gent over there. 'E looks like a fat purse. Care to 'ave a go at 'im?"

Hawk swung his gaze in the direction Ned indicated. A foppish gentleman lounged against a pillar at the side of the nave. The man's appearance certainly spoke of wealth, or rather shouted of it. A short-waisted doublet of embroidered satin gaped open to reveal a snowy silk shirt beneath. The ribbon-bedecked sleeves of the doublet were fashionably short and lapped over shirt cuffs dripping with lace. Bright ribbon loops adorned his petticoat breeches— a new style which Hawk found ridiculous—and large lacy cannons fell from garters at the gentleman's knees and flounced almost to the tops of his rather high-heeled pumps. Bright ostrich plumes added garish color to his hat. Even in the multihued confusion of Paul's Walk, the man stood out as gaudy.

"I think that one's silver isn't worth the risk of getting close to him," Hawk quipped. "He's bright enough we might go blind."

"Pah!" spat Ned. " 'E's an easy cony to catch." He turned to One-Eye. " 'Awk 'ere used to be the best goddamned cony catcher in London. Moll Cutpurse and me, we taught 'im everything we know. Now 'e's spent so much time playin' King of the Thieves, organizin' nip and foist and flick till they wanna puke, 'e's lost the touch."

Hawk's mouth slanted up at Ned's gibe. "You think I've lost my touch, do you? It has been a while since I was out on the street."

"Pays to keep yer 'and in, Cap'n."

Hawk's eyes lit upon a soberly but richly dressed man who looked Puritan to the core. "How's that for a cony?" he asked Ned.

Ned followed the direction of Hawk's gaze. "Yer always lightin' on the God-hawkers."

"It's a small return for them lighting rather heavily on me."

"At least the cove looks like 'e's got somethin' worth nippin'."

Hawk gave Ned and One-Eye a predatory grin. "Let's find out. As you say, it's good to keep one's hand in."

Hawk followed casually behind the Puritan gentleman as he ambled out the door into the churchyard. The sober fellow paused outside the door, his attention caught by the sermon that was still being spouted from the pulpit at Paul's Cross. Hawk strolled up and halted beside him, tilting his head as if interested in the preacher's haranguing, which had switched from morals to politics.

"The man has the right of it," Hawk commented amiably as the preacher caught his breath. "Richard won't be the leader that Oliver was."

The Puritan glanced his way, agreement in his face. " 'Tis God's curse on England that he took Cromwell in the prime of life, just punishment for the way we've allowed public morals to slip. Even being Cromwell's son, Richard won't be able to steer the country back upon the paths of righteousness."

"Indeed!" Hawk concurred.

The man was about to receive a firsthand demonstration of the sadly lacking public morals. Ned and One-Eye had slipped out of the nave into the yard and were hovering like wolves ready to close in for the kill.

"Oliver Cromwell was a man with a rare gift of leadership," Hawk continued. "I fear we'll not find another of his stamp."

"We need a strong hand at the helm of government in these restless times," the Puritan confided. "One hears more and more talk of inviting young Charles Stuart to return." He shook his head sadly. "Debauched son of an evil tyrant. What a sad end that would be to our noble triumph."

"It would," Hawk acknowledged sadly. He gave a tiny shrug and turned one palm toward his companion, the signal calling for the bump. Ned and One-Eye promptly began a convincing exchange of shouts which ended in blows.

"My goodness!" Hawk exclaimed in horror. "The things one sees in public places these days!"

No one else paid the brawling duo much mind, as such things were commonplace enough to rate disregard. Neither did Ned and One-Eye earn much attention when they flailed their way directly into Hawk and his intended victim.

"I say!" the Puritan complained as he was knocked to his knees.

"Off with you, villains!" Hawk yelled. He bent to help the Puritan to his feet as Ned and One-Eye disappeared into the crowd. "Criminal! Simply criminal! Where is the constable when such scoundrels knock a worthy citizen from his feet?"

"Indeed!" The gentleman staggered upright and accepted Hawk's assistance in straightening and brushing dirt from his clothing. "Thank you, good sir! We can see what state England is coming to!"

"Can't we, though! I do hope you've sustained no injury."

"I think not."

"How fortunate. I believe I shall go back to my house. At least there a man is still safe!"

"For the time being," the man commiserated. "Go with God, sir."

"And you also."

Hawk melted into the crowd, grinning widely once the fool was out of sight. Ned and One-Eye materialized.

"Get it?" Ned inquired.

"What do you think?" Hawk replied. He lifted a heavy purse from his belt, a purse formerly in the possession of the talkative Puritan.

"Ye 'aven't lost the touch after all," Ned conceded.

"We just did a good deed," Hawk told them. "Old sobersides will find his road to heaven much smoother without having to worry about this measure of worldliness." He held up the purse for their admiration. "Back to the Lion to celebrate!"

The celebration started by hiring a hackney to carry them to Southwark, a rare luxury. They were in fine spirits after their small triumph, but Hawk's jovial mood departed when the cab passed a family walking along Watling Street. A craftsman by the look of him, the husband held a gangly boy by the hand, while the wife cradled an infant in her arms. As they passed, the boy looked up at his father and laughed at something the man said.

No matter how much time passed, Hawk would never

stop wincing at such common reminders of what he had lost.

Back at the Lion, Hawk brooded while Good Mary served the trio her best ale. Mary was the proprietress of the tavern, and she always made a point of serving Hawk herself, claiming as her own the privilege of waiting upon the man who controlled the better part of London's underworld business. The "Good" added to her name did not come from her morals, or from the ale she made—though the brew was excellent—but from other earthy talents she possessed.

Even Good Mary couldn't break Hawk from his mood on this afternoon, however. While Ned and One-Eye drank their ale and regaled the house with their little victory, Hawk brooded over a piece of paper he pulled from his coat. On the paper was an ink sketch—one of many such sketches he had drawn over the past three years. In clear, bold strokes he had depicted the face of a woman. Her features were classically elegant with large eyes, thick lashes, gracefully arched brows, a slim nose turned up slightly at the tip. The illustration showed a small smile bringing out twin dimples on the woman's cheeks, but the woman looked cold and haughty in spite of the smile.

Ned set down his ale and peered at the sketch. "Every time you draw that gentry mort, she looks more like a witch," he commented.

Hawk chuckled unpleasantly. "I don't think she'd like that description."

"Why d'ye keep drawing 'er? Yer drawin's found 'er for ye, didn't they?"

It had taken a year for Hawk to learn Jane Alexander's whereabouts—a well-kept house on Great Queen Street in the West End. He'd handed his sketches to as much of

London's underworld as he could reach, and as a friend of
Moll Cutpurse, who was practically a legend in criminal
circles, he could reach a good part of it. The reward he
offered for information was collected by an enterprising
nine-year-old street urchin, who'd recognized Mistress Alexander in the market at Cheapside and had followed her
home. From then until two months ago Hawk had a man
on the Alexander house staff reporting to him—a groom
by the name of Todd. The man had been hard to subvert,
but everyone had his price.

"The drawings found her for me," Hawk replied brood-
ingly. "For all the good it's doing me now."

"Make way, ye clods!" Moll Cutpurse's booming voice
announced her arrival as she tramped through the tavern
door with her usual lack of grace. Dressed in a man's doublet and breeches, her yellowed teeth clamped down on a
pipe, she was hardly distinguishable as a woman. Anyone
who mistook Moll for a man, however, would likely feel
the sharp edge of her tongue if not the hard ball of her fist.

She clumped over to Hawk's table. "Why so glum, lad?
Business 'as been jumpin', the money rollin' in, and there
ye sit lookin' like Doom 'imself."

Hawk spared a brief smile for Moll as she pulled a stool
under her broad behind and sat down. A part of everything
he got went into Moll's deep pockets, so she knew every
shilling he collected from the organization of nips, foists,
divers, and cony catchers that he employed. She knew everyone in his network, knew how much of their take went
to him in return for his protection and training, knew better than anyone else in London's underworld what that
take was. Moll didn't trust anyone, even Hawk, whom she
had dragged from the gutter and nursed back to life and
health. But Hawk trusted her. Only Moll knew that most of

Hawk's take from his carefully organized criminal network went overseas to help support the English court in exile and royalists who had fled the country.

"We're celebrating, Moll," he told her. "Mary!" he shouted across the din of the tavern. "Serve up an ale for Moll."

One-Eye held up the filched purse for her inspection.

"Been out on the street again, 'ave ye?" Moll asked.

" 'E's keepin' 'is 'and in," Ned related.

"Always said ye were a natural at it. Ye don't lose a natural talent." She fixed Hawk with a cunning eye. "Why so glum?" she persisted.

"Pah!" Ned answered for Hawk. " 'E saw a kid today."

Moll nodded. Children always turned Hawk broody.

"I've tried to plant two men on the Alexander staff since Todd was let go. Both have been turned away. I haven't the devil of a notion of what's happening over there with Gideon."

Moll grunted thanks to Good Mary as the proprietress set another ale on the table. " 'E's all right, lad. 'E's a lot safer with the lady than 'e would be 'ere, no matter what's goin' on."

Moll had told Hawk the same thing over and over again since he'd first found Jane Alexander and vowed to go after his son. The underworld life was no place for a child. She repeated that indisputable fact every time he weakened with longing for his Gideon.

Just then living, breathing evidence that Moll was right strolled into the tavern in the persons of Walter Sykes and his little assistant. Walter was a diver, a thief who uses a small child to wriggle into rooms through narrow spaces—a window, a chimney flue, a blocked doorway. Sykes sat down at a table and bellowed for bread and ale. The child with him, a lad of about ten years, started to sit also until the diver pushed him aside with a hefty cuff.

"Ye've gotta earn yer food, ye miserable little bugger!" Sykes cuffed the boy again for good measure, then looked around the room as if for approval. "Tried a lift last night on the Cheapside, and the little bugger couldn't get through the cellar window!"

The boy backed away from Sykes's scowl. His face was red where the man had hit him, and one eye was already starting to swell.

"Been feedin' 'im up too much!" the diver told the house.

"I can't help it!" the boy pleaded.

His remark only deepened the scowl on the diver's face.

"Can't work if I can't eat!" the child declared with a hint of belligerence.

"Come 'ere, ye worthless whelp!" Sykes grabbed the boy by his frayed and dirty coat. "I'll teach ye to mouth off at me, ye little—!"

He raised his fist to beat the child, but a viselike grip arrested his arm. The diver turned in a fury, then froze as he looked into the calm face of the Hawk.

"You're abusing the one who's keeping you in lodgings and ale, Sykes."

" 'Tisn't yer business, 'Awk." Sykes tried unsuccessfully to wrest his arm from Hawk's grip. "Besides," he growled, "the boy ain't earnin' 'is keep!"

"Children grow. That hardly rates a beating."

The tavern grew silent. Hawk's words were quiet with a deadly calm.

"I ain't yer man," Sykes sneered. "Ye can't tell *me* what to do like ye do most o' the gallows bait around 'ere!"

"I don't work with bullies who abuse children," Hawk

stated quietly. "That doesn't mean I can't tell you what to do." He released Sykes's arm with a violent shove that sent the diver back over the table and crashing into the wall. Sykes staggered up, drew a knife from his belt, and lurched forward. Hawk easily avoided his clumsy rush, and the diver stumbled into the circle of the tavern's other customers, who had drawn close to watch the entertainment. They grabbed him by the arms, turned him around, and pushed him back toward Hawk with a raucous cheer.

Sykes brought his knife up in a wicked arc. Hawk blocked the slicing uppercut by grabbing Sykes's wrist. With the other hand he reached out for the diver's neck, circled the scrawny column with his fingers, and relentlessly squeezed. The knife dropped, thudding on the packed dirt floor. A harsh gurgle escaped Sykes's throat.

His victim's purpling face didn't bother Hawk as once it would have. In the world where he now lived, rules didn't exist. Fights were deadly battles; a man won by whatever means he could. Chivalry, honor, and fair play were for gentlemen, and Hawk no longer counted himself in that elite group.

At the last moment before Sykes passed out, Hawk released his deadly grip. "Get out," he ordered in a level, dangerous voice.

Sykes staggered and rubbed at his throat. He motioned the boy to follow him as he retreated toward the door. The child, wide-eyed, shook his head.

"Stay here if you want, boy," Hawk offered.

"The lad's Walter's son," a man chimed in. "Ye can't take a son from 'is father."

"Yes, you can," Hawk insisted. "It's been done before. Get out," he repeated to Sykes.

Sykes hesitated a moment, then fled. Hawk turned to the

diver's son. The boy straightened his spine and stood perfectly still, but his eyes were wary as Hawk moved toward him.

"What's your name, boy?"

"Little Tate."

Hawk grinned. "Not so little anymore, are you, Tate?"

The boy looked as though he didn't know whether to grin or to cry.

Hawk reached out and put a hand on the lad's shoulder. "It doesn't matter now if you choose to grow, Tate. Come over to the table and get something to eat."

Good Mary brought out the best from her kitchen—fish stew, mutton, cheese, hard bread, and a mug full of milk. While the boy attacked the meal, Hawk pulled out his sketch and stared at it moodily.

"I know a family in Lincoln's Inn Fields who'd pay handsomely for such a fine boy," Moll Cutpurse told Hawk. "They're good folks who'd treat 'im like a son."

Hawk looked up from his sketch and fixed his eyes on Tate. "What say you, boy? Would you like to live with gentlefolk? Learn to read, write, and turn your nose up at rogues such as us?"

Tate's eyes grew wide. He paused in his chewing. "I wouldn't never turn my nose up, sir!"

Hawk smiled.

"But I'd like to read and write." The boy turned awe-filled eyes toward Moll. "Would they take me? Really?"

"Aye," she said with a nod of certainty. "They would, boy."

"Make the arrangements then, Moll. And tell the family to keep their money to use for the lad." He smiled at Moll's scowl. "I'll make up your part of the profit out of my pocket. I'll have no part of selling a child."

Moll shrugged, and Hawk turned his attention back to the sketch. Jane Alexander stared up at him from the drawing. The hint of a smile that curved her mouth seemed full of contempt.

Suddenly Hawk was flooded with disgust—for himself, for the life he led, for the whole stinking Puritan England. It was past time for him to fetch his son and get out of the country.

"Mary! Bring me paper and a quill!"

"Aye, Hawk. Right 'ere. Ye be the only cove o' me acquaintance what knows 'ow to use such things."

Hawk hastily composed a note. "Tate, lad, are you familiar with the City?"

"Aye, sir."

"Then run this to Colonel Terence Colbert in Cornhill Street. He's well known and should be easy to find."

The boy wiped his mouth on his sleeve and reached out eagerly for the missive. "I'll find 'im, sir!"

As Tate rushed off on his errand, Hawk leaned back and once more retrieved the sketch from his coat. Without taking a last look he crumpled the drawing in his hand and let it drop to the floor.

"Ye need to eat more, mistress!" Charity scolded Jane as she walked through the dining room door with a basket of hard bread. "Though the fare left in the larder isn't such to set a mouth to watering, and we've no cook to serve it the way it should be served!"

Jane looked up from her plate, where the boiled pork and cabbage congealed in an unappetizing mass. Even if her supper had consisted of tender boiled capon and fine wine, she couldn't have shown a fitting enthusiasm. Exhaustion sat upon her like a lead weight. Eating was simply a necessary chore she must perform before seeking the comfort of her bed.

"It's no wonder you've no appetite at this time of the night," Charity continued. She set the bread down before her mistress. "We've buttermilk ye should finish. 'Tis the last of it, and it'll turn bad soon. For certain it wouldn't have lasted so long if the young master were here, or your grandmother, either."

Should Charity keep her hands as busy as her mouth, Jane thought wryly, the house would be in a much better state. Not that Jane could find it in her heart to much blame poor Charity for her complaining. For the past week the housekeeper had tackled the work of the house alone while Jane spent the days and evenings taking care of poor old Mistress Thackeray next door. All the other staff had been dismissed weeks ago because of financial difficulties, and she'd sent Grandmother Margaret and young Gideon to her sister in Kent when she took on the duties of nurse to her neighbor.

How lonely the house was without Giddy, and even Grandmother Margaret's absence left a void. They'd been gone for three weeks now. The letters they exchanged only partially eased the aching emptiness, but Jane was glad they'd not been here while she might have brought contagion home to one of them. The very young and very old were so susceptible to illness.

"Ye're pale as ashes, mistress. Can't ye eat?"

"I've really very little appetite, Charity. But thank you for serving the meal."

"Ye've run yourself into the ground caring for that woman," Charity complained, folding her arms indignantly across her ample bosom. "She's a rich one, and should've hired herself someone to see to her. Or at least she could've paid you so we could put some decent food in the larder."

Jane shook her head. "Mistress Thackeray has been my neighbor since I first moved into this house nine years ago as Colonel Alexander's bride. I could hardly leave her in the care of servants who wouldn't go near her room for fear of the plague."

Charity paled and retreated a step. "You never said the woman had plague!"

"She didn't. It was another fever that carried the poor lady off. But the stableman's daughter died of plague a month ago, and he had the rest of the staff in a panic. Foolish man."

"Aye," Charity agreed, but a doubtful frown still darkened her face. "Ye always hear of some person or another being carried off by the plague. Especially in the City. 'Tis always everyone's fear that the pestilence will spread."

"Don't you start the foolishness as well," Jane admonished her firmly. "Mistress Thackeray, God rest her soul, did not have the plague."

"Yes, mistress."

Jane looked at her plate and sighed. "The hour is late, Charity. You needn't stay up just because I am dawdling over my food. Take yourself off to bed, and I shall see to the mess."

Charity didn't hesitate. "If you say so, Mistress Alexander."

"Don't forget to say a prayer for Mistress Thackeray's soul."

"As you say, ma'am. 'Tis sorry I am to hear of the old lady's passing."

The house was blessedly quiet after Charity took her talkative mouth to bed. Jane sat at the table for a short while, enjoying the silence, then rose and cleaned the supper mess from table and kitchen. Charity did not keep the kitchen as clean as Jane would have liked, but Jane didn't have the energy to undertake the job so late at night. She remembered back to the time—such a short while ago, really, but it seemed years—she had had enough money to support the staff needed to keep the house and garden in good order. The funds that Oliver Cromwell allocated to care for the widow of a good friend had dwindled when the great man fell ill, and stopped when he died. Thaddeus Alexander, though a distinguished and respected soldier, had very little wealth through his family, and now Jane had no wealth at all.

In the refuge of her bedchamber Jane allowed her shoulders to slump. She removed her coif and loosened the severe chignon that the cap had covered. A heavy mass of brilliant gold cascaded to her waist. After brushing her tresses until they glistened in the candlelight, Jane deftly twisted the heavy mane into a loosely braided rope that hung down her back, out of her way. Then she washed her face and hands with cold water that stood in a porcelain basin on a table near the clothespress.

The bed beckoned, a longed-for haven of rest. Jane considered neglecting the day's last duty, but years of daily discipline won. She could almost hear her father's voice echoing in her mind: One cannot improve without looking inward, he had frequently lectured his daughters. For their own education and salvation he had bade them write out their thoughts and contemplate their shortcomings, so that they could better correct their courses in life. Jane had faithfully obeyed his stricture every day of her life, no matter how tired she was or how many other things demanded attention. Tonight was no exception.

She sat down at the small scriptore that stood beneath the bedchamber's one window, took out a worn, leather-covered volume, and began to write.

Mistress Hope Thackeray died this night, may the dear Lord rest her soul. Though I know that the death of an upright and God-fearing person should not be a cause for grief, still I find myself succumbing to dejection. Perhaps I could forgive myself if my melancholy stemmed wholly from the loss of my sweet neighbor, but I fear it is as much my own circumstances that darken my spirit. I should stop whining about my lot and remind myself that despair is sin, and self-pity is an invitation to the Devil to set his clutches upon my soul. Still I ask myself, how is a gentlewoman widow with little property and no fortune to support herself, a growing child, and an aging grandmother? Not to mention to find the money for Giddy's tutor. I can run my household without servants, but Gideon must not be deprived of his education. The Bible tells us that God will provide. But how?

The answer to that question came to Jane even before she closed her little volume—the same answer that she had rejected so many times over these past weeks. She could take charity from her sister Sarah and her sister's husband Geoffrey. Such dependence would be a sore blow to her pride, but pride was a sin also, was it not?

She sighed, put aside her journal, and knelt on the bare floor to pray. Dutifully she put in a word for Mistress Thackeray's soul, begged forgiveness for her own pride and lack of faith, then gave thanks that Gideon would soon be back in her life. Prayers done, Jane removed her clothing, set the garments neatly in the clothespress, and slipped naked into bed. The bed linen was cold against her bare skin, but she was too tired to notice. Neither the cold nor her many problems could keep her awake this night. She fell asleep thinking that if despair were truly a sin, then the Devil must be on his way to claim her. Try as she might, Jane could see very little hope for the future.

Hawk pressed himself against the wall of the darkened entrance hall of the Alexander residence. Outside, Ned guarded against unexpected intrusion. Little Mistress Puritan was fortunate that she lived in a West End neighborhood, for the latch on her door was no barrier to a thief who knew his business. If the house had been in the City itself, it would have been robbed and robbed again until it had nothing left of value.

He waited, silent and still as a statue. In front of him was the parlor entrance, and through the parlor Hawk could see a dining room, which no doubt led to pantry, kitchen, and servants' quarters. Stairs flanked an entrance hall and led upward into darkness—to bedchambers. No sound came from either upstairs or downstairs; no light disturbed the dark. The house and its residents were peacefully asleep.

Finally Hawk moved. With stealthy wariness he climbed the stairway. Not a board creaked on his ascent; not a footfall sounded. He reined in his impatience in favor of caution. His son waited just a few feet away, and a week hence, arranged by the royalist agent through whom Hawk had funneled funds these past years, a ship would carry father and son away from England, to a place where they could take up their lives where they had been interrupted three years ago. Hawk ached to dash up the stairs and scoop Gideon into his arms, so long had he waited to see his son's face once again. But one false step might alert the house, and then there would be hell to pay.

Hawk gained the top of the stairs and began a systematic search for his son, chamber by chamber. The first two rooms he checked were empty and smelled mustily of disuse. The dwelling had obviously been designed for a larger family than it housed. The third chamber was much larger, and plainly not a nursery. A coal fire glowed dimly on a grate in the fireplace, and by its light Hawk could see a softly rounded figure in the four-poster bed. One arm lay atop the bedclothes, and alongside it, a pale rope of braided hair. Mistress Jane Alexander herself. Hawk's fist tightened at his side as he backed out and silently shut the door.

Three other chambers opened onto the gallery where Hawk prowled. All were empty. A moment of panic made him stop and catch his breath—he who in the last three years had learned to despise and discard fear. The thought of completely losing Gideon was the only thing that could inspire him to terror.

His son was not here. Only servants would be sleeping downstairs, and all reports he'd received from this house assured him that Gideon was a pampered member of the family. Where the hell was he?

Hawk backtracked and slipped once again into the master bedchamber. Since Gideon was not here for him to steal silently away, he would have to deal with Mistress Alexander herself. Such a confrontation had not been part of his plan, but something in him rejoiced all the same. For three years he'd carried the memory of Jane Alexander's face looking through the barred slit of his prison cell, telling him that Gideon was hers. Hawk smiled to think what expression that solemn, self-righteous little face would wear when she realized that Matthew Hawkins had returned to claim his own.

Silently he moved across the room. For a moment he simply stood and looked down at the figure that seemed so small in the huge bed. One pale, slender arm lay atop the bedclothes. The heavy rope of her hair, gleaming even in the dull light of the coal grate, lay upon her chest. Her face looked younger than it had appeared in the many drawings he'd sketched of her over the last three years. Younger, more innocent, without a hint of mockery or contempt on her sweet, elegant features.

Hawk scowled. What did he expect, fool that he was? The damned woman was asleep! Of course she looked innocent.

It was Hawk's fearsome scowl that met Jane's eyes when she woke to the sight of a figure looming over her in the darkness.

4

Suspended between waking and sleeping, Jane at first thought the scowling face was her worst nightmare become real. Her evil thoughts had summoned the Devil himself—a dark incarnation of flesh, power, and menace. The demon's face was in shadow, but Jane could see the hellish gleam in his eyes as they devoured her soul. She lay frozen with terror, unable to move, or even breathe.

The intruder reached to his belt and drew a knife. The action jarred Jane out of her trance. She started to rise. He pushed her roughly back to the mattress and pressed the deadly tip of his knife to her throat. The prick of cold steel brought Jane fully awake at last. This creature was not the Devil, she realized. Satan had no need for a blade. The demon shredded souls, not flesh.

"Do you know who I am?" the man asked.

Jane gave a tiny negative shake of her head, too terrified to make a sound.

"Look at me!" he demanded, leaning closer. "Take a good look at me!"

The dim glow from the coal grate made a sinister landscape of his face. Desperately she examined his features—the wickedly curved brows, the stern line of his mouth, the agressively jutting nose, the thin scar that marred one cheek. If she had seen such a face before she would re-member it. It would haunt her nightmares and keep her from sleep.

"Do you know me now?" he growled.

Jane shook her head again. The man was mad. Bedlam had thrown open its doors. The fearsome prick of the knife at her throat tightened her every nerve. She was going to die. Jane was sure of it. She closed her eyes for a final prayer. The feather mattress sagged as the madman sat down beside her on the bed. Jane could almost feel the heat of him, smell the warm scent of leather, smoke, and sweat that clung to him.

"I am Matthew Hawkins, Mistress Alexander."

Her eyes flew open. He hovered above her—frighten-ingly close.

"Do you know me now?"

Matthew Hawkins! Matthew Hawkins should be dead or living out his wretched life in a cane field on Barbados. This man could not be Gideon's father!

"Do you know me?" he persisted.

He looked nothing like the gaunt, filthy convict she'd seen in Fleet Prison. Except perhaps for the wide, arrogant mouth and the angry flash of his eyes—and the nose. The nose was the same.

Slowly Jane nodded, realizing the truth. She would rather he be the Devil.

"Have I changed a bit?" he sneered. "Perhaps the scar offends you. I was careless in a gutter fight and let a knife get to my face."

Jane simply stared at him in dismay.

"Once, Mistress Alexander, I was a gentleman who lived quietly and minded my own affairs. Thanks to your Lord Cromwell, I now am a creature who prowls the night, a disease that feeds on the lifeblood of London. I have no regard for virtue, or morality, or honor, or even life itself. I tell you this so you don't mistakenly comfort yourself that I must have a remnant of decency left within me. I don't. I warn you not to trifle with me, mistress."

Jane was already stiff with fear. The rogue didn't need to convince her further.

"Now tell me the whereabouts of my son."

Mention of Gideon sparked a bit of courage. She didn't answer.

"I've already searched the rooms," he told her. "I know he isn't here. Tell me where he is and I'll spare you."

"He isn't here," Jane said softly, trying to keep her voice steady.

"I know he isn't here!" Hawk snarled.

"He's beyond your reach."

The rigid anger of Hawk's face almost conquered Jane's resolve. She was so afraid that she thought she might disgrace herself by being physically ill. But nothing would make her allow this man to touch her son.

Hawk took the knife from her throat, briefly tested the edge with his thumb, then slid it back into its sheath. "Think well on the consequences of your stubborness, Mistress Alexander."

She looked him steadily in the eye. "You can do what you want, Lord Chester. I will never tell you where Gideon is. His safety means everything to me."

"You think he would not be safe with his own father?"

"You are not Gideon's father," she told him calmly. "I don't know how you escaped your sentence, or where you've been hiding all this time, but you sacrificed every right to being Gideon's father by the traitorous activities for which you were condemned."

"Did I indeed? Yet you still persist in thinking I am a lord, with a lord's delicacy in dealing with women." He gave her a look that made her want to melt into the mattress so that he could not reach her with his knife, his hands, his fists.

"My life means nothing beside Gideon's safety," she declared, hating her voice for wavering.

He stood, and for a moment Jane thought she imagined amusement in his wry smile. "Your life isn't at stake," he assured her. "Something much more precious."

Jane's eyes widened in horror as Hawk began to remove his clothing. "What . . . what are you doing?"

He flashed her a grin which would have done the Devil himself proud. "Preparing for bed."

Jane watched in horror as he shrugged off his shirt and unlaced his breeches. The sight of broad, bare shoulders and muscle-ridged chest froze the thoughts within her brain. When he sat down on the bed to pull off his boots she could only stare at the wide expanse of his back and the flow of muscles in his arms.

"I . . . !" She choked as he peeled the breeches down from his hips and slid beneath the bedcovers. Her mind was numb. She couldn't think.

"You've taken a lover, my good little Puritan widow."

He slid his hand about her bare waist. She shrieked and jumped from the bed. His leering smile followed her, and with horror she realized she was naked. She snatched at the bedsheets to cover herself, but not before she felt his gaze slip over her like a warm hand. He smiled his approval. Jane grew hot and cold at the same time.

"I have *not* taken a lover, you villain! I would kill myself before letting you touch me!"

"You'll not kill yourself," he told her. "And there's no

need for me to touch you. My being in your bedroom, in your house, is enough. Your servants, your neighbors, your friends will think poor Jane Alexander has strayed to the wicked ways of the world."

He rose from the bed, manifestly unashamed of his shocking nakedness. Jane felt the breath leave her body. He seemed bigger than life, more than human, his maleness a ghastly force that pressed her to retreat. But the bedclothes she clutched to her body allowed her no slack to move.

"What will the clergy of your most pure Church believe, mistress? Will the priest decry your sins from the pulpit when he learns of your transgression? Will you have your head shaved and be whipped at the cart's tail for being a whore?"

"This is nonsense!" Jane cried. "Get out of my house at once, before I call a constable!"

"A constable?" He didn't appear at all worried. "How are you to call a constable when I don't intend to let you out of my sight until I am finished with you?"

"You cannot assault a woman in her own home!"

"Certainly I can!" he said cheerfully. "Your friend Cromwell and his cronies assaulted innocent people in their homes without a twinge of conscience, and I daresay his successor will make it a habit as well."

Jane felt as though she were in a particularly dreadful nightmare. In the normal, waking world one didn't converse with a stark-naked man while one's own fragile modesty was preserved only by a bedsheet.

"Besides, mistress"—Hawk's voice grew more serious, and it rang with a note of threat that Jane couldn't mistake —"I will do anything I must to retrieve my son. If I have to ruin you, leave your reputation in a shambles, even if I have to take your pretty neck in my two hands and wring Gideon's whereabouts from your throat, I wouldn't hesitate or blink an eye at the consequences to you."

His threats were enunciated slowly, as though he were making sure she understood every single syllable. Gradually he moved toward her. Jane yanked desperately at the tether that held her in place, her eyes growing wider at every step Hawk took. The sheet jerked loose. Jane stumbled back, still clutching the material to her naked body, until her back bumped against the cold plaster wall.

"Do you understand me, Mistress Alexander?" Hawk asked quietly. He stopped an arm's length in front of her.

For a moment Jane could scarcely breathe. He filled her vision, and everywhere her eyes moved they rested upon bare male flesh, or, worse, Hawk's face—calm, merciless, unyielding.

"I think you had better tell me where my son is," Hawk said. "I am his father. I wish Gideon no harm."

That he did not have the same concern for Jane was plain on his face.

"For three years I've been a fugitive running with the wolves of London. One misstep, one inattentive moment could have cost my life. I've learned to gutter-fight with knives, cudgels, rocks, and fists. I made my living tricking fools and robbing gulls. And not one moment of that time did I not think about Gideon, somewhere in my mind, wondering if he was happy, wondering if he remembered me, wondering what kind of nonsense you were stuffing into his head.

"Now I've come to take him back. My time in the gutters is over, and so is his time with you."

Jane couldn't resist looking into Hawk's eyes. She recognized his pain for what it was, for she had felt the same agony when her own son died. Such a reminder made her even more determined not to lose another son.

"Now, Mistress Alexander." Hawk's voice was very quiet, with a tone that made Jane want to disappear into the wall. "Are you going to tell me where Gideon is? Or are you coming back to bed?"

The next morning dawned dreary and gray—almost as gray as Jane's face when she entered the kitchen to face Charity. Hawk was one step behind her. The housekeeper looked up in surprise as they came through the door.

"Charity, I'm afraid we have a guest."

Charity set aside the loaf of barley bread she was slicing, looked Hawk up and down, and then glanced at Jane in surprise. " 'Tis early in the morning for a call."

Hawk smiled with charming innocence. "Not an early-morning, but a late-night call, Mistress Charity."

The housekeeper's brows shot up.

Jane's face grew hot. She frowned at Hawk. "You needn't imply that . . . that . . . !"

"That what? That I slept in your bed? 'Tis the truth."

Charity's eyes grew wide.

Jane's flush deepened. "Pull your eyes back in your head, miss. 'Tis the truth he was in my bed, but I didn't keep him company there!"

Hawk shrugged, as if the detail were unimportant.

"This is Gideon's father, Lord . . . Master Matthew Hawkins, fugitive from justice, and, from what I glean of his ramblings, criminal at large."

"Hawkins. Hawkins . . ." Charity pondered aloud. "Oh!" Charity bustled backward until the kitchen table blocked her retreat. Her eyes fastened on the thin scar that marked Hawk's cheekbone. "He's the Hawk!" She drew in a panicky breath. "I heard of him in the markets. Everyone knows of him and that hawk face with its scar! The street boys call him the King of Thieves."

"He's king of nothing!" Jane snapped, irritated by Charity's fearful awe. She gave Hawk a cold gray glance. "He's merely an amoral jackanapes who thinks bluster will intimidate me into giving up Gideon."

"Bluster, mistress? I don't recall any bluster. I simply said I would keep you company until you tell me where the boy is."

Charity gasped. "Tell him what he wants to know, mistress! Please! Look at those eyes of his! He'll kill us all if you cross him!"

"Don't be ridiculous, Charity! He's not going to kill anyone—or cause any other harm, either." Jane gave Hawk a quelling glance. He answered with a devilish grin. "Harming us will not gain him his purpose. Animals like him thrive on fear, and when they cannot terrify, they are helpless."

Charity's consternation escaped her mouth in a fearful whine. "Oh, mistress! You don't know men like him!"

"Be quiet, Charity," Jane commanded calmly. She put a hand to her head, which was beginning to throb.

The housekeeper looked in despair at Jane's determined expression, then gave a little cry. "I'll tell you where he is, Master Hawk! I'll tell you!" She rushed to Hawk and sank to her knees.

"Charity, no!"

The housekeeper ignored her plea. "Gideon's gone to stay with Sarah—Mistress Jane's sister."

Hawk's face grew intent. "Whereabouts is this sister Sarah?"

"In the country!"

"Where in the country?"

Charity's face grew white at the look Hawk gave her. Jane closed her eyes, fearing the housekeeper's next words. All her courage was for naught, the humiliation, the terror, the cold, uncomfortable night spent in a chair watching the monster she was sure would leap upon her at any moment. All for naught.

"I—I . . . don't know," Charity stammered. "She lives in a big house in . . . in Kent! That's it!"

"Who is her husband?" Hawk's voice grew tight.

"Some man . . . He's a baronet," she added hopefully.

"A nameless country baronet," Hawk returned bitterly. "That's a great help!"

Charity burst into tears. "Don't kill us," she sobbed.

Jane breathed for the first time since Charity's recital began. She pulled the girl to her feet. "He's not going to do violence to anyone," Jane assured her. "Master Hawkins fights with weapons less clean than knives and swords. He uses humiliation and degradation to get his way."

"Oooooh!" Charity wailed.

"Now set the table for breakfast. We will try to pretend this nuisance"—she scowled at Hawk—"isn't here."

As Charity wept her way out the kitchen door, Hawk smiled maliciously. "Do you have any other servants for me to frighten?"

"You are absolutely without scruple!"

"Exactly what I tried to convince you of last night, my stubborn little Puritan."

"You say that word as though it were a curse."

"It is. A curse on England, and, more particularly, a curse on me. Now, mistress, what other servants do you have? Perhaps they will prove more knowledgeable than Mistress Featherbrain."

"I have no other servants for you to bully."

"You expect me to believe—"

A scream from the dining room interrupted the hostilities. Jane rushed for the door. The sight that met her eyes snapped the last rein she held on her temper. Charity cowered in a corner of the room, sniveling and shrieking, while a bandy-legged little demon of a man postured before her and growled like a beast, obviously enjoying the housekeeper's terror.

Jane, however, was not in the least terrorized. After she had spent hours being stalked by a wolf, this little man seemed but a weasel in comparison.

"Get out of my way!" Jane brushed Charity's tormentor aside, hurried to the frantic housekeeper, and put her arms around the girl. "Hush, Charity! Control yourself!"

Charity whimpered.

"I see you've met my comrade-in-arms, Ned Crow." Hawk sauntered into the dining room and ignored Jane's glare. "Ned, meet Mistress Jane Alexander and her housekeeper Charity. . . ."

"Brown," Jane provided coldly. "Charity Brown."

Ned growled again as Charity cringed.

"Shame on you both for frightening an innocent girl!"

"Don't look so innocent to me." Ned's face fell, as if his ferocity had been a mere game and Jane had spoiled his fun.

"Of course these estimable ladies are innocent," Hawk drawled. "All the world knows that Puritans are the most innocent of God's creatures—innocent in this case even of good sense."

"Damned if you don't come up with the fanciest talk sometimes! Ain't 'e somethin'?" Ned directed a winning smile toward Charity, who whimpered within the circle of Jane's comforting arms.

"Behave yourself, Ned," Hawk warned, "or Mistress Charity won't allow you any breakfast."

"You expect us to feed you?" cried Jane.

"Of course. How else would you treat your guests?"

"I'd offer you the same fare I use to rid the cellar of rats!" She turned and swept indignantly back through the kitchen door, her gray wool skirts swishing around her ankles. Charity scurried like a frightened mouse in her wake.

Ned's hoots followed the women through the door.

Hawk just smiled and shook his head. "Methinks the lady needs a lesson in hospitality."

Breakfast was a poor affair. Jane sat stiffly as Charity set before them barley bread with pork and cabbage left over from the evening before. Water was the only beverage.

"This would rid the cellar of rats, all right." Hawk grimaced at the meager fare. "Charity, if you value your life, you'll bring some real food to the table."

" 'Tis good enough for Mistress Jane to eat, then 'tis certainly good enough for the likes of you."

Jane smiled. Charity had rapidly lost her fear once Jane explained that their reputations, not their lives, were at stake. Propriety meant a bit less to the housekeeper than Jane would have liked.

"You mean to tell me this is what you normally eat?" Hawk asked.

Jane took a bite of cabbage and managed not to grimace. "Sometimes we have rice or oysters. Turnips and beans also."

Ned made a face. Nevertheless, his fork was busy stuffing cabbage and pork into his mouth. He gave Hawk an apologetic look. "'Abit," he explained. "A smart man don't turn down food."

"This is hardly a meal fit for a lady of your station," Hawk commented. "You have a rather odd idea of culinary taste. Is this what you've been feeding my son?"

"Your son has never suffered for lack of food," Jane told him coolly.

"If he's been forced to eat such as this for the past three years, Gideon must have a stomach of iron by now."

"The past six months we've been forced to . . . economize. My husband left me no fortune, and my only pension was through Lord Cromwell's generosity."

"So now Cromwell's dead you're without a quid, is that it?"

"It's not that bad," Jane said. "We're making do."

"With greasy pork and cabbage washed down with only water? I had better fare than this in the prison cell you bought me." The old resentment for that humiliation came to surface in Hawk's voice.

Jane regarded him with cool gray eyes. "If I'd known then that you were a villain as well as a traitor I would have saved my coin."

For a moment the two of them matched stare for stare. Jane was the first to drop her eyes.

"Aye," Hawk admitted. "I'm a veritable villain. If you'd had any sense when you stole my son, you would have used that coin to buy my death instead of wasting it on decent food and bedding. I'm sure the gaoler would have been just as happy with that bribe as with the other."

Jane was silent.

"You should've known I would come back for Gideon if it was humanly possible."

"It should not have been possible," Jane said quietly. "No one returns from slavery in Barbados."

"I didn't quite make it to Barbados. I escaped on the way to the ship." He grinned. "Without the strength of those lovely big meals you provided, I doubt I could have done it."

Jane clenched her jaw.

"As things stand I should think you'd be glad to have one less mouth to feed. You should be thanking me for taking Giddy off your hands."

Jane raised her face and met Hawk's eyes without flinching. Her voice rang with quiet pride. "One does not give up a child because of hard times. Gideon is my son."

"Nay, madam. Gideon is *my* son. And you will have no peace day or night until you tell me where he is."

The rest of the meal passed in silence. When Jane told Charity to save Hawk's almost untouched portion, Hawk countermanded Jane's order.

"Don't you dare, Charity. Throw the slop to the swine."

"We have no swine, other than them what's sittin' at this table."

Jane suppressed a smile, and Hawk raised a brow. "Well, mistress, these swine are not going to eat such fare again."

"I believe the King of Thieves expects to be fed like a true king," Jane said.

Charity merely snorted and took Hawk's plate. Ned hurried to finish the last morsel of pork before she could take his as well.

Jane rose. "You gentlemen may have the entire day on your hands to lounge at table, but Charity and I have work to do."

"She's a 'ard one," Ned commented as Jane left the room.

"Aye." Hawk followed her with thoughtful eyes. "For a soft-looking little lass she's a hard one. She'll probably have Giddy sweeping chimneys to earn his bread."

Jane donned the heavy shawl that hung by the pantry door. "I'm going to the carriage house to fetch the washtub," she told Charity.

The housekeeper glanced toward the door into the dining room, then in the direction of the neighboring house. Jane nodded. She certainly would slip over to the neighbors and ask them to alert a constable. This devil Hawkins wasn't half as clever as he thought. "Gather the laundry, Charity, and put the kettle on to heat."

"Aye, mistress."

If the two villains were listening to the exchange, they would believe the women were going about their daily work—Jane hoped. For the benefit of eyes that might be watching, Jane picked her way through the muddy garden to the carriage shed, where the washtub was stored. The shed had a back door not visible from the house, and the back door led straight out to the hedge that separated her house from the neighbor's. The hedge was thick, but not impassable. She wondered how long the authorities would take to come to her aid.

"No carriage?"

Jane halted, her hand reaching for the latch to the back door. She turned slowly. Hawk smiled at her from where he leaned on the front stall. He nodded toward the washtub that was propped against one wall.

"Isn't that what you came for?"

"What?" Her heart pounded. How had he followed her so quickly and quietly? Was he half cat?

"The washtub," he reminded her gently.

"Yes . . . certainly. I was just . . ."

"You couldn't have been thinking of leaving. I know you're much too intelligent a lady to try anything so foolish."

"I was . . ."

"Because if you think I've treated you badly so far, you wouldn't like what I'd do to you if you tried to turn me over to the law."

Jane raised her chin a notch. She refused to let the Devil intimidate her. "I don't frighten as easily as my housekeeper, Master Hawkins. There's no power on earth that can make me give you what you want."

His eyes bored into hers. She saw something in those calm hazel depths that did indeed frighten her—more than shouts or rages or threats would have frightened her.

"I have all the power I need to get what I want, Mistress Jane. For your own sake you should believe that."

Just as she thought he might raise a fist or indulge in some other display of masculine temper, Hawk smiled. A twinkle in his eyes dispelled some of the tension. He glanced around at the four empty stalls, the gardening tools that hung on the harness rack, the washtub propped against the wall where the coach had once stood.

"Did you eat the horses? It might have been an improvement on this morning's fare."

Jane frowned impatiently. "Of course we didn't eat the horses!"

Her face colored as Hawk's smile turned to a teasing grin.

"We sold the coach and horses. Such luxury is beyond my means right now."

"Then we'll need to hire a hackney to get to the market."

"Indeed!" She crossed to the washtub and hefted it onto

her hip. *"You* may go wherever you wish!" Her disgusted look proclaimed her wish that he would take a leap off the edge of the earth. "But *I* will be staying here to help Charity with the laundry."

"You'll have a much better time going to market with me. Come along."

Before she could prevent him he took the tub from her with one hand and appropriated her arm with his other hand. He towed her out of the carriage shed across the garden to the kitchen, where Charity gave a little shriek at their contentious entrance.

"I am not stepping a foot from this house in your company!" Jane told Hawk when he stopped to set the tub on the floor. She managed to yank her arm from his grip. "And I'm certainly not going to be seen in a public market with the likes of—!"

"You're certainly not going without me," he countered, arms folded across his broad chest. "And you *are* going. If you think I'm going to put up with such slop as we had this morning, you're sadly mistaken. Gutter rats eat better than you do."

"I have no—"

"I have plenty of money."

"Will you let me finish a sentence?"

He grinned tauntingly. "Most of your sentences don't seem to be worth finishing, mistress. Where's your cloak? It's cold outside."

Jane turned to Charity, who gaped at them from the coal stove. "Fill the washtub with water, Charity. We haven't all day to get the washing done."

"Yes, Charity," Hawk echoed. "Fill the tub. Ned will help you with the laundry." He raised his voice. "Ned!"

Jane and Charity objected at the same time, but Charity's voice drowned out Jane's softer protest. "I'm not letting that rodent of a man near my wash!" the housekeeper declared, bristling.

"Lord but this house is full of argumentative females!" Ned stuck his head in the kitchen door. "Did ye know this 'ouse ain't got no silver? It ain't even got no jewels, and what coin there is wouldn't buy a decent meal at the Lion!"

"There's only one valuable I want from this house, Ned, and he's not here."

Ned shrugged. "Don't 'urt to look."

"I'm taking Mistress Alexander to the market, Ned. Stay here and help Charity with the laundry."

"What?"

"You heard me. A little soap and water will do you good."

"Done without it fine so far." Ned slanted a look at the glaring Charity. "But maybe if the right woman . . ."

Hawk took Jane's arm and steered her from the kitchen. "They'll be all right," he assured her when she cast a worried glance backward. "Ned's not nearly as villainous as he would have people believe."

"I'm not going anywhere with you," Jane insisted. "You can't order me around like a slave and expect me to obey."

"What are you going to do about it?" Hawk asked. "As you might have gathered, ladylike objections don't sway me very much." In the entrance hall he handed Jane her cloak. She squared her jaw, tightened her mouth to a determined line, and refused to take it.

Hawk merely smiled, then placed it around her shoulders. She jumped as his hand brushed across the nape of her neck.

"Getting out of the house will improve your disposition," he remarked.

She moved stiffly as he guided her out the door.

Hawk sighed. "Something ought to be able to improve your disposition."

5

The hackney driver's impassive face hid a knowing smirk, or so Jane imagined, as Hawk took her arm in a most familiar fashion to assist her into the cab. Every eye in the neighborhood had to be watching her leave the house in a man's company. The same eyes would see them return, watch for Hawk to leave, and when he didn't, draw conclusions even more damning than the ones they must be drawing at this moment. Jane felt her face grow hot at the very idea of what her neighbors must be thinking.

"Mistress Alexander, my dear, you appear most uncomfortable."

She glared at him.

"All you have to do is say the right words," he reminded her.

Her lips compressed to a tight line.

"Stubborn to the last, I see."

The hackney jolted up the street and turned toward the City.

"Where are we going?" Jane asked in a strained voice.

"I know a good man in Cheapside who sells the best tea in London. Or perhaps you would prefer chocolate."

"Tea and chocolate are for the wealthy, Master Hawkins. Such extravagance is—"

"Sinful?"

She flashed him an exasperated frown. "Not sinful. Unwise."

"No one has ever accused me of wisdom," he said with a smile.

"I imagine not!"

"I think we must also have some good Rhenish wine, or perhaps some Bordeaux; a chine of beef for roasting; perhaps a tender haunch of venison, some chicken, or mutton; for dessert some almonds and raisins, oranges, marmalade comfits."

Jane's mouth watered in spite of her irritation. "I certainly haven't the means for such luxury."

"Of course you haven't," he conceded. "It's only too obvious you haven't the means for much of anything. If I'd known my son was enduring such privation—!"

"Gideon lacks for nothing!"

"Indeed?"

"In my care he is loved. He is taught that true beauty lies not in the physical world and true wealth is not counted in silver and gold. What would he have learned with you, Master Hawkins?"

Hawk's smile faded. He had no answer.

"I will have none of your rich food, sir. Do you hope to discover Giddy's whereabouts by bribing me with venison pasties and marmalade comfits?"

Her barb made him smile again. "I wouldn't make the mistake of thinking you so easily bought, mistress. Your very stubbornness makes me believe I will be living with you for a good while, and I've no intention of eating sour cabbage and pork all that time."

Jane pressed her fingers to her temples, where her head throbbed quite uncomfortably. "Your quest is hopeless,

Master Hawkins. You can ruin my good name, make my household into a purgatory—as you are apparently determined to do—you can do the worst you are capable of doing, and still I won't tell you where to find Gideon."

Hawk's face settled into a strange, fearsome calm. "My dear little Puritan, you could not imagine the worst I am capable of doing."

For a moment Jane's breath caught in her throat. His expression made her recall with some distress the furious animal of a man who had smashed his fist against the bars of his prison door and called her an unspeakable name in Fleet Prison, and also the man who had pinned her to her own bed with the cutting edge of a knife held against her throat.

Then Hawk's mouth lifted in a crooked grin that dispelled the menacing oppression that had settled into the coach. "I don't believe you're nearly as obdurate as you think, Mistress Alexander."

The hackney clopped past Fleet Prison—an unpleasant reminder to Jane of where she'd first met the rogue who now tormented her. If she had followed Grandmother Margaret's advice and stayed home that day, this nightmare would not have happened. They joined the traffic crowding through Ludgate into the City. Silence stretched so tightly between them Jane thought she would scream. Hawk's eyes were on her constantly—Jane felt them and was suffocated under their weight even as she refused to return his gaze.

They passed the huge edifice of St. Paul's and turned north toward the markets on Cheapside before Hawk broke the silence, speaking casually as if no tension existed between them.

"You might regard the food as yours, you know. After

all, you have fed, housed, and clothed my son for three years. Consider that I owe you quite a debt for that."

Scorn gave Jane the courage to meet Hawk's eyes. "Gideon is not *your* son, Master Hawkins. You forfeited all right to that beautiful child by your treasonous and criminal conduct. Gideon is *my* son. I will not give him up."

"Gideon is your son, is he?" Hawk lifted a brow. "Strange, I don't recall begetting him with you. That's something I'd remember, I'm certain."

Jane's face grew so hot she feared the roots of her hair might spring up in protest. She pulled her gaze away from his mocking eyes and stared toward the crowds on the street. Surely there was someone out there who would help her. In this center of enlightened civilization, a scoundrel like Hawk couldn't simply walk into a woman's life and terrorize her at will.

As if reading her mind, Hawk shook his head with mock sympathy. "Would you like to summon a constable?" he asked quietly. "That would provide fodder for the gossips, wouldn't it? Widow turns her criminal lover over to the authorities. Jane Alexander leads double life—chaste Puritan by day; by night doxy to the King of Thieves. I think the City would enjoy such a tale."

Jane remained silent, but she wanted to cry. The villain was right. No one knew better than she how her people diligently sought out not only their own sins but others' sins as well. Too many would be eager to believe the tale of a young widow falling from grace in so lurid a fashion. She'd been correct the night before when she'd thought Hawkins was the Devil. He was indeed either the Devil himself or the Devil's closest kin. No mere man could be so base.

"Here we are." Hawk tapped the roof of the coach as a

signal to stop. He jumped out and reached up a hand to assist Jane. "Are you ready to do some shopping, my dear?"

The day deteriorated from that point on. Cheapside seemed to crawl with curious eyes, all looking at Jane being escorted on Hawk's arm. Even when they finally returned to Great Queen Street she could find no refuge. Hawk tagged along at her heels like an unwanted shadow. No matter where in the house she went or what she did, she had but to turn to find him watching her, his face calm, confident, his gaze silently letting her know that he could outlast her in any kind of waiting game. Ned kept a similar watch on Charity. The housekeeper's sour glances and biting remarks only made the little man grin. The madder Charity became, the more he seemed to enjoy himself.

The midday meal was a strained affair. Hawk partook heartily of the morning's purchases, supping on venison pasty, hard yellow cheese, rice, sweet custard, and Rhenish wine. Jane would have none of the rich fare. While Hawk devoured his feast, she satisfied her appetite with cabbage soup and a portion of old cheese that had been molding in the larder these past weeks. Holding to her principles gave Jane a certain righteous satisfaction. Unfortunately, satisfaction of conscience held very little comfort for her stomach.

"I do admire your stubbornness," Hawk conceded with a smile. He cut a slice of sharp yellow cheese and bit into it with relish. "I've always thought women had a more practical nature. Eating cabbage soup while so much finer fare is available—that certainly does deserve some kind of prize for willful bullheadedness."

Jane watched as Hawk took another bite of cheese. He smiled his satisfaction, then sampled the sweet custard.

The man was a master of temptation, she decided. She really shouldn't watch his gluttonous display, especially with her stomach rumbling from the sour cabbage soup.

She rose abruptly, almost overturning the bench. "The soup needs more salt," she answered the query of his raised brow.

"I would think the soup needs more than salt."

Clenching her spoon, Jane considered rapping Hawk's knuckles with the implement as he reached for another venison pasty. The villain would only enjoy her slip from dignity, she decided. But the temptation was still great. She marched off to fetch the salt from the pantry.

The sight which met Jane's eyes when she stepped into the kitchen unraveled her already frayed temper. "What do you think you're doing?" she demanded.

Startled, Charity choked on the bite of sweet custard she had just stuffed into her mouth. In front of her on the kitchen table was spread a feast similar to the one Hawk was enjoying in the dining room. Ned Crow's plate also held a mountain of rich food.

"Master Hawkins said the food was for us all!" Charity muttered around the custard.

"Master Hawkins is not master here! The members of this household eat what *I* provide. We do not take the charity of criminals and traitors, and we do not succumb to the hungers of the body at the expense of our souls!"

The housekeeper obviously would have preferred to not be included in Jane's *we*. She watched forlornly as her mistress snatched the plate from beneath her nose and emptied the contents into the garbage pail.

"There is plenty of soup, Charity, and cheese and bread. Tomorrow you and I will go shopping to replenish the larder—with items more suited to our budget."

Charity made a face. "I don't see no harm in taking a windfall what falls into your lap."

"Just consider how this food was purchased," Jane retorted. "The money was no doubt gotten through"—she scowled at Ned's wide grin—"through ways we daren't imagine. Honest fare will sit easier on your stomach, Charity, and on your conscience."

Charity looked unconvinced. "That cabbage soup don't sit well on anything, mistress."

"Tomorrow we will buy some fresh vegetables and beef trimmings. And perhaps some oysters."

The housekeeper grimaced. Oysters, as far as she was concerned, rivaled sour cabbage in appeal—even though the inexpensive shellfish were popular with the lower orders of London dwellers.

The day got worse as the clock ticked on. Hawk followed Jane to the garden to watch with wry amusement while she repaired the fence that had let rabbits into her squash during the autumn months. Then he sat opposite her as she worked at her mending in the sunroom off the parlor.

"Are you not rather bored sitting there staring?" she asked him sharply.

Hawk merely smiled. "Watching you is anything but boring, Mistress Alexander."

She looked up suspiciously. "What do you mean by that?"

"I mean you are quite a singular woman, in spite of being a Puritan. You fill a man's eyes with your grace."

For once Jane could detect no mockery in his tone, and somehow the lack of it frightened her. She put aside her mending and pressed a hand to her head, which ached again. "If you'll excuse me, Master Hawkins, I feel in need of a nap."

He rose when she did. "I'll not excuse you, dear lady. But I'd be happy to join you."

Her head throbbed even more painfully. Jane wanted to cry for the hundredth time that day. "You really intend to leave me no privacy?"

He shook his head. "You can end this invasion with a few words, mistress."

"Not in your lifetime, Master Hawkins. I shall find another way to be rid of you."

"I think not."

At supper he blatantly enjoyed his sumptuous meal while silently mocking her less than adequate one. Charity's silent sulking about not being allowed to partake of Hawk's bounty didn't help. Jane tried to ignore Hawk's mocking eyes, Charity's sullen pout, and the unappetizing portion on her plate while she concentrated on devising a plan to be rid of her intruder. No scheme came to mind, however hard she thought. And all the while Jane felt the weight of Hawk's eyes. That silent gaze reduced her mind to a confused muddle and weighed like lead on her very soul.

After supper she retired to the library. If she couldn't lose Hawk, perhaps she could lose herself in reading. Hawk followed, of course. Jane could feel his eyes on her back as she selected a book and sat down in a chair facing the window. She heard him rummaging along the wall of bookcases that stood behind her late husband's desk.

"Rather narrow selection you have here," he commented. "Donne, Milton, Thomas Fuller, Hobbes—don't you read anything besides these religious ponderings?"

Jane looked at the volume she had selected blindly from the shelf: Jeremy Taylor, *A Discourse Concerning Prayer.* At this moment she had no desire to contemplate the subtleties of prayer. Prayer would not get her out of this tangle.

"Ah!" Hawkins exclaimed as he perused the lower shelf. "Marlowe, Shakespeare." He grinned at Jane. "I wouldn't have believed it of you, mistress."

"Those are your volumes," she replied coldly. "Gideon's nurse brought them for the boy, thinking they might be of some comfort to him, as you had admired them so."

He sobered. "Do you let him read from them?"

"I don't prevent him. But after the day spent in worthwhile learning directed by his tutor, Giddy has little use for such reading."

"In other words, you stuff his little mind so full of religious drivel that he can't appreciate good literature of a broader scope."

Jane closed the *Discourse Concerning Prayer* with a snap. "Drivel, Master Hawkins? Religion is what separates man from beast. But then, I would hardly expect a creature such as you to appreciate the difference."

"No. Of course not." He sat on one corner of the desk and regarded her with a provoking smile. "I'm sure you consider only the enlightened members of your own narrow sect as worthy to be called men. All the rest of us are beasts. Isn't that right?"

"I—!"

"Isn't that right?" he insisted.

"Men who ignore the truth and have no concern for their souls are little different from the animals in the fields."

"Of course you and the rest of your sober and somber Puritans are so certain of what is truth and what isn't."

"The truth is in the Bible for all to read," she told him.

"Is it?"

He took a Bible from the shelf and sat down in the chair opposite her, his eyes sparkling. If Jane didn't know better she might think he was enjoying himself.

"What knowledge do you have of the Bible, Master Hawkins?"

"A passing acquaintance," he claimed. He opened the volume. "Here is a truth straight from a saint's mouth: 'Judge not, that ye be not judged. For with what judgment ye judge, ye shall be judged, and with what measure ye mete, it shall be measured to you again.' Matthew, chapter seven, first and second verses. Perhaps, mistress, you should not be so quick to condemn all who do not agree with you as evil."

Jane smiled serenely and took the Bible from his hands. She read from the same chapter. " 'Wide is the gate, and broad is the way, that leadeth to destruction, and many there be which go in thereat: Because strait is the gate, and narrow is the way, which leadeth unto life, and few there be that find it.' Also Matthew, chapter seven, verses thirteen and fourteen, Master Hawkins. What a pity you do not have the wisdom as well as the name of that saint."

"You think God is setting Puritans to guard His strait and narrow gate?" he asked with a doubtful chuckle.

"Who better?" she replied jestingly. "I would hardly expect to see *you* guarding His gates."

He laughed. "I'll grant you that point."

Hawk's laugh made Jane smile in spite of herself. It was a clear laugh full of humor, gentleness, and just a touch of self-mockery. Not at all the chortling of a devil.

"Have you ever read Shakespeare, mistress?"

"Of course not."

"You should." He placed the Bible back upon the shelf and took down one of his own volumes of Shakespeare.

"Wisdom and truth are found not only in the Bible, mistress." He scanned the pages for a moment, then read:

> " 'Roses have thorns, and silver fountains mud;
> Clouds and eclipses stain both moon and sun,
> And loathsome canker lives in sweetest bud.'

From Shakespeare's Sonnet thirty-five. And more." He flipped pages and read again.

> " 'When to the sessions of sweet silent thought
> I summon up remembrance of things past,
> I sigh the lack of many a thing I sought,
> And with old woes new wail my dear time's waste.' "

He seemed to reflect a moment on the words, then smiled wryly. "From his Sonnet thirty."

"I see no particular wisdom in those lines," Jane commented sourly.

"Because you haven't learned their truth by sad experience. Would you like something sweeter? A love sonnet, perhaps?"

Jane opened her mouth to protest such worldly drivel, but before the words were out of her mouth Hawk was reading again.

> " 'When in the chronicle of wasted time
> I see descriptions of the fairest wights,
> And beauty making beautiful old rime,
> In praise of ladies dead and lovely knights,
> Then, in the blazon of sweet beauty's best,
> Of hand, of foot, of lip, of eye, of brow,

I see their antique pen would have expressed
Even such a beauty as you master now."

As Hawk's eyes left the page and fastened on her face, Jane felt her skin heat with embarrassment.

"Of course, if it's poetry of love that moves you, I'll agree the Bible has no equal. Have you read the Song of Solomon?"

"I've read the entire Bible several times over."

"Did you enjoy the Song of Solomon?" He reached for the Bible again and rapidly leafed through the weighty volume.

Jane's face grew even pinker. "I don't know what you mean."

Hawk looked up and smiled. "Sadly enough, I think you're telling the truth. Take this passage, for example—"

"No! I mean, this is ridiculous, Master Hawkins." Jane stood abruptly. "I came into the library to read, not to indulge in meaningless debate over matters that are not disputable. I'm not even sure any longer what we discuss. You have a very confusing way about you, sir!"

"Thank you." He gave her an unrepentant grin. " 'Tis an art that takes practice."

"I would think you come by it naturally!" She shoved the *Discourse Concerning Prayer* back into its place on the shelf. "Since I am apparently to be prevented from peaceful study, I will leave you to continue your discussion with yourself—since you find yourself such an erudite and amusing companion. Good night, Master Hawkins."

Jane breathed a sigh of relief when she closed the library door behind her. She wished she could seal it shut and trap the Devil within. He could read his silly sonnets and morbid recitations to his heart's content and spare her the headache of having to listen to his useless spoutings. Her head was pounding again, the drums of a hundred regiments rolling painfully through her brain. For a moment she allowed herself the luxury of slumping against the wall, her head pressed against the cool molding of the library door. Then she straightened and climbed the stairway to her chamber.

The blessing of privacy settled about Jane in comforting silence. She took the linen coif from her hair, unfastened the gorget that covered the neckline of her bodice, and reached for the lacings that fastened at her back. The lacings put up their usual struggle. Jane's hair came loose in the battle, flowing down her back in a golden flood and making matters even worse. The unannounced opening of her chamber door caught Jane in a very awkward position.

"Need help?" Hawk drawled.

Jane jumped like a startled doe.

"That looks damnably hard to reach."

"Get out!"

Hawk ignored her demand and sauntered toward her. Jane clutched the half-unfastened bodice to her chest and backed against the wall.

"Get out!"

"You didn't think I was going to let you out of my sight, did you?"

Gently he pried her away from the wall and turned her around.

Jane didn't object. She couldn't. For the first time in her life she was dumbfounded. Her brain whirled in confusion, her body stood rooted to the spot, ignoring her demands to flee or at least spring into action and club Hawk soundly with a fist. She was speechless and numb as Hawk reached for her, but not so numb that she couldn't feel the warmth of his hands on her shoulders and the strangely tantalizing brush of his fingers against her skin as he set about the task of unfastening the rest of her laces.

He turned her around to face him again, to face that wide mouth slanted upward in a mocking smile, the expectantly cocked brows, and calm hazel eyes—more brown now than green—regarding her in gentle amusement. Hands on her shoulders, he held her at arm's length.

"If you're going to wear such inconvenient clothing, you really should hire a lady's maid."

Jane couldn't force an appropriate response from her numb lips. The man's audacity was beyond a sane reaction.

"You might get someone who could advise you on fashion. Those drab gowns you wear and that ugly little cap over your hair gives a man the impression that you're as plain as a little brown sparrow. But you're not plain at all."

Hawk stood staring at her. She could feel his eyes take in the disarrayed tumble of her hair, the mortified blush on her cheeks, the expanse of naked skin above the bodice she clutched to her breasts. The numbness that held her to the spot gave way to a tingle that began between her legs and spread to her belly and breasts. The air within her lungs quivered, her heart seemed to shiver with every beat. Even her lips trembled; she bit them in fear of revealing this strange weakness.

"Please leave me alone," she pleaded. She had gone past anger to abject humiliation. If begging would end her torture, then she would beg.

"Certainly," he agreed amiably. "As soon as you tell me where to find my son."

A whimper of distress escaped her throat, in spite of her attempt to bite the sound back. He put a finger to her lower lip and pried it from between her teeth. The finger lingered at her mouth until she jerked her head away.

"You're making your lips bleed."

Jane clenched her teeth, wanting to cry.

"Tell me where Giddy is and I'll leave you alone. You won't ever have to see me again."

She was silent. Her jaw squared in determination.

"Until then, my chaste and modest little Puritan, I'll be your shadow, day and night. I'll never leave your side. Those sad gray eyes of yours won't move me, and all the weeping in the world won't rid you of me. If you hope some shred of honor within me will soften me to your plight, you hope in vain. I have no honor left. All that is left to me in this world is my son."

The pathos of his words, of his self-confessed iniquity, touched something in Jane's soul. The touch was light and brief, however, and immediately wiped away by a touch of another sort. As though drawn against his will, Hawk reached out and gently brushed a strand of hair from her cheek. The look in his eyes when he did so—eyes suddenly gone dark and fathomless as the night—jolted Jane from her trance. She jerked back and whirled around, giving him her stiff, unyielding back.

"You are the Devil himself," she accused bitterly.

"Not quite the Devil," Hawk said. "Perhaps the Devil's advocate in a world that needs a touch of the old imp."

"I suppose you'll not even give me the privacy to disrobe."

She heard his deep chuckle behind her. "If I were to be so noble, no doubt you'd club me the moment my back was turned. You needn't worry that you'll surprise me with anything I haven't seen before."

Jane closed her eyes in agony. Would the nightmare

never end? She refused to turn back toward him, but heard his boots clump across the bare wood floor to her wardrobe. A moment later he presented her with a white cotton night rail.

"Judging from last night, I'd guess you sleep naked as a wood nymph—one of the few sensible things about you. But tonight you might prefer to wear this."

She snatched the garment from his hand and clutched it to her. Stoically she fastened her eyes upon the blank, whitewashed surface of the wall in front of her, as if she might find written there something that could help her. Rustlings behind her and the creak of the bed indicated Hawk's continued presence. Finally she resigned herself and slipped the night rail over her head, pulling it down quickly as her bodice fell to the floor. She stepped out of skirts and petticoats hidden beneath the folds of white cotton.

Hawk was ensconced firmly in her bed by the time Jane turned around. Not deigning to look at him, she marched to the wardrobe and neatly hung her garments, then took a brown wool blanket from the linen chest, wrapped it around herself, and sat down on the straight-backed wooden chair in the corner.

"That appears to be an uncomfortable place to spend the night."

She gave him a shriveling look. "Are you suggesting I sleep in the bed with you?"

He shrugged. "You can sleep wherever you please, as long as you sleep within my sight."

He leaned toward the bed table to douse the lamp. At the simple movement, muscles rippled in his shoulders and arms. Swarthy, lean, and hard, his bare torso seemed sinfully out of place against the white of her bed sheets. The lamp snuffed out, and in the darkness the image of that masculine torso stayed etched on Jane's eyes.

"Good night, Mistress Jane Alexander."

Jane answered him with resentful silence. She sat without moving, her spine as straight and stiff as the back of the chair. Gradually her eyes accustomed to the darkness. The dull glow from the coal grate peopled the chamber with black shadows and dim red light, transforming it from her sacred refuge into an earthly version of hell. For the first time since Jane could remember, she had not ended the night with a journal entry and prayer. If she prayed now, her prayer would be a sinful one—a request for the Lord to visit some particularly unpleasant punishment upon the monster in her bed. She sighed, allowed her shoulders to slump just a bit, and massaged her aching head.

For a long time she sat still, listening to Hawk's breathing. When it settled to the even rhythm of sleep, she rose quietly and tiptoed to the door.

"Ah, ah!"

Jane jumped at Hawk's warning and pulled her hand away from the latch.

"If you try that again you *will* end up beside me in this bed. Tied, if necessary."

She released a long breath of exasperation.

"Don't test my patience, mistress. I warned you that I'm a man of no honor. You wouldn't like me when I'm angry."

"I don't like you now."

"Fair enough."

Jane could hear the insolent grin in his words, could feel his eyes follow her as she made her way back to the chair. Suddenly something flew at her out of the darkness. She shrieked, but her attacker was only a pillow launched from bed.

"Sleep well," Hawk said with a chuckle.

The next few days of Hawk's intrusion were even worse than the first, except that meals were considerably better. Ned not only kept as close an eye on Charity as Hawk kept on Jane, but while he made a pest of himself he also turned his hand to cooking. The little man was a passable chef—better than either Charity or Jane, who had shared kitchen chores when Jane had been forced to let Cook go.

Jane could no longer resist the temptation of fresh buttermilk, vension, and a chine of beef roasted to a turn. Likewise, to require such abstinence of poor Charity carried a principle much too far, Jane decided. If they must suffer from the presence of these criminals in their home, then they might as well enjoy what few benefits the rogues brought with them.

Jane had to draw the line at her housekeeper's loose behavior with Hawk's knavish companion, however. Ned managed to charm the girl from a hissing cat to a purring kitten in less than two days' time. His dubious charm had little to do with Charity's transformation. The housekeeper warmed to any person or thing that lightened her work load, and when Ned took over the cooking chores—claiming that they would all starve if Charity was trusted with meals—he found a way to the housekeeper's heart.

Jane enjoyed a rare moment alone at the dining table after dinner when Charity confided her opinion that Ned wasn't such a villain, and perhaps the infamous Hawk wasn't such a scoundrel as marketplace and street gossip made him. The men sat within sight in the parlor, locked in a low-voiced discussion.

Exhausted from three nights of poor sleep, Jane all but

snapped the housekeeper's head off. Nor did she apologize when Charity huffed indignantly from the dining room. Another night loomed ahead of her, a night of sitting in an uncomfortable chair, plotting ways to get rid of her unwanted guest while he snoozed pleasantly in her bed—snoozed but never slept so soundly that she could catch him at a disadvantage. The thought put Jane in no mood to watch Charity's speculative, appreciate gaze fasten on either man who was within sight. She wouldn't have such licentious behavior in her house.

The very next day Jane's worst nightmare came true; her private hell became a public one when a delegation of three ladies from her church congregation came to call. Her first thought when Charity announced visitors was to plead illness. In truth she felt not at all well. Before she could make her excuse, however, Hawk instructed Charity to show their callers in. The delighted grin upon his face made Jane's heart sink.

The visitors filed into the parlor, a somber regiment of three marching as if to the strains of a hymn. They sat themselves down on the settee, their feet side by side in a neat row and their hands folded primly in their laps. Jane grimaced inwardly. Of all the members of her congregation, these three were the last she would want to call: Mary Clark, whose gray hair and wrinkled face gave no hint of the moral zeal contained within her aging spirit; Lady Danfield, a middle-aged dragon who ruled the ladies of the congregation with the same strict discipline with which Lord Danfield ruled the gentlemen; and lastly Barbara Childs, youngest of the three and self-appointed arbiter of the congregation's morals.

There they sat on Jane's settee, a nightmare come true. Hawk flashed them a smile, one that Jane was sure would set ordinary women all aflutter. The only response he got was a disapproving frown from Lady Danfield.

Jane sat down in the chair opposite the settee, seemingly as calm as her callers. "What a pleasure to see you ladies," she began. "May I offer you some refreshment—hot cider or a nice glass of buttermilk?"

Lady Danfield turned her disapproving look upon Jane. "No, thank you, Widow Alexander. We are here because we were concerned," she stated bluntly. "You were not in church yesterday."

Jane felt as though Lady Danfield had hit her with a club. Yesterday was Sunday? How could she have forgotten? She had never in her life missed a Sunday service, not until Matthew Hawkins barged into her world and turned it upside down. "I . . . haven't been feeling well at all."

Mary Clark frowned in prunelike censure. "If you've the strength to rise from bed, then you've no excuse to shirk your duty to the Lord."

"You're right, Mistress Clark. I am sorely at fault."

All three ladies gave a little nod of satisfaction at Jane's acknowledgment, then turned their heads, as if puppets controlled by a single string, toward Hawk.

"I don't believe we've met," Lady Danfield said coldly.

"Indeed, I haven't had the pleasure, my lady." Hawk smiled, his eyes twinkling.

Drums of doom pounded painfully in Jane's head.

"I'm Linus Gardner, Jane's . . . cousin."

The heads turned in unison back toward Jane. "You've never mentioned a cousin, Widow Alexander."

Before Jane could speak Hawk moved to her side and placed a familiar hand on her shoulder. The heat of his touch burned through to her very soul, making her want to cringe. "There are so many cousins in our family, I'm not surprised she chooses to ignore us. But we've become very close on this visit."

"Indeed!" All three spoke together, their voices crackling with disbelief.

The smile Hawk gave Jane added fuel to the ladies' indignation. It was just the right touch to make them certain she and Hawk were wallowing in sin. What could she say to defend herself? The truth? "The truth will set you free," the Bible said, but in this case the truth would condemn her just as surely as the lie.

She shrugged off Hawk's proprietary hand. "My . . . cousin . . . likes to think of himself as quite the knavish rogue," Jane confided calmly. "In truth he is quite an ordinary dullard who shocks people for his own entertainment." She met the gleam in his eye with a sour look that should have left no doubt in the prim ladies' minds that Hawk was not her lover. "He has the habit of dropping in uninvited on people who have very little use for him, family or no. The pity is he hasn't learned to depart as quickly as he comes."

Jane's denial did little to soften the disapproving faces across from her. They would believe what they wanted to believe. Sin—discovering it, discussing it, deploring it, and condemning it—was a cornerstone of the Puritan way. Without it some lives had very little meaning.

The ladies rose as one. "We will ask the Reverend Morley to call," Lady Danfield told Jane, more of a threat than a promise. "I'm sure he will have some wisdom to share with you."

None of the three deigned to look at Hawk as they marched out of the parlor. Jane went with them, waving Charity aside and holding the door for them to leave. Mary Clark turned to Jane as she crossed the threshold.

"I see every evidence of lewd behavior in this household, Jane Alexander. I don't know who that man is, but he's set you on the road to perdition. It's a well-known fact that young widows living without proper guidance are the Devil's favorite target."

"I assure you everything in my household is most proper," Jane said. Then with a hint of reproach: "You should know me better, Mary."

"Hmmph!" was Mistress Clark's reply.

Jane heard Hawk's chuckle as she closed the door behind her self-appointed jury.

"If that was an example of Puritan womanhood, then the sect is bound to die out in no time—all on its own."

Jane leaned against the door for support. Her legs felt too weak to hold her. Never in her life had she been so embarrassed. She had always been the model child, the modest maid, the virtuous wife, the rock of righteousness upon whom never so much as a chastising glance fell. Now, all the eyes of her congregation, friends, people in the market and on the streets, even servants, would be following her in condemnation. Not because of any sin she could atone for, but because of Matthew Hawkins, traitor, criminal, self-styled Devil's advocate. She wanted to scream and cry and the same time.

She did neither. The ingrained habit of self-control took charge as she returned to the parlor. "Are you quite satisfied?" she inquired, her hands balled into fists at her sides.

Hawk leaned back in her late husband's favorite chair, his feet propped upon an ornately carved oak side table. "What do you think?" The provoking smile didn't leave his face. "I'll not be satisfied, Jane, until I get what I came for."

"You've done your worst," she said in a tight voice. "You can see I won't give in."

"I've done my worst." He repeated her words with a chuckle, then shook his head. "No, my dear innocent. I could do worse. Much worse."

Fury burned in Jane's chest, tightened her throat, pressed behind her eyes. Control began to slip. "How dare you come into my house, intrude in my life, ruin my good name! If there is any justice in heaven or on earth, someday you'll be sorry!"

"That's the pity of it," he mocked. "There is no justice. Not in heaven or on earth."

The headache that had plagued Jane for the last few days suddenly swelled to intolerable pain. It combined with her fury to send red spots dancing before her eyes. "Leave! Get out! Just leave me alone!"

When he simply sat there, his insolent form wavering slightly in her gaze, Jane whimpered, "Get out!" She bombarded him with the closest thing at hand, as she might throw stones at the rats that invaded her vegetable cellar.

Hawk caught the missile, looked at it, and smiled. "Attacking with a Bible, are you? I suppose it's an appropriate club to bludgeon me with."

His words thundered in Jane's head to join the flashes of pain that ricocheted off the inside of her skull. The last thing she saw before darkness claimed her was the fading of Hawk's smile.

6

For a moment Hawk merely stood and stared at the motionless heap on the parlor floor. His brain refused to register the fact that Jane Alexander had fainted. The little widow didn't seem the sort of female to swoon. She should have flesh of steel to match her determined spirit, strength of body equal to her vigor of mind. That she didn't came as a shock.

"What in hell?" He knelt beside her and pressed his fingers to her neck to feel for a pulse. Her skin was dry and hot, her breathing shallow. A gush of panic flooded his veins. Had *he* done this to her? Was the woman so puny that a bit of vexation could lay her low?

Impatiently Hawk chafed Jane's hands and gently slapped her flushed cheeks. "Mistress Alexander, for God's sake wake up!"

If hearing the Lord's name taken in vain didn't rouse her, nothing would.

"Mistress Puritan, quit this nonsense and get back on your feet, goddammit!"

Jane lay still as death.

"Jane!" Her name was almost a plea. He hoisted her into his arms. "You insist on carrying this much further and you're going to be mortally embarrassed. Charity!" he shouted. "Get in here and see to your mistress!"

Hawk carried Jane up the stairs, noting in dismay how light she was, how the bones of her hip cut into his belly. Why had he not noticed she was so thin and fragile?

"Charity!" he bellowed as he lay Jane on her bed. "Get up here, dammit! Where is that woman?"

He bent over to loosen Jane's bodice just as the housekeeper bustled into the chamber. She shrieked when she saw Hawk hovering so closely over Jane's body.

"What're ye doing? Get out! Get away! Foul lecher!" She rushed to the pitcher on the dresser and brandished it above her head.

"Don't be a fool, woman! Would I have called you in here if I was bent on rape? Your mistress is ill."

Charity's manner changed abruptly. "Ill? Oh, dear Lord! She's ill!"

"That's what I said. I'm sure she'd rather have you tending her than me."

Charity pressed both hands to her heart, as if that organ were in danger of failing. "Oh, dear! It's the plague! She must've got it from poor Mistress Thackeray. I told her she shouldn't be nursing that old woman! I knew she'd bring it home!"

Hawk looked at Jane, then at Charity. The whole house had gone mad. "She doesn't have the plague, you silly girl. She merely fainted. Maybe the ague, or a woman's fit."

What did Hawk know about women's vapors? His wife, God rest her soul, had fainted at least once a month, sometimes more often—from distress, overabundance of emotion, tight corsets, strong doses of sun, mysterious female complaints, and sometimes, Hawk suspected, as a ploy to get his attention. Once again he reflected, with a touch of panic, that Jane Alexander didn't seem the sort of female for such weaknesses.

"If it's not the plague," Charity whined, "then it's something just as bad. Mistress Jane caught it from Mistress Thackeray, and we'll catch it just the same. Oh, mercy! If she dies I'll never get my back wages!"

Jane chose that moment to moan. Her face was even more flushed than before.

"Lord preserve us!" Charity whimpered.

Hawk's patience reached its limit. He rounded on the housekeeper with a vengeance. "Stop sniveling, woman! I'll make you wish you had the plague if you don't get some cool water and clean towels up to this chamber. And send Ned for a physician. Where is the closest?"

Charity retreated a few steps from his anger. "There's one lives in Lincoln's Inn Fields."

"Tell Ned to fetch him. And hurry."

"Yes, my lord!"

Hawk paced the bare floorboards for a few lengths of the room, then turned a disgusted glance on Jane. She looked all too vulnerable and innocent lying there with dark honey lashes feathered against flushed cheeks. A stray twinge of sympathy caught him unawares, until he reminded himself that she was a Puritan, she had stolen his son, and even now she kept him from Gideon.

"What the hell am I to do?" he asked her still form. "Goddammit, where is that woman?"

He bellowed for Charity again. A moment later Ned stuck his head in the door.

"Did you bring the physician?" Hawk demanded.

"What physician? What're ye snarling about up here, 'Awk? I can 'ear ye all over the 'ouse."

"Charity didn't tell you to fetch a physician?"

"Hain't seen 'er." For the first time he looked at the figure on the bed, then stepped into the room. "Hoo! What'd ye do to the lady?"

"I didn't do anything to her, dammit! Much as I'd like to. She fainted dead away, out of the blue. I told Charity to have you fetch a doctor. There's one lives in Lincoln's Inn Fields."

"Right away, Cap'n!"

"Go!"

After Ned left, Hawk bellowed once again for the housekeeper, who seemed to be taking a great deal of time about fetching cool water and clean towels. When she didn't appear, he took upon himself the task of making the patient more comfortable, afraid to leave her side to hunt down the truant maid.

Hawk had undressed his share of women, but never one so limp and unresponding. Jane lay in his arms like a child's rag doll. He scarcely noticed the female body that lay exposed to his gaze as he removed her bodice, skirt, petticoats, corset, and chemise. Maneuvering her limp form into a soft cotton night rail, he took distant note of alabaster skin, full, rose-tipped breasts, and slim legs, then filed the sight in his mind for later appreciation. He also noticed the unladylike roughness of her hands and the protrusion of ribs and hipbones. The fear that she was seriously ill made him curse under his breath. Just at that moment, speaking profanity aloud within hearing of Jane's ears didn't seem right.

Hawk pulled the room's one chair next to the bed and sat staring at the slight girl lying there. He'd hardly done her justice in his sketches, Hawk decided. Her features were much finer than he'd remembered, her brows more gracefully arched, the lashes that curtained her eyes thicker. Her hair—he'd seen very little of her hair in that meeting through his prison door. It was soft and fine and lustrous lying against the pillow in tangled chaos—a crown of glory she concealed from view under plain starched linen.

"That in itself is a sin," he told her softly. "To hide such God-given beauty as if it were a shame."

At the sound of his words she tossed and moaned, throwing the covers off and tangling them in her legs. When he untangled her, her skin was even hotter to his touch than it had been before. How long had it been since Charity left to fetch water and towels? Hawk had lost track of the minutes passing as he'd sat and indulged in pointless admiration. Cursing the housekeeper, who no doubt was making up excuses to stay out of her mistress's sickroom, Hawk decided to fetch water and towels himself. He picked up the water pitcher just as the door opened to admit Ned.

"Good! You're back. Where is the physician?"

" 'E won't come, 'Awk. Says 'e'll 'ave 'is pay first."

Apparently the doctor knew of Jane's poor circumstances. "There's an example of Christian charity for you."

Ned shrugged. "The quacks are always more interested in a cove's pockets than anything else."

"He'll get his pay," Hawk declared. "I'll fetch the scoundrel myself."

Ned's mouth twisted into his version of a smile. "The mort's got no money."

"I do," Hawk said.

"Why bother?" Ned insisted, cocking his head. "If she dies, won't 'er sister bring the boy and come to bury 'er?"

Hawk gave his confederate an unbelieving stare.

"That's a mighty frown for a man 'oo's found the answer to 'is problems."

Hawk hadn't been aware of frowning, but he discovered Ned was right. A fierce scowl furrowed his brow. The thought of Jane Alexander's dying didn't sit right in his mind, in spite of the possible benefits.

"The mort's caught yer fancy," Ned said accusingly.

Hawk snorted. "Not likely." His eyes strayed to the unconscious girl on the bed. "A man's got to admire her grit, though."

"Aye," Ned admitted, smiling crookedly. "That a man does."

"We've no assurance this sister would come," Hawk said, not meeting Ned's eyes. "If Jane Alexander dies, I might never find Gideon."

Ned chuckled. "And 'er a Puritan, no less. 'Oo woulda' thought—the 'Awk and a Puritan mort."

Hawk gave his friend a look that could have frozen the Thames in July. "Are you through with your prattle?"

Ned grinned gnomishly. "For now."

"Then tell me where to find this greedy physician."

Jane woke to a darkened room. The gray gloom pressed in on her, pulsing with heat in time to the pain throbbing inside her skull. She felt weighted down by lead. Her bed seemed to spin slowly, tilt this way and that until she had to close her eyes to stop the sensation. When she opened them again a face swam into view above her—a goblin straight from hell, she first thought. Then she realized the face belonged to Ned Crow.

"Awake, are ye?"

Jane could manage only an inarticulate moan.

"Aye. That's the way ye look, too. 'Awk's gone to fetch a physician."

She closed her eyes again. The world still spun, and her own breath seared her skin when she exhaled. The fever was the same one that had killed Mistress Thackeray. Jane knew the course of the illness, for she had sat with her poor neighbor day and night, bathed her fever-wracked skin, comforted her while she raved in delirium, and listened helplessly while she wept in pain. Now Jane must follow the same bitter road.

She didn't fear the prospect of death. That was not what made her heart twist in agony. Her fear was for Gideon. Who would care for her dear Giddy if she died? Her sister Sarah might, but Sarah had five children of her own to care for, and she and her husband Geoffrey had never approved of Jane's taking the boy in the first place.

Jane opened her eyes again. Ned still hovered over her like a misshapen, frowning gargoyle. The frown was one of concern, she was surprised to note, and his eyes, usually the hard black of a snake's, softened with a touch of sympathy.

"Where is . . . ?" Her voice caught in her throat. Even speaking was an effort.

" 'Awk?" Ned supplied.

Jane nodded—an excruciating effort.

"Gone to fetch the quack. I told you before."

She shook her head, not remembering. "Tell me . . ." If she died, Hawk would most surely take Gideon. Sweet, frivolous Sarah wouldn't have the determination to hold the child. "Would . . . would Hawk be a good father?"

Ned's brows shot up in surprise. "Is it that on yer mind, mistress? Ye just tell 'Awk where the boy is and see what kind o' father 'e is. 'E's been chompin' at the bit to fetch that boy all the three years I've knowed the man. 'E knowed where Giddy was. 'Anded out drawin's o' you all over town till someone told 'im where ye live. Then after all that 'e left the boy 'ere 'cause 'e knew it was better for Giddy, but it 'urt 'im some. More than some, if truth be known."

"He's a violent man," Jane whispered sadly, as if to herself.

"'Awk'd never lift a finger to a child, mistress. Ye should'a seen what 'e did to Walter Sykes fer beatin' on Little Tate. Near beat 'im to a pulp, 'e did!" Ned hesitated at the look on Jane's face. "Maybe that weren't the thing to tell ye, considerin'. But 'Awk loves that boy, mistress. Ain't you nor the law nor anything else goin' to keep 'im away from 'is son."

Jane closed her eyes on a new flash of pain that lanced through her head. As it lessened, she sighed. "As long as I live, Gideon is *my* son."

"Well, now," Ned told her with a crooked smile, "for some reason 'Awk seems mighty determined that ye're gonna live, mistress, though it seems foolishness to me, considerin'. But I guess you'd pull through anyway. Any mort with the grit to stand up to Ned Crow isn't likely to duck under at a bit o' fever."

Jane sensed the little man was actually trying to cheer her, in his own twisted way. She attempted a smile.

"That's better," Ned said approvingly. "There's nothin' like a bit of a smile to cure a fever. 'Ere's somethin' that'll make ye smile. I'll show ye how I earned a livin' in the yard at St. Paul's when I first got off ship. Used to be a tar in the merchant fleet, ye know. 'Ere now. Watch!"

From Jane's dresser he took a hairbrush and a porcelain box of hairpins. He emptied the contents of the box onto the dresser, took the brush and the box in one hand, the box's lid in the other, then with a bow and a flourish toward the bed, proceeded to juggle them with great dexterity.

"Used to juggle any item the crowd would give me—up to five or six. Couldn't go much more'n that."

Right in rhythm with his juggling he picked the empty candlestick off the bedside table and added it to his act.

"There now. That brought milady a smile, didn't it?" He began a little dance in time to the motion of his hands. "Better still—if some gull hands me a worthy item, I make it disappear!"

Suddenly he was juggling only three things. The porcelain hairpin box was nowhere to be seen. He stopped, letting the brush, the lid, and the candlestick drop into his hand one by one, then opened his bulky vest and revealed the box. "A fellow what's good at it can earn a pretty piece o' coin this way. And any gull stupid enough to fall for the act deserves to be fleeced."

"Ned," Jane said, hovering between a smile and a grimace of pain, "it is wrong to take advantage of fools."

"Nay, mistress. We're all fools. And we all get fleeced in our own time."

The door opened and interrupted Ned's foray into philosophy.

"What's going on here?" Hawk demanded.

"I was entertainin' the lady with a bit of jugglin'," Ned explained.

The black-clad physician who followed Hawk into the room gave Ned a look of disbelief.

Ned shrugged. "She was talkin' gloomy. No sense dyin' sad."

The doctor was a thin, ascetic-looking man with an expression to match his somber garb. He looked at Hawk and Ned in disapproval. "This is most unorthodox. Where is the lady's attendant?"

"Avoiding the sickroom like the plague—literally," Hawk told him.

The physician looked at his patient and sniffed. "Very well. If you . . . gentlemen will leave me to my examination . . ."

Ten minutes later the doctor emerged from Jane's chamber with a look of dour satisfaction on his face. "You are a relative?" he asked Hawk in a dubious tone.

"You might say I'm part of the family."

"A cousin," Ned added with a smirk.

"Indeed!" The physician gave them both a jaundiced stare, then shrugged. "Your . . . cousin . . . has camp fever, or jail fever, it is sometimes called. 'Tis unusual in people of quality, but not unheard of. You will find that a scarlet rash is developing on her skin. It will spread and get worse, and her fever will most likely rise until it either breaks or she succumbs."

Hawk glanced toward the door of Jane's chamber, his heart sinking. "Is she likely to die?"

"I have no way of knowing the outcome, but it is quite possible." The physician skewered Hawk with a sharp glare. "Sin leads to retribution, sir, and illness is often the consequence of wickedness. 'Tis the best advice I can give you and your *cousin*—along with a warning that this fever, like sin, is contagious."

"If it's wickedness that brings on illness," Hawk countered, "then that lady in there should be the healthiest woman alive."

"Indeed! Satan stalks the unwary and brings down those that are complacent in their piety."

Hawk lifted one brow in sardonic disgust. "If piety is the best medicine you can offer, sir, then you're no use to me. Ned will show you to the door."

"My fee?"

Hawk counted out a number of coins and placed them in the physician's hand.

"This is only half the amount!" the doctor objected.

"For half a job. You diagnosed but didn't offer a treatment other than God's mercy, which is a quality I've come to mistrust. Go now before I decide you've not even earned the fee in your hand."

Hawk's voice was low, but the physician retreated a step from the look in his eye. "You, sir, are a knave!"

"A fact I acknowledge with no argument."

Hawk ignored Ned's frantic signaling for attention as the doctor flounced out. His flash of anger was entirely unreasonable, he acknowledged to himself. After all, it was he who had set about destroying Jane Alexander's reputation. But hearing that self-righteous vulture defame her character had been one straw too much for his temper.

"Ye should've told the quack to send word to 'er sister to come and nurse. Where's yer 'ead?"

"I doubt he'd know where her sister's to be found. Besides, if we're *cousins*"—he slanted Ned a chiding look—"we should know things like that, shouldn't we?"

· Ned snorted his disgust.

"Go find that lazy housekeeper and tell her that her mistress doesn't have the plague, and she's been exposed to the fever by just living here, so she might as well come see to the nursing duties."

Twenty minutes later Ned found Hawk in the sickroom with a sleeping Jane. He reported that Charity was nowhere about the house or garden, and her personal things were gone from the room off the kitchen where she slept.

"How do you know where the woman slept?" Hawk asked, one brow raised.

Ned shrugged and grinned. "She was willin'. I was 'ot."

Hawk grimaced and glanced at Jane, who slept, still as death itself. "Now I suppose we have to worry about the damned housekeeper going to the authorities."

"Nah!" Ned opined. "That'd be too much bother for such as 'er."

"And there's no one left to see to Mistress Alexander."

Ned looked at Hawk and smiled slowly.

"Goddammit!" Hawk snarled.

"We could leave. Ye know the boy's in Kent. Could be we might still find 'im."

"Leave her to die?"

"Likely she'll die anyway."

"But if she doesn't, she may still tell me where Gideon is."

Ned chuckled dryly.

"Leave off," Hawk warned gruffly. "I'm not yet such a monster as to abandon a woman to die alone."

" 'Specially this one," Ned tossed over his shoulder as he sauntered out of the chamber.

Especially this one, Hawk admitted to himself. A woman who loved so fiercely that she would defy known criminals, stand firm in the face of threats, and sacrifice everything, even her precious reputation, for the sake of a child—such a woman did not deserve to die alone and helpless. Had Jane been a man, Hawk would have admired her, even though they were adversaries; but she was a woman, and he didn't know quite what to make of her. He knew only that he couldn't leave her to die.

"My life was peaceful once," he told the sleeping woman. "Your kind remedied that three years ago. They took my freedom, and you took my son." He smiled pensively. "Now you add the final stroke, woman. Becoming a criminal was bad enough, but now you make a damned nursemaid of me. You'd better live through this, Jane Alexander. Elsewise I'll never get even."

Hawk's plans were going awry one by one. "Zeus does not bring all men's plans to fulfillment," he quoted to himself. Homer, *The Iliad*—a piece which Jane Alexander had not read, or if she'd perused the epic poem, no doubt she'd condemned it as heathen wickedness. But she would no doubt appreciate his discovering the truth of that particular line.

But plans could be mended. At this moment Hawk was waiting to do just that. For an hour he'd been sitting at the Rose and Briar Tavern. Colonel Colbert was late. Hawk had discovered long ago that the royalist agent enjoyed being late, as if making people wait for him somehow gave him the superior edge.

Hawk had sent Ned with a message to Colbert soon after the physician pronounced sentence upon Jane. On returning with Colbert's reluctant agreement to a meeting, Ned had related the colonel's displeasure. But Colbert would come, Hawk knew. He didn't dare refuse. Not with all that Hawk could reveal about him if he cared to.

The taproom was crowded and noisy. Already Hawk had turned down three advances from enterprising whores and narrowly missed being sucked into a brawl at the next table. Here in Alsatia—a district between Whitefriars and Carmelite Street, with the Thames to the south and Fleet Street to the north—the streets were rough and the taverns and stews rougher. The brawlers, whores, and drunkards made Hawk feel right at home. Here he needn't worry about Puritan ears listening to his words or the eyes of the law noting his movements.

He did, however, worry about leaving Jane in Ned's less than tender care. Hawk thought about the little man's juggling act in Jane's sickroom earlier that day. Juggling and demonstrating criminal sleight of hand, of all things! Ned had few succoring instincts. Except that Jane *had* been smiling at his silly act, amazingly enough.

Colbert's entrance interrupted Hawk's thoughts. The colonel blew into the tavern along with a gust of icy wind. Shutting the door behind him, he scanned the room, then ambled casually to the bar and ordered ale. At least, Hawk imagined, Colbert probably thought his gait was casual, but the rigid bearing of the military was bred into the man. Fortunately, almost everyone else in the room was too drunk to notice.

Nothing else about Colbert would have tempted anyone to guess the man to be colonel of a fine regiment of horse. His clothing was that of a tradesman, and a poor one at that. His face was shadowed by a broad-brimmed sugar-loaf hat. His buskins were scuffed and covered with the mud of the street. Into his right boot was stuffed the riding quirt he was never without.

Ale in one hand, Colbert grabbed a chair from another table and sat down opposite Hawk. He took off his hat, revealing brown hair short-clipped in the style of the Roundhead and blue eyes sharp as a cold wind at sea.

"What's this about?" he said without preliminary. "I thought not to hear from you again until you were with the King."

The raucous noise of the tavern gave them enough privacy to speak without dissembling.

"My plans have changed," Hawk told him.

"What do you mean? The arrangements have been made. Everything is set."

"I'm still going, with a short delay. I haven't been able to locate my son."

Colbert snorted in disgust. "Your son! He's done well enough where he is."

"He has done well enough, I suppose," Hawk agreed. "But I haven't."

"Pah! I went to great trouble to arrange for you to travel as a manservant to Lord Carleton. What would you have me do while you're looking for this son of yours?" He took a gulp of ale and wiped his mouth upon his sleeve.

"Make other arrangements, Colbert. I need another month."

"Make other arrangements," Colbert mimicked. "As easy as that. Would you have me risk my neck further by strolling the docks and asking which ship's captain would be willing to take on a fugitive rebel? Damn it, Hawkins! Every contact I make is a risk of exposure!"

Hawk was unsympathetic. He leaned forward and fixed Colbert's eyes with his own. "That's the hell of playing both sides at the same time, Colbert. Whichever side wins, you reap the benefits—as long as you can keep the secret that you've been working for Charles as well as Cromwell."

"Damn you, Hawk! Are you casting a slur upon my loyalty to Charles?"

"Not at all." Hawk chuckled sourly. "I'd be the first to say a man's first loyalty should be to himself."

"My philosophy exactly." Colbert's thin lips twisted into a sarcastic smile. "Which is why I refuse to put myself at further risk for your whim. You may take your son or leave him where he is. The matter's of no consequence to me. But if you wish to leave England, you'll leave with Lord Carleton in a week's time."

Hawk's eyes narrowed at Colbert's tone. "Don't try to tell me what I will or will not do, my friend." The words were quiet, and the silence that stretched between the two men even quieter.

As the silence lengthened, Colbert's smile grew strained. He knew Hawk well enough to sense he was treading on dangerous ground. "We are all servants of the King," he temporized. "Sometimes personal desires must be sacrificed for the Cause."

"I think I've sacrificed enough in the last few years," Hawk replied with deceptive mildness. "Charles would be the first to admit I've served him well. He and his courtiers have been eager enough for the money I've funneled through you into their deep pockets."

"And now he's eager to have you join him in Europe. He needs men such as you."

"He'll get me," Hawk assured him. "Charles's victory is my only hope of regaining I've lost. But first I find my son."

Colbert snorted in impatience.

"You can make other arrangements easily enough, Colbert."

"You try my patience," Colbert snapped. "And the patience of the King."

Hawk smiled unrepentently. "How long did Charles try to wrest *his* son from Lucy Walters's clutches? I think he'll understand my plight."

Colbert grimaced. Charles's affection for the bastard he'd sired with his longtime mistress—now estranged—was a matter of embarrassment for his supporters. Even more embarrassing was Mistress Walters's claim that she was Charles's legal wife, and their son his heir. For years she had held the boy like a bludgeon over his father's head.

"Kings often give themselves more latitude for foolishness than they give their subjects," Colbert warned.

"Perhaps that's a warning you should heed yourself. I wonder how Charles would feel about the percentage of my profits that you have withheld for yourself?"

Colbert had the grace to flush.

"A reminder of who holds the cards in this game," Hawk said gently. "I'll leave England in a month, Colbert. If I'm forced to travel on my own, and I'm caught, then you might start to worry—about the government, about the King—take your choice."

Colbert's mouth tightened to a thin line. For a moment he simply stared at Hawk in resentful silence. He finally relented. "Very well. In five weeks' time I sail to Holland on government business—a meeting with the Stadtholders about the House of Orange and their support for Charles. You can sail with me as a diplomatic assistant. You'll be on your own from Holland to Antwerp, which is where the King expects you."

"Good enough."

"We sail on the *Mary Catherine* out of London on January twenty-seventh. If you aren't there, I'll sail without you."

"I'll be there," Hawk assured him. "With my son."

Colbert stood up and gave Hawk a final frown. "You're a hard man, Matthew Hawkins."

Not nearly as hard as he should be, Hawk thought as he watched Colbert leave the tavern. If he had half the sense God gave a sparrow, he would leave Jane Alexander to her fate and go to Kent. He and Ned could probably find

Giddy. It wouldn't be easy, but then, nothing ever was. But if he left, the little widow's stubborn spirit would haunt him the rest of his days.

Hawk had a sudden vision of Jane's cool gray eyes, calm no matter what threats he threw her way; her curvaceous mouth, so soft in rare unguarded moments; the upward tilt of her slightly imperfect nose. He smiled without meaning to smile, caught himself at it, and grimaced.

He wasn't getting soft. Jane could die if she pleased, and he'd not turn a hair as long as she first told him where to find Gideon. Hawk would care for her only because for three years she had nurtured his son. He owed her this at least.

That was the only reason he would stay, Hawk told himself. He almost believed it.

Jane was not a good patient, and Hawk's ability as a nurse left much to be desired. Miserable and embarrassed, Jane fought every intimacy that her illness forced upon them. Her Puritan modesty stretched Hawk's patience to the breaking point, and his insistence on ignoring her protests fired her heretofore unrevealed temper. Her moods swung wildly; one moment she lashed out in hot anger and the next she wept in tearful protest. Hating such weakness, she wept even more, perplexing her reluctant nurse until Hawk felt as though he himself might weep from sheer frustration.

"If you want to wrestle," he warned her on the third day of her illness, "I assure you that I'll win."

He shook out a clean bedgown, draped it across his shoulder, and turned back the bedcovers. They had been through this battle twice on the previous day, because Jane's alternate sweats and chills and Hawk's efforts to get food and liquid down her throat dirtied her garments almost as soon as he managed to get them on her.

Weak as she was, Jane tried to slap away Hawk's hands as he unfastened the lacings of her gown.

"Don't fret." He propped her limp form against his shoulder and lifted the gown over her head. "What's under your gown doesn't hold any surprises for me."

She tried to wriggle from his grasp, struck out at his chest with her fist, then sagged against him, exhausted from the effort. Tears overflowed her eyes and dribbled down her cheeks.

He pulled the clean gown over her head and threaded her arms through the sleeves.

"Please," Jane croaked as he laid her back on the pillows and brought the bedcovers up to her chin. "Leave me alone. Please." She turned her face into a pillow already wet with her tears.

"What would you have me do, mistress?" Hawk asked sharply. "Leave you to die?"

"Charity," Jane whispered into the pillow.

"She's gone, as I've told you ten times already. I would gladly turn my duties over to her or anyone else, for that matter. Yesterday I tried to hire a nurse, but the only two women who applied for the position declined after learning the details. I don't know whether they were more frightened by the contagion or by Ned's looks."

She didn't respond to his weak attempt at humor. Hawk sighed in exasperation.

"There's no one to tend you except me, mistress. And I've no intention of leaving you to your death, not when you're my only link with Gideon." He smiled grimly and sat down upon the edge of the bed. "Unless you'd care to tell me where he is."

Jane's hands fisted around a wad of sheet. She shook her head.

"I thought not. To tell the truth I doubt even that would rid you of me. It's just my contrary nature to force you to live—if only for the pleasure of seeing you face me once you're well. That wall of dignity you've built around yourself is going to be missing a few bricks, isn't it?"

Jane glared at him, sighed, and closed her eyes.

Two days later Hawk would have been glad to have Jane rant at him or protest his ministrations. She no longer had the strength to fight him, or even to care when he changed her gown or helped her with those natural but undignified functions that had so embarrassed her earlier. Nor did she shrink from his touch when he bathed her with cool water and spread salve over the rash on her face, neck, breasts, and belly. In fact the caress of his hands seemed to soothe her. Her quiet acceptance of such intimacies alarmed Hawk more than the delirium in which she called out for her lost baby and dead family. Even in her raving Jane called her husband Colonel Alexander. What a relationship they must have had, Hawk mused cynically, where the man who had lived with her, bedded her, and planted his seed in her belly must still be addressed with such rigid formality. Hawk thought of his long dead wife Gloria. She'd been a timid, obedient girl, and they'd had more courtesy than closeness in their short marriage; but Gloria had certainly never called him Lord Chester.

More than anyone else, however, Jane called for Gideon. The boy shone in her fever-bright eyes, and love softened her voice in imaginary conversations with her adopted child. Hawk tried to harden his heart, telling himself that those were conversations *he* should have had with his son, had not the Puritans—those hypocritical self-styled paragons of Christian virtue—condemned him for helping a friend in desperate need. He forced himself to remember that Jane Alexander was one of those hated Puritans, that the softness in her voice was for the son she had stolen from him.

"Giddy!" she whispered in the small hours of the morning. Hawk had been dozing in the chair he had pulled over by the bed, but he awoke instantly at the sound of her voice. She sounded almost normal, as if the child she spoke to sat beside her, as he doubtless did in her fevered dreams. "Not all boys are allowed to have baby bunnies, darling. But you may keep them if you learn all your verses this week." Her mouth curved into a smile. "No, dear. Todd will tolerate them if we tell him he must, but I don't expect he'll help us feed them."

Jane had told him once that rabbits overran her little garden. He could picture Giddy finding a nest of the creatures and adopting the babies. He wasn't surprised. Gideon had always had a soft spot in his little heart for dumb creatures—dogs, horses, even birds. Hawk was surprised that the staid widow had allowed the boy to keep his prize. He grinned at the thought of her using the baby rabbits as a bribe to make the boy do his lessons. Hawk himself had often resorted to bribery while teaching Giddy to read. Not that the boy wasn't bright or interested; Gideon simply couldn't sit still more than five minutes at a time.

Hawk's smile faded as he pictured Gideon the last time he had seen the boy. His son had been weeping in the arms of his nurse the night the army dragged Hawk out of his house, and the damned captain in charge of the detail had refused even to give Hawk time to say good-bye. How much had Giddy changed in these past three years? He would be taller, with much of the pudgy baby fat gone.

Would he remember his father? Had Jane Alexander told the boy his father was a debauched scoundrel? Did she make him repent on his knees for his father's mortal sins as well as his own small ones?

Hawk dropped his head into his hands. "Gideon," he whispered, despairing.

"Giddy," Jane repeated softly.

7

While Hawk cared for Jane, Ned Crow sharpened his talents as a housewife. All things considered, he decided after a few days, the straight life did have a few things to be said for it—good food, a bed free of lice and fleas, and a warm fire in the evening to take the chill off a man's toes. He felt as though he were on holiday. The cooking was nothing. For the most part he had only himself to feed, as Hawk and the woman ate hardly at all. As for cleaning—what were a few dust balls here and there, a little mud on the kitchen floor, a bit of grease on the stove? They didn't merit his attention. The only piece of drudgery he couldn't avoid was the laundry, for Hawk insisted that the woman's bedgowns and linen be washed daily. He'd always been a strange one about being clean, had Hawk. But all in all he was a good fellow, a talented thief, and a hell of a fighter, so Ned forgave him for it.

The only thing really taxing about Ned's current situation was the boredom. Before Mistress Alexander had taken sick, the house had entertainment aplenty. The Puritan woman was an amusement in herself, standing up to Hawk the way she did. Her cool looks and unruffled stubbornness were enough to drive a man to murder. Hell, the woman refused to be cowed by Ned Crow himself, and that took a load of nerve, not to mention plain foolishness.

Charity had provided even better entertainment—the sort Ned was always anxious for. Plump, rosy-cheeked, and willing, that was how Ned liked his women, and Charity fitted the bill better than most he had bedded. The girl might come from Puritan stock, but she had the instincts of a she-cat in heat. They'd had a merry time indeed once she'd gotten over her screeching and pouting. Of course, if Mistress Alexander had discovered Ned plowing her maid, no telling what entertainment would have followed. The lady might have had his ears, or something much more precious. Quiet, staid, and proper women were the very worst when they finally cut loose—a fact Ned had discovered to his dismay several times in his life.

Now, however, the mistress and housekeeper both were gone, the mistress to her bed, and soon probably from this world, and Charity to who knew where. Ned was so bored he was beginning to talk to the dust balls that congregated in the corners. He could have scrubbed down the floors, polished the stairway banister, or washed the dishes that filled the washtub, but such activities seemed unnecessarily virtuous—not to mention dull. So instead he entertained himself by following his criminal instincts. Such a house as this had to have something of value that would compensate Ned for the trouble and boredom of the last few days. He was determined to find it.

Ned prowled the rooms of Jane's house like a bloodhound sniffing for a trail. He went through cupboards and found nothing but linen, sewing supplies, worthless crockery, blankets, a few medicinals, uncarded wool, a drop spindle for spinning yarn, and a small stash of coins that would hardly tempt the poorest thief. The kitchen and pantry yielded nothing other than flour, sugar, an old butter churn, laundry soap, and the edible delicacies that Hawk had provided. Ned could satisfy his appetite there, but not his avarice.

It was the desk in the library that finally yielded Ned his treasure. He spent a few amusing minutes going through Jane's papers, glad that Hawk had taught him how to read and figure. Before this day he'd seen very little use in the skills, but now they were proving their worth. One drawer held Jane's accounts. Ned discovered, much to his amusement, that even when the lady of the house had possessed money, her servants had been robbing her. The man of business who handled her affairs was as much of a thief as Ned was. There was true Puritan spirit at work! In another drawer Ned found a miniature of a man he assumed to be the mistress's husband—an arrogant-looking bastard with his gold braid and haughty expression. Ned assumed the same mien as the face in the miniature, jaw thrust out, mouth stern, nose tilted up and eyes fixed straight ahead. He was able to maintain such dignity only a moment before he laughed and tossed the miniature back into the drawer.

He was about to move on when his searching hand lit on several bundles of letters tied together with string.

"What 'ave we 'ere?" he wondered aloud, regarding the bundle with gleaming eyes. He cut the string, opened a letter, and smiled. How fortunate that Jane Alexander and her sister were such faithful correspondents. Sarah Stratford Winford was a meticulous lady, it seemed. At the head of every missive she'd penned the name of her dwelling in Kent—Three Oaks Manor—and the very first letter Ned scanned mentioned a trip to the nearby town of Canterbury. How easy it all was!

Ned was a nosy person and quite proud of it. One could stumble upon many interesting tidbits of information by prying into other people's business. Sarah Winford's correspondence with her sister, for instance, yielded a wealth of details that right now seemed useless, but someday might prove helpful. The letters covered the span of years since Sarah's marriage ten years ago to a Sir Geoffrey Winford. Ned's seeking eyes found reference to Mistress Alexander's own wedding, which occurred one year after her sister's, when Jane was but sixteen. Numerous pages of Lady Winford's missives extolled the Winford children. Long letters also comforted Jane on the loss of her husband, then the loss of her child. Along with the required sympathy, Sarah dispensed a tactful dose of scoldings for Jane's lack of correspondence. Later letters congratulated Jane on her resolute spirit and refusal to give in to depression, then prattled on with news of the Kentish countryside (a devilishly dull part of the country, Ned surmised), and talked of things that would interest only women. Ned pawed through the rest of the letters until he found mention of Hawk's son Gideon. Lady Winford admitted having doubts about Jane's rashness in taking the boy in, but admitted graciously that the child had breathed life back into Jane's spirit.

Ned grunted with satisfaction and retied the letters into their original neat bundles. This story was almost as good as the mopey plays and poetry Hawk liked to read—and just as sad. Mistress Alexander was going to lose the child who had restored her to happiness. Hawk would ignore the lady's pleas and take him away, and Ned would help. After all, Hawk was the boy's father. When Hawk lost Gideon, he was just as tortured as when the widow lost her baby son.

Still, Ned felt a pang for Jane's plight. A woman with the guts to stand up to the Hawk and the fearsome Ned Crow deserved a better fate, more was the pity. Perhaps she would have the good sense to die from her fever.

Ned found Hawk in Mistress Alexander's chamber, dozing in a chair beside her bed, his hand cradling hers as she slept. The little man smiled crookedly and cleared his throat.

Hawk started awake, saw Ned, and hastily withdrew his hand.

"Yer problems're over, 'Awk." He tossed the bundles of letters into Hawk's lap. "Look'ee what I found. The sister's married to a country gent name'a Winford. They live at Three Oaks Manor near Canterbury. Easy as priggin' a purse from a blind man."

Hawk looked at the bundle with dull eyes.

"Ain't ye glad ye taught me 'ow t'read?"

Hawk rubbed his brow. "If I recall, you were the one who had to be convinced of the worth of that endeavor."

"Aye. Well, least we know now where yer Giddy is, even if the mort dies."

Ned had to smile at the bleak expression on Hawk's face. "Ye're not jumpin' up and down, praisin' me cleverness fer this discovery, 'Awk."

Hawk got up and stretched. "You're very clever, Ned."

"Kind'a you t'say so. When do we leave?"

"When Mistress Alexander recovers."

Ned snorted skeptically, went to the bed, and stared down upon Jane's ashen face.

"She'll give ye trouble if she lives," Ned ventured. "More trouble than ye want."

"I think I can handle one puny little widow woman."

Ned had never thought Hawk a fool, but now he wondered. "Best for ye both if she dies. But I'd hate to be Death knockin' on this one's door if she didn't wanna go." He shook his head. "Read the letters," he advised as he left. How glad he was that he had neither conscience nor heart. Both made life too damned complicated for a man.

After eight days of illness Jane opened her eyes and swam up from the depths of fever and delirium. The world did not spin quite so badly as before; her head hurt awfully, but not with the blinding torment that drove her into oblivion. The next day she felt well enough to be embarrassed when Hawk changed the bed linen and her night rail, and to wonder at his odd smile when she struck his hands away from the ribbon tie on her gown. The next day she was hungry. Her fever had broken.

With Jane's recovery came the awful awareness of all that had happened during her illness. When she realized that Christmas had come and gone, she wept, still too weak to control the frequent emotional bouts of tears that plagued her. Christmas was a holiday forbidden to Puritans; its celebration had been outlawed when Cromwell took control of the government. But Jane and her household had always had a small, discreet celebration of the yuletide. For her it was a precious time of the year, and missing it grieved her sorely.

As Jane's body took its own slow time in recovering, many things grieved her. She was hurt that Charity had deserted her and wept whenever she thought on the disloyalty. She was horrified that Ned now ruled in the kitchen and the rest of the house had been neglected, and she chafed at Hawk's command that she stay in bed.

She challenged Hawk one late morning when the sunlight streamed through the window and beckoned her to be up and about and doing. "I am still mistress of my own house. Who do you think you are to order me about like a child?"

Hawk lounged upon the window seat in mere shirt-sleeves and breeches. With one booted foot on the seat and the other leg stretched casually out in front of him, he looked entirely too comfortable in her bedchamber. "I'm the man who saved your life," he claimed with a grin.

Jane couldn't deny it. Her recollections of the eight days past were brief flashes that confused nightmare with reality, but she remembered enough to know he was telling the truth. "You're right," she acknowledged stiffly. "I am in your debt, but you don't own me, Master Hawkins."

He cocked a brow in her direction. "I wouldn't want to own you, Mistress Alexander."

"Then perhaps you'll permit me to rise and tend to my household."

"Your household has survived without you for this past fortnight. It can endure another few days."

Jane's stubbornness returned faster than her strength. Later that same day Hawk found her in the kitchen, her hair—still damp from a washing—coiled at her neck, an apron covering the somber brown dress that was only half-laced in the back. He had spent the past hour reading in the library, thinking her asleep, and here she was trying to scrub the multilayered coating of grease from the cook-stove. Ned slouched in the corner, regarding her as though she'd just escaped from Bedlam.

"What the hell do you think you're doing?"

Jane straightened and turned. "Master Hawkins," she said patiently, "did you know that profanity is punishable by law?"

"Certainly." He grinned, folded his arms across his

chest, and leaned back against the kitchen doorframe. "My habits are quite littered with things that are punishable by law."

"So I've noticed." She turned back to her scrubbing. "If you insist on remaining in this house, you might take note that it is a house that honors God in speech and habit."

"I doubt that a little innocent cursing offends God overmuch," he reasoned.

She breathed an exasperated sigh, stopped her scrubbing, and propped herself against the stove top with stiff arms.

Hawk motioned Ned to be gone with a jerk of his head. "You're being foolish, you know," he said to Jane once the little man had left. "If you fall ill again, I just might decide to charge for my nursing services." He strolled forward and took her by the shoulders. "Turn around and straighten up so I can fasten your laces. If you insist on being out of bed, we can't have you looking like a hoyden."

She jerked away as his fingers sought the back fastenings of her bodice, but the sudden motion made her dizzy, and she swayed back against him.

"See, you haven't even the strength to put up a decent fight." He pushed her upright again and pulled the laces tight. Somehow the task seemed more intimate than any he had performed during her illness.

"Master Hawkins, please." A flush crawled up her neck to her cheeks. " 'Tis indecent."

"Now, mistress, I would think we were through with such silliness after the past few days. Besides, 'tis just as indecent for you to walk about with your bodice so insecure."

"Master Hawkins . . ."

"You should think about hiring another girl now that

Charity's gone. I can't be your lady's maid forever, you know."

"Master Hawkins!" She whirled around to face him and nearly lost her balance. "You are the King of Irritants, not the King of Thieves."

"Illness doesn't set well with your temper, does it, mistress?"

She moaned.

"Sit!" He pulled a stool beneath her backside and pushed her down. Propping one foot on the coal bin and leaning on his bent knee, he regarded her sternly.

"I'm not ill," she declared. "Just vexed."

"You're going back to bed."

"No, I'm not. Your Ned has left my house and kitchen a disaster. I have work to do."

"Is there something in your Puritan dogma that doesn't allow a sick person to rest?"

"I am no longer sick. Industriousness is a virtue, sir, though I'd not expect you to know that. Pampering is good for neither the body nor the soul."

"Did you never learn that sometimes it is wise to be kind to yourself?" he asked gently.

"You are a fine one to speak of kindness."

He sighed, straightened, and looked out the window at the unusally cloudless sky. "I know what you need."

"I need you to leave me alone," she told him firmly.

"You need some fresh air and sun. The day is a fine one for January. Suppose we go for a ride."

She regarded him with strained patience. "I have no coach, no carriage, and no horses, Master Hawkins."

"A problem easily solved," he returned brightly. "We'll hire a hackney."

"I have work to do. Such idleness is not—"

"Mistress Alexander," he began with admirable tolerance, "you are in no condition to be as sober and industrious as your overactive conscience would like. Neither have you the strength to resist should I carry you back up to your bed. Which is it to be—an outing with some fresh air, or to bed?" He folded his arms across his chest with determined finality and merely smiled in the face of her glare.

An hour later they drove along the Strand toward Westminster. On their left, the houses of the great—the Palace of the Savoy, Russell House, Durham House, York House, and Northampton House—seemed to doze in the unusual January sunshine. Ahead in the distance lay St. James's Park, beautiful even with its trees winter-naked and its grass sered brown by the January cold.

Hawk sat beside Jane in the small, one-horse wagon that passed for a carriage. Their rented steed was a bit shaggy in his winter coat, and the clip-clop of its feet was a slow rhythm of lethargy. Hawk remembered the fine matched team he'd kept in his stables along with a glass-windowed private coach. He'd prized that team as much as his blooded saddle horses, often unseating his groom and sitting on the driver's box himself. Driving them—feeling their spirit and energy flow through the reins into his hands —was exhilarating. Quite a different experience from lounging behind the shaggy rump of a rented nag whose three gaits were walk, trot, and stumble.

He glanced at Jane. She sat stiffly beside him, her hands primly folded on the lap robe. The chill air colored her cheeks in shades of soft rose, and the sun glinted gold off hair that peeked from beneath her linen coif. Her lips, he noted, must be the envy of every woman who saw her, so perfectly were they formed. Her eyes also—their cool gray hinting at depths that many a man would long to explore.

The thick fringe of honey-colored lashes, the pale, perfectly arched brows, the clean, graceful line of jaw and brow—all in all it was a face of almost pristine perfection. The slight flaw of her upturned nose and the hint of a dimple in her cheeks only softened the perfection to beauty.

Hawk dragged his gaze back to the horse's behind, which was a far safer subject of contemplation.

" 'Tis a nice day, is it not?" he asked the stiff figure beside him.

Jane slid him a sideways glance, afraid to look directly at him. The white line that ran from temple to cheekbone caught her eye. How strange that the scar didn't mar his fine looks, just as his depraved and violent life hadn't seemed to mark the gentlemanly mien he tried so hard to deny.

Jane no longer knew what to make of Hawk or how to react to him. Before her illness, he had been an object of fear and contempt, but now she owed him more than derision. The man had saved her life, after all. She had no illusions about his motive; he still entertained false hopes that she would direct him to Giddy. Still, his care had shown a gentleness and patience that didn't spring from the mere necessity of keeping her alive. Hawk possessed a well-hidden core of humanity she hadn't suspected until now. There was more to him than the cynical criminal without mercy or honor.

" 'Tis a fine day indeed," she answered. "I can't remember ever seeing a January day so bright."

"Was I not right? Fresh air is what you needed." He slanted her a cocky smile. "Are you feeling halfway human again?"

"I'm quite human, I assure you. Ofttimes too human."

Hawk slapped the reins on the horse's rump and their pace increased by a small measure. They rode a few moments in silence. Hawk studied Jane quite openly. Jane, aware of his appraisal, still refused to meet his gaze. Normally not a woman to shilly-shally, she couldn't for the life of her resolve how to behave to the man. Hawk was no longer a stranger. How could he be when he had performed intimacies upon her person that would have made a husband blush? He had fought by her side in a battle with death, and together they'd won. Yet still he was a threat to her life's happiness, a brute without honor who had already destroyed her good name and would gladly destroy anything else he felt necessary to get what he wanted. He was power without remorse, intelligence without conscience, the devil's advocate in a world already dominated by evil.

And still she owed him her life.

"I think I would like to go back now," she said. She needed to be alone to think. Having him so close beside her muddled her mind.

He pulled off the road and stopped the carriage. "Jane . . ." he began. His face grew stern, and the gleam of sympathy that shone through the dark determination in his eyes frightened Jane even more than his frown—so much so that she dared not call him to task for the presumption of her given name. "Jane . . . I know where Gideon is."

Her heart jumped, then seemed to stop. She closed her eyes.

"Ned found some correspondence of your sister—Lady Winford of Three Oaks Manor in Kent. It should be easy enough to find."

When she'd gained enough control of herself to speak,

Jane said, "Then you have what you want. Why are you still here?"

Hawk sighed and shifted his gaze to a clump of trees on the side of the road. "When you came to my prison cell that day, I was furious. Cromwell took everything I had, then you took my son—to raise him in the image of what I hated most in the world. I vowed that if some miracle delivered me I would have my revenge."

"Is revenge as sweet as you'd thought?" she asked bitterly.

"No." His eyes remained on the clump of trees, his mouth slanted upward in self-mockery. "For three years I sustained my fury against you, only to find that things are not quite what I'd thought them to be. You gave Giddy a home when he needed one. You loved him."

"I still love him. I will always love him."

He looked at her finally, his eyes dark with a demand that held her gaze to his. "You ask why I am still here. Why don't I travel to Kent and be done with it?" He idly flicked one of the reins against his knee. "I could do that. Over the past years I've learned well the art of being a thief. Stealing a boy would be little different from stealing anything else. On the other hand, a kidnapping might scare a year's growth out of my son. And if your sister or her husband tried to prevent me . . ." He trailed off, leaving the picture to her imagination.

Jane's lips tightened in distress.

"I don't want to frighten Gideon. I do want what's best for him." He paused, and an ironic smile twisted his lips. "Perhaps I've decided that he needs a mother more than he needs a father."

Jane held her breath. Her eyes widened in disbelief.

Hawk's gaze slid back to the clump of trees at the side of

the road. "I want to see him. Take me to Three Oaks and be my ticket into that house. I just want to see him."

"You jest!"

"No."

"Are you saying you won't take him from me? Why should I believe you?"

"Because I could've been gone from here to fetch my son anytime for the last week, and I'm still here."

Jane willed him to looked at her, so she could see the truth or lie in those changeable eyes. But he kept his face averted, refusing to meet her gaze. "If you intend to leave him," she challenged him, "why not just go?"

He shook his head emphatically. "Gideon is my son. I want to see him before I leave England."

Jane closed her eyes again, hoping that shutting out the sight of Hawk's face might help her think. She didn't dare believe him. He was a traitor and a criminal. For three long years he had plotted to retrieve his son. This abrupt decision to leave England without Gideon didn't make sense.

Too much about Matthew Hawkins, ex-Lord Chester, didn't make sense. A callous criminal, he had cared for her with the gentleness of a . . . a—she shied away from *lover* and substituted *husband* instead. A man robbed, he had come to the aid of the one who had taken what was most precious to him. He dreamed of regaining his child, only to give him up once he'd found him. None of it made sense! None of it!

Perhaps, Jane thought hopefully, Hawk didn't love Gideon as much as she did. Or perhaps, her conscience countered with an uncomfortable prod, he loved the child more. He was thinking of Giddy's best interests. Since Hawk had reappeared, alive and well, had Jane stopped once to consider that Gideon might actually choose to go with his father, given the chance? No, she hadn't. So who loved the child more?

"Where are you going?" Jane asked quietly.

Hawk hesitated a moment. "I'm going to the Spanish Netherlands to join the King," he finally said.

"Then the charge of your being a traitor was true, for all your denials."

"If a supporter of the King is a traitor, then aye, that's what I am, though three years ago, when I was arrested, I didn't give a fig for either King or Cromwell. I've spent these last three years skimming the profits of London's underworld and sending them to Charles and his court."

Jane arched a pale brow. "Lord Cromwell would've thought it appropriate, I'm sure, that Charles be supported in such an unworthy manner."

Hawk snorted. "Cromwell's friends have little right to take young Charles to task, not after what they have done to this poor country. I would have supported the Devil himself if I thought he could oust the Puritans from England."

"I'm sure there are some who would say that you have."

"Enough, mistress! You're stalling, and I'm in no mood to argue politics." Hawk scowled. His gaze finally swung around to meet hers, his eyes dark, blank, unreadable. "Will you take me to Gideon so that I may see him before I leave the country, or must I go myself? The consequences of my going alone will be on your head."

Jane listened to her own heartbeat as she groped for an answer. Something inside her wanted to believe the man had good in his soul. He had saved her life; he had trusted her with the dangerous information of his traitorous crimes, his dangerous destination. Sometimes in life one had to trust, even if the trust was unwise.

"I will take you to see Gideon," she said.

Late the next morning, Hawk drove around the house on Great Queen Street and parked a small coach with a matched team of two dapple grays in front of the carriage house.

"Where did you get that?" Jane questioned as she and Ned came out into the garden. She looked at the equipage with wide eyes.

"I didn't steal it, mistress, if that's what you mean to imply. I bought it."

"Bought it with what?"

"I think I told you once before that I had plenty of money."

"Ill-gotten gains," she said with a half smile.

"You won't think this ill gotten when you are so comfortably riding to Kent. Ned, do you think you can drive this rig?"

"I c'n drive anything, 'Awk!"

"They've got spirit, these two."

"Ain't an 'orse born that c'n outsmart Ned Crow! 'Orses an' the ladies, they all like a firm 'and now and again." He smirked.

"Then take them up the road and try them out. You have two days to woo these beauties before we put them to serious work."

"Aye, aye, Cap'n!"

Hawk jumped down as Ned scrambled up to the driver's box. He watched with a smile as the little man shook out the lines and, with a gentle hand, urged the team forward.

"Is there nothing Ned cannot do?" Jane asked in amazement.

"Not to his way of thinking," Hawk said. "We criminals have to be jacks-of-all-trades, you know."

She cast him a wary look. "Are you so proud to be a criminal?"

"I'm proud to no longer be the fool I once was."

"What fool is that, Master Hawkins?"

"The fool who thought if he minded his own business and left others in peace that they would do the same for him."

She shook her head in resignation. "Dinner is waiting. Ned prepared a fish stew. He still insists on doing the cooking."

As Hawk followed Jane into the dining room, he smiled at her tone of resentment. She had nothing to complain of Ned's cooking. As Hawk had said, the man was a jack-of-all-trades. What she resented was that Ned, just as determined as Hawk that she rest, wouldn't let her into her own kitchen, and the fellow had even stooped to dusting the furniture and scrubbing the floors to prevent Jane from doing it.

Jane dished out the fish stew and put it on the table with slices of still-warm bread.

"This would go well with ale," Hawk said.

"You can make do with buttermilk, I'm sure." She lowered her head for a brief, silent prayer before getting up to fetch the buttermilk and cheese.

Hawk shook his head wonderingly. Most of the women of his acquaintance liked nothing more than being waited upon. Jane was the first woman he'd known, including his late wife, who truly practiced what she preached. Sobriety, thrift, asceticism, and industriousness comprised the Puritan way. In Hawk's jaundiced opinion, few Puritans carried their principles deeper than a surface show. Jane, however, lived what she believed. He had to give her credit for that. Her Bible-thumping narrow-mindedness was aggravating, but at least it was honest. For that matter, she was not as narrow as many of her sect. She had taken in the child of a royalist, she had kept Hawk's books for Giddy instead of burning them, and—this thought brought a smile—she slept buck naked, a comfortable, sensible, and very un-Puritan-like habit.

"What are you smiling at?" Jane asked.

"Gideon," he lied. If she knew what had really made him smile, she might dump her dinner upon his head.

She dropped her gaze. " 'Tis a noble thing you're doing, Matthew Hawkins. Gideon truly will be better off with me."

Hawk didn't answer. The joy of retrieving his son was marred by his regret at taking Gideon from Jane. He had spent the last three years thieving, cheating, and lying. He had black deeds aplenty on his conscience, but none bothered him quite as much as lying to Jane Alexander. He had no intentions of leaving his son behind when he sailed for the Spanish Netherlands, but he needed Jane's cooperation to ease his way into Three Oaks Manor.

She looked up from her plate, meeting his gaze. As always, her gentle gray eyes were clear and ingenuous. Her innocence made his guilt strike even deeper into his heart. Jane Alexander was a damned Puritan, part of the establishment that had taken everything Hawk had—his title, his home, his business. Jane herself had been the one who took his son. She didn't deserve his sympathy; she wasn't worth a moment's guilt.

Once Hawk had believed all that. It had been a comfortable thing to believe. He wished he could believe it still.

"Tomorrow we'll take the new coach and go shopping."

"There's nothing we need," Jane said. "In two days we leave. Any food left in the pantry will simply spoil."

"Food is not what I intend to shop for. You'll need some new clothing for the trip to Kent." The tried and true way for a man to assuage his conscience where a woman was concerned—buy her clothes.

She smiled, as though amused. "I need no new clothing, Master Hawkins."

"Your clothing is all so . . . plain." He tried to keep guilt from his voice. "Surely for a visit to your sister you could indulge yourself a little."

"I've no need to indulge myself," she said. "My gowns are plain because I am a sober person."

He shook his head. "God's world is beautiful, Jane. He clothes it with emerald grass, cerulean seas, flowers, birds, autumn leaves. Why do Puritans think it a sin to follow God's example and clothe themselves accordingly?"

Jane chuckled tolerantly. "Are you playing the Devil's advocate again?"

"No," he answered with a smile. "This time I am playing advocate for Mistress Jane Alexander."

"Such ostentation is not my way, Master Hawkins. It leads to vanity."

"A simple traveling dress, then." He held up a hand to ward off her objection. "A sober traveling dress. Brown, or gray. You can't get much more sober than gray."

"I've no need for a new dress," she insisted. Her eyes twinkled. "Even a sober one. If I didn't know better, I'd think you were trying to bribe me. I've already agreed to let you see Gideon."

He conceded his motive. "I would like to find a way to repay you for that kindness."

"You've repaid me ten times over by giving up your determination to wrest him from me." The twinkle in her eye changed to gratitude. "I know what a sacrifice that is. Matthew Hawkins, you are not quite the devil you would have me believe."

The woman did know how to twist the knife of guilt! And she didn't even know she was doing it. Suddenly the fish stew no longer seemed palatable. "Well," he concluded, "if you won't allow me to repay you with clothing, I trust that at least you will have no objection to my spending the next two days seeing to some work that cries to be done here. When you return, you will have better luck engaging a new housekeeper if the place is repaired."

Jane's dinner must have taken on the same unappetizing aspect as Hawk's, for she swirled it with her fork but made no effort to eat. "I don't know that I'll be returning," she admitted. "I've come to realize that my present circumstances do not allow for maintenance of a household . . . and there is Giddy and his education to think of."

Hawk heard the sting of lost pride in her voice.

"I shall probably sell the house and move in with my sister. She and Geoffrey have offered several times."

"You'll still need the house in good repair even if you sell it."

"Yes." She met his gaze, and Hawk could see her effort to regain her spirits. "No doubt such honest work will do your soul good, sir."

Her smile bit into his conscience. Until lately Hawk hadn't known he had enough conscience left to hurt.

Hawk's conscience took a beating on another score as well. For endless days he had played nursemaid to Jane.

He'd dressed her, bathed her, even caressed her at times without a single lustful thought entering his mind. Now, however, the blush was back in her cheeks and the gauntness left by the fever had filled out to an attractive firm roundness. Now he remembered the alabaster quality of her skin. Now he remembered the firm thrust of her breasts, the long, smooth columns of her legs, the inviting flare of her hips. Now she came to his dreams at night. Asleep, his defenses lowered, he conjured up the woman beneath the starched Puritan shell. More than once he awoke with her name on his lips, a dream interrupted in the throes of lust, his body hot, sweating, fully erect, and swollen with need. How fortunate that Hawk granted Jane her nightly privacy now that she had agreed to take him to Giddy. If she'd seen him in such a state, she would have demanded he sleep in the carriage shed, no doubt.

Jane herself made matters worse, for the woman inside her more than once peeked through her chaste and proper manner. The morning after she refused his offer of clothing, Jane came across Hawk in mere shirt and breeches, kneeling in the doorway between kitchen and dining room to repair a hinge. It was a job that Ned had promised to do, but Ned couldn't be pried away from the new coach and team, so Hawk had set about the repair himself.

"I had no idea that gentlemen of your rank had a talent for such mundane things," she commented.

He looked up at her with a crooked smile. "Over the past several years I've learned quite a few things that are not becoming to a gentleman of my former rank." He emphasized *former* with a bitterness she couldn't miss.

"I didn't say anything about unbecoming, sir. Honest labor is always becoming, no matter what your station in life."

He rose and she tried to brush past him into the kitchen at the same time. The moment their bodies collided, they froze, her breast to his chest, her belly to his hip. For that moment, a tiny instant that seemed to set time all out of kilter and stretch into eternity, Jane didn't move. Hawk didn't move. Neither of them dared to breathe.

The sound of Ned bringing the coach around the house broke the spell. Jane jumped like a scalded cat, oversetting her balance in her alarm. Hawk reached out and caught her by the shoulders, steadying her and for a moment holding her from escaping his touch.

Jane colored. Hawk released her before she could fight to pull away. Her mouth opened and closed several times before she managed to speak.

"I . . . I must get to the kitchen," she babbled. Clearing her throat, she continued more calmly. "I must set the kitchen straight. 'Tis a fine mess, and Ned can't see past your new coach."

"Your new coach," Hawk insisted. "You should rest. I'll set Ned to the task of cleaning the kitchen."

"No. Really. I feel the need to be doing something today."

He gave her a doubtful look.

"I'm quite well, Master Hawkins. You needn't care for me any longer, you know."

As she turned into the kitchen, Hawk realized he'd gotten used to caring for her. Oddly enough, having her dependent upon him was a pleasant feeling, too pleasant a feeling.

He was getting soft—no doubt about it. Softness was not something he could afford right now, softness of feeling, of determination, of conscience. Hawk had learned the hard way that to survive in this world a man had to put aside such pleasantries, along with morals, ethics, philosophies, and preferences. For the last three years hate had kept him alive. He hated the Puritans and what they'd done to England, he hated King Charles for being fool enough to get his head lopped off and plunge England into this mess, he hated what he had to do to stay alive. He'd hated Jane Alexander for taking his son.

Hawk wished he could still hate Jane. Instead, he was beginning to hate himself.

Jane insisted on delaying their departure when she realized they would be leaving on a Sunday. Traveling on Sunday was forbidden. The law stated that people should not only refrain from serious travel, but from "vainly and profanely" walking as well. Such bans were much more loosely enforced since Oliver Cromwell's death, but Jane put her foot down. They would not start for Kent until Monday. On Sunday they would attend church and attempt to repair her damaged reputation.

Hawk's old cell in Fleet Prison would've been a more inviting prospect to him than a Puritan church. He couldn't very well let Jane attend alone, though. She might come to her senses and set the law on him. Likewise, if he forbade her going, she might have second thoughts about taking him to Gideon. He could take the boy alone if he had to, but the task would be neither easy nor pleasant.

The services were as bad as Hawk had feared. He was introduced as Jane's cousin, the story given more credence by the news that they were soon to set out for a visit to Jane's sister. Still, not everyone was convinced. Finding sin in others, Hawk mused, was much more entertaining than rooting it out of oneself. Jane bore with the pursed mouths and disapproving stares very well, Hawk thought. He himself wanted to knock a few people on their morally upright asses.

For two long hours he sat in a wooden pew listening to an earnest, long-faced man regale the congregation with his version of wisdom. Much was said of sin, reason, self-control, self-reform, and the dangers of any activity which might be construed as pleasurable. Nothing was said of joy, beauty, tolerance, or mercy.

Among the somber-faced listeners he recognized the women who had called to inquire about Jane's absence from church—Lady Danfield, looking every bit the old dragon that she was, Mary Clark, her wrinkled face giving her a deceptively harmless appearance, and Barbara Childs, whose nodding head signaled her agreement with every dreary point the preacher made. How dare those spiteful hens appoint themselves to judge an honest and courageous woman like Jane Alexander! For a moment Hawk allowed himself to forget that he was the one who had set out to destroy Jane's good name.

He gave a sideways glance to Jane, whose head was bowed in concentration. She looked like an angel, even in drab gray. The color of her gown made her gray eyes seem all the brighter, and nothing could hide the clean delicacy of her profile nor the hint of humor in the dimple that dented her cheek. As if the Devil himself whispered in Hawk's ear, thoughts that were entirely unholy flooded through his mind and heated his body. It was sin itself that a woman like Jane Alexander should be stifled in the narrow confines of the Puritans' moral straits. She was beautiful, intelligent, courageous, and had a gentle humor that shone through her studiously somber mien. Some enterprising man should come along and give her a nudge from the pedestal of her stiff virtue. A little innocent sin would do her good.

As if hearing herself in Hawk's thoughts, Jane looked over at him and smiled her gentle smile. Suddenly Hawk wished that enterprising man could be himself.

8

Jane left London for Kent with mixed feelings. Bouncing down Great Queen Street in the unaccustomed luxury of a new private coach, Jane twisted to look back at her house out the glassed window.

"I worry about leaving it empty," she told Hawk.

"No one will bother it."

He spoke with a confidence that reminded Jane of his underworld connections. He was leader of the wolves, she remembered. If he told the pack not to close in on this particular unattended house, then undoubtedly they would obey. The thought reminded Jane uncomfortably that Hawk was not quite the amiable fellow he sometimes appeared to be.

The vulnerability of her empty house was not the only thing that made Jane uneasy. Since her illness she'd developed a new awareness of Matthew Hawkins. His resonant voice, the sometimes cruel, most-times gentle curve of his lips, the breadth of his shoulders, the wicked arch of his brows—all this produced in her an uneasiness that was frightening and pleasant at the same time. She had never understood all the churchmen's talk of sinful lust until now. Her late husband, though she held him in respect and affection, had never inspired such feelings in her, and certainly no other man set her heart to thumping and her stomach to flipping. Now, however, she understood lust. She was infected with the sinful malady, and she suspected she was not alone in her turmoil. The gleam in Hawk's eyes was all too apparent when he looked at her.

Their unnatural intimacy during her illness must have afflicted them so, Jane reasoned. It was for good reason that such familiarity was permitted exclusively between those who were properly wed, and then only in moderation. Such powerful physical yearnings were unwise even within marriage. Jane could understand why. They were disruptive, disorienting, and entirely annoying. Being confined in the coach for several days with Hawk was going to be a trial indeed.

On the other hand, she was glad to be paying a visit to Sarah, and glad to be leaving the smells, sounds, and filth of London for a while. All things considered, a potentially disastrous situation had worked out for the best. If her illness and the resulting intimacy had brought Hawk to the conclusion that he should leave Gideon with her, then Jane thanked God she'd been sick. She would be willing to go through a hundred such days of misery if the agony allowed her to keep the boy.

She had much to be thankful for, Jane mused. Even her good name seemed to be at least partially restored by her appearance in church with her *cousin*. The lie weighed a bit on her conscience, though when she'd complained about it Hawk teased that her lie nullified his, and in the total sum of things they'd neither one sinned. She'd had to laugh at his twisted reasoning. Her laugh brought a smile to his face and sparked the gleam that so often lighted his eyes. He liked to see her laugh, he commented. Jane remembered how his words had made her heart lurch so that she abruptly stopped laughing.

"You are awfully silent," Hawk said from the opposite corner of the coach. At the beginning of the journey he'd sat directly across from her, but Jane slid to the opposite corner the moment their knees touched. "Are you feeling well?"

"I'm quite well, thank you. It's just that I have much to think about." She turned her head to look out the window. They had left London behind and now trotted through the countryside south of the city. Even in the doldrums of winter the vista of meadows and hedgerows was lovely, drawing her eyes with their peace.

"You are in fine looks today." He grinned. "Though I must say that dark brown doesn't become you. I've never met a female so opposed to enhancing her own beauty. Yours is considerable, you know."

Jane didn't stammer with embarrassment as she might have three weeks ago. She was becoming accustomed to Hawk's provoking comments. "We Puritans choose to cultivate the beauty inside, sir, not the fleeting beauty on the outside."

For a moment Hawk's face grew dark. "I might accept that statement of Jane Alexander. I doubt its truth when applied to most of your sect."

She gave him a tolerant smile. "I fear that we are as prone to sin as any other human beings. But we recognize our sins, think upon them, and strive to overcome our wicked natures and bring ourselves closer to God."

"I'll admit the truth of part of what you say," Hawk conceded. "You Puritans think about sin more than anyone ought to—your sins, other people's sins, the world's sins. Makes you a damned uninteresting lot. If I were God, I certainly wouldn't want heaven to be overrun with a crowd of moralists who ignore the beauty of a flower to nitpick about the dirt on its petals."

Jane raised a brow. "But then, you aren't God, are you, Master Hawkins?"

"Unfortunately, no." He favored her with a disarming smile. "If I were, the world would be run quite differently, I assure you."

"I can imagine."

"For one thing, females as fetching as you would never be permitted to wear such drab colors, nor cover their glorious hair with an ugly linen coif."

"Then all you care for is the surface appearance of a person. Have you no appreciation for inner beauty?"

"It's my opinion that appearance often mirrors the person within. Were I God, mistress, no one would waste time in the cataloguing of sins—theirs or anyone else's. Life would be a gift to enjoy, and harmless pleasure a form of worship—as it should be."

She smiled at the outrageous statement. "I suppose the Lord has told you personally that it should be thus?"

"Of course He did. Shame on you, Mistress Alexander. I thought you had read your Bible."

"I have."

"Then you recall Psalm sixteen, verse eleven: 'Thou wilt shew me the path of life: in thy presence is fullness of joy; at thy right hand there are pleasures for evermore.'"

"I'd hardly think that refers to the kind of pleasures that you would promote, sir."

"Are you so sure of my wicked character?" he inquired lightly. "Consider Ecclesiastes chapter nine, verse seven: 'Go thy way, eat thy bread with joy, and drink thy wine with a merry heart.' And also chapter eight, verse fifteen of the same book: 'Then I commended mirth, because a man hath no better thing under the sun, than to eat, and to drink, and to be merry: for that shall abide with him of his labour the days of his life, which God giveth him under the sun.' "

"You're more familiar with the Bible than I would have thought," Jane admitted.

"The difference between us, Jane, is that I don't read the Bible to the exclusion of all else."

"And also," she noted with a gentle smile, "that you seem adept at quoting only verses that validate your own opinions."

"A habit I picked up from listening to religious zealots."

Jane found the logic of some of Hawk's views confusing. She had to admire his gift of argument, even though she knew his purpose was merely to provoke her. Hawk's philosophy was almost as seductive as the man himself. Both were dangerous and wicked, she reminded herself, no matter what verses he could quote to justify himself. If she were wise she would close her ears to his words. She had slipped quite far enough into the paths of wickedness—yielding her modesty to this man, lying about him to her congregation, traveling unescorted through the countryside with him. She needn't slip even further by listening to his outrageous arguments against what she knew to be right, good, and proper.

"Would you like me to tell you of Gideon?" she asked, steering the conversation to a safer topic.

The rest of the day they spent in discussion of a matter they both agreed upon—that Gideon was the brightest, most clever, and sweetest child in England. Hawk obviously approved when Jane reported that the boy was singularly unimpressed by his tutor's exhortations to self-examination, self-criticism, and sober conduct. Improvement of his soul didn't rank high in Gideon's priorities. But he was still very young, Jane explained, and she didn't completely agree with her church's philosophy that every child's spirit must be broken to the good of his salvation.

"Do you dare disagree with your church?" Hawk asked with the tilt of a mocking brow.

"Nothing on earth is perfect," she answered readily.

"Except Gideon, of course."

Jane laughed ruefully. "I suppose I can be overwhelming when I get on the subject of Gideon."

"A fault we share, I'll admit."

Jane continued to laugh when she described some of the child's antics in avoiding his lessons. It wasn't that Giddy wasn't bright, she explained, just that he had too much energy by far to sit for more than five minutes in one place.

Before Jane knew it the sun rested on the horizon and Ned pulled the coach into the courtyard of the inn where they would stop for the night. With a belated twinge of conscience, she realized that she'd spent the whole afternoon chatting with a criminal and traitor, just as though they were fast friends. Had he been a brother or a husband she could have been no more familiar with the man. A tardy blush climbed to her cheeks for such a lapse of propriety.

"Wait here with Ned," Hawk ordered as he stepped from the coach. "I'll obtain lodging for us."

Jane watched as he walked to the door of the inn, making his way through the gaggle of geese and chickens that littered the courtyard. A mongrel dog sniffed at his knee as he went by, and Hawk absently bent and scratched its ears. Now she knew where Gideon got his fondness for animals.

Suddenly the plight of father and son made her sad, in spite of herself.

The inn was clean, as was the innkeeper, a portly little man with a jovial tilt to his mouth and a reddish face that matched his hair. He greeted Jane with great civility when Hawk returned to escort her from the coach. The taproom was quiet, Jane noted with relief, and if either of the two serving girls was one of the strumpets who supposedly plied their trade in such places, at least they didn't look the part.

"Best in the house for ye, milord!" The stout innkeeper led them up a narrow staircase at the end of the taproom and showed them to a pleasant room with a wood fire—such luxury!—crackling in the fireplace. The chamber was large enough to accommodate several damask-upholstered chairs, a table, a washstand with a flower-painted matching pitcher and basin, and, dominating all else, a large curtained bed. A window, its shutters standing open, overlooked the stable and carriage house that sat a little distance from the back of the inn.

"This is lovely," Jane said, surprised. She wondered if Hawk's room was as nice. He must have had to pay a small fortune for such accommodations.

"I'll see that your dinner is brought right up, milord. Me son will help your man with your trunks."

"Milord?" Jane lifted a fair brow as the innkeeper left.

"Good rooms are more easily obtained by the Earl of Chester than the fugitive Matthew Hawkins."

She smiled sadly. "You lie without even giving it a thought, don't you?"

" 'Tis a skill I've found useful," came the unrepentant answer. "Besides, the title was once mine, and God willing, will be again someday."

She took off her cloak and hung it neatly on a peg beside the door. "I doubt God being willing would matter much to a man like you."

He grinned. "I haven't yet convinced you that God is on *my* side?"

"Not quite."

Ned and the innkeeper's son arrived with the trunks at the same time two serving maids came to lay out dinner. Jane urged Ned to sup with them, but he refused.

"Nay, mistress. Rooms like this'un gimme the shakes if I'm in 'em too long. Only time I gets inta such fancified places is when I'm priggin' the silver or liftin' the jewels. Keep thinkin' I'm gonna get meself nabbed." He ogled the maids to see if they were impressed, puffing up like a rooster when they eyed him with alarm.

Jane threw him a stern look and he reluctantly deflated.

"Don't pay him any mind, ladies," Hawk told the girls. "Ned isn't dangerous at all. But unless that supper is set out soon, I might be tempted to snap off one of your heads as an appetizer."

The girls merely giggled. Unwise of them, Jane thought, to be fooled by looks and fine clothes into thinking Hawk the less dangerous of the two men. The maids hurried to their task, however, casting surreptitious admiring glances at Hawk as they worked. Ned delayed until they were ready to leave. With a broad wink at Hawk, he followed them out the door. A few seconds after he shut the door behind them, one of the serving girls gave a squeal that ended in a giggle.

Jane shook her head. "That man shouldn't be turned loose on the civilized world."

"Do you still think this is a civilized world?"

"It would be, if people would follow their consciences instead of their desires."

He held out a chair for her to sit at the table. "Is that what you do, my stern little Puritan?"

She colored a bit. "Not always."

He chuckled and sat down opposite her. "An honest answer. You could almost cure my sinful cynicism with your refreshing honesty, my dear lady."

She blushed again.

They ate in silence—an excellent supper of cold roast goose, boiled capon, olive pie, and sweet tarts—until Hawk spoke his thoughts aloud.

"I'm anxious to see how Gideon reacts when he discovers his father is alive. I assume you told him that I was dead."

"I did," Jane admitted with a frown. "I . . . I don't believe you should tell Gideon that you are his father."

The bite Hawk was lifting to his mouth stopped midway. "Why?"

"Can't you see how . . . confusing it would be for the child?"

Hawk put down his fork. His lips tightened into a tense line. "Just how else will you explain my presence?"

"There would be any number of ways." Jane was tempted to remind Hawk that he was the expert at lying, but the look on his face forestalled her. Anger would have impressed her much less than the sadness she saw there. She was accustomed to Hawk's anger; this sad vulnerability was something she hadn't expected.

"I would like Gideon to know," he said.

"Of course you would. But think of poor Giddy. What will he think to have his father suddenly rise from the dead and then leave him?"

Jane remembered the pain of losing her own son. How much sadder for Hawk, whose son was alive but beyond his reach. Even though it was within his power to snatch the boy away, he voluntarily surrendered him for the child's own good. After Hawk's noble sacrifice, how could Jane deny him the comfort of having his son know he was still alive? Yet she had to think of what was best for Gideon.

"My friend," she said quietly. "If I were a fairy in a child's story I would wave my magic wand and take your misfortune away, for in spite of all the differences that lie between us, I believe you're a good man. But nothing can undo the past, and the best we can do is look to the future. Can you not put off the truth until Gideon is older and better able to understand?"

Hawk gave her a strange look, surprise mingled with sadness, warmth with bitterness. "My little Puritan asking me to lie?"

One corner of her mouth twitched up. "I suppose I must admit that there is a place for less than the truth."

"A lie," he insisted.

"Very well, a lie." He had the most aggravating way of pointing out her imperfections. She sighed and continued. "Surely you will return to England in the years to come. Once Gideon is more mature, he can be told the story of how you had to flee, and he'll understand. If you'll let me know where you are, I'll write you about his progress."

Hawk was silent, his eyes hooded in a way she didn't quite understand.

"It grieves me to see your sorrow," she told him quietly. "Your anguish reminds me so much of my own when I lost my child. You must remember that you're not really losing Giddy. He'll still be alive, and well, and safe." Moved by the pain she imagined in Hawk's face, Jane reached out sympathetically and covered his hand with her own. Their hands touched with a shock of warmth and intimacy. Jane withdrew in haste, coloring at the realization of what she'd just done. "I—I'm sorry," she stammered, and averted her face.

"You embarrass much too easily." Hawk forced a lightness into his voice. "You really should toughen up those tender sensibilities of yours."

"You mock me."

"Not at all. I am merely amazed that a woman could reach your age and still retain such tender innocence."

"You're quite mistaken." She refused to raise her eyes. "I'm far from innocent."

Hawk smiled. "Eat your supper, mistress. The food will get cold."

He watched as she picked at her food, her cheeks still burning. Naïve little Puritan, to feel sorry for a rogue such as he, to think him noble and grieve for his pain in giving up Gideon. If she only knew that any pain in his expression emanated directly and most ignobly from his groin, which ached from her tempting nearness.

A day confined in a small coach with Jane Alexander was torture that no man should have to endure. Hawk had been without a woman for much too long, and Jane Alexander, despite her studied plainness, was as fetching a female as he'd ever known. His hand burned where her fingers had touched it.

Hawk stabbed a bite of roast goose and forced himself to eat, though with a sexual appetite raging he had little appetite of any other kind. He was a greater scoundrel than he had believed of himself, Hawk mused bitterly. Jane Alexander's only crime was that she was a Puritan, and an honest Puritan at that. Contrary to his first bitter assessment, she had taken his son out of love, not out of greed and malice. She was an innocent, and though she talked of sin, Hawk would wager that she scarcely knew what sin was. Yet he had deceived her about Gideon and fully intended to take the boy from her. He had lied to her, letting her think him noble when he was corrupt. Worst, all day he had tried to concoct a just reason for seducing her. Having her this close to him was like waving a nectared rose in front of an eager honeybee. His conscience gave him a dozen reasons why he should leave her be, but his desire gave him one powerful reason to take her.

The small part of honor that was left to him hoped that his conscience won.

Jane raised cool gray eyes to his. While he had trotted along the road to losing his composure, she had regained hers. "I suppose we've not really settled the question, have we?"

Hawk had difficulty remembering just what question they'd been discussing.

"Think about what I said, Master Hawkins. Think about Gideon."

Hawk's conscience took another swing at him. The subject of Gideon's knowing his father was alive was not at issue, if Jane only knew it. Because Gideon was leaving with Hawk, and Jane would be left alone.

"We can talk about it again tomorrow," she offered. "To tell the truth, I'm very tired. Perhaps on the way to your room you could ask the maids to come clear away the dishes."

Hawk smiled and shook his head. "This was the only decent room the inn had available. I'm afraid you'll have to put up with me for one more night."

She stared at him for a moment, her gray eyes wide. "You're jesting," she said hopefully.

"No."

"I . . . really . . . that's impossible. Oh, dear! What must the innkeeper think, and the maids. They think we're . . ."

"Married," he provided. He raised an amused brow. "Knowing how you value your reputation, I told the innkeeper that you're my wife."

She stood abruptly, almost oversetting the table. "Wife? You told him I was your wife?"

"Aye. How does it feel to be a countess?" He lounged in his chair, rather enjoying the sight of her building to a fury. Since her illness she'd scarcely had the energy to work up a good mad, and damned if the woman wasn't attractive when she was angry—her color high, her gray eyes dark and flashing.

"That is . . . is unconscionable, sir! Really!"

"What would you have me do?" he inquired lightly. "Tell the man that we're lovers?"

"We are *not* lovers!"

"A regrettable fact," Hawk admitted. He couldn't resist provoking her.

"And I will not have you telling whomever you please that I'm your wife!"

"It seemed the easiest way to handle the problem."

"The easiest way to handle the problem is for you to sleep in the stable with Ned and the horses."

"I've done my share of sleeping in gutters, alleys, and tavern carriage houses. It's a habit I don't intend to take up ever again. Including tonight."

"Master Hawkins!" Her voice slowly changed from indignation to a plea for reason. "We can't sleep in this room together!"

"Mistress Alexander." He rose and set his napkin upon the table. "I thought you one of the most sensible females I've ever had the pleasure to meet, and here you disappoint me by throwing a fit over something as unreasonable as this. For the past month I have lived in your house, and for three of those weeks we slept in the same room. I've washed you, fed you, dressed you, and performed other tasks for you that I'm sure you'd rather I not mention. I've also listened to you snore."

"What?"

"Don't be embarrassed. You sound just like a kitten purring. It's really a very feminine snore."

She turned away for a moment, and he pictured her struggling to hold together the frayed tatters of her dignity. She was entirely too much fun to bait, Hawk decided. If she were plain and dull, he would have much less trouble acting the gentleman.

When Jane faced him again, her spine was admirably straight. "Sir . . ."

The tone of her voice was not a good omen, Hawk reflected wryly.

". . . while all that you say is true, I never willingly shared a room with you, nor did I willingly allow all those intimacies you insist upon reminding me of. When first you shared my room, only brute force gained you the privilege, and when I was sick, I had no control over anything I allowed or did."

Hawk smiled. "Do you now?" His conscience was losing. The sight of her intoxicated him with desire. She was too much of a woman to stay a chaste widow, whether she realized it or not.

"What do you mean?" she demanded hesitantly, as if knowing very well what he meant.

Hawk answered her with a silence that spoke volumes into the tension between them. Somewhere in the depth of her gray eyes, the tight curve of her lips, the rapid rise and fall of those well-hidden breasts was an uninitiated passion begging to be set free. It set Hawk afire, and he guessed that Jane felt it too, somewhere within her, when the spark in her eyes slowly turned from indignation to dismay.

"I think you've been denying your own nature much too long," Hawk said with deceptive calm.

She held up her hand as though to ward him off, though he hadn't made a single move toward her. Her head shook a denial, whether of him or herself Hawk didn't know. "You've tried to woo me to the ways of the world since you first stepped foot into my house. You might believe you've succeeded, simply because I've been forced to compromise myself to things that are beyond my control. But you're quite mistaken. My virtue is not that easily assailed."

He grinned wickedly. "Nothing worthwhile ever is."

She drew in a sharp breath. Silence hung between them, shivering with tension. Then suddenly, unexpectedly, she laughed. "Matthew Hawkins, when I first saw you crouching above me in the night, I thought you were the Devil. Now I know I was wrong. You've not the deceitful slyness of the Devil. You may be a rogue, but at least you're an honest rogue."

Hawk raised a brow. He felt as though he'd suddenly wandered into the wrong scene in a silly romance. Wasn't this the part where the virtuous female was supposed to cringingly defend her honor and declare she would rather die than submit? Not that that was exactly what he had planned. The truth was, this scene being rather spontaneous, he didn't have much of anything planned. But why the hell was Jane laughing?

"I vow, sir, I don't know where you conceived this desire, but at least I am fairly warned."

He gave her a puzzled look.

"I know you too well to fear that you will force yourself upon me," she explained. "For an entire week you slept in my chamber and never touched me. When I was ill and at your mercy, you saved me. You're not half the villain you think you are."

Hawk snorted in disbelief.

"You may sleep in the stables. Here—" and she handed him the extra blanket that lay at the foot of the bed.

Hawk tossed it aside. He shed his doublet and began to unbutton his shirt. "I am *not* sleeping in the stable. After all, 'tis my money that pays for the room."

Jane glared at him. She picked up the blanket. "Very well, then, *I* will sleep in the stables. I'm sure there is a stall there that will provide more privacy than I would have here!"

"Be my guest!" he snapped.

Hawk winced as the door closed behind her. She'd shut it very quietly—only Jane Alexander would refrain from slamming a door when she was angry, Hawk reflected sourly. The woman was unnatural, and she had all the reasoning power of a pea. If she was so damned sure he wouldn't rape her, why march off in a huff to the stable?

He pulled off his shirt, boots, breeches, and hose and tossed them in a pile with unaccustomed carelessness. After he doused the lamp and climbed into bed, he remembered the dishes.

Damn the dishes! he thought. The maids could fetch

them in the morning. And damn Jane Alexander. How could a stiff-necked little Puritan put a man in such a heat?

Hawk supposed he should admire Jane for sticking to her straitlaced principles. But the ache in his groin kept him from appreciating this latest example of her sincerity. She wrapped her virtue around her like some damned holy cloak, and someday she was going to smother that bright spark of warmth, joy, and passion he saw winking from the few rents in that pristine shroud. The thought bothered him a hell of a lot more than it should have.

Jane would be back, Hawk was certain. Her anger would wear thin, and she'd find that a stable was no substitute for a firelit room with a mattress and warm quilts. When she returned, he decided, he'd play the gentleman and let her have the bed. He'd slept on more floors than he could count. One more wouldn't matter. She could close the damned bed curtains, if she wished. That should give her enough of her precious privacy.

Hawk lay awake as the fire sank to a mere flicker. The sounds of the inn quieted. The room grew cool. When Jane finally returned the floor was going to be a damned cold place to sleep.

He let his thoughts wander, wondering when he'd started to think of Jane as a woman instead of a Puritan enemy. Perhaps that very first night, when she'd scampered from her bed in panic and given him a brief glimpse of full breasts and slender legs before she snatched the sheet to her body. Perhaps when she was ill and lay helpless in his arms, weeping in delirium. In all but the carnal sense he knew Jane better than he'd known his wife, and he'd certainly done his best to remedy that last area of unfamiliarity tonight.

Hawk smiled, thinking of Jane's indignation. She'd been

tempted by the same feelings as he, or she wouldn't have been half so upset. If she weren't such a staunch little saint and he such a determined sinner, they'd suit very well. He chuckled aloud at the thought, picturing him and Jane walking arm in arm, a dozen of their children following with Gideon in the lead. The vision shifted suddenly to the bed where they made all those children—Jane's gentle welcoming smile, rose-tipped breasts beneath his hands, long legs eager to wrap around his waist and hold him inside her.

"Dammit!" he cursed aloud. Once more he was swollen to the point of pain, fool that he was. "Where is that woman?"

More than an hour had passed and she hadn't returned. Damned stubborn female. She might prefer the horses to him for nighttime company, but he couldn't very well let a lady stay in such a place.

He swung out of bed and hurriedly pulled on boots, breeches, and shirt. Suddenly anxious, he left the room with breeches only half-laced and shirt unbuttoned.

That stubborn woman was coming back if he had to carry her over his shoulder!

9

The night was black as a whore's soul, with moon and stars swallowed up by clouds that breathed a cold dampness into the air. The inside of the stable was equally damp and dark, the chill only slightly diminished by the musty warmth of horseflesh.

Hawk cursed himself for not bringing a candle. He groped along a wall, hoping to find tinderbox and lamp, but instead found Ned—or rather, tripped over Ned.

"Owf! What the bugger—!"

"Ned! It's Hawk."

"Goddamn it!" Ned growled. "Ye tryin' ta break me ribs?"

"Where's the lamp?"

Ned scuffled to his feet. " 'Ere it is."

A flint sparked and the lamp suddenly cast a dim glow across a long row of stalls on one side of the stable and, facing the stalls, a hodge-podge of coaches brought in to shelter from the night dampness. Harnesses hung from the stall partitions and from pegs pounded into the walls. Saddles straddled the rafters. Straw, hay, and manure were everywhere.

Ned prodded tenderly at his injured anatomy. "Fine sort of a thief you are what can't see in the dark!"

"You should expect to get kicked if you make your bed in a doorway."

Ned chuckled. "That's the purpose. Wanted ta stop any gents from comin' in afore they could discover yer lady and make sport of 'er."

Hawk grimaced. "She's hardly *my* lady."

"Reasoned you two 'ad an upset about that."

"You can stop grinning like a randy cat and get yourself gone for a while. I need to talk to the lady in private."

"Aye, aye, Cap'n!"

"Where is she?"

"Marched 'erself back to a stall next ta that bay mare. Stickin' with the females, she is," he chortled.

"Get yourself gone, Ned. And thanks for standing sentry."

"Someone needs ta watch over that little lass," he said cryptically.

Jane looked most uncomfortable curled into the corner of her stall. Propped against a pile of dirty straw, her eyes were squinched tightly shut, as though she would force sleep to come.

Hawk's quiet approach didn't rouse her. He rested his arms atop the chest-high stall door and cleared his throat. Her eyes popped open in alarm.

"Don't you think you've made your point, mistress?"

She hastily pushed herself up to a sitting position and brushed the straw from her hair. Her gown was wrinkled and adorned with hay, and her coif sat askew on her head, spilling bright gold hair in a tangled fall about her shoulders. Hawk noted that her disarray didn't detract one bit from her beauty.

"Have you come to trade places with me?" she asked

stiffly. With an uneasy glance she took in his unbuttoned shirt and half-laced breeches.

"No. I've come to tell you that you may come back. I promise not to lay a single finger upon you."

For several heartbeats she didn't answer. Her eyes moved resolutely from his partly bare chest to his face. "I never thought you would, Master Hawkins."

"Then perhaps it's your own desires you fear."

She faltered a moment, and a telltale flush crept into her cheeks. "I fear nothing!" she said with a bit too much determination. " 'Tis propriety that concerns me. I can't stay with you on the pretense of being your wife, and, despite what has occurred in the past, for me to sleep in the same room with you would be the height of impropriety. Even you should be able to understand that, Master Hawkins. After all, you were once a gentleman. Though gentlemen such as you regularly flout the rules of propriety, surely you have at least some small understanding of the rules you ignore."

"What I understand is that you cannot sleep here, and I will not. Propriety be damned, mistress. You are coming back to the room with me."

She stood. Straightening her spine, squaring her jaw, she looked prepared for a fight. "No," she answered simply.

"I assure you that you are much more likely to be assaulted in this stable than in our room."

"Assault is not what I am concerned about, as I said before."

"Well it should be. You don't have the common sense of a babe in arms—marching off to sleep in a stable because of a fit of prudishness! For an intelligent woman, mistress, you haven't a brain in your head!"

She simply raised her stubborn chin another notch. "I shall go back to our room only if you remain here."

"Not likely, mistress! You'll go back to our room if I have to cart you over my shoulder like a sack of flour!"

"Touch me," she threatened in a quiet voice, "and I'll turn right around and go back to London."

"I don't think so. Because I'll see Gideon with or without you, and you and I both know that it will be better for Giddy—and better for you—if you are at my side when I see him. Just think what notions might occur to me if you're not there."

From a heated flush Jane suddenly grew pale. Even through his anger Hawk hated himself for saying it.

"That's not a threat, mistress. Just a fact. You'll do what's best for Gideon. Now come back to our room so we can both get some sleep." He opened the stall door and stepped in.

Jane's agitation seemed all out of proportion to the situation. She backed away until the stall partition halted further retreat. "I'll not sleep in the same room with you, Master Hawkins. You can just stop your foolish bluster and leave. I'll do just fine here in the stable, I assure you."

Hawk shook his head. "Mistress Foolish, I warned you."

He reached out for her, but quick as a frightened doe she ducked under his arm and darted out of the stall.

"Goddammit!"

Jane proved herself inexperienced in the game of chase, for within moments she ran herself into a corner where the back wall of the stable, piled high with dirty hay and straw, met the last stall of the row.

Hawk walked slowly toward her. He should have had the sense to leave the little witch alone, but somewhere in their argument the battle had changed from Hawk against Jane

Alexander to Hawk against all of the Puritans who had England cramped by their joyless, rigid doctrine. He wasn't about to let himself be bested.

"You'd better get away from that horse," he warned.

Jane glanced quickly at the big black stallion that occupied the stall against which she stood. He was a nasty-looking brute who looked ready to join the battle.

Hawk took advantage of her diverted attention and grabbed at her. This time he was prepared for her attempt to dodge and brought her up short as she tried to get past him. Her fist connected with his jaw with near lethal force.

"Dammit! You've got the instincts of a Billingsgate tart!"

Jane rounded on him again. He ducked, plowed forward, and scooped her onto his shoulder, just as he'd threatened.

"Now be still!"

She only grew more frantic. Her desperate struggles threw Hawk off balance. They crashed against the stall, which sent the stallion into fits of kicking. Then they lurched drunkenly into the straw piled against the back wall. The straw slipped under Hawk's feet and they fell together into the pile, Hawk on top, legs entwined with hers, his bare chest mere inches above Jane's face.

They both froze. Hawk felt the twin mounds of Jane's breasts against his bare chest, the pressure of her hip against his groin. The scent of her filled his nostrils—soap, lilac water, hay, and the smell of woman all mixed together with the acrid odor of fear.

He shifted a bit and looked down into her wide-eyed face. "For a proper lady, you surely are the damnedest hellion I ever knew." Before she could defend herself he lowered his mouth to hers. The temptation was too great for any man to resist. Jane stiffened beneath him, then went limp. Her mouth opened, unresisting, to the probing of his tongue.

Hawk groaned into her mouth. She was sweet, so sweet, her mouth like honey, just as he'd known it would be. Beneath his hands, her tangled hair was silk, her skin warm satin. Every inch of him felt her pressed against him. His body suffused with heat. He thought he would explode when Jane's hands came to his shoulders, slipped around his neck and down his back in a soft caress that made him quiver. Her tongue began a tentative dance with his own.

Jane sank into a world of sensation. She forgot anger, fear, even propriety in Hawk's assault upon her senses. The feel of his lips, the thrust of his tongue, the weight of his body upon hers unleashed a raw instinct she couldn't control. She itched to touch him, so she did. Her fingers touched the day's rough growth of beard, twined through thick silken hair, traced the breadth of powerful shoulders, and roved down his back. Muscles like molten steel rolled beneath her hands. He pressed her down, helpless, while he stole her breath, her very will. No virgin, she knew exactly what bulged hot and hard against her belly, and the feel of him pressed against her sent her spiraling into a place where conscience and caution didn't exist.

Hawk released her abruptly. Jane opened her eyes to see him panting above her, looking down at her as a tiger might regard a juicy hunk of meat. Still awash in sensation, she could only lie beneath him and return his stare, feeling a similar hunger take command of her own body. This was what she had feared when she refused to go back with him to the inn. She herself was her downfall, not he. It was not his strength she dreaded, but her own weakness.

Slowly the chill air of the stable crept between them.

The touch of coolness slowed the whirl of Jane's senses. Warmth and desire ebbed from her body; remorse and fear rushed in to fill the void. She closed her eyes and drew a deep breath of air laced with shame. Her very soul trembled at her loss of control.

With a fist on Hawk's bare chest she pushed him off her and scrambled to her feet. Somewhere in the back of her mind she noted that Hawk looked as stunned as she felt. He reached out to help her up.

"No!" She cringed from his touch.

"Jane . . ."

"Don't touch me!"

He backed away from her. Jane averted her eyes. Half-laced, his breeches did nothing to hide the state of his arousal. The sight made her dizzy with a feeling she didn't want to remember.

"I'm sorry." His words were quiet. Hawk himself looked as though he'd been granted a vision of a side of himself he didn't find entirely welcome. "You act as though I'm going to eat you alive. I assure you I'm not."

Jane couldn't meet his eyes. She knew as well as he that Hawk had been the one to break the kiss. There would have been no need for him to rape her, if completion of their passion was what he sought. She was shameless!

"You'd best set yourself straight," he told her. "You can't go back into the inn looking as though you've just been tumbled in the hay. Someone might be up and about."

She heard the smile in his voice and still refused to raise her eyes.

He came forward to brush the straw from her hair and straighten her mussed bodice. His hands were warm where they touched her. His fingers traced the tracks of her tears from eye to chin, and she didn't seem to be able to move.

He bent to pick up her linen coif. Jane remembered the precise moment it had slipped off at the urging of his hands. His fingers had raked gently through her hair. The memory made her shiver.

He handed her the coif. "Come on." Docilely she allowed him to take her arm and followed him out of the stable. "You see what a danger a stable can be?"

"I'm all right," she said—not really to him. More to herself. "I'm quite all right."

"Of course you are." He didn't sound convinced.

When they got to their room, he rolled a blanket and laid it lengthwise on the bed. "You can take the side by the window; I'll take the side by the door." He placed her hairbrush in her hand. "There's still straw in your hair. I'll give you a few moments to get into your bedclothes."

When he returned, she was huddled under the covers, her night rail buttoned tightly beneath her chin. He doused the lamp, undressed, and climbed into bed. Jane turned away from him, feeling the fragile barrier of the rolled blanket at her back. Her hands gripped the edge of the bed. She could hear Hawk breathing not two feet away from her.

The arrangement was terribly improper, but seemliness hardly mattered when some uncontrolled wanton part of her had already cast her principles to the wind. To insist on an outward show of propriety now would be both hypocritical and meaningless.

Jane closed her eyes, longing for the forgetfulness of sleep. Twenty-five years she had lived, through marriage and childbirth and widowhood, and in all that time she had never suspected she had such lust buried within her body.

The church clergy were right. The Devil certainly did sneak up on those complacent in their piety.

For what seemed hours she clung to the edge of the bed, listening to Hawk toss restlessly beside her. He, it seemed, was having no more luck than she in wooing sleep.

Sleep did finally come, but even sleep was no escape from Hawk or the feelings he had awakened. Her dreams sent him to her. Again she lay beneath him, his hand caressing her breast, the swell of his male organ witness to his desire. She lay frozen, unmoving, helpless as he moved himself upon her. His mouth came down to hers, and she sank into darkness. He devoured her, ate away at her soul, and she neither cried nor struggled as he fed upon her— because it was a lovely feeling, being devoured.

"Do you think I'll eat you alive? See what can happen in a stable?" The words echoed in her head, and in the distance her name sounded somewhere like the chime of a bell. Jane. Jane. Hawk's voice, and from his mouth her plain name sounded like a melody. Jane. What a lovely feeling, having him press her down into the hay, panting over her, his hunger lighting his eyes like a tiger's in the darkness.

"Jane. Jane."

The voice surrounded her.

"Jane."

She opened her eyes. Hawk was indeed leaning over her, speaking her name.

"Wake up. 'Tis time to be on our way."

For a moment Jane lingered between dream and reality. The room had scarcely grayed with dawn, and in the half-light Hawk's face seemed to hang above hers. She focused on his lips, desire stirring to the memory of what his mouth could do to hers.

"Wake up!"

"Wh . . . what?"

Reality finally surfaced through the cobwebs of sleep. The dream fell away, leaving only a confused aching in its place.

"Get dressed," Hawk ordered. "I'm going down to help Ned hitch up the team." His voice sounded tired.

He had dressed before waking her, Jane noticed as he threw his gabardine over his shoulders and went out. She sat up and wearily rested her head against her drawn-up knees, wondering if Hawk might feel just as awkward about their night as she did.

They left an hour later after breaking their fast on cold mutton, cheese, and creamy milk fresh from the inn's cow. As they pulled out of the courtyard, Jane kept her eyes fastened on the floor of the coach. What little sleep she'd gotten the night before had left her more exhausted than if she'd had none at all. She felt drained and shaky, ill prepared to face Hawk with her usual cool equanimity. She didn't even want to face Ned, whose knowing smirk set her nerves on edge.

She was making a veritable ninny of herself, Jane mused, and such behavior was quite unlike her. She had always had the calm confidence of one who has herself well in hand, one who is secure in her strength, assured in her self-discipline. The ripe age of five-and-twenty was hardly a time to discover a side of herself that was like a stranger—a stranger who would flout convention and travel unescorted with a unprincipled rogue, who would feel stirrings of unholy lust for the scoundrel and succumb at the first temptation. She hardly knew what to expect of herself anymore, and the uncertainty was fearful.

Jane had to admit an ironic humor to the situation, however. Her sister Sarah had frequently chided her for being the family's "little holy darling," as Sarah used to put it. "Saint Jane," Sarah had frequently named her when they were out of their parents' hearing. Even Jane had thought herself quite dull and predictable. She had pictured herself growing old as another Grandmother Margaret, stiff, unyielding, and proper. The picture hadn't pleased her, but then neither did this strange, undisciplined, improper self that had surfaced of late. Jane supposed it served her right after all these years of easy piety to be shown that she was made from weak flesh after all.

On his side of the coach, Hawk mused on the difficulties of being somewhere between a rogue and a gentleman. He couldn't deny to himself that the discovery of only one room left at the inn hadn't been unwelcome. Somewhere inside him had been the hope that Jane might succumb to the woman he saw hidden in her eyes, and he hadn't been above pushing her a bit. He was rogue enough to try his luck. He hadn't, however, meant to frighten her and send her fleeing to the stables. And he certainly hadn't planned to assault her when he went to fetch her back. Raw instinct had bested what little of the gentleman was left to him. Jane Alexander could make his blood boil, and only the horrified realization of what he'd been about to do had saved him from making a bastard of himself and a victim of her. He had come to admire her—not for her principles, which were nonsense, but for her honesty in living by them. Yet he tried his damnedest to make her violate them. He had hoped for better from himself.

Still, it was interesting to note that his little Puritan melted down quite nicely when properly aroused.

They traveled at a good pace along the road that led past Rochester toward Chatham. Jane remained silent, not brooding or sulking, but an introspective silence that weighed on Hawk's conscience. After an hour of feeling his conscience become heavier and heavier, he decided that an apology might be in order.

"Jane . . . ," he began, then hesitated, one corner of his mouth tilting upward. "I think after last night we are familiar enough with each other that I might call you by your given name."

Jane raised a calm but melancholy face to meet his gaze. "After last night there might be a number of things you could call me." She smiled, diffusing the bitterness of her words. "I think, all things considered, Jane would be most appropriate."

"I apologize for last night, Jane. I . . . didn't mean to frighten you, or cause you grief."

She regarded him for a moment with eyes that seemed to see much more deeply into his soul than Hawk wanted her to see. "No," she said quietly, "I don't believe you did. Tell me, Matthew . . ."

He smiled as she returned the familiarity of using his given name.

". . . is your determined assault on my values and virtue merely a skirmish in your war against those who caused you injury?"

The woman had more perception than a sheltered and innocent Puritan widow ought to have. "You're much too hard on yourself." He shook his head ruefully. "I'll admit that I thought once or twice that seducing a lamb from the faithful fold would be a pleasant bit of revenge, but you underestimate your attraction as a woman. You're quite beautiful, you know."

The flush that came to her cheeks was entirely appealing, Hawk decided.

"You're not only beautiful, but you have a quality that some women—even some plain women—have that lures a man more strongly than beauty. Passion, sensuality, vitality —it's a mixture of all of those."

"I don't—"

"Jane." His soft voice cut off her denial. "You do, whether or not you recognize it. I'm afraid last night you overwhelmed any shred of honor I have left. What I did was a grave mistake, and I apologize for it. I didn't treat you last night as you deserve to be treated, and I vow it won't happen again."

He meant it, Hawk realized. Jane Alexander was beautiful in more ways than one. She was too fine a woman to be trifled with.

Her eyes drifted uneasily away. She studied the passing scenery, presenting Hawk with a profile that he suddenly craved to draw. He wondered if he could capture the unhappy tension that lent such a sense of tautness to her fine features.

"The fault was not only yours," she said quietly, still looking out the window. For a moment she was silent, thinking on her own imaginary sins, Hawk suspected. When she finally met his gaze her eyes held the hint of a twinkle. "Though certainly most of it was. I do hope the good Lord takes that into account when He assigns penance for the deed."

Hawk chuckled. "If God considered both of our accounts, my little Puritan, He'd surely mark the sin against mine, since one more drop added to an ocean of transgression will scarcely make a difference. Besides," he added with a smile, "a kiss is hardly such a sin."

Jane dropped her gaze, and Hawk wondered if she was

thinking how close their little tumble in the hay had come to being much more than a kiss.

"It was a very foolish thing we did," she concluded.

"Yes," he agreed quietly.

"Perhaps it would be best forgotten, since neither of us can claim innocence, and therefore neither can truly claim to be wronged."

"That is very generous of you."

Most women, Hawk mused, would have taken the excuse to sulk for days. Jane offered to forget the whole thing, though Hawk knew he wouldn't forget the feel of her sweet mouth and pliant body.

"Jane Alexander," he said with a smile, "you're a remarkable woman."

"Thank you." The smile that spread from her lips to her eyes was almost mischievous. "But surely not your sort of woman."

"Touché," he returned with a grin. "To tell the truth, I'm not entirely sure what my kind of woman is."

"You were married." The inflection of her voice made her words as much a question as a statement.

"Yes, I was married. My wife was the daughter of a wealthy London merchant. Her father was in the wool trade, as was I. Gloria was sweet, and a bit timid. She would never have dreamed of pitting her will against mine or saying nay to whatever I asked of her."

" 'Tis as a wife should be to her husband."

Hawk chuckled and regarded her skeptically. "Noble words, mistress. Were you so meek to your husband?"

Her dimples appeared. "I was a very well-behaved wife, sir. A Puritan woman is taught to cultivate reserve and tactful silence in her husband's presence."

"Forgive me," he said with a grin, "but somehow I can't

believe it of you. If you've any meek obedience, it's well hidden."

Jane tilted her head and smiled. "You are not my husband. There's no reason for me to bow to *your* wishes."

"As you have unmistakably demonstrated," he agreed. His tone was light, but he reflected in a more serious vein, wondering if he would want another wife like Gloria, were he to marry again. Their life together had been harmonious enough, but it had also been dull. Thirty or forty years of such a lackluster relationship could be a sore trial.

"Losing your wife so early in your life together must have been a great sorrow," Jane said sympathetically. "After losing my . . . husband, I was cast down for a very long time."

Hawk suspected she was thinking of her dead son, not the man she had called—so formally—Colonel Alexander.

"Gloria would have suffered greatly when I was arrested," he said. "She wouldn't have known what to do or to whom she could turn. Her parents died shortly after we were wed. I suppose in a twisted way it was best that she died before she could be overtaken by my misfortune."

"But you escaped."

"Aye. And still I've no life to offer a woman, nor does my life seem likely to settle down soon. I'd not ask a wife to share my lot."

"Nor a child."

Hawk looked up into her gentle regard. She still thought him a martyr of sorts. Her face was full of compassion for his sacrifice. His conscience pricked at him, and he tried to ignore it.

"Nor a child," he lied.

Their fragile harmony continued as morning flowed into afternoon. As the weather held fair, they dined in a meadow beside the road, the bread, cheese, cold goose, and apple tarts packed that morning at the inn spread out on a blanket between them. Ned quickly ate his portion and retired to the coach for a nap, complaining with a wicked smile in Hawk's direction that his sleep had been interrupted one too many times the night before. Hawk sent him on his way with a glare. Jane colored brightly.

"You've no need to worry about Ned," Hawk assured her. "He wouldn't say anything to your family—or to anyone else for that matter—to embarrass you." He waved a goose leg toward the coach. "In fact Ned's as staunch a defender as you'll ever have. He'd probably slit the throat of anyone who defamed you"—he grinned—"except me, of course. He's taken a perverse liking to you. Admires your grit."

Jane glanced toward the coach with a gentle smile. "For a villain, your Ned is really quite a good fellow."

Hawk shook his head. "Don't mistake him for that, mistress." His eyes caught the smile that lingered on her face. "You have quite the smile of an angel, did you know that, Jane Alexander?" He reached out a hand and tentatively touched her cheek. "In fact, sometimes I think you are an angel."

Jane pulled away from his touch and looked away. "You should certainly know that I'm not." She seemed to gather her courage, then steadily met his gaze once again. "And if I were indeed an angel, you'd be doing your very best to tarnish my halo, I think."

Hawk chuckled, discarded the drumstick he'd been eating, and leaned back upon the brown grass. "Only you can truly tarnish your halo, Mistress Angel. Our downfall ultimately comes from within ourselves; only we can bring about our own dishonor."

Jane tilted a dubious brow. "Such philosophy is not what I've heard from you before, sir."

He shook his head. " 'Tis true dishonor I speak of, not misfortune. Cromwell and his Puritans made me a criminal, but I made a rogue of myself." He looked up at the pale cold sky. "Were I to be truly honest, I'd have to admit that even my misfortunes can be laid at my own door. Had I really been a royalist, I wouldn't have been waiting for Cromwell to arrest me. I so arrogantly held myself above the struggle, thinking politics and the battles of government beneath me. So the monster I ignored rose up and bit me."

Jane plucked a blade of winter-dry grass and twirled it between her fingers. She wasn't sure she wanted to know this side of Matthew Hawkins. The hardened, callous, debauched royalist—no matter how attractive and, at times, appealing—was much easier to hold at a distance than the philosophical, somewhat vulnerable man who sat with her now. When he was gone, every time she looked at Gideon she would think of Hawk and wonder what he truly was. It was so much easier to be indifferent to a person, especially that person's pain, when one didn't know him well. Jane was coming to know Hawk uncomfortably well.

"If you truly were not a part of the uprising that spring," she asked, "why weren't you cleared at your trial? That is what trials are for, is it not?"

Hawk snorted, and she saw the old bitterness creep back into his eyes, turning them cold and dark.

"Puritans are much more eager to condemn than to find the truth. Condemnation is their talent. They condemn everything—pleasure, merriment, art, life itself." He gave her a strange look. "They've even condemned you, Jane. They've taken a sensitive, warm, and beautiful woman and cramped her into a mold as dry and lifeless as that blade of grass you're torturing."

Jane dropped the blade of grass as if it had burned her fingers, then resolutely picked it up again. "You're wrong," she told him, shaking her head. "My life is full of joy. You simply have the wrong eyes to see it."

Hawk merely smiled. His astute regard was disconcerting. No matter how well they knew each other, Jane reflected, their worlds were much too far apart to ever truly touch. The sorrow she felt at recognizing that truth was frightening.

10

Three Oaks, the Winford home in Kent, couldn't rival the great houses of the nobility for grandeur, but for peace and tranquillity no ostentatious mansion could match it. Three stately oaks stood guard in front of the three-story brick edifice, and countless others lined the curved drive and presided in royal fashion over the acres that surrounded the house and gardens.

Jane and Hawk caught a glimpse of the manor as their road crested a rise just to the south of the Winford holdings. The morning fog had burned off, and the house appeared to sleep in pale morning sun, the high vertical windows that marched along its facade shuttered against January cold. Bordering one side was a walled garden, and in back, a vast expanse of well-trimmed lawn sloped from the tiered stone terrace to a lively river which tumbled north on its way to join the Thames.

"An impressive place," Hawk commented.

Jane glanced at him in surprise, for Hawk had been very quiet on this last morning of their journey. His lively and ofttimes provoking conversation had lapsed into brooding silence.

"Yes," Jane answered. "Geoffrey and Sarah do very well. Most of these prosperous farms we've passed this morning owe rents to the Winford manor, and that gives them a very comfortable income on top of Geoffrey's private fortune. His father and grandfather did quite well in trade. 'Twas his grandfather who was given a hereditary title by King James."

"Ah. My grandfather."

Jane frowned, puzzled. "I beg your pardon?"

"King James was my father's father—on the wrong side of the blanket, of course. I suppose that will be another black mark on my account in heaven," he added with a wry smile.

"I hardly think your grandfather's sins could be laid at your door," Jane told him, a light of mischief in her eye. "If Geoffrey knew, he would be most impressed, I'm sure. He is very conscious of lineages, titles, and whatnot. Even his own very minor title impresses him."

"I thought you said once that Sir Geoffrey was Parliament's man—a republican."

"Oh, he is in word and deed," Jane assured him. "My brother-in-law comes from a staunch Puritan family and married into another. He had little choice in supporting Oliver Cromwell. But at heart he is very impressed by royalty. If he knew Gideon had such blue blood in his veins— even from the wrong side of the blanket—he would have spoiled the child rotten over these past weeks."

At mention of Gideon, Hawk's face tightened.

Jane regarded him sympathetically, imagining his turmoil at the prospect of seeing his son for the first time in three long years. She chattered on, trying to ease the tension.

"My sister Sarah was married a year before I wed Colonel Alexander—ten years ago. How long it seems now. Sir Geoffrey was considered quite a catch when he came to

London to seek a suitable wife. My father was quite pleased when Sarah attracted his eye. But of course our families had been acquainted for years.

"They have five darling children now, and much prefer the country to London," she continued. "Geoffrey only travels to the City occasionally for the sake of business. He's still in the wool trade."

Hawk was silent.

"If anything were to happen to me," Jane said quietly, "Sarah and Geoffrey would see to Gideon's welfare. I'm sure after you meet them you'll feel much better about Giddy's prospects."

"I'm in no doubt as to Gideon's prospects," Hawk answered cryptically.

Jane fell silent, wondering about his last remark, then decided to deal with a subject that had bothered her for some days.

"Matthew . . . ," she began. The hesitation in her voice brought Hawk's eyes up to hers. "I hesitate to lie to my family, but I wonder if it is safe to introduce you by your real name."

Hawk's expression hardened. "You didn't hesitate to suggest lying to Gideon."

"That . . . that is quite different."

He paused a moment, his hazel eyes darkening to a melancholy hue. "My name is hardly a household word, and this far removed from London, there's very little anyone could do, even if your family takes exception to my past. Spin too many lies and you'll be caught in your own web."

She looked doubtful.

He smiled. "Competent lying needs practice, Jane, and you've had very little, I think."

"But you agree that Gideon . . . that we should not let him know who you are."

Hawk averted his gaze and stared out the window. They had turned onto the manor's long drive, and naked-limbed oaks marched by in measured precision. "For now," he agreed quietly. "Only for now."

The Winfords were surprised by Jane's arrival, but greeted her effusively. As blond as her sister, Lady Winford was short, rather plump, and gowned quite becomingly in lavender-and-rose silk. Sir Geoffrey, stout, balding, and almost as short as his wife, chuckled approvingly as Sarah enfolded Jane in a hug the moment she stepped from the coach.

"There now, wife! Did I not tell ye that all that worrying was for naught?"

Sarah held Jane at arm's length. "Mercy, but you're thin! All this time and not a word! Jane, I was frantic with worry —almost ready to dispatch poor Geoffrey to London to see if you were well! Haven't you been eating, dear? Why didn't you let us know you were coming? This isn't your coach, is it? I thought you sold yours."

"Wife, give the girl a chance to catch her breath." Sir Geoffrey cast a guarded look at Hawk, who stood watching the sisterly reunion. "And give your sister a chance to introduce this fellow here."

Sarah noticed Hawk for the first time, it seemed, and her eyes widened. "Oh, my! Jane?"

Jane saw the confusion in her sister's face. With a tiny sigh of apprehension she gestured Hawk to come forward. "May I present Master Matthew Hawkins. Master Hawkins . . ."

Hawk smiled at her return to formal address.

". . . allow me to introduce my sister, Lady Winford, and her husband, Sir Geoffrey Winford."

"My pleasure," Hawk said with a nod.

Both Winfords looked at him curiously, then eyed Jane as if further explanation was expected. Sir Geoffrey cleared his throat. "Hawkins . . . seems I know the name. You related to the fellow Hawkins—Earl of Glouster, no, Chester . . . Earl of Chester—who had the big warehouses down by Queenhithe? Quite a big wool house, that. Shrewd businessman, the fellow was. Hanged, I b'lieve. Some royalist mischief."

Hawk smiled, unperturbed, while Jane's heart leapt into her throat. "The very same, Sir Geoffrey. Unfortunately, title, warehouses, and business were stripped from me for the alleged mischief you mentioned."

Sarah gasped. Jane closed her eyes.

"I say!" Geoffrey exclaimed. "Thought you were dead!"

"My sentence was lifted at the last moment."

Jane finally understood what Hawk meant about practiced lying. The man was an artist.

Both Winfords still looked taken aback.

Sir Geoffrey cleared his throat, a rumbling that sounded startlingly loud in the strained silence. "Uh . . . I'm sure 'tis an interesting story, my good fellow—how you came to be reprieved and made the acquaintance of our Jane here. But let's finish the telling in the parlor, shall we?"

"By all means," Hawk assented easily.

"Splendid. Uh . . . splendid. Your man can take the coach around back and then get himself something hot in the kitchen. Sarah?" he prodded his wife, who still stared at Hawk with seeming fascination.

"Oh, yes!" Sarah started to life. "By all means . . . into the parlor and I'll have Mathilde bring refreshments. Have you broken your fast?" she dithered. "Oh, of course you have. 'Tis almost noon. But you must have some tea or coffee at least. Buttermilk for you, Jane? I vow you need something sweet and rich to fill you out!"

"No, Sarah. Nothing, thank you."

A rather portly, red-haired butler greeted them in the hallway and took their wraps. Upon spying Jane, his florid face broke into a smile. "Nice to see you again, Mistress Alexander."

"Thank you, Connor."

"Connor," Sarah ordered, "open the shutters in the parlor and stoke the fire, please. 'Tis much too gloomy in there. And have Mathilde bring in tea and pastries, please."

"Yes, my lady."

Sarah led the way into the parlor and arranged herself becomingly on a plush settee while her husband stood before the fire.

"Do sit down, Jane dear," Sarah urged. "This is all most mysterious, I must say. I trust you won't tell me that the two of you traveled here alone and unescorted."

Jane did not sit. Neither did Hawk. Jane knew him well enough to feel his tension. It infected her as if it were her own. Outwardly calm, he cast his eyes into every corner of the house that was within his sight. She knew what he sought.

"Sarah, where is Gideon?" Jane asked.

"Jane . . . !" her sister objected.

"I will explain all, Sarah. But first tell me where Giddy is."

"He's upstairs with the other children and their tutor. And Grandmother Margaret is taking a late-morning nap." She laughed, distracted already from the mystery at hand.

"He is such a handful, my dear. He doesn't like the idea of lessons at all, you know, and has told us several times that a guest shouldn't be required to sit for such schooling. Then he objected to taking lessons with the girls. He is much put out by Melissa, though it is most entertaining to see him try to deal with her. She is quite taken with him and tags constantly at his heels. I fear poor Giddy thinks our little Melissa is one cross too many to bear."

Sir Geoffrey cleared his throat. "Sarah," he reproved gently.

"What? Oh, yes! So Giddy is quite well, my dear. But we are most anxious to hear—"

"Now, sir!" Geoffrey picked up the thread of his wife's question. "Did you travel all this way from London with my sister-in-law? 'Tis most improper, if you did."

"Geoffrey," Jane said, "let me explain."

"Please do." He harrumphed expectantly.

"I admit the impropriety of all this—calling on you unannounced, traveling for three days unescorted in the company of Master Hawkins—"

"Oh, Jane! You didn't!"

"Let her finish, Sarah," Geoffrey chided his wife.

"And as Geoffrey suspects, I'm sure," Jane continued quietly, "Master Hawkins did not have his sentence lifted. He escaped it."

"Oh, dear!" Sarah gasped. "Jane! What can you be thinking!"

"The important point is that Master Hawkins is Gideon's father." Jane's admission cut off her sister's protest and left stunned silence in its place.

Geoffrey took but a moment to recover. "By Gad, Jane! You told us the boy's father was dead!"

"A mistaken assumption, I assure you." Hawk's deep

voice made all eyes turn his way. "The truth is, as Mistress Alexander says, I escaped the fate that Cromwell planned for me and lay low for three years. Now I am about to leave England, and I persuaded this kind lady to allow me some time with my son before I go."

"A rebel!" Geoffrey growled.

"Or patriot," Hawk countered, "depending on your point of view, sir."

Jane sat down, feeling the silence press in around her. Sarah had grown white as her lacy linen collar, and Geoffrey frowned pensively. No doubt they were both contemplating the consequences of having a fugitive in their home, even if the chase for him had died three years ago. She hated to involve her family in this mess, but she owed Hawk at least a little while with his son.

"Master Hawkins saved my life, Geoffrey. I fell ill with the same fever that took Mistress Thackeray." Jane's eyes shifted to Sarah. "I wrote you of her being sick."

"Yes," Sarah said, for once at loss for words.

"Charity deserted me, but Master Hawkins, who had come hoping to find his son, stayed and cared for me. He's a good man." She felt Hawk's eyes upon her, the sudden bemusement in his regard. "And for my sake I hope you will find it in your hearts to accept him as a guest."

Geoffrey rose and moved ponderously to the fireplace, there staring into the flames. After a few moments he sighed. "Daresay you might have the right of it, Hawkins. Never a finer man lived than Oliver Cromwell, but his whelp Richard—pah! The government's more chaos than order since Cromwell's death. Could be the only solution to the problem is a return to a limited monarchy. If Richard don't start showing some promise, the whole country'll be crying for young Charles to come back and take his father's throne."

"Geoffrey!" Jane admonished. "You don't mean that!"

"Indeed I do, girl!" He cleared his throat and turned toward her. " 'Tis quite a surprise you give your sister and me. Didn't think you had it in you to be running off on such adventure. You've compromised yourself most foolishly, you know."

"She hadn't much choice, sir," Hawk broke in.

"What's that you say?"

"Mistress Alexander knew I was determined to see Gideon—one way or another. 'Twas only for the boy's own good she was willing to accompany me here."

Jane held her breath as she watched her brother-in-law consider Hawk's implied threat. She didn't release it until the set of Geoffrey's shoulders relaxed. "Stripped your title, did Cromwell? Rum deal, that. But doubtless you'll have it returned when the political pendulum swings back."

" 'Tis Gideon he cares about, Geoffrey, not the silly title."

Geoffrey threw a sharp look at Jane, then a conciliatory smile toward Hawk. "Women, bless them!"

Sarah fluttered to her feet. "Well, now that all that's been settled"—she looked to her husband to ensure that everything had indeed been settled—"you should refresh yourselves. Where *is* Mathilde with the tea and pastries?"

"Really, Sarah, we don't need anything," Jane told her.

"But of course you do! Look at how thin you are, and dinner isn't for two hours yet. Come, let's go into the withdrawing room—it's so much warmer."

Sarah took Jane's arm and urged her along. Sir Geoffrey and Hawk dawdled behind. Somewhat to Jane's surprise, they seemed deep in cordial conversation about the wool trade in London.

"Master Hawkins's story is very touching," Sarah confided quietly, "but I must express the opinion that learning of a dead father come to life is going to be very confusing for poor little Gideon. Unless of course he's taking the boy with him to wherever he's going."

"He's not," Jane said firmly.

"Then perhaps when he returns to England with the King, as Geoffrey says—"

"Geoffrey is wrong, I believe, Sarah. England will never accept another king."

"Well, of course, I have very little opinion on such things. But as a rule Geoffrey is right in his estimations."

"Besides, Master Hawkins agrees that Gideon is better off with me."

"Does he?" She looked at Jane doubtfully, then Mathilde caught her eye. "Where are the refreshments, Mathilde?"

"Coming, my lady."

Sarah sighed as the slight little pox-faced woman bustled toward the kitchen. "Good help is so difficult to find. But of course you know. Imagine Charity deserting you like that! Absolutely criminal! Why, you could have died!"

Jane let her sister ramble on, accustomed to her dizzying jumps from subject to subject. She pondered uneasily on Geoffrey's unexpected congeniality with Hawk, realizing that she should have guessed that once her brother-in-law discovered that Hawk was an earl—in disfavor or not— Geoffrey would become the soul of hospitality. She didn't want them too friendly. After all, if conflict arose, Jane wanted her family on her side.

Moments later the stream of Sarah's chatter was interrupted by the men's joining them. At the same time Mathilde returned with tea—a luxury introduced into England several years ago but far too expensive for Jane to afford—and a plateful of little spiced sugar-frosted cakes.

"Sarah," Geoffrey said. "Perhaps we should call the children down."

Jane felt Hawk tense rather than saw it.

"Oh. Of course. What have I been thinking! Mathilde, please go upstairs and tell Master Sterling that the children may join us until dinner."

Hawk didn't take his eyes from the parlor entrance until the small herd of children thundered down the stairs into the entry hall and from there bounced into the parlor. The youngsters spied Jane immediately and surrounded her with welcoming cries. She greeted each one with a warm hug, feeling Hawk's eyes upon her as she did so, then lost them one by one to the lure of tea and pastries.

"Children!" Sarah scolded. "Mind your manners!"

Her command was echoed by the tutor as he followed them into the room. Tall, thin, with wispy brown hair, he had an unmistakably harried look about him.

"Thank you, Master Sterling," Sarah said. "I have them in hand. They'll return to their studies after dinner."

A relieved-looking Master Sterling nodded and took his leave.

"Children"—Sarah suddenly assumed the air of a general—"line up to be introduced nicely to our guest, then you may each have one pastry."

The youngsters formed an irregular stairstep of children as Sarah introduced them one by one.

"Thomas is our eldest. He is nine." Thomas bowed gravely, then lost his practiced dignity in a wide grin. Even at nine he was the image of his father.

"Trevor is eight." Plump and fair, Trevor resembled his mother right down to her merry blue eyes.

"George is seven." Taller than Trevor, George stood very straight to make sure everyone noticed the fact.

"Deidre is five." Painstakingly curled brown ringlets and a stiff little gown of velvet and silk made Deidre appear a miniature lady, but the twinkle in her eyes suggested otherwise.

"And Melissa is four. Melissa, dear, take your fingers out of your mouth. Ladies do not suck on their fingers." Melissa sucked away, paying her mother no mind, and regarded Hawk with solemn brown eyes.

Sarah frowned, perplexed. "Where is Gideon?"

"Gideon!" Jane scolded. "Leave the pastries and come here to be introduced."

A sheepish Gideon sprang up from in front of the settee, licking sugar from his fingers. Jane took him by the shoulder and led him to the end of the line of Winford children, where Melissa promptly removed her fingers from her mouth and grasped wetly onto his sleeve. The boy sighed.

"This is Gideon, who is very tall for eight years of age."

Gideon grinned, stretching his few freckles and lighting the lively green of his eyes. Jane ruffled her fingers fondly through the silky black curls that tumbled about the boy's ears. They were very like his father's, she noticed—and took her hand away. "Make your bow, Gideon."

"Gideon," Hawk acknowledged the boy's quick bow.

The raw ache in his voice made Jane's throat hurt with sympathy. She circled the boy's shoulder with a possessive arm. "Gideon," she said brightly. "This gentleman is Master Matthew Hawkins."

Giddy's eyes drifted back to the pastries, which the other

children were also eyeing in anticipation. Jane saw there was no help for it.

Sarah took over. "One pastry each, children. Gideon must go last, since he's already had his share. If Master Sterling were still in the house, young man, I would send you back to your lessons while the other children ate their treats."

Giddy made a move of disgust and ducked from beneath Jane's restricting arm. He bounced over to join the other children, oblivious of Hawk's eyes following him as a starved man might follow a loaf of bread.

Unmindful of the impropriety, Jane laid a gentle hand on Hawk's arm. "You hoped he would remember you, did you not?"

Hawk sighed.

"Three years is a long time to a child, Matthew—an eternity."

"An eternity to me, also. He's grown. No more baby fat and dimples. Lean and fit as a little monkey."

Jane laughed softly. "An apt description of our Gideon." Self-consciously she took her hand from his arm. "Sarah, since the sun is shining, why don't we finish our tea, then take a walk by the river. It will do the children good to bounce off some of their energy."

Geoffrey harrumphed. "Splendid idea! Do take the herd somewhere, Sarah. I've some accounts to look at." He glanced at Hawk. "This tea is a brew for women. Care to take a brandy before dinner? Hmph. No, suppose not. Well, don't let m'wife talk your head off. She does more chattering than walking."

The children consumed the tea and pastries with great gusto, then led the way from the house, shrieking with delight as they emerged onto the tiered terrace and thence to the wide lawn that sloped down to the river. They cavorted like puppies released from a kennel, tumbling across the grass, chasing one another and rousting out a few unfortunate ducks that had been sunning by the river.

"You indulge them impossibly, Sarah," Jane told her sister, the warmth in her tone belying her words.

"Geoffrey and I don't hold with the belief that children must be broken in spirit to be saved from evil, as well you know, Jane. Giddy is the wildest of the bunch."

Jane smiled acknowledgment. For all the religious and disciplinary laxity of the Winford household, Jane couldn't help thinking it compared favorably to the rigid atmosphere in which she and Sarah had been raised. "What would we have done if we'd been given a chance to tumble around like this as children?"

"We wouldn't have known what to do. Or at least you wouldn't have." Sarah's eyes shone merrily. "I certainly would have."

They sat on the grass in the sun while the children played hide-and-seek among the trees that stood along the river. George and Gideon had talked Hawk into a contest of throwing rocks at trees. Little Melissa had transferred her affection from Gideon to Hawk. She hung on his leg as though he were a favorite, oversize doll. Between his turns at rock throwing, Hawk hunkered down and allowed her to play pat-a-cake with his big hands. Melissa's face shone brighter than the midday sun.

"My goodness, but Master Hawkins is a well-set-up man, don't you think, Jane? That black hair and those green eyes—"

"They're not green," Jane corrected her. "They're hazel."

"Oh. Well, they looked green to me, just like Giddy's.

He's a very handsome man, though he has a harder look than I would credit to be gentlemanly. Still, he's an earl—"

"Was an earl," Jane corrected again.

"And perhaps will be again. You must have been very concerned when he appeared, knowing how precious Gideon is to you. Is he very bitter about his troubles?"

Jane answered Sarah's questions and made absent-minded responses to her chattering while she watched Hawk with the children. Even at such a distance she could feel the warmth of the smile he gave little Melissa and hear his laughter with the boys. Deidre, apparently jealous of her little sister, joined the circle around Hawk. She was the shiest of the Winford children, but even she seemed captivated.

This was a side of Hawk that Jane hadn't seen. How could a man who was savage enough to virtually rule the London underworld, vicious enough to once have held a knife to her throat, have such patience with children? Would she ever understand the man?

"Jane, dear! Have you heard a word I've said? Jane?"

"What? Oh, yes. Of course I have, Sarah."

Sarah passed a shrewd glance from her sister to Hawk, who, with the boys, was skipping stones across the water. Melissa's hanging from his leg put him at a disadvantage, but he didn't complain. "He's a surprising man, your Master Hawkins."

"He's certainly not *my* Master Hawkins."

Gideon tossed a rock and laughed at some comment that Hawk made. Jane could almost see the light in Hawk's eyes—eyes that would be almost golden now, the color of his contentment that she'd seen only a very few times. He flung a rock which skimmed over the surface of the water in a series of tiny skips. Giddy hollered and clapped Hawk on the back, and Hawk responded with a friendly grasp of the boy's shoulder. Jane could feel the tension of that grip almost as if it were her own flesh that Hawk held as though he would never let go. With a strange ache in her heart she let her gaze drop to the grass upon which she sat. When she raised her eyes again, father and son were again apart, and Giddy was competing with George, Thomas, and Trevor to find the best skipping rocks left on the riverbank.

"Well of course I didn't mean he was *your* Master Hawkins," Sarah denied. "I must say that you're not at all yourself today, Jane. But then, you've been ill, haven't you? Being sick can have strange effects on the character, you know. And I certainly didn't mean to imply that there was anything improper between the two of you, in spite of the horrid circumstances."

"No, of course you didn't. And you're right." Jane smiled. "Master Hawkins is a surprising man in many ways."

Dinner was in the midafternoon—later than Sarah would like it, she confided to Jane once they were seated for the meal. The cook, however, insisted upon the late hour. It had taken a miracle to persuade the woman to leave London for the country, and if Sarah dared suggest dining at a boorishly early hour, she would probably pack and leave. The children had already eaten, supervised in their manners by their tutor, and were now reluctantly back at their lessons.

The Winfords' dining table was the height of luxury, having upholstered oak chairs instead of mere stools for the diners to sit upon. Grandmother Margaret sat in her chair as though it were a throne. Just across the table from Hawk, she divided disapproving glances equally between him and Jane, and still had some censure left over for Sarah.

"That was an exceedingly short prayer," she commented as Geoffrey said the amens to the grace. "You girls remember your parents' house? Your father and mother never sat down to a meal without a full half hour of Bible reading first, and dinner conversation was restricted to discussion of whatever passage was read from the Good Book. 'Twas the same in my own house."

"So you've informed us, Grandmother," Geoffrey answered in an unperturbed voice. Sarah looked at Jane and rolled her eyes heavenward, confirming that Jane was the only one in the family who had the patience to put up with the stern old lady.

Margaret shifted her glare to Hawk as the servants brought in the soup course—a fish soup with pieces of eel, cod, and shellfish. "So you are the Matthew Hawkins whose crimes brought us the boy Gideon."

Jane grimaced. Hawk had been introduced simply as Master Hawkins of London. Trust her grandmother to have a memory so sharp she never forgot a thing!

Hawk seemed to enjoy the old lady's disapproval. "My crimes were neglible," he told her. "But since that time I've managed to live up to the republic's poor opinion of me."

"Hmph!" was Margaret's reply. "You're a bold one, I'll give you that."

"As are you, madam."

Grandmother Margaret actually seemed to enjoy the exchange. "I suppose it's too much to hope that you've come back for the boy."

"Grandmother!" Jane and Sarah objected at the same time.

"I've come to see my son. Then England will be rid of me for a while."

"Well, don't be thinking to bring your high-living King into England, sir. England's become a God-fearing land, and we've no use for such dissipated profligates."

Hawk smiled. "I'm sure the dissipated profligate wouldn't dream of going against your wishes, madam."

"Hmph!"

If Hawk had not won over Sarah and Geoffrey before, he had them in the palm of his hand by the time the sweet tarts with raisins were served. Jane watched in amazement as he turned on the charm. Even Grandmother Margaret had been wooed from acid to merely sour.

He was all things to all people, Jane mused with her own bit of sourness. Just enough discreet flattery to have Sarah cooing, enough sober attention to Geoffrey's opinions to have that one puffed in satisfaction, and a wry combativeness that somehow seemed to please Margaret. How easily he fooled them.

After dinner the men took their cigars into the library. Grandmother Margaret retired to her chamber for prayers, leaving Sarah with an admonishment not to indulge in her usual after-dinner wine. "Your digestion doesn't need it," the old lady warned, "and neither does your soul."

Delighted to disobey, Sarah motioned for Mathilde to bring a decanter of sherry and two glasses as the ladies adjourned to the withdrawing room. "I don't envy you having shared your house with Grandmother these past years!" She poured Jane and herself a glass of sherry. "You're the only one of the family who's ever gotten on with her. Even Mother and Father could scarcely abide her. These last few weeks she's been with us have been . . . Well, I'd forgotten what a truly crusty old soul she is."

Jane smiled and sipped at her sherry. "I wouldn't say Grandmother and I got on . . . exactly. I simply regard her as an exercise in patience." She sent a worried glance in the direction of the library.

"Oh, don't worry about Geoffrey and your Master Hawkins. They'll be talking about nothing more interesting than politics and wool. Even if Master Hawkins let slip one of your secrets, Geoffrey wouldn't hear, I vow. He's forgotten that most men occasionally find women a temptation."

"Master Hawkins and I have no secrets." Jane felt a twinge of guilt, for that statement wasn't precisely true. She wouldn't want her family to know about those horrid days when Hawk had flagrantly exposed her to gossip. No matter what repairs she attempted, she would never be able to erase all the tarnish from her name. There was also that unfortunate incident in the stable. Indeed, she shared several shameful secrets with Hawk, and Sarah had a gleam in her eye that told Jane she hadn't fooled her sister for one minute. "The things you imagine, Sarah! You've really grown quite worldly, you know."

"Pooh!" Sarah waved off Jane's gentle reprimand with a wave of her hand. "Being married to Thaddeus Alexander made you much too serious, Jane. I remember a young man who courted you just before the colonel came along— what was his name? I don't remember. Anyway, he was quite handsome and knew how to smile. You should have married him."

Jane arched a fine brow. "Colonel Alexander was Father's choice for me. I saw no reason to set my will against his. I was content with my husband, Sarah."

"Poor Jane." Sarah smiled and shook her head. "Always the steady, reliable, obedient one. Your husband turned you into a mouse with all his sermonizing about duty, sobriety, and responsibility."

Jane rose and went to the window. Looking into the fading afternoon beyond the glass panes, she pensively swirled her wine. "I am not such a mouse as you think, Sarah."

Sarah poured herself another glass of sherry. "Up until now you certainly have been a mouse!" She giggled. "A very dear mouse, but a mouse just the same. The only time you ever stepped out of the bounds of being a perfect wife —then a perfect widow—was when you took in Gideon. And, of course, now—all this flitting around with Giddy's father," she teased. "I vow the man must have put a spell on you to make you loosen up so!"

Jane turned almost as red as the wine.

"See, my dear!" Sarah laughed softly. "You never could lie."

"You don't know Master Hawkins as I do," Jane warned.

"Assuredly not," Sarah chortled.

"Sarah . . . !"

"Oh, don't blush so, Jane. If I'm not mistaken, the man fancies you, and you might do worse. He has money and a title, or he will when the King takes power. Geoffrey says England is starting to cry for the monarchy's return, and if he's right, you would be very fortunate to have a staunch royalist offer for your hand. Besides," she gushed, "I think it's romantic. He's very handsome, with just a touch of mystery about him that makes him all the more interesting."

Jane shook her head. "You don't have any idea what you're talking about, dear."

Hawk was anything but romantic. He was dangerous, criminal, callous, vengeful, lustful, and in a strange, contradictory way, gentle and vulnerable when one least expected it. But he wasn't romantic. Any attraction Jane felt for him was a foolishness she could easily conquer with good sense and a bit of discipline.

Or so she hoped.

11

❀ ❀

"I say, Master Hawkins! You're an early riser, I see." Sir Geoffrey rubbed his hands together briskly as he sat down across from Hawk at a table spread with cheese, fruit, bread, fresh milk, and slices of hot pork. "Splendid habit, getting up with the sun! Gives a man a healthy appetite—invigorates a man's spirit!"

"Indeed it does," Hawk agreed.

"Jane tells me you've blood ties to the Stuarts." Geoffrey speared several slices of pork and heaped them on a plate along with bread and cheese. "Ain't surprised—you've got the dark looks of 'em. Suspect when you leave England you'll be going to Europe to help young Charlie's cause, eh?"

Hawk arched a brow.

"Oh, Jane's not been letting out your secrets, if that's what you're thinking. Not that I for one would trust a chattering woman with any information I wanted to keep under wraps, but Jane ain't as silly as most. She's got a head on her shoulders." He stuffed a bite into his mouth and continued to talk around it. " 'Tisn't hard to deduce, though, that kin to the royal family would be wanting to help Charlie back to the throne. Not that I don't wish you well in the venture. Myself, I didn't hold with the old King's habits.

He was a papist if you ask me, and a damned arrogant tyrant. But Parliament ain't much better, and old Cromwell's son Richard—pah! We'd be far better off with a reasonable king, I say!"

Sarah and Jane came into the room together. " 'Tis early in the morning to be bending the man's ear," Sarah chided as they sat down. "Master Hawkins isn't here to hear your politics, husband."

"That's right," Geoffrey said. "Where is that boy of yours?"

Jane and Sarah both gave Geoffrey a quelling look. "Geoffrey, dear, we're all agreed that 'tis best for Giddy not to know that Master Hawkins is his father," Sarah reminded him.

"Hmmph! Fine day when a man can't acknowledge his own son. This England's in a sorry state, I tell you!"

Jane glanced at Hawk uneasily, but his face revealed nothing of what he felt.

"Well, 'tis a fine morning for January—dashed unusual, this weather we've been having. I'll show you my lands, if you like, Master Hawkins. Young Gideon can come as well. Master Sterling'll bless me for taking the boy off for the morning, I'd guess."

"I'd like that," Hawk said.

"Geoffrey!" Sarah scolded. "How will I explain to the other children that Gideon gets this special treat?"

Sir Geoffrey snorted. "You explain too much, my dear. Children should not require explanations, they should simply do as they're told."

Sarah huffed in dissatisfaction.

"If you don't mind," Jane interjected. "I would like to go, too."

Geoffrey looked at her in disapproval. "Didn't know you rode, m'dear."

"I think she'd learn to ride if she didn't," Hawk said. His knowing smile brought a flush to Jane's face.

Sir Geoffrey was correct. Jane wasn't a horsewoman of any skill. But she would have ridden a camel if need be rather than let Hawk take Gideon out of her sight. The little party rode slowly for her benefit and for Giddy's, for Gideon was little better on horseback than was Jane, though he tried very hard to imitate Hawk, who sat his saddle as if he was part of the horse. They rode north for a ways along the river, then cut into Geoffrey's favorite hunting woods, which at this time of year had only a few brown and shriveled leaves clinging to the trees and was pungent with the smell of dead vegetation.

Hawk and Geoffrey chatted like old friends, about politics, about current markets for wool in Europe, about the problems of running estates. Jane learned that Hawk had possessed several holdings before his arrest—two in Hampshire and one in Dorset. Hawk complimented Sir Geoffrey on his horseflesh—the baronet's pride and joy. He also commented favorably upon the acres of meadows and woods and the prosperous-looking farms that comprised the Three Oaks domain. Before they had ridden an hour, Jane was sure that Geoffrey would back Matthew Hawkins for king given an ounce of encouragement.

Jane herself felt less congenial, and her ill humor grew as the outing lengthened. All her energy was required to stay on her horse, even though the little mare was as gentle and biddable a creature as anyone could ask. Her backside ached, her shoulders grew more stiff by the minute from trying to stay upright in the ridiculous sidesaddle, and her knee was never going to be the same after spending the morning wrapped around the sidesaddle's knee horn.

Geoffrey's eager deference to Hawk did not improve Jane's mood. She had feared offending her family with Hawk's visit—after all, he was a rebel and a criminal, albeit at times an amiable criminal. He had practically murdered her in her own bed, ruthlessly compromised her good name, mocked her way of life, and attacked her virtue. But instead of regarding Hawk with disapproving eyes, Sarah and Geoffrey seemed to subtly reproach Jane for separating the man from his son, making her the villain, not Hawk.

Of course Jane hadn't filled them in on the details of Hawk's criminal past, nor his offenses toward her. Still, they should have more sense than to be so easily taken in by a charming rogue.

Giddy's piping voice pulled Jane from her sour musing. "Are we going back to London, Aunt Jane?"

From the first day Giddy had come to her, Jane had instructed him to call her Aunt Jane. No matter how she longed for the title of Mother, she felt that would be too much of a trespass on the poor dead lady who had borne him.

"We might decide to stay here for a while," Jane told him. "Maybe a long while. Would you like that?"

"Ever so much!" Gideon declared. "George and I went fishing last week, and I caught two fish that Cook fried for my dinner. George caught a bigger fish, but he only caught one, and I caught two."

"That's splendid, Giddy," Jane said. "You must show me how to fish sometime soon."

"I will, but ladies aren't very good at fishing. That's what George says."

"Some ladies are very good at fishing," Hawk inter-jected. He reined his horse back until he was even with them, leaving Geoffrey to his own company. "My mother was quite the fisherman. She was also very good at tennis, and she could outshoot my father, which angered him im-mensely."

Gideon's mouth fell open. "Was she a lady?"

"Most definitely a lady," Hawk replied with a smile. "A countess."

"My mother was a real lady," Gideon said, not to be outdone. "Only she's dead. And my father was an awfully rich lord who was friends with the King."

"That's most impressive," he told the boy. "Where is your father now?" His conversational tone masked the ten-sion in the question, but Jane sensed it all the same.

"He's dead too," Gideon said matter-of-factly. "He was friends with the King," he continued, as if that in itself was enough explanation. "Sometimes I get sad when I think of him. I don't remember him, and Master Peabody, my tutor in London, says I won't see him in heaven. Master Peabody says friends of the old King are all sinners who ignore the will of God and they'll burn in hell."

Jane drew a horrified breath. "Giddy! He didn't tell you that!" Guilt pricked at her. She should have monitored Gideon's tutor more closely, but she had no idea Master Peabody would feed the boy such nonsense. "Did he really say such a thing?"

"Yes, he did."

A curtain seemed to fall over Hawk's expression. His face seemed carved from granite, but the cold glitter in his eyes made a frisson of fear skitter down Jane's spine. It was just as well foolish Master Peabody wasn't within

Hawk's reach, considering Matthew Hawkins's lamentable adeptness at violence.

"Master Peabody was wrong, Gideon," she said vehemently. "I'm positive that your father is not burning in hell. We must leave God to judge as He sees fit and not usurp His authority to ourselves."

Gideon had lost interest, however. He but shrugged and trotted ahead to ride beside Geoffrey. Jane hadn't the courage to raise her eyes to Hawk's.

"The morning draws on, doesn't it?" Geoffrey twisted in his saddle to speak to Jane and Hawk. "Best be getting back. This afternoon I must leave for London—business, y'know. Would you care to accompany me, Hawkins? You're an old hand at these dashed shipping problems. You might enjoy yourself."

"I think not," Hawk said.

Jane sighed and shook her head. If Geoffrey had forgotten that his guest was a fugitive and a criminal, at least Hawk had not.

Directly after dinner Sir Geoffrey left for London. After good-byes had been said, Jane, Sarah, and Hawk took the children for another walk along the river, even though the unusual January sun that had favored them these last few days had ducked behind gathering clouds. The children were delighted with the romp and drew Hawk into their games as though he were one of the family. Gideon in particular seemed taken with him. The boy's affection was only natural, Jane told herself. Even though Gideon didn't recognize his father, blood called to blood. Their affinity shouldn't have made her jealous, but it did.

Hawk's ease with all the children discomfited Jane. Men were not supposed to be so drawn to the little ones; that was a woman's special realm. Hawk in particular should not have fallen in so readily with their silliness and laughter. This facet of his character didn't fit with Jane's notion of how a rebel, a criminal, and a self-confessed scoundrel should behave. She watched the children swarm around him on their afternoon stroll, she listened with amazement when they returned to the house and his quiet second of Sarah's order that the children go back to their lessons immediately silenced all objections, and she fought her envy at supper as Gideon sat beside Hawk and talked nonstop about Geoffrey's promise to take him hunting with the Winford boys. Jane kept foremost in her mind that Hawk was making a noble sacrifice for his son and she shouldn't begrudge him Giddy's closeness while he was here to enjoy it.

Late that night, Jane sat at the little writing desk in her chamber and tried to mold her emotions into written words. Days had passed since she had written in her journal. Never before in her life had she been so neglectful of her spiritual record keeping. Since Matthew Hawkins had come into her life, it seemed all her good habits and self-discipline had gone by the wayside.

She opened the journal and penned:

January 24, 1659

I have been unkind today. In my thoughts I have allowed jealousy and resentment to trample the charitable feelings I should have for Matthew Hawkins. Sarah and Geoffrey, who have accepted Master Hawkins in true Christian charity, have been kinder to him than I who owe the man my life. Yet I am resentful of my family's ready acceptance of a man whom I know to be a dangerous rogue—for all his feigned charm and manners. Worse, the natural affection Gideon gives his father inspires me to wicked envy. If I were less selfish, I would be happy to see this troubled man have a happy interlude with his son.

As I usually am not prone to such strong and unruly emotions, I fear I am dealing poorly with the effect Master Hawkins has upon me. The pendulum of my sentiments toward the man swings from fear and resentment to admiration and—I will have to admit—warm affection. There is much to admire in the man, despite his shortcomings. Perhaps Geoffrey and Sarah are not so wrong to be taken with him, and I should work harder to be more generous in my forgiveness. Though he is worldly, carnal, unprincipled, and—I believe—capable of savagery when he thinks it necessary, still he has dealt gently with me, for the most part, and has made a most painful and noble sacrifice regarding his son.

Jane paused in her writing, reluctantly facing the truth that in spite of her mixed feelings, she'd conceived a most unwise affection for Matthew Hawkins, the Hawk, King of Thieves, Prince of Rogues. She continued, reflecting that years in the future she would read this day's entry and laugh at herself for a fool.

I confess that my resentment for the way Master Hawkins has charmed my family stems most ignobly from a desire on my part to be the only one with a soul generous enough to recognize the nobility hidden so deeply within the villain. Instead, I find myself to be sadly lacking in that very virtue of generosity. I shall try to do better in the days to come.

Jane closed her journal and looked toward her bed. It didn't seem inviting. She would never be able to sleep with her mind whirling and her conscience smarting. Everyone else had retired. The house was quiet. She looked out the window to the small formal garden that Sarah had culti- vated at the side of the house. The moon, mostly obscured by clouds, cast an uncertain light on naked hedges, skeletal trees, and graveled walkways. Despite its winter barren- ness, the garden seemed to call her. A touch of fresh air was just what she needed to clear the confusion from her brain, Jane decided. She donned her wool cloak, slipped silently from her chamber, tiptoed along the upstairs gal- lery past stern portraits of illustrious Winford ancestors, hurried down the stairs, and let herself out the side French doors into the cold, moon-shadowed garden.

As Jane silently left the house, Hawk paced the carpeted floor of his own chamber, wide awake, counting off in his mind every detail of the night's coming adventure. He hoped Ned was fairly gentle with the stable master. He'd tried to impress upon his confederate that Three Oaks was not the back alleys of London, and their purpose was clean escape, not mayhem. Ned had agreed with a wicked grin that was anything but reassuring. The little man was as anxious as Hawk to be gone from this place, though for different reasons. Hobnobbing with honest servants in a placid country home was not Ned's idea of a good time.

Hawk walked restlessly to the window, hesitated, then frowned out into the night. The moon's uncertain light re- vealed a figure walking the garden path. Jane. He recog- nized her even though she was swathed in a voluminous cloak to ward off the cold.

Hawk smiled. There walked his only regret in this adven- ture—Jane Alexander. In a few more hours he would be out of her life forever, and she out of his. He would miss her. Damned but he would! Prim, cool, and virtuous, the woman had managed to get under his skin in a manner that none before her had—not even Gloria.

Hawk remembered how furious he'd been that nightmarish day in Fleet Prison when Jane had given him the news that Gideon was safe with her. Safe, indeed! That his son had been stolen by a Puritan had seemed to Hawk one of the cruelest blows fate had dealt him, and all during the three years that followed the fury had seethed within him —fury against fate, against Cromwell, against Puritans, and against Jane Alexander. Small wonder Jane had thought him the Devil that first night when he'd stolen into her bedchamber. He'd had the Devil within him, certainly. A streak of malicious cruelty had prompted him to lay that knife against her throat. He thought if he was cruel enough, savage enough, she wouldn't hesitate to hand over the boy. How wrong he'd been. He could have drawn blood with that knife and she wouldn't have given in. He could have abused her as foully as any man could abuse a woman, and still she wouldn't have budged. There was more to Jane Alexander than met the eye. She was as stubborn as she was softhearted, as courageous as she was innocent; and like most innocents, she was too trusting. Trust would be her downfall.

Jane would hate him after this night's work, with good reason. She didn't deserve what he was doing to her. Gideon couldn't have had a better mother, for all the Puritan nonsense she had stuffed into the boy's head. And Hawk could not have had a more innocent victim. She was not the schemer he'd thought her, nor the haughty, self-righteous, judgmental hypocrite he'd imagined. Jane Alexander was as beautiful inside as she was out—an extraordinary woman. Hawk wouldn't forget her. Nor would he let Gideon forget her. He was sorry to be the cause of more pain in a life that had already had more than its share.

Hawk watched awhile as Jane strolled the graveled path below. There among the naked trees and empty rose gardens she looked hauntingly lonely. Soon, he reminded himself guiltily, she would be even more lonely.

"Bloody hell! Just what the hell do you expect me to do?" he asked his conscience aloud.

No answer came, at least none he wanted to hear. With a sigh Hawk fetched his long gabardine coat from the wardrobe and threw it over his shoulders. There was time for a last good-bye before he left.

Hawk found Jane sitting on a marble bench, her face lifted to the elusive moon. The frosty pale light turned her skin to smooth alabaster and her loose hair to pure silver. She had the look of a marble angel, so much so that Hawk found himself treading softly, as though he were trespassing in a holy place, not simply walking in a garden late at night.

"Jane."

At his quiet greeting she gasped and shot up from the bench, the silken veil of her hair swirling around her shoulders as she whirled to face him. "Hawk . . . Matthew!"

She took a startled step backward and stumbled. Hawk reached out to steady her balance. For a moment they stood frozen with his hands gripping her shoulders. He didn't want to release her, Hawk realized. But he did release her, slowly, delaying to straighten her cloak upon her shoulders where he had mussed it.

Hawk's hands felt cold when he finally dropped them back to his side. Cautiously Jane backed off a step, seeking the safety of distance.

"You're out very late," he said.

She clutched her cloak more tightly around her. "I couldn't sleep."

"Neither could I." He fisted his hands at his sides to keep from reaching for her again. "You look cold."

"No, I'm fine, really. It's not so cold out here, even though the clouds have been moving in all afternoon."

"I saw you from my window," he admitted. "Thought you might like some company."

Just then the moon ducked behind a cloud. The night became very dark, but the silver glow still seemed to rest upon her hair and lashes—she was still an unearthly silver angel. How he wished that she weren't! Had fate cast Jane Alexander in some less virtuous role—a barmaid, a courtesan, or one of those merry ladies who pretended to virtue merely as part of an elaborate courting game—Hawk wouldn't have hesitated to make her his mistress. But then she would no longer be Jane. Part of her charm lay in her stubborn morality.

They moved together down the graveled walk, each absorbed in thought. Jane frowned at the path ahead of them, but Hawk suspected her mind was far from the garden.

"Matthew, I'm sorry for what Giddy's tutor told him."

"What?" He should have guessed that her mind was on Gideon.

"About all royalists being sinners bound for hell. That was a horrid thing for anyone to tell a child. I didn't realize that Master Peabody was so indiscreet. When we come to live with Sarah, Giddy will be under the supervision of Master Sterling, who is much more . . . open-minded."

"Open-minded, eh?" He arched a brow. "Does that

charming apology mean you no longer believe I'm bound
for hell?"

"I think you're bound for the Spanish Netherlands."
Jane's impish smile destroyed the angel illusion and reminded Hawk how warmly human she could be. "Where
you go after that is in God's hands. I wouldn't presume to
appropriate the judgment to myself."

"Unlike most others of your church." His words were
more teasing than bitter. Somehow, being with Jane Alexander eased much of the bitterness in his soul.

The path guided them around a fountain that in summer
spouted water from the upraised beaks of four marble
swans. Beside the fountain was a bench. They sat.

"What did you tell Gideon about me?" Hawk asked.

"I told him the truth—or at least what I thought was the
truth. He thinks you died fighting for what you believed
in."

"And you told him that what I believed in was wrong."

A moment passed before Jane answered. "I thought to
let him draw his own conclusions. Apparently Master
Peabody had more definite ideas. I'm sorry, Matthew. I will
have a talk with Gideon."

They walked on in silence, and Hawk could sense her
chagrin. He wasn't concerned about what the tutor had
said to Giddy. Shortly the boy would know without a doubt
that his father was not burning in hell—not yet, at least.

The house loomed up before them. The night had gotten
colder, the clouds thicker and lower. A heaviness in the air
warned of snow. They'd walked a complete circle of the
little garden, and now the time had come to go in, to take
his leave of Jane and get on about the business at hand.

"I must leave soon," he told her. This very night he
would leave, but he couldn't tell her that. How did he say

good-bye when he was the only one who knew that a good-bye was in order?

"Giddy has a natural affection for you," Jane said quietly—almost sadly, Hawk thought. "He'll miss you, I think."

Hawk felt a prick of conscience. Giddy wouldn't miss him at all, but the boy might miss Jane.

"If you'll write me once you reach your destination," Jane said, "I'll keep you informed on Giddy's progress."

Hawk stopped in the middle of the path, took Jane's arm, and turned her toward him. "I've been very hard on you at times," he admitted. "But I hope you'll remember me with some charity at least."

She looked at him with her heart in her eyes. For all her stiff virtue, she wasn't indifferent to him, and she hadn't the deviousness to mask her feelings. Hawk wished again that they had met under different circumstances—a different time, a different battle, with both of them on the same side instead of in opposing camps.

"I'll remember . . ." She paused as though seeking the right words. "I'll remember that you're not nearly the rogue you think you are."

She would regret those words in the morning, Hawk reflected sadly.

"And I'll never let Gideon forget that his father was a gentleman, and a good and courageous man."

A light snow was beginning to fall, in spite of the fact that the moon had reappeared. Feathery flakes landed in Jane's hair, glittering like a halo in the pale moonlight.

" 'Tis your opinion that has my concern," he told her. "Not Gideon's."

A snowflake landed squarely on the tip of her upturned nose. Hawk smiled and brushed it off with his finger. Before she could move he gently brushed her lips with his, a hand at her neck holding her momentarily for the brief caress. He drew back, and his hand trailed down her arm to gently squeeze her hand. She trembled. Frightened of him, Hawk wondered, or herself?

"Not another assault on your virtue, little Puritan," he assured her. "Just simple affection. I won't forget you, Jane."

Jane looked after Hawk as he turned to leave. She raised a hand to touch her burning lips, thinking that now she owed her journal at least one more confession.

Hawk watched tensely until Jane disappeared from the garden. He listened to her soft footfalls climb the stairway and sound along the gallery to her chamber. For thirty minutes after her chamber door closed behind her, he stood quietly, listening for a sound that might indicate she was still awake. There was none. The time had finally come.

His few personal belongings slung across his back in a duffle, Hawk stole silently to the room Gideon shared with young Trevor. Silent as a hunting cat he opened the door and slipped in to kneel beside Giddy's bed.

"Gideon." His hand poised above the boy's mouth, Hawk whispered again. "Gideon."

"What . . . huh?"

Hawk gently covered the child's mouth with his hand and raised a finger to his lips to command silence. "Are you up for an adventure?" he asked the boy softly.

Gideon's eyes brightened as he nodded.

"Just you and me," Hawk whispered. "Don't wake Trevor."

Eager to join in the conspiracy, Giddy quietly climbed out of bed.

"Clothes," Hawk said. Fortunately, Gideon was a sloppy little tyke. His clothes lay in a pile by the clothespress, and it took only moments for him to pull on shirt, breeches, and doublet. When Hawk motioned for the boy to follow, Giddy tiptoed out of the room with elaborate stealth, his boots dangling from one hand.

"Where are we going?" the boy whispered eagerly as they silently descended the stairs.

In the kitchen they stopped for Gideon to pull on his boots. Hawk took off his cloak and wrapped it around his son, then guided him through the pantry and out the back door toward the stables. "We're going on an adventure," he answered. "Just you and I."

"Really? Not George or Trevor or Thomas or anyone?"

"That's right."

"Even Aunt Jane?"

"Not her either."

"Will she be mad?"

Mad was probably a mild word for what Jane would be, Hawk thought. "It's a surprise," he explained. "Wait here for a moment. I'll be back."

Hawk left Gideon outside the stable door. He wasn't certain that the scene inside would be fit for an innocent boy's eyes. Ned met him with a shielded lantern just inside the door. The little man motioned toward the tack room, where Henry the stableman lay sprawled against the wall.

" 'E's all right," Ned said as Hawk bent over the unconscious man. "I can be gentle as a little lamb when I want. 'E'll 'ave an achin' 'ead is all."

"Good work, Ned."

"I allus do good work," Ned claimed. "Saddled three 'orses. 'Is lordship's best."

Hawk counted out appropriate payment for the horses and left the coins on the unconscious stableman's chest. "Let's get out of here."

Gideon gave the three horses a doubtful frown when Ned and Hawk led them from the stable. "Where're we going?" he asked again. This time his voice was not quite as eager as before.

The time had come for the truth, Hawk decided. "We're going to London, Gideon."

"Why?"

"Because you and I are going on a journey. At the docks in London we'll meet a ship that will take us across the sea to the Netherlands."

Giddy's eyes grew wide. He backed up a step.

"Gideon." Hawk knelt beside him. "Your father isn't dead. "I am your father, and I've come to fetch you so that we can be a family again, just as we once were."

"No! My father's dead."

"I'm not dead, Gideon. I escaped."

"No!" the boy denied, his voice rising. "Aunt Jane said my father's dead, and she wouldn't lie!"

"Jane didn't lie, Giddy. She believed I was dead."

"Does Aunt Jane know where we're going?"

"No. She doesn't. But you're my son, Gideon. I love you, and you belong with me."

"We'd best get out of 'ere, 'Awk." Ned swung aboard his horse and looked uneasily toward the dark house.

"Come, Gideon. Get on your horse." Hawk took the boy's arm and tried to help him mount, but Giddy tried to jerk away. Hawk almost lost him and tightened his grip. "Gideon, we must leave."

"You're not my father!" the boy insisted.

"Get on the horse," Hawk commanded.

"If you're my father, then why didn't you come for me sooner?" Giddy demanded.

"I'll explain later. Just get on your horse, son."

"No!"

This was taking much too long, and Gideon was painfully loud. At any moment the house might awaken. Hawk's jaw clenched as he thought of the consequences of being discovered. His grip on Gideon tightened. Giddy squeaked in pain and flailed at Hawk with his fists.

Hawk cursed himself for reducing his son from a boy eager for adventure to a terrified child.

" 'E's not gonna ride," Ned stated the obvious.

"I'll carry him."

Hawk scooped the kicking, flailing boy into his arms and climbed with his burden into the saddle, thankful that the stable was far enough from the house that Giddy's cries would most likely go unheard. Ned swatted the third horse on the rump and sent him trotting back into the barn.

"Let's go," he told Ned.

" 'Bout time," Ned grumbled.

They spurred their horses toward the main road.

"Aunt Jane! Aunt Jane!" Gideon wailed.

The boy's cries rang painfully in Hawk's ears. This was not how he had picture their reunion—not at all. But he had no choice, no choice but to hurt and betray Jane Alexander, no choice but to kidnap his own terrified son.

"No! Please! I don't want to go! Aunt Jane!"

Every word battered at Hawk's tortured heart.

12

❀ ❀

"Mistress Jane. Mistress Jane."

Jane's eyes opened to the sound of Mathilde's timid summons. Her chamber was still gray and cold with the dawn.

"Mistress Jane, are you awake?"

"Hm?"

"Wake up," the maid insisted. "Something terrible's happened, mistress."

That brought Jane fully awake.

"Master Gideon's gone. My lady told me to wake you."

"Gideon . . . what? Gideon's gone?"

"Aye, mum."

Her heart sank. "Bring my robe," she told Mathilde.

Sarah and Grandmother Margaret both awaited her in the withdrawing room. Both were in dressing robes with hair disordered from sleep.

"Oh, Jane! Jane!" Sarah babbled, and wrung her hands.

"The boy's gone," Margaret said in a disgusted voice. "And your Master Hawkins with him."

"What?" Jane's voice was deadly quiet. She looked to Sarah for confirmation.

"Henry from the stables came up just minutes ago. He . . . oh, Jane! I can hardly believe it! He said someone hit him on the head, and when he woke, two of the horses were gone."

"And so was your Master Hawkins and his son," Margaret finished for Sarah, folding her arms across her thin chest. "A third horse was saddled and still in the barn. We can only guess that your rebel friend and his man couldn't persuade the boy to ride away on his own, so one of them dragged him up in front of the saddle."

"He left payment for the horses on poor Henry's chest," Sarah wailed. "Oh, Jane! I still don't believe it! He seemed so . . . so charming!"

Jane gripped the back of the settee to steady herself. She closed her eyes, wishing desperately to open them and find herself in her own bed, waking from a nightmare. But when she opened them again, a pale Sarah and a stern Margaret still awaited her reaction.

"I've been a fool," she said with a calm she didn't feel.

"I told you that boy would be trouble!" Margaret reminded her with satisfaction. "As if taking in a royalist cub wasn't enough, now you've disgraced yourself with his father and brought shame to the whole family."

"Oh, do shut up!"

Both Margaret and Sarah gasped at Jane's outburst.

"Gideon is not trouble! He was never trouble! And my only disgrace is stupidity!"

"Jane," Sarah pleaded, "you're overwrought."

"How could I have been so criminally naïve!" Jane hit the settee with her fist. "I trusted him! I even felt sorry for him, even though I could see well what he was! How could I have let myself be seduced into believing him?"

"Good riddance to the both of them, I say!" Margaret declared.

"Grandmother . . . !" Sarah warned timidly.

Jane paid no mind to Margaret's acid comment. She was busy mentally cursing Hawk and kicking herself. Gideon was gone. Her heart ached so that she could scarcely breathe, and on top of that unbearable pain was the sting of Hawk's treachery. She'd been used, her emotions and weaknesses played as a fine violinist played his strings. Heartlessly, callously, and with cold calculation, Hawk had betrayed her.

Jane began to pace, seized by a terrible urgency. "I *must do* something! I *must* get Gideon back!"

"We'll send a messenger to London!" Sarah suggested. "Surely the authorities . . . !"

"Matthew Hawkins has been dodging the authorities for three years!" Jane scoffed.

"We'll send for Geoffrey, then. He'll know what to do." Both Jane and Margaret snorted at that idea.

Jane desperately tried to think. What could she, a powerless widow woman, do against Matthew Hawkins? He was clever, dangerous, ruthless, wealthy with ill-gotten criminal profits, while she was . . . she was what?

Jane pictured living the rest of her life without Gideon, without his mischief, his pranks, his bright curiosity, his affection. She felt herself wither down to nothing, robbed of her husband, the child of her body, and now the child of her heart. Life stretched ahead in days, months, years of bleak, barren nothingness.

She wouldn't let it happen! Matthew Hawkins might have bested Cromwell, bested the army, and bested the authorities. No doubt he thought he'd bested Jane Alexander most easily of all, but he didn't know her as well as he thought. She would follow him to hell if she had to. Somehow she would get the resources and find the courage, because without Giddy life itself scarcely mattered.

"I'm going to London," she declared. "I'll stop him."

"You're mad!" Margaret croaked.

Sarah blanched. "Jane! You're not thinking!"

"I am thinking," Jane replied quietly, calm now that she had made her decision. "I'm thinking of Gideon—frightened, confused, bound for a world of danger and debauchery with Matthew Hawkins. I know where Hawkins is bound. With good fortune and speed on my side I might reach London before they sail."

"And do what?" Margaret ridiculed. "What can you do against this man other than inform the authorities—and they will no doubt believe you a madwoman."

"I'll think of something!" Jane assured her. "Without Gideon my life is . . . empty. I've nothing more to lose."

"What nonsense!" the old lady scoffed. "You could lose much more than your life in pursuit of this debauched royalist. You could lose your reputation, your very soul, you foolish girl!"

"I don't care what I lose," Jane said firmly. "I just want my son."

Somewhere behind Jane's anger and worry, a little voice reminded her that Gideon was Hawk's son, not hers.

Two days of very hard traveling brought Jane almost to London—almost, but not quite. When night fell, Henry, the Winfords' stable master and coachman, insisted on stopping at an inn a mere hour's drive from the city gates. No one with an ounce of sense traveled England's roads at night, he said, and Sarah agreed. An early morning's start would get them to London in good time, she told Jane, and there was nothing that could be done at night in any case.

Exhausted, frustrated, and on edge, Jane gave in with ill grace. Even as she paced the inn room she shared with

Sarah, Hawk might be sailing for Europe, taking Giddy far beyond her reach. Her hands balled into fists, she leaned against the windowsill and stared out into the cold night, wishing that she could see through the darkness and over the miles that separated her from Gideon. Where was he? Was he frightened? Was Hawk taking good care of him? She felt a familiar stab of fear pierce her heart. If Hawk allowed one hair on the boy's head to be hurt, then she would make him long for the fate he escaped three years ago. Jane now had something in common with Matthew Hawkins—they shared the need for revenge.

"Jane, dear! Do come away from the window and eat something. The food is tolerably good, I must say, and you'll accomplish nothing by making yourself sick again."

Sarah sounded as though she were talking to one of her children, Jane thought. Her sister no doubt thought her mad as a loon, the way the plump little matron had clucked despairingly through the last two days as Jane urged Teddy to drive the team harder. If one of Sarah's children had been kidnapped, she would have been just as frantic as Jane, but Sarah had never understood that Gideon had become Jane's child as much as George or Deidre was Sarah's. She understood Jane's anger and disappointment, but not her frenzy. Indeed, Jane had scarcely been able to prevent her sister from delaying the pursuit even more by dragging two trunks full of clothing and her lady's maid with them to London.

"I really have no appetite," Jane told her.

"Well, you must eat! I will not have you wasting away and falling ill. You've scarcely eaten a thing since we started. The pork pies are very good, and there's boiled capon—one of your favorites. Starving yourself is not going to help retrieve Gideon."

Jane obediently sat down at the small table where Sarah had already finished her meal. She felt her sister's sympathetic glance.

"Jane, my love, you realize you must try to be reasonable about this. We may not be able to get Gideon back. The boy is Master Hawkins's son, after all. The authorities may not be much interested in pursuing a royalist rebel with the country coming around to favoring the monarchy again. After all, if your Master Hawkins has connections to Prince Charles, he may someday be a man of some power and influence."

"I will get him back." Jane's voice was flat and determined. She didn't want to listen to reason. She could listen only to her own pain. "Somehow I will get him back."

Sarah sighed.

Jane assured herself that if she had to call the authorities down on Hawk, she would. He was a criminal as well as a rebel—a fact Sarah didn't know—and surely the London police as well as the army would want him.

She forced herself to eat, reminded painfully of a similar meal she had shared with Hawk in a very similar inn. The rogue had tried to seduce her that night. Remembering how readily she had succumbed to his wickedness still made her blush with shame. The very next day she had smiled and laughed with him, allowing his charm to lull her into trust. She had even admired the man in an odd sort of way, fool that she was. How he must have laughed at her naïveté—every time she gave him her sympathy, every time she reminded him of his noble sacrifice, every time she insisted that he wasn't the villain he purported to be! Had he relished knowing that he would betray her? Was her pain part of his vengeance on the Puritans who had ruined his life? His gentle kiss in the Three Oaks garden—affection, he claimed, not seduction. Remember him with charity! A fine parting mockery!

"Jane. You're not eating."

Gideon's sweet face rose up in Jane's mind—sparkling green eyes and mischievous smile transforming into the hazel eyes and the scornful smile of Hawk's wide, arrogant mouth. The boiled capon and pork pies turned to sawdust, and the few bites she had taken lay in her stomach like lead.

"I'm sorry, Sarah, I cannot eat."

"I can't eat," Gideon complained. The beef stew and rich cheese set before him were the best the Lion had to offer, but he stubbornly refused to eat.

"If you don't eat, you won't grow," Hawk told him in a conversational tone. "Do you always want to be so small?"

"I'm not small," the boy insisted. "Aunt Jane says I'm big for my age."

"You're big for eight," Hawk agreed. "But if you don't eat, you'll be the same size when you're eighteen. How will that look?"

Giddy screwed up his face in disbelief. "It's a sin to lie. Aunt Jane told me so."

"Do you think I'm lying?" Hawk asked innocently.

"Yes."

"It's also a sin not to eat when your father tells you to."

"It's a bigger sin to lie," Giddy insisted.

Hawk shrugged. "Suppose we both reform. You eat, and I'll stop lying."

Gideon snorted in contempt, but he relented so far as to stab a piece of beef and stick it into his mouth.

Hawk smiled at his small victory. Small victories were all he won these days. Giddy no longer denied that Hawk was his father, but with a child's lack of logic, he alternately castigated Hawk for the three-year desertion and then demanded to be returned to Jane. Hawk's explanations couldn't penetrate the boy's sulkiness, and his declarations of affection made no impression. Giddy's eyes brimmed with hurt—and a touch of fear. Both cut Hawk clear through to his soul.

Once they were clear of England, Hawk told himself, Giddy's resentment would fade. Tomorrow they sailed with the morning tide—such a short time, but each hour seemed a week. Hawk wanted nothing more than to be gone from this shore.

The Lion Inn was no longer the haven it once had been. A month ago Hawk had been king here. He still was, to judge from the attention Good Mary showered upon him and the respectful, almost fearful greetings he got from the patrons. But with Jane's memory fresh in his mind and Gideon at his side, the inn seemed squalid, its customers—the underworld predators who had been his fellows for three years—unfit for Gideon's acquaintance.

"Say, 'Awk! 'Aven't seen ye in a while. Gone inta divin', 'ave ye? The boy looks a bit big fer it, but 'e looks like 'e's got the guts."

"Kelly." Hawk greeted the fellow who sauntered up to their table. Tufts of red hair stuck out from under a dirty knit cap, and the man's words were carried on breath that reeked of rotten teeth and sour ale. "This is my son," Hawk explained.

"Owww! Is 'e the one! Finally fetched 'im back, did ye? 'E fer sale?"

"No."

Giddy's eyes had grown wide. "Why did he want to buy me?" he asked as Kelly headed for the bar.

"Don't worry about it, Giddy. No one's going to take you away from me again."

Giddy shot Hawk a resentful look that made it clear that he didn't want to stay with him anyway. Then the boy's eyes were caught by the activity several tables away. "What're they doing?" He pointed with his knife to where one of Mary's barmaids sat on the lap of a bewhiskered, gentlemanly-looking fellow whom Hawk recognized as one of London's foremost picklocks, or charms, as they were known in the underworld lingo. There wasn't a lock made that Danny Carsten couldn't conquer, but right at this moment Danny was intent on conquering the sham virtue of the woman on his lap.

Their game was a common one. The whore played the maiden, slapping and scolding as Danny's hand wandered over her wares. She pretended to be horrified when he dipped into her bodice and pinched a nipple, but there was laughter in her voice and the glint of anticipated coin in her eyes as she scolded him.

"Ye know ye can't resist me, Gert." Dan chuckled as he pushed down her bodice and groped to contain the spill of her bosom, which was certainly more than a handful even for a large man like Danny. "I'd wager ye 'aven't been proper laid since yer last time with me."

She squealed in protest when he lowered his mouth to her breast, but at the same time her hand dived between his legs to urge him on. Within moments her attempts at a maidenly squeal lowered to an urgent cooing as his pelvis jerked up toward her hand and his own hand slipped under her skirt.

No one paid the couple the least mind except Gideon, who was wide-eyed. "He's hurting that lady," Giddy said. "Shouldn't someone help her?"

"He's not hurting her, Giddy. He's . . ." How to explain tavern sleaze to a curious eight-year-old boy? "They're playing a game."

Gideon considered for a moment. "They don't look as if they're playing. I think they're fighting."

"Let's go up to our room, son. We've got to be at the ship before the sun rises, and you'll sleep through the sailing unless you go to bed."

"I don't want to get on a ship."

Another disagreement was forestalled by Ned's timely arrival. He strode up to their table, a grin on his swarthy face and an expectant arch to his brows. "It's all fixed." He lifted a small duffel for their inspection. "I'm ready."

"Ready for what?" Hawk queried patiently. At least Gideon was distracted from the public foreplay.

"I've decided ye need a keeper, 'Awk. I'm goin' with ye."

Hawk sighed. "You are?"

"Aye, Cap'n. I'm signin' on as crew."

"I thought you were going to keep the organization going."

"Moll can do that. Just left 'er. She sends 'er best."

"We've already said our good-byes."

"Aye. So she said. Told me to keep you outta trouble." He smirked cockily. "Truth is, I've an itch to be off this rotted island. A man needs to expand 'is experiences."

Hawk gave him a knowing smile. "Who do you owe money to this time?"

Ned gave him a hurt look.

"Who is it?"

"Oyster Bill," Ned admitted with a grimace.

"I'll pay him for you."

"Nah. No need. It's more fun to keep 'im guessin'. I won't be no trouble."

"Colbert may think otherwise."

"You'll 'andle 'im. You always do." He grinned at Gideon. "Ahoy there, Giddy lad. What do ye think of the ol' Lion, eh? 'Tis a grand place, ain't it?"

"I hate it!" Giddy said with vehemence. "It's a dreadful place, and I don't want to be here!"

Ned took the boy's anger in stride, just as he had all the way from Three Oaks. "Well, then, tomorrow yer daddy and me'll take you to a better place—aboard a lovely big ship. Ye'll like that."

"No, I won't! I won't like it one bit! I want to go back to Aunt Jane!"

Hawk sighed as he met Ned's eyes over the boy's head. Morning couldn't come too soon.

Morning couldn't come too soon for Jane, who had no patience with the long hours of the night. She slept not at all, but instead sat up and watched out the window as the stars played hide-and-seek with the clouds in the night sky, and at the first sign of gray on the horizon she woke Sarah.

At Jane's prodding they were on the road within the hour, taking bread and cheese from the inn to break their fast along the way. They reached the docks at Billingsgate just as London's haze was turning red with the day's first light.

"We must find a ship going to the Spanish Netherlands," Jane told Sarah. "How many could there be? Surely not more than one or two every week, and Hawk only had a few hours' head start on us."

Sarah patted her sister's hand. "I'm sure he can't have sailed, my love. We'll send Teddy to make inquiries along the dock."

"I'll go with him."

"You won't! Jane, this is Billingsgate, for pity's sake! There are sailors and dockhands and . . . and . . . every sort of trash on the docks. You won't get out of this coach and make a spectacle of yourself!"

Jane got her way, however. She cared little for appearances, as long as she found out which ship awaited Hawk and Gideon, and Sarah could do nothing to dampen her determination. She trailed along beside Teddy, fidgeting impatiently as he questioned the dockhands, sailors, and merchants that crowded the quays even at this early hour.

Finally an impressively bearded ship's officer took the time to answer them with something other than an annoyed grunt. "My good man—and dear lady." He acknowledged Jane with a tip of his cap. "England and Spain are indulging in hostilities right at the moment, so one simply doesn't sail from London to the dominions of Spain, you see." He took in the distraught blanching of Jane's face. "However, if one was very determined to reach the Spanish Netherlands, one might sail to Holland and from there go overland south to your destination. Or you might find another ship at The Hague to take you south to Bruges. The *Mary Catherine* sailed for Holland just a few minutes ago, and I'm sure she carries several who will land at The Hague and do precisely as I've outlined."

He pointed down the foggy Thames, and Jane could see the dim bulk of a merchantman in the direction he indicated. Her heart suddenly felt hollow. Gideon was on that ship. Something inside her—the part that had been mother to him for three years—felt his presence out there in the gray river mist, heading out to sea. Her hands balled into fists at her sides as a hopeless, angry frustration rose up to choke off her breath.

"Another ship should be sailing at the end of the week, I believe. Madam? Are you quite all right?"

The chivalrous concern in the officer's voice penetrated Jane's frustration. Perhaps there was hope yet. "Sir, are you an officer of one of these vessels?"

"Yes, mistress, I am," he said with some condescension.

"Then perhaps you have access to one of those . . . those boats that are used to go back and forth between ships?"

"A longboat?" He frowned. "Well, that's true, but . . ."

"I *must* get out to that ship and speak with its captain, sir. There is a criminal aboard who has kidnapped my son."

"Indeed!"

"If you could take me out in your boat . . ."

The officer tugged thoughtfully at his beard. "It's not that easy, mistress. Perhaps you should notify the authorities."

"It would be too late. The ship will be out to sea. Sir! My eight-year-old son is aboard that ship with a ruthless man. The captain must be informed that he is transporting a fugitive, and I must retrieve my child!"

"Well, now . . ." The officer looked helplessly at Teddy, who simply nodded—whether in agreement with Jane's story or sympathy with the officer's predicament neither could tell.

"Good sir!" Jane pleaded. "Do I look like a woman who would spin such a tale if it weren't true?"

"Of course not, dear lady." The man looked out toward the ship, fast disappearing in the morning fog, then back to Jane.

Jane wished she knew how to flirt, how to wheedle and cajole and appeal to a man's instincts to get what she wanted. But all she could do was look at the man's face and pray. "Please!" Whether she was begging God or the ship's officer she didn't herself know.

"Very well." The officer sighed. "It'll do no harm, I suppose. As it happens, I have a boat and crew waiting to take me back to my own ship, which is standing out in the river. I'll tell them you're a late passenger for the *Mary Catherine.*"

"Oh, thank you!"

"Come along, then."

"I shan't be a minute. I've only to tell my sister where I go."

Sarah was firmly set against the plan, but Jane was deaf to reason. Gideon was drawing farther away from her every minute, and she refused to argue.

"If you must pursue this madness, then Teddy will go with you."

"No, my lady!" Teddy shook his head adamantly. "Ye may dismiss me if ye wish, but I'll not be setting no foot aboard no little boat. I've the sense to stay on firm land."

Sarah fumed. "Then I will accompany you."

"You certainly will not!" Jane replied.

"You cannot go alone!"

"Sarah, 'tis bad enough I'm making a spectacle of myself without dragging you along. Geoffrey would never forgive either one of us."

"Then take this, at least." Sarah held out a leather purse of coins.

"I don't need money, Sarah. I shall be back with Gideon directly."

"Yes, of course you will. But perhaps you will want to reward the gentlemen who are taking you out to the ship."

"All right." Jane took the purse and put it inside her

cloak. "I haven't time to argue. Thank you, Sarah, for being such a dear. I must go now."

Sarah shook her head as Jane hurried down the dock toward the waiting boat. Her sister was mad, she was sure of it. She only hoped that the Lord had a legion of angels interceding for poor, foolish madwomen on this day.

The pull to the *Mary Catherine* seemed endless, with the ship growing very little closer and the fog becoming thicker the farther out on the river that they rowed. Jane ignored the oarsmen's curious glances and the officer's discreet but sympathetic inspection. Did he believe her story, or did he think her a madwoman for importuning him so? It didn't matter, as long as he took her to Gideon.

After an anxious eternity, the longboat came within hailing distance. "Ahoy the *Mary Catherine!*" called the bearded officer. "Ahoy there!"

A faint hail returned, muffled by the fog.

"We've an important message for Captain Jakes."

After a few moments, the lumbering merchantman turned into the wind and dropped what few sails she had upon her yards. Jane's heart lurched when the longboat bumped against the huge hull.

"You'd better go up," the officer advised Jane. "You won't want to be bandying your words about for all the crew to hear."

"Oh, mercy!" Jane bent back her head to look up the hull, which seemed several stories tall.

"Send down a sling!" the officer yelled up to the deck.

The contraption that Jane rode up to the *Mary Catherine's* deck did nothing to ease Jane's nerves. In spite of the calm air, the sling swung precariously out into empty space as it was hauled up. Jane divided her fearful attention between the wooden hull that threatened to smash her when the sling swung toward the ship and the cold gray river that swirled beneath her when it swung outward. When she arrived on deck, her eyes were wide, her knuckles white, and her stomach was threatening to create a spectacle of its own.

"Madam!" came a terse voice. "What is the meaning of this?"

The voice belonged to a burly man with curling eyebrows and side whiskers that seemed to jump with every word he spoke. His Dutch accent was so marked that Jane almost failed to understand his words. But there was no mistaking his tone. He was very angry indeed.

"Are you the captain?" she asked, extricating herself from the sling with the help of a grinning sailor.

"Captain Jakes," the man provided impatiently. "Who are you, madam? And what is this about a message for me?"

Jane felt her earlier certainty slip away. She was a demented fool. What if Hawk and Giddy were not on this ship? This angry captain, the kind officer who had brought her out, the crew—they would certainly think her deranged, and she would have caused untold trouble for no reason at all.

"I . . . I believe you have a fugitive on board," she said, trying to put confidence into voice. "A dangerous criminal has abducted my son, and I believe he is bound for Europe on your vessel."

The captain eyed her contemptuously. "You are mad, madam! You stop my ship to babble of fugitives and kidnappings? Are you the port authority? No!"

"You must believe me! The man's name is Matthew Hawkins, and he is a traitor and a criminal."

"This is preposterous! Go back to Bedlam, madam, where you belong."

Jane suddenly felt a cold frisson travel down her spine. She had to be right. Hawk was on board. She could feel his eyes burn icy holes in her back.

The men on deck shuffled uneasily or touched their forelocks as her eyes lit upon them, one by one. Hawk didn't duck or lower his eyes when she spotted him. He looked straight at her, and she could feel rather than see the cold green anger in his eyes. Her heart gave a lurch. "That is the man," she said quietly to Captain Jakes. "That is Matthew Hawkins." Even as she felt the triumph of vindication, Jane regretted exposing Hawk, but she knew of no other way to retrieve Gideon.

Captain Jakes turned a furious scowl on Jane's prey as Hawk strode boldly forward.

"Jane! What are you doing here?" Hawk's voice held no hint of fear or hesitation.

Jane scowled. Shouldn't Hawk be hiding, or diving overboard to swim for safety from the law's retribution?

"Do you know this woman, sir?" the captain demanded.

"Indeed," Hawk said regretfully.

"This is the man!" Jane repeated.

"This man is not your Matthew Hawkins, madam! He is Master Linus Gardner, who is assistant to a prominent army officer on a diplomatic mission. Do you expect me to believe a man with such credentials is your fugitive?"

"No . . . yes! He's—"

"And yet you seem to know this woman?" The captain ignored Jane and turned to Hawk with the question.

"She is my wife," Hawk said, his voice containing just the right amount of regret, shame, and chagrin.

Jane sputtered.

"Unfortunately, Captain, as you can see, she is quite mad. Since our son was born she's had delusions that I am a spy or some kind of a criminal. She once believed I was an infamous highwayman holding her for ransom. Another time she thought me a desert chieftain in Africa holding her prisoner among a host of slave girls. Her delusions are very hard on our son, so I take him with me whenever I must travel."

"Well, confound it man! What is she doing here?"

"I left her in her sister and brother-in-law's care. She must have slipped out and pursued me. When I left she was ranting about my kidnapping the boy."

The boy in question added credence to Hawk's story just then by coming up on deck, spotting Jane, and running to her with glad cries. Ned followed after him, tipped his cap to Jane, and asked Hawk, "What's she doin' 'ere?"

"Escaped," Hawk told him with a lift of the brows.

Ned paused a moment, then simply shrugged. "Oh."

"Well, sir!" Captain Jakes growled. "If we could end this reunion, perhaps you can send your wife back to her keepers before we lose the tide."

"He lies!" Jane protested, hugging Giddy to her.

Hawk stepped forward and gently pried Giddy from Jane's embrace. "Gideon, am I your father?"

"Yes," Giddy admitted with a grimace.

Hawk gave the captain a regretful smile. "Unfortunately, Captain Jakes, I can't very well send my wife back to find her way in the city alone—not in her current state of distress. If you would consent to an additional passenger for this trip, I will arrange return passage for her with a suitable escort once we have reached The Hague."

Captain Jakes snorted in disgust. "Do what you will, sir. We must be on our way."

"No!" Jane cried. "This is impossible! This man is not what he says!"

"Just keep the foolish woman out of trouble aboard my ship!" the captain thundered. He turned on his heel and bellowed orders that sent his crew to the rigging.

A chill that had nothing to do with the cold morning seized Jane's heart. She turned slowly to Hawk, who arched one devilish brow and smiled.

13

"Of all the idiotic, rabbit-brained stunts! Do you realize the danger you put yourself in? What did you do—walk the docks like some Billingsgate tart until you found a long-boat full of sailors willing to give a female a ride?" Hawk's fist hit the doorframe, which buckled with the power of his blow.

Jane retreated a step, alarmed by the violence of his fury. He filled the doorway, blocking any chance of escape. Against the bronze of his face, his scar traced a thin line of angry white.

"You don't have the sense God gave a mouse, do you?"

Jane gathered her frayed courage around her righteous indignation. "You lied to me! You betrayed my trust, twisted my goodwill into weakness, and used it to gain your own selfish ends!"

"Yes, I lied to you, you foolish woman! I would have lied to God himself to get Gideon back. Lying to *you* gave me no pause at all." Hawk's fists balled at his sides as he advanced, but he stopped at the sudden fear on Jane's face. With some difficulty he contained his anger. Once he'd been a gentle man; no more. Now there was a constant bitterness in him that burned most times in slow, danger-ous silence but erupted on occasion with frightening violence. But Jane, if she only knew it, had little to fear, for his anger was more for himself than for her. She was a foolish innocent who was pulled into danger because of him. "Jane," he continued in a calmer voice, "I'm sorry. Lying to you did give me pause. I apologize for the grief I've caused. But you must understand that Gideon is my son, and he should be with me."

"What does Giddy say to that?" Jane asked caustically.

"Giddy will come around," Hawk assured her. "I'm his father, and he's very young. When he's older those three years with you will be an interlude he scarcely remembers."

Jane's lips tightened. She seemed to fight an inner battle, and the truth of Hawk's statement finally won, coming into her eyes with a sadness that faded the cool, clear gray to pools of mist. She turned away and stared fixedly at the fog beyond the cabin's one small porthole. Hawk couldn't remember ever before seeing her square little shoulders slump in such a way.

Hawk resolutely shut his heart to a renewed twinge of conscience. Gideon was his son, and Jane was going to have to accept that fact. He had not liked lying to her, or leaving her hurt and grieving. And he should have controlled his temper better. But the little fool had made the situation infinitely worse by charging into the lion's den and trying to beard her betrayer in his own lair.

What surprised Hawk more than his conscience was his own reaction to Jane's unexpected appearance. Leaving her in Kent had been hard. He was not yet tired of baiting her while he watched her struggle with an all too human temper. Nor was he weary of watching her smile or luring a sparkle into her eyes, watching cool gray soften to warm mist. Their conversations and debates had yet to bore him, and her looks, her voice, her movements still captured his interest as no other woman's ever had. In short, when she swung over the ship's rail in the sling, a ray of sun broke through the dreary gray of the depression that had held Hawk in thrall since he rode away from Three Oaks. Now that the first flush of his anger had faded, Hawk was selfish enough to be glad she was here and ruthless enough to keep her here during their short crossing to The Hague. There were legitimate reasons for detaining her, but mostly Jane was a prisoner for his own amusement, Hawk admitted. Such a thing was less than he expected of himself. He truly had become a rogue.

"Well, now, my foolish little Puritan," he said to her back. "What shall be done with you?"

Her shoulders squared with a visible effort of will and she turned around. "What you *should* do is give me Gideon and send us back to the shore."

He arched an admiring brow. "I've never met a woman quite as stubborn as you are. You really have muleheadedness down to an art. You should be grateful I'm such a patient and tolerant man most of the time."

"I'd be grateful to see you rotting in prison where you belong," she snapped.

He shook his head. "There's the rub, you see. If I'd sent you back with that longboat you so foolishly commandeered, you'd be off to the authorities, and, knowing you, you'd keep after them until someone believed you. By some slim chance the army might still be interested enough to try to apprehend me before I reach the Spanish Netherlands, and though the chances are small that they would succeed, I'd rather not bother with it. So you see you've put me in a bind where I'm forced to compromise you even more than I have already."

"The ship's officer who conveyed me to your ship will report you to the authorities."

Hawk smiled, a cat playing with a mouse. "I think not. I spun him just as fine a tale as I did our captain."

She bit her lip, then said with less confidence, "Surely Sarah will set them on you."

"No, Jane," he said gently. "Sarah will complain to her husband, and Geoffrey is too concerned with what power I might wield on the monarchy's return to risk offending me. Besides, he will think himself well enough acquainted with me to know that I'll let no real harm befall you."

"That's nonsense!"

"You know it's not." He pushed himself off the door and walked over to her, noting how she steeled herself against backing up at his approach. He took her hand; it curled into little ball of ice in his. "It's true, you know," he told her quietly. "I'll not let any harm befall you despite your foolishness. With good winds we will be at The Hague in just a few days. When we land I'll arrange for your passage back to London, where you can pester the army and the police as you please. By then I'll be with the court in exile and it will be too late for them to do me any harm."

She was silent, refusing to meet his eyes.

"Until then you will be my poor mad wife. Giddy can move in with Ned and Colonel Colbert's manservant, and you will stay in this cabin with me."

As if only now coming to life, she jerked her hand from his. "I will not stay in any cabin with you."

He took her chin in his hand and gently forced her head up so that her eyes met his. "We had this argument once before. Do you remember who won?"

Her eyes were the cool gray slate of disdain.

"I won," he reminded her. "Here there's no stable for

you to run to. There's just a ship full of randy sailors and a captain who's already not too pleased with you. For your own safety's sake you aren't going to make any trouble."

Jane considered for a moment. A desperation in her eyes made him think she feared herself more than him.

"You move in with Ned," she proposed. "Giddy and I will stay here."

He released her, his thumb caressing her cheek as his hand fell away from her face. "No one would believe it," he said with a tolerant smile.

"Believe what?" she asked defensively.

"That a man wouldn't insist upon sleeping in the same cabin—in the same bed—with a wife as beautiful as you, be she mad or not."

The blood drained from her face.

"Don't worry, my little Puritan—a pretense only. I made a promise to you some days ago that I would never again assault your precious virtue—and whatever else I am, I'm a man who keeps his promises." He laughed suddenly. "Quoting from your favorite book: 'Who can find a virtuous woman? For her price is far above rubies.' "

"Proverbs thirty-one," Jane said as if in a trance.

"Verse ten," he added. "I've no such price to pay, Jane. Your virtue is safe. But I won't guarantee the rest of the men on this vessel, so stay in this cabin unless you're with me."

She didn't answer. He left her standing in the middle of the cabin looking lost and deflated. Closing the cabin door, he wondered if he'd just told her another lie.

Jane simply stood for a few moments, staring at the door that had closed quietly behind Hawk. She was at a loss. What could she do? She was trapped, helpless, a sparrow at the mercy of the hawk.

And Hawk was right. She'd been a demented fool to come after him. But she couldn't have placidly accepted that Gideon was gone. The pain of losing her child had prodded her to rush headlong into action without thinking. But even had she known the outcome, she probably would have tried anyway.

With a sigh, Jane sat down upon a bunk. Her headlong rush had certainly dumped her into trouble far over her head. She had delivered herself into Hawk's power—and into a situation that was so frightening that she dared not even start to be afraid, unless the fear, once admitted, would so overwhelm her that she would indeed become the madwoman the whole ship thought her to be. It was bad enough to be on a ship whose crew thought she was mad, whose captain was "none too pleased with her," as Hawk had succinctly phrased it, and whose destination was a land where she knew not a single soul. It was bad enough to be forced to depend upon a traitorous criminal who lied more often than he told the truth and who would abandon her without a thought if it suited his purposes. But worst of all was being forced to share an intimate cabin with a man whose wickedness would try the forbearance of a saint and whose undisciplined anger would make the bravest of angels cringe behind her wings.

There was much in Hawk that was frightening. Beneath the education and culture that enabled him to quote the Bible and his wicked Shakespeare simmered a violence that appeared just often enough to remind her he was dangerous. That lamentable ferocity contrasted sharply with the gentleness with which he usually treated her, yet if she took one step too far in trying his temper . . .

"Foolishness!" Jane chided herself aloud. The sound of her voice made her fears seem not quite so real, just as a whistled tune might dispel unknown ghosts on a gloomy night. Female hysteria was overtaking reason, she tried to persuade herself. Nothing was so dark as she imagined. Hawk had never truly touched her in anger, and even though he seemed quite angry with what he called her foolishness, she was the one who truly had cause for anger. Hawk had lied and deceived. He had taken unmerciful advantage of her trust and betrayed every kindness she had shown him. She must cling to her anger, which was righteous and just, and let that anger wash away her fear—and wash away, also, the ghost of unwanted desire that still curled through her body at the sight of him.

Jane tried to gather her tattered composure as she looked around her prison, which was a closet of a room crowded with four bunks stacked two high against the inner and outer bulkheads. A trunk—Hawk's, she assumed —was lashed to the foot of the bunk on which she sat, and close to that, a washstand was securely fastened to the outer bulkhead just below a single porthole. On the same bulkhead a lantern was bracketed so it wouldn't fall during rough weather. Pegs had been driven into the inner and aft bulkheads for hanging clothes, and under the opposite bunk stood a chipped chamber pot. Those items completed the cabin's rough appointments. Jane sighed. No matter how few days the journey lasted, it was going to be a very long trip.

A timid knock on the door interrupted her gloomy thoughts.

"Who is it?" she asked suspiciously.

"It's me!" came a young voice.

"Gideon!" Jane hurried to the door and flung it open. "Giddy!"

He rushed in like a small whirlwind and wrapped himself

around her, his curly black head buried in her midsection. Jane felt the warmth of his embrace all the way through to her heart.

"Gideon, are you all right?"

The boy pulled back to arm's length and beamed up into her face. "I'm all right now."

"You haven't been frightened, have you?"

"No, Aunt Jane. I wasn't frightened at all. Really!"

Jane ruffled her fingers through his hair. "And I wasn't frightened for you, because I knew Master Hawkins would take very good care of you." The lie pained her, but harsh reality demanded that she try to ease Gideon into accepting Hawk in his affections. She could not try to keep Giddy's heart with her when the rest of him must go with his father.

Giddy screwed his face into an expression of distaste. "Is Master Hawkins really my father?"

Jane sat on a bunk and drew the boy to stand in front of her so that their eyes were nearly on a level. "Yes, Gideon. Master Hawkins is really your father."

"You told me my father was dead."

"I thought he was," Jane said softly. "But I was mistaken."

"Why didn't you tell me he was my father when you came to Aunt Sarah's?"

Jane sighed and ran her hand gently up and down Gideon's lean little arms. How did she explain lying to a child she'd told never to lie? "I was wrong," she admitted. "I should have told you. But I thought it would bother you, and Master Hawkins meant to leave you with me when he left for Europe. He changed his mind, as you can see."

"Did you come to take me back?" Gideon asked hopefully.

"I can't take you back right now, Gideon." Jane tried to keep her voice matter-of-fact, free of the pain that twisted her heart.

"Sometime soon, then?"

"I don't know," she said. "That depends on your father. He wants you to live with him."

Giddy grimaced. "I don't like him."

Jane felt an unexpected sympathy for Hawk. For three years he had dreamed of having his son back. Now Gideon's antipathy must have turned his triumph to ashes.

"He loves you very much," Jane said quietly. "Your not returning that love must hurt him terribly."

Gideon considered a moment, as if he had never realized that he wielded a power to hurt. "If he loves me, why did he leave?"

"He didn't want to leave," Jane assured him. "I'm sure the army dragged him off kicking and screaming, just as I used to drag you off to bed sometimes when you were smaller. He came back for you as soon as he could."

Gideon bit his lip in concentration. "I still don't like him. He doesn't play games the way you do, and sometimes when he gets real quiet you can tell he's yelling inside."

Jane stifled a smile, wondering how Hawk would feel if he knew his son read him so well. "Maybe you can teach him to play games," she suggested.

Gideon screwed up his face.

"I think you'll learn to like him, Gideon. He has some fine qualities, and I suspect you'll grow up to be very much like him."

"Bleaaah!" His tongue came out to signal his disgust.

Jane sensed that Giddy was beginning to enjoy the debate a bit too much. She knew from experience that trying to reason with him now would be useless, so she smiled and patted the bunk beside her in invitation for him to sit. "Tell me what has happened to you since you left Aunt Sarah's. I'm anxious to hear."

Giddy brightened immediately. He loved an audience, as Jane well knew. "I got to ride a horse all the way to London," he told her.

"How exciting!"

"Well . . . I was riding with Master Hawkins most of the time, but it was better than riding in a coach!"

"Maybe Master Hawkins will teach you to ride as well as he does."

Giddy ignored the idea. "And we stayed at an inn where a dirty-looking fellow tried to buy me."

"And I would guess that your father told the man you weren't for sale."

"Well, yes. He said no one was going to take me away."

No one, Jane mused sadly, especially a Puritan widow named Jane Alexander.

"And there was a man pinching this woman, and I thought he was hurting her but Master Hawkins said he wasn't."

Jane closed her eyes, reluctant to imagine exactly what Gideon was relating.

"And then this morning while it was still dark we met this army fellow and came onto the ship."

An army fellow? Interesting. Captain Jakes had also mentioned that Hawk, under the name of Gardner, was traveling as assistant to a prominent army officer.

"And Ned's been showing me all the parts of the ship. Did you know he used to be a sailor? He says sea salt's in his blood. Do you suppose that's really true?"

"Ned was just using an expression, Giddy. He meant that he's spent much time at sea."

"Oh. Well, he sure knows a lot about ships. And the sailors are nice. They tell me what they're doing, and one showed me a swing called a bosun's chair and hauled me up in it almost as high as the lower yard—that's what those crosswise poles are called, you know."

Jane tried not to show her concern at the picture of Giddy swaying above the deck in some sort of flimsy swing. They were only in the river, she reminded herself, with scarcely any sail on the poles. Surely when they reached the open sea Hawk would forbid such dangerous pastimes.

Gideon prattled on about his adventures aboard the *Mary Catherine*. He seemed to have crowded a great deal into one morning, Jane thought, and if he truly was distressed over leaving her, he wasn't letting it ruin his fun. Suddenly she envied the resilience of childhood.

Gideon left after a short time. Ned had promised to take him belowdecks where the cannon were kept. He'd even asked special permission of the captain, Giddy informed her. The boy was already growing apart from her, Jane thought sadly as he bounced out of the cabin.

The day dragged after Gideon left. Being alone with her own fears and regrets made the hours seem impossibly long. She was almost grateful when Hawk appeared with a tray of fish stew, roasted beef, bread, cheese, and wine. A crewman followed him into the cabin with a second tray. Looking at Jane askance, as if she might launch into a mad fit at any moment, he set the tray upon a bunk and left without a word.

"Dinner," Hawk announced. "I thought you might not be up to dining with the captain and officers, though we are invited."

"Thank you," she said in a chilly tone. The man might have won, but she didn't have to be a sport about it.

" 'Tis a shame we don't have a proper table, but these merchantmen lack the amenities of some of the larger ships, and I'm not in the first rank of passengers."

She arched a fine brow. "You mean to say you didn't tell the captain you were an earl with connections to the royal family?"

"Certainly not," he said with a chuckle. "That would have earned me quarters in the brig, I'm sure. Would you prefer this bunk or that one for your dining table?"

Jane sat down and accepted his offer of one of the trays, though she didn't feel the least bit hungry.

"Did Gideon visit you?" Hawk asked, his voice carefully casual.

"Yes, he did. We had a pleasant visit. He told me all about how he wasn't a bit afraid when you dragged him away from Three Oaks. He also had some interesting tales about the inn where you and he stayed in London."

Hawk grimaced.

"If you're determined to destroy the morals I tried to instill in Gideon, at least have the goodness to do it a bit more gradually. I'm afraid drinking and carousing will come as a bit of a shock to him."

Hawk toyed absently with his food. If she didn't know better, Jane would have thought he looked chagrined.

"That was a mistake," he admitted with a sigh. "I didn't remember the Lion as being so corrupt until I took Gideon there."

"Gideon was quite impressed," Jane said with a waspish edge to her voice.

"So I gather."

Jane picked at her dinner, feeling the oppressive silence press in upon her. Finally, Hawk looked up from his plate.

"Other than that, how was he?"

"Who?"

"Gideon!"

She was being deliberately obtuse, Jane knew, and was immediately ashamed of herself. Rubbing Hawk's face in the ashes of his victory was useless cruelty.

"He thinks he doesn't like you," she told him quietly. "I imagine that he's told you that in no uncertain terms."

"He has," Hawk replied tersely. He went back to his dinner, attacking the beef as though it had somehow offended him.

"He'll change his mind," Jane predicted. "As you so firmly told me, in a few years all the time he spent with me will be but a dim memory. He'll come to understand why you had to leave, and no doubt he'll come to hate Puritans just as much as you do."

Hawk sighed and set aside his tray, apparently having no more appetite than Jane. He got up and paced from the porthole to the door and back again—all of two strides each way. His size made the cabin seem even smaller than it was.

"I don't think I hate Puritans anymore, Jane."

"How generous of you," she said wryly.

His mouth slanted into a rueful smile. "You're bitter. I suppose I don't blame you. But it's true, just the same. You've taken a measure of hatred away from me, my virtuous little Puritan. You should congratulate yourself for that. By letting me meet your sister and her husband— good people, if I may say—and by showering my son with love and devotion, you've made me realize my hatred was misdirected, even useless. I'm sure that account book in heaven that you Puritans so worry about is overflowing with praise for your good deed in drawing the venom from my fangs."

Jane stood up and went to the porthole, gazing out at the damp gray mist that made sea and clouds seem to blend as one. The weather fitted her mood. Amazed at her own spitefulness, she acknowledged that she didn't want to do this man a good deed; she didn't want to make his soul more at peace with itself. She wanted to scream her anger at the injustice of it all.

"Jane."

The soft voice so close to her ear startled her from her black thoughts. She turned and found herself caged against the bulkhead by his arms.

"I never meant to hurt you, not since the night I first saw you lying in your bed, looking as though a mere breeze could blow you away and a solid tap could break you. I wish you would believe that."

Pride asserted itself. "Don't worry about me, Master Hawkins. I don't break so easily."

He smiled. "I know that now. But all the same, I'm sorry to cause you pain."

She turned her face away, refusing to meet his gaze.

"I meant what I said in the garden, Jane. Believe it or not, my heart harbors a great deal of affection for you, however you may scorn that heart as a black lair of the Devil. I wish you could try to understand at least a little. Gideon is my own flesh and blood. In my place, would *you* have willingly given him up?"

Jane refused to answer. She didn't want to listen. Hawk's deep voice was as seductive in his reasoning as it was in other things.

He sighed and moved back from her. "I see you're determined to cast me in the role of implacable villain. But hear me in this, Jane Alexander. There are villains blacker than I on this ship. This is a dangerous game you've entered, and as long as you're in it, I'm your best protection against harm. So don't batter too harshly on your shield."

Jane shook her head. "With one breath you say Gideon belongs with you, and in the next you boast of the dangerous way of life you drag him into. Where is the reason in that, Matthew?"

"Give it up, Jane. All the words in the world won't change my mind."

A knock on the cabin door forestalled her retort.

"Come in," Hawk called.

A man stepped into the cabin. He was tall with close-cropped brown hair, icy blue eyes, and a ramrod-straight bearing. Jane's nerves jumped in shock as she recognized him. Five years had passed since she had seen him, but he looked much the same. She hadn't cared for him much when, as a close friend of her husband's, he had frequented their house on Great Queen Street. Now she felt the same feeling of automatic antipathy. It was his eyes, she decided. They reminded her of a lizard's eyes, and just now they regarded her with a great deal of surprise.

Hawk did not look happy with the intrusion. He made introductions reluctantly.

"Jane, this is an associate of mine." He deliberately left out the name.

Jane supplied it. "Colonel Colbert. How are you, sir?"

Colbert considered her coldly. "Mistress Alexander. It's been a very long time."

Hawk looked from one to the other. His eyes narrowed. "You two are acquainted."

"Colonel Colbert was a friend of my late husband's."

"Indeed." Hawk's face might have been carved from granite.

Colbert snapped his attention away from Jane. "I had a few matters to discuss with you, Hawkins, but I can see that you're busy. It can wait until later."

"Don't let me delay your business, Colonel," Jane said.

"A delay is of no consequence, madam. It is good to see you again. I wish you a good journey."

As quickly as he had come, he left.

"So that is the high-ranking army officer you are in league with," Jane said, looking sharply at Hawk. "Of all the men in England to turn toward the monarchy, Colbert would have been my last guess."

Hawk eyed her speculatively from beneath lowered brows. His frown was all out of proportion to her comment, Jane thought, and a shiver of premonition ran up her spine.

"She's got to go. There's no help for it. She simply must be removed from the picture." Colonel Terence Colbert paced the length of his cabin, his steps clicking with military precision on the deck. His cabin, as befitted his rank, was larger than Hawk's—four strides from bulkhead to bulkhead, but that still was not room enough for him to pace off his anger.

Hawk lounged against the stacked bunks like an indolent but watchful cat. "What do you mean, she's got to go?"

"My God, man! The woman knows me! She knows my name, my rank—she even knows my regiment. And she knows of our connection. The lady is no half-wit, Hawkins. She can put two and two together as well as anyone else.

Her knowledge could compromise my position as a royalist agent and even cost me my life!"

"The risk of that is small." Hawk folded his arms across his chest. "She has little interest in politics, and her family —a sister and brother-in-law —are about as promonarchy as one can get and still be a Puritan."

"Poppycock! She's the widow of one of Cromwell's staunchest supporters, and she must still have acquaintances high in the government. She'll have my neck in a noose."

"You're overreacting," Hawk said calmly.

Colbert whirled on him in a cold fury. "Let me tell you something, Hawkins. This is a very harsh game I play. Very harsh indeed. I have managed to stay alive because I am a cautious man. I don't take chances. That woman—that widow of my old friend whom you plan to send back to England—is a noose waiting to tighten around my neck. I won't have it, I tell you! Get rid of her!"

"Kill her," Hawk clarified.

"Exactly!"

"No."

Hawk's calm refusal was like a stone dropped into still water. The ripples spread through the ensuing silence in tangible waves. Colbert's face grew rigid, his eyes dark and expressionless as a snake's.

"No, is it, Hawkins?"

"You won't touch her," Hawk elaborated. "Neither will I. Neither will any of your men."

Colbert snorted. "What is the woman to you that you would risk my life and the royalist cause so that she might continue her drab little existence?"

Hawk was silent for a moment. Cold hazel eyes regarded Colbert with unnerving steadiness. "I think you overrate your contribution to the rebellion when you equate your safety with the royalist cause. But even so, she's small threat to you. Jane Alexander is a little rabbit existing in a world of wolves. She seldom pokes her nose outside her den."

" 'Tis easy for you to dismiss the danger!" Colbert scoffed. "You are not the one at risk. If you won't take care of the matter, Hawkins, then I will!"

Hawk's eyes flashed with anger, but his voice was deadly calm. "Colbert, we've worked together for over two years. You know I'm a man who keeps his promises, and I promise you this. By harming one hair on Jane Alexander's head you'll be signing your own death warrant."

A muscle in Colbert's jaw began a rhythmic twitching. "You *are* a fool! Do you realize against whom you are pitting yourself?"

Hawk was unimpressed. One brow inched up in casual scorn. "That question goes both ways, Colbert." He said no more, but his silence was ripe with threat.

For a moment the two men stared at each other like two wolves hungry for blood. Colbert was the first to look away.

"What assurance do I have that this woman won't compromise my safety?"

Hawk sensed partial surrender in the relaxation of Colbert's rigid stance. "I will take her with me to Antwerp," Hawk told him. "That should keep you safe enough."

Colbert pulled his riding crop from his boot. The quirt was always with him, even when he was miles away from any horse. Now he studied it minutely. "You will be gone much on the King's business. How will you be sure that she stays where you put her?"

"She'll stay," Hawk assured him confidently.

"She'll stay," Colbert mimicked. He slapped the quirt

against his boot. "If she doesn't stay, Hawkins, if she returns to England or anyplace where she can do me harm, I will take care of the matter myself."

"You won't need to. But my promise still stands. Do her harm and you can start counting your days."

Colbert didn't reply as Hawk unlatched the cabin door and let himself out into the companionway. With a vicious swipe the colonel lashed the quirt across the bunk where Hawk had been leaning.

Up on deck, Hawk gratefully breathed in the cool, damp air. Jane was going to spit like a kitten in cold water, but the situation was her own doing, he reasoned. He wondered why he himself wasn't more upset. Could it be he was glad that he had an excuse to hold her for a bit longer?

That thought in itself was frightening.

14

❀ ❀

"What did you say?" Jane's voice was calm, but underlying the calm was an ominous note of fury that seemed to echo in the small space of their cabin.

"I'm sorry, Jane. I didn't intend this," Hawk told her. "But it's the only solution to the problem. When the King manages to return to power I'll arrange your passage back to England. Then Colbert will no longer be endangered by your knowledge of his loyalties."

"Lack of loyalties, you mean!"

He shrugged. "As you wish."

Jane turned her back, skirts whirling around her legs with the suddenness of her movement, shoulders squared in stiff defiance, fists balled tightly at her sides.

"Believe me, you wouldn't like your friend Colbert's answer to the situation."

"I don't like *your* answer!"

Hawk sympathized with her distress. He'd done nothing but hurt her from the moment he stole into her life. He didn't want to hurt her anymore, but in this matter he had little choice. Colbert would make good his threat, and any revenge Hawk might wreak on the man would be little help to Jane in her grave.

"It won't be for such a long time," he said rationally,

trying to appeal to the reason she so prided herself upon. "England is beginning to cry for Charles's return. Within a year he'll be King in truth as well as claim, and Colbert will be safe."

Jane turned to face him. Her face was pale, making her eyes look as dark as the night outside the glassed-in porthole. "You can't be serious about this! It must be a jest!"

"I'm sorry. It's no jest."

"What have your idiotic politics and spy games to do with me? I am no danger to Colonel Colbert!"

"Colbert deems otherwise," Hawk said gently. "Believe me, Jane, returning to England right now would put you in grave peril. Colbert is a ruthless man, and he's not above taking his own measures to ensure that you're not a threat to him."

She stared at him in cold silence, her eyes devoid of that spark of warmth which had survived even the worst of their other battles. Hawk steeled his heart, reminding himself that what he did was for Jane's own good. If she hadn't so foolishly pursued him, she wouldn't be in this mess.

An imp of conscience, though, reminded him that she had not pursued him, she had pursued Gideon. Had Hawk not done much the same thing to retrieve his son?

"In any case," he said gruffly, "you have no choice. For the time being you'll stay with me. Colbert will be satisfied, and you will be safe."

Jane gripped her skirts with both hands in a seeming effort to strangle the material. "Colbert is a ruthless man!" She mocked his words. "How ruthless a man are *you*, Matthew Hawkins? What are you doing to me?" A note of desperation crept into her voice. "You stole my child, my reputation, now you steal me. What will I have left when you're through?"

Hawk refrained from telling her how close she was to having nothing left if Colbert had his way.

"What terrible thing did I do to you that you single me out for such revenge?" she continued softly. Her voice was more sad than accusing.

"You know that isn't the case." He reached out to comfort her, but she shrank away, retreating as though his hand were a venomous snake. He dropped his arm back to his side. "I'm doing this to protect you."

"I can protect myself, if need be."

He shook his head sadly. "You couldn't protect yourself from a mouse. Right now I'm the least of the evils besetting you."

She huffed her disbelief. "I've seen no evidence that the colonel is evil, but I've seen more than enough to attest to your character!"

He smiled ruefully. "True. You'll just have to take my word that you're better off in my hands than in his."

Jane refused to meet his eyes, fixing her gaze out the porthole. The gray gloom of her eyes matched the dark, cold mist that colored both sky and sea. "You once had everything taken from you, and now you do the same to me," she said quietly. "What will you force me to be—your servant, your . . . mistress? How will you explain me to people who wouldn't approve of your kidnapping a harmless widow? Surely not everyone in the Spanish Netherlands is as criminal as you are."

"Harmless, are you? I'm relieved to hear it."

"Harmless compared to you!"

He refused to take offense. "You're right, of course. Not many men have reached the heights of villainy that I commonly tread. A few might raise their eyebrows if I introduced you as an abducted prisoner. But I'm sure we can

concoct a plausible excuse for your bearing me company."
He cocked his head and considered her at length. "You'd
make a poor servant," he speculated. "Much too insolent,
always wanting your own way, and unable to take direction.
No one in his right mind would ever hire you."

He was glad to see a flush rise to her cheeks and a flash
of indignation light her eyes.

"As for being my mistress—that's an arrangement that
would be entertaining, but I doubt you'd be cooperative,
and I did, unfortunately, make you a promise of honorable
treatment."

What had started as a faint blush turned her face hot
scarlet.

"Unless, of course, you'd care to release me from that
promise."

"Certainly not!"

He laughed. The vehemence of her words dispelled his
worry that he'd beaten her down to nothing. "Of course, if
I had a less lurid past and a more hopeful future, or if I
was the gentleman I once was, I might offer marriage at
this juncture. Unfortunately, my prospects are doubtful,
and my guess is that you wouldn't find such a rogue as I
suited to your high standards."

Surprise brought her eyes around to meet his. "You're
not serious, of course!" She gave him the chance to con-
firm or deny, but his mocking smile didn't change. "If you
were serious," she continued indignantly, "I'd say you were
the one in this room who deserves to be named mad. Marriage, indeed!"

Marriage, indeed! Hawk agreed silently. The idea was
ridiculous, of course—he marry a starched and virtuous
widow—a Puritan at that!—with nothing to bring to the

marriage except herself. He was a fool for even joking about the idea.

Jane remained coldly silent, her arms crossed, her spine straight and stiff as tempered steel.

Hawk sighed. "Perhaps the best plan would be to simply introduce you as Gideon's governess once we reach The Hague."

"It's obviously been a long time since you were a gentleman, Master Hawkins. No respectable governess would travel alone with a man unescorted by anyone but a small child."

Hawk shrugged. "It's the best I can offer under the circumstances."

She sniffed her displeasure.

"Think of the cloud's silver lining," he suggested with determined cheerfulness. "You'll be with Gideon. That's what you wanted, isn't it?"

At mention of Gideon her face softened. "This will be very confusing for him."

"Yes," Hawk agreed. But not nearly as confusing as it was for his father, he added silently. He didn't want to think about the night ahead, or all the nights to follow. Fate had chosen a scoundrel for a task that would make a saint sweat. "Giddy will adjust," he assured her. "He inherited that talent from his father."

"I'd hate to think what other traits the poor boy inherited from his father."

He needn't have worried about beating Jane down, Hawk realized. "Well, madam. If our discussion is at an end, would you like to escape this cabin and show your face at the supper table? You've only a short while to parade about as a wife before you're reduced to the status of a mere governess."

Jane narrowed her eyes. The better to aim the sharp silver spears they were shooting, Hawk reflected wryly. "If I were really your wife," she said, "I'd take great pleasure in making you miserable for the rest of your days."

He smiled as she took his proffered arm. "I'm sure you would."

Hours later Jane lay awake in the upper bunk—somehow it seemed to offer more privacy than the lower. Her skirt and bodice—the only clothes she had—hung neatly on one of the pegs driven into the bulkhead, modestly draped over her petticoats, stockings, and corset. The clothing swayed with the gentle up-and-down motion of the ship.

The cabin was cold. The blankets that covered her weren't sufficient to the task of keeping her warm, for she had only her shift to sleep in, and the shift seemed less than nothing at all. Most of the nights since she'd been widowed Jane had slept naked—a comfortable and probably sinful habit that she'd seen little harm in as long as she slept alone. But in this wretched bunk she felt more vulnerably nude than when she'd climbed into bed at home wearing only her own skin—because this night she wasn't to sleep alone. At any moment the cabin door would open and in would walk Hawk.

She turned restlessly, started to drive her fist into the flimsy pillow, then stayed her hand and gently rearranged her intended victim beneath her head. Fist pounding was too reminiscent of one of Giddy's tantrums. It was also reminiscent of the darker side of Hawk's nature—the anger and violence that sometimes erupted from beneath his sardonic shell. But Jane was neither a child nor a person ruled by her base emotions. She could control herself, or at least she should be able to control herself, no matter what problems and frustrations beset her.

The evening had left a bitter taste in her mouth and the ship's food a queasy feeling in her stomach. Supper had been unbearably awkward with the captain, officers, and three other passengers scarcely acknowledging her existence. Hawk had stared at her in brooding silence, imbibed heavily, and answered the other diners' attempts at conversation with a minimum of words. Their table companions had talked not at all to Jane, and covert and curious glances in her direction confirmed that every one of them believed her mad, or at least eccentric past the point of forgiveness. Colonel Colbert was there, eyeing her as a python might eye a rabbit. The very unpleasantness of it all had forced her to leave with her meal half eaten.

Hawk hadn't made the evening any easier. She'd felt his eyes weigh her down as she excused herself from the company, but he hadn't followed her retreat. He'd probably postponed his return so that she could suffer the tension of waiting for him. He was good at making her suffer—uncannily good.

The bunk was uncomfortable, almost as uncomfortable as her thoughts. Nighttime was a magnifying glass where problems were concerned, Jane found, and sleep was a luxury beyond reach. Even had sleep tried to claim her, Jane wouldn't have succumbed. She would not let herself be so vulnerable while at any moment Hawk could come into the cabin. Only when he was safely lost to sleep could she lose herself also. Until then she would stay awake.

She stared up at the deck above her head and wondered how a woman as obedient, devout, and just plain dull as she was could get into such a mess. God and Satan must have made another bargain, Jane decided, only this time they chose a weak-willed widow to torture instead of the patient Job, and the widow wasn't excelling at being wise, strong, or godly. If she'd had her journal, she'd be awake half the night spilling confessions of her wrongdoings onto the pages.

Confession one, she composed for an imaginary page: her heart still jumped in wicked excitement whenever Hawk was near—in spite of his offenses and her very justified anger. Dear God, she had almost hoped that his jesting proposal had been real! What foolishness!

Confession two, a more serious transgression: one tiny part of her was glad not to be sent back to England, sinful and irresponsible as the feeling was. One hidden corner of her soul rejoiced not to return to the lonely house on Great Queen Street or the charity of Three Oaks, to the scoldings of her grandmother and the pity of her sister, rejoiced to be going with Gideon—and with his father. That wicked spark of gladness winked like a tiny, solitary star through the dark layers of despair that enveloped the rest of her.

Confession three: Jane found she couldn't discover a third iniquity, though surely it existed. Though of course the two already confessed would keep the celestial record keeper quite busy enough marking debits to her heavenly account.

Jane had no idea how much time had passed when Hawk finally did come into the cabin. For all her wakefulness she lay still, feigning sleep, hoping he didn't see her small jump as the door closed behind him. The odor of alcohol accompanied him into the tiny cabin. He was drunk, Jane concluded—wickedly, dangerously drunk.

He wasn't so drunk, however, that he couldn't make his way around the cabin—at least for the most part. Jane flinched at the sound of some part of his anatomy making harsh contact with the edge of the lower bunk. The phrase he muttered was certainly not fit for a lady's ears. She heard the clothes rustle from his body. The buttons of his doublet clinked as they hit the deck, and his boots landed with a sharp thunk as he discarded them.

Then there was silence, and that was the worst of all, because when Jane couldn't hear what Hawk was doing, her imagination pictured him for her. She lay quietly, scarcely breathing. He was not in the bunk below her, for she hadn't heard the ropes creak with his weight. So he stood somewhere in the darkness, still, silent, watching her.

Jane knew he was watching her. She could feel his eyes upon her, like a tiger's eyes, shining in the darkness, burning and hungry for prey. As her nerves wound tighter, Hawk simply stood there, not moving, not speaking. The timbers of the ship continued their rhythmic creaking. The hull murmured with the passing wash of the sea. Those background sounds only emphasized the silence. Jane heard not a sound from Hawk—not a breath, or the scuff of a foot, or a sigh. But she could feel him. She could feel him just as surely as if he'd laid his hand upon her. His silent, eerie regard held anger, sorrow, and desire. She could feel them all, but mostly she felt the desire. Her lungs could scarcely expand, so great was the weight of his dark passion. Her skin tingled with the imagined nearness of his hand to her body. His arousal seemed to fill the tiny space that closeted them. It reached out to her, wrapped around her, caressed her, terrified her.

Jane was a widow, well acquainted, she thought, with men's needs, but this silently stalking desire was an animal she hadn't known existed. She felt helpless before its power, caught somehow in its potent, invisible claws. If

Hawk made a move toward her, she would be incapable of stopping him. God help her, she doubted that she would even try to stop him.

She lay perfectly still, imagining she could hear the vibration of her own nerves. Finally the darkness emitted a sigh—nearly inaudible—followed by the quiet scuff of a foot on the deck and the creak of ropes in the lower bunk. The thickness of the air seemed to relent, and she could breathe again. Still Jane lay awake, listening to the tossings in the lower bunk, staring into the darkness, wondering and ashamed at the regret that mingled with her relief.

The next day dawned a damp, cold gray, but the sea was smooth and the winds steady. The two masts of the *Mary Catherine* rose into the mist and disappeared as if they'd been swallowed by the sky. White sails billowed in the gloom, looking like ghosts flying over a somber sea.

In the ship's waist sat Ned and Gideon, sheltered from the wind against the bulkhead that rose to the deck above. Ned sat cross-legged, weaving his hands through the air while Gideon tried to imitate his movement.

" 'Ere now! That not it! Through, up, under again, and through the other direction." Ned took the short section of rope from Gideon's fumbling fingers and demonstrated. "See there, 'ow easy it is."

"You make it look easy," Gideon said with a grimace. "But it isn't easy for me!"

"It's easy when ye practice enough. Try it again."

Gideon succeeded only in getting his fingers more knotted than the rope. "It doesn't matter!" he declared. "I didn't want to be a sailor anyway!"

Ned shook his head. "Sailin's a fine profession, lad. I were a sailor, me father was a sailor . . ."

"Where did your father sail?" Giddy asked.

Ned chuckled darkly. "Who knows. 'E coulda been any number of sailor men who came to me mother's 'ouse. Coulda been a merchant tar what traveled to the Orient and the Americas, or coulda been a sailor in the great English Navy what can't be beat upon the high seas."

"You don't know who your father is?" Giddy asked with wide eyes.

Ned winked. "I likes ta think that I got a whole crowd o' fathers. That way if I meet an old fellow I admire, I c'n think that could be me dad. And if I meet an old fart not worth the air 'e breathes, I c'n say that weren't me father—there's too many other possibilities. Ye see?"

Gideon twisted his face in confusion.

"Now a high-class fellow like you," Ned continued, "ye know who yer father is. No doubt about it. An' ye c'n be proud of 'im, too. Though I tell ye plain, 'e's no better at knots than ye are."

Ned's head motioned toward Hawk, who sat a short distance away, his back propped against a coil of rope. Engrossed in sketching, he was oblivious that their attention had turned his way.

Gideon's mouth bowed down at the mention of his father. For a moment he considered in sulky silence, then slanted Ned a look from under thick black lashes. "Really?" he asked. "Master Hawkins can't make knots any better than me?"

"Yer father wasn't born to be a sailor," Ned affirmed. His voice dropped to a confidential whisper. " 'E told me once that sometimes 'e even gets seasick. 'E's a bit of a landlubbler, yer father is."

"Hmmph!"

"And ye must call him Master Gardner while we're on

the ship," Ned continued softly. "Either that or call him Father, since ye're 'is son."

Giddy scowled as if calling Hawk Father was out of the question. "Why Master Gardner?"

"If 'e used 'is real name, the constables might find 'im and put a noose around 'is neck." Ned's brows shot up. "Ye wouldn't want that, would ye?"

Giddy looked undecided.

Just then Jane came through the hatchway and stepped onto the deck. Her eyes seemed dark and bruised in a face much too pale. She clutched her cloak around her as though she was cold from much more than the damp sea air.

Hawk glanced at her and scowled. She scowled back.

"Now there's a pair who could use a cup o' common sense!" Ned quipped.

Giddy didn't hear him, though. The boy shot up as soon as Jane appeared and raced over to her. He held out the rope with the bowline that Ned had just knotted, jumping up and down in an excitement he hadn't shown when Ned had tried to teach him the knot.

Ned looked over at Hawk, who was frowning toward Jane and Giddy. He didn't look any less wan than Jane, his jaw clenched against what might have been pain, his lips compressed to a tight and uncompromising line. The fools were their own worst enemies, Ned decided—so caught up in their fancy ideas and cross-purposes. Any idiot could see that the two of them had the itch for each other, and getting in nature's way wasn't healthy as far as Ned was concerned. When he had an itch, he scratched it and let tomorrow take care of itself.

Ned unfolded himself from the deck and strolled over to Jane and the boy. The crew on the deck and in the rigging had all stopped what they were doing to watch as Jane greeted Giddy. Ned recognized the look in some of the eyes—it was a look he had seen often enough around a pretty woman. Others regarded her with that special fear that was reserved for those touched by madness. The woman needed protection, Ned decided, and better he provide it than Hawk. From the looks of Hawk, the poor lady needed protection from him more than from the curious crew.

"Mornin', Mistress Jane."

She greeted him with a hesitant smile. "Good morning, Ned. Giddy was just showing me the knot you've been teaching him."

" 'E's a bright lad."

"It's hard to move your fingers in the cold," Giddy told her. "Otherwise I would've done better."

"I'm sure you'll do just fine if you practice."

"That's what I told 'im," Ned agreed.

She moved toward the rail, Gideon clinging to her skirts. Ned went with her, feeling Hawk's eyes follow him. Let the fool be jealous, Ned thought cockily. It would do him good to see that he might not be the only one trailing after Jane with his tongue hanging out.

"A lady like you shouldn't be paradin' around deck alone," he told Jane. "These sailor men ain't got the manners o' the gentlemen ye're used to."

Jane smiled and arched a fine brow. "I doubt they'd bother a madwoman."

"Some of 'em would bother a sea snake if they thought it was female. Beggin' yer pardon."

"Then I'm grateful for your company." She gripped the railing and gazed sadly out to sea, back over the ship's wake toward England. "I've never seen the sea before," she admitted. "It's a bit frightening, isn't it?"

"Nah!" Ned denied. "No more'n anythin' else."

Her knuckles grew white against the dark teakwood of the rail as she looked down to where the sea surged in great bursts from beneath the hull.

"The sea's a mindless thing," Ned told her. "Not nearly as dangerous as people. Them's the ones ye got to watch out fer. A lady with yer grit can't be afeared a the sea, not when yer not afeared a the Hawk. Hell, ye ain't even scared a ol' Ned Crow."

Jane looked up from the heaving water and regarded Ned with friendly curiosity. "Are you something to be frightened of, Master Crow?"

"Aye. To be sure! I'm a fierce one."

Her eyes traveled from his sharp, swarthy face with its mutilated ear down to where Giddy clung confidently to one of his hands. Ned scowled at the amused twinkle that appeared in her eyes.

"Don't let appearances fool ye, mistress! If ye're gonna be out in the world, ye oughta learn to tell the difference between a real through-and-through villain like me and a fellow who's got just the surface coating of mean." He nodded toward Hawk. "Now 'Awk there, 'e's a smart fellow. Picked up cuttin' purses and cony catching like he was born to it. 'E's good with a knife, even better with 'is fists, and 'e learned to put on enough mean to lord it over most a the nips and foists in London—leastwise those over in Southwark where we 'ad our lodgin's. But Hawk ain't the genuine article rogue that I am. I'd bet a heap o' money on a guess he won't be 'appy till 'e's settled down with a kid on each knee and a pretty wife waitin' in 'is bed, beggin' yer pardon."

"Is that what you'd guess?"

Jane slanted him a smile that convinced Ned the lady was not as somber and serious as she'd like the world to believe. It also let him know that she was well aware of what he tried to do. Ned was unashamed. Someone had to put in a good word for Hawk. The fool was certainly bungling the job on his own.

"Every man and woman has a choice, you know, Ned. We choose whether we are to be good or evil, gentleman or rogue, saint or sinner. You chose your road in life; Matthew chose his also. If he wanted a child on each knee and that pretty wife, he could have had them."

"Beggin' yer pardon, mistress, but ye don't know much about the world, do ye? If you'da seen the 'Awk when I first found 'im . . . 'Is only choice was to live or die—and to live 'e 'ad to learn what I taught 'im. 'E 'ad no more choice about that than you 'ave about bein' dragged off across the sea."

Jane smiled archly. " 'Twas my own behavior that led me here, Ned. Though I may now regret what I did, I acted from my own choice. In the same way Matthew Hawkins's decisions led him to where he is now."

Ned shook his head. "Ye really don't know much about livin', mistress. Giddy's got more sense than you 'ave."

"I have?" Giddy piped up happily.

"Ye 'ave!" Ned confirmed. " 'Awk'll teach the boy 'ow to grow up, Mistress Jane. I'd wager 'e could teach you somethin' about that if ye'd let 'im."

Jane slanted Ned a knowing look. "I wonder if Matthew appreciates what a good friend you are to him."

"Oh, aye," he told her with a grin. "I keep remindin' 'im ever' time 'e forgets."

* * *

Hawk watched the threesome at the rail with mixed feelings. He'd ordered Jane to stay below, too aware of the danger to both Jane and to Colbert should she say the wrong thing. Not that anyone on this ship would believe a word she said. He'd done his lying well. The crew looked at her with the fear ignorant men reserved for ghosts and the mad.

He chose not to make a fight of it. She was safe enough with Ned, and Ned seemed more than willing to put up with her. Gideon followed her like a lost pup—an appropriate analogy, he thought.

Hawk looked at the sketch he had just completed. Over the past three years his drawings, once versatile and varied, had depicted only one subject. He had added details to the sketch at the last moment when Jane had unknowingly offered herself as live model. The penciled figure was drawn from the waist up, one hand clinging to a ship's rail as she gazed out over the water. Her eyes were wide, awestruck with the vastness before her and tinged slightly with apprehension. Tendrils of windblown hair escaped her coif and the hood of her cloak, blowing across her face and softening the angles of chin and cheek, which were sharper by far than the last time he had sketched the same face.

This sketch was different from the other portraits in more than the sharpness of features grown too thin. Her expression held a quality of innocence and sensuousness at the same time—a rich blossom still folded tightly in upon itself, waiting for the warm breath of gentle passion to release it from its own coils.

Hawk stifled an urge to crush the sketch in his hands. He was tired, having gotten no sleep the night before as he lay in his bunk feeling Jane's presence above him—so close, and yet far beyond his reach. He had been stinking drunk when he'd gone to their cabin, almost out of control. The arousal that Jane's proximity inspired ached the entire night, easing only at dawn as a raging headache and uneasy stomach came to replace it. The more he was near the damned woman, the more she got under his skin, and now he was stuck with her for God only knew how long. Last night he'd nearly broken that stupid promise he'd given her. How would he survive the many nights to come?

He looked again at the sketch, admiring not his artistic talent but the clean, feminine profile of his model. The drawing was quite different from the first he'd done of her; the woman was quite different than he'd initially thought her after that nightmare meeting in Fleet Prison.

For the first time since the horrible night when he'd been arrested, Hawk felt a tide rushing in to overwhelm him. Something inside him was out of control.

15

Jane sat on her bed, quill in hand and paper awkwardly arranged upon her lap. A bottle of ink stood precariously on the wooden post of the bedstead. There was no table in her modest chamber; neither was there a writing desk. Governesses did not rate anything better than servants' quarters in this house.

Jane poised the quill, then hesitated in thought. What could she say to her sister that was reassuring and yet not untrue? Finally she began to write.

January 31, 1659—The Hague, Holland
My dear Sarah,

   I imagine you must be frantic with worry by now, but be assured that I am unharmed and safe. I have longed to write to you, but aboard ship there was no paper to be had except from the captain, and he and I were not on such terms that I could make such a request. I am presently at The Hague in the company of Matthew Hawkins and Gideon. We are guests in the home of William and Anne Kipdorp, who are close friends of the Princess of Orange, who, as you know, is Prince Charles's sister Mary. Naturally they are avid supporters of Charles and, as do all that I have met here, refer to him as King

Charles II of England. They are quite confident about Charles's coming to power.

As to why I am here—you can guess that my plan on the docks at Billingsgate went awry. Master Hawkins defended himself against my accusations by convincing the captain of the *Mary Catherine* that I am his mad wife. Now, because of political considerations which I cannot explain, Master Hawkins is determined to keep me with him on the Continent until Charles has won England. He has introduced me as Gideon's governess, so all is as proper as possible under the circumstances.

In truth, I have seen very little of Master Hawkins. After the first night on board ship he left me to inhabit his cabin alone. I suspect he slept in the crew quarters, which part of the ship I certainly did not see, but Gideon told me of it. Neither has he been much present since we landed at The Hague. He has been about his business with his associates and has left me under the watchful eye of Anne Kipdorp. From that lady's vigilance, I would guess that she knows I am here unwillingly.

I did entertain the thought of trying to arrange passage back to England with the purse you gave me, but Mistress Kipdorp has prevented me from having any time to myself. The one brief day we have been here she escorted me to a modiste's to purchase clothing suitable for a governess. (My trunk was lost at sea, Hawk explains to anyone who is curious. The man lies as naturally as he breathes!) Once back in the confines of her house she saw to it that Giddy and I were together under the vigilant eye of her housekeeper—a formidable German woman who speaks no English at all but has been instructed, I'm sure, that Gideon and I are not to leave the house without escort.

Poor Gideon alternates between fits of unhappiness and excitement. Demands that I take him back to England mix illogically with enthusiastic accounts of his adventures aboard ship and the new places we will soon see. He has formed quite an attachment for Master Hawkins's companion Ned. Though I'm sure Ned is quite as fierce as he insists, the man is gentle and patient with Giddy—more so than Gideon's father, I might add. For all Matthew Hawkins's love for his son, he cannot seem to say the right words to draw Gideon to him. Boy and man seemed great friends at Three Oaks, before Giddy learned that Master Hawkins is his father. Now Gideon will scarcely speak to him. In spite of all that has occurred, I feel a certain sympathy for the poor man.

As for myself, my spirits are as high as could be expected. The future's uncertainty worries me, and I long to be back in England. I do not believe, however, that Master Hawkins is the sort of man who would intentionally harm a woman. Please prevent Geoffrey from sending a rescue, which I suspect he might. I am really quite fine, and for Geoffrey to raise a fuss would only cause trouble and embarrassment. If I have learned one thing from this unfortunate adventure, it is that Matthew Hawkins is neither to be trusted nor trifled with.

How strange, dear Sarah, to remember our childhood when you were always the one getting into scrapes. Now you are safely at home leading an exemplary life while I —who never disobeyed our parents, never put a foot outside the bounds of what was wise, decent, and proper —have embarked on the most improper and foolish adventure of all. I hope someday we will both be able to laugh about this as we sit in the garden at Three Oaks and sip lemonade on a warm, peaceful summer day.

Tomorrow we leave to travel overland to Antwerp, which is to the south in the Spanish Netherlands. The time required for that journey will depend on the roads, which I hear are quite muddy and, in places, icy. When we are established in that city, I will write you again.

Please do not worry about me. I am made of stronger stuff than you know, and with God's help, I will survive this very well. Give Geoffrey and the children my love. I miss you all.

Your loving sister,

Jane signed her name and sprinkled the paper with sand to set the ink. She tried not to wonder how long it would be before she saw Sarah or England again.

That evening, Jane tried to ask the stern housekeeper Frau Carr about posting the letter, using signs as best she could and pointing to the envelope. The housekeeper's eyes remained blank in her square, stolid face as Jane repeated her pantomine, then the woman growled something in German. The only words Jane understood were "Frau Kipdorp."

Mistress Kipdorp was scarcely more receptive to Jane's request. The Dutch matron regarded her as though she'd asked if she might fly to the moon. "You will have to talk to Lord Chester about that," she told her in a frigid voice.

So Hawk was back to being Earl of Chester. She shouldn't have been surprised, Jane reflected. Naturally Charles's supporters would give no recognition to acts of Cromwell's government—especially an act stripping a royalist of titles and lands.

"Lord Chester" returned to the house long after supper, which the Kipdorps ate in the formal opulence of their dining room and Jane ate with Giddy in Giddy's chamber. Hawk refused to post Jane's letter without first reading it.

"It's personal," she told him coldly. "There's no need for you to read it."

Hawk regarded her just as coldly from his chair in the Kipdorps' library, where he sat with feet casually propped on a richly upholstered stool and a brandy on the table beside him. "I'm not interested in prying into your personal correspondence, but I do need to ensure you haven't written anything that you shouldn't."

Her chin rose by a stubborn notch. "Then I will simply give you my word that nothing in my letter refers to Colonel Colbert. I assume he is the one who inspires your worry."

Hawk was just as stubborn. "I either look at the letter or you don't post it."

"You doubt my word?"

He merely smiled and raised one brow. The light from the fireplace cast his face in a particularly devilish mold, and Jane knew a sudden and unreasoning flash of anger.

"I fear you've mistaken my habits for your own," she said. "You are the one who lies to suit his own purpose, not I."

If the barb hit its target, Jane couldn't see its effect in Hawk's calm hazel eyes. He merely held out his hand for the letter. Sullenly she surrendered it. The contents held nothing so intimate that she need be embarrassed, but the principle of having her privacy invaded vexed her. Having her word judged as less than sterling vexed her even more.

She stood with spine stiff and face fixed while Hawk read. When he handed the letter back, his expression was as cold and blank as her own.

"You may give it to Mistress Kipdorp to post. Tell her to check with me if she hesitates."

Of course, Anne Kipdorp would be another person who believed Jane lied as a matter of course. She wondered what Hawk had told the lady about his son's "governess."

"Was that all you wanted?" Hawk asked, his mouth a forbidding line.

It wasn't all Jane wanted, but he knew that. She wanted to return to England, she wanted to be once again among people who loved and trusted her, and—strangely enough —she wanted the Hawk who had kissed her in Sarah's garden and had almost been her friend. In only a few short days the man whom Jane remembered coaxing her back to life, charming Sarah and Geoffrey, and playing games with their children was fast becoming only a memory. He had changed into the Matthew Hawkins who now sat so forbidding in front of her and treated her as though she were poison. Before he had been mocking, provoking, disrespectful, impertinent, and scornful—and sometimes uncomfortably insightful. Now he was simply cold, full of enough disdain to freeze the Thames in July. Somehow the change in him gave her as much distress as being abducted. It hurt almost as sharply as losing Gideon, though she was ashamed to admit it.

She wanted to say something to bring back the old Hawk. The Devil's advocate was far preferable to this cold aristocrat.

"Was there something else you wanted?" he asked.

"No. Nothing."

"We leave in the morning."

"So our hostess informed me."

"Do you have everything you need?"

"Mistress Kipdorp was very generous with your coin in purchasing for me a wardrobe suitable for a governess."

"I told her to not skimp. I assume the modest clothing of a governess will suit your Puritan tastes well."

"Well enough, thank you."

"Then I will see you in the morning."

"Good night, then."

"Yes. Good night."

Hawk watched Jane leave the room. He felt poised on a knife edge: one tip of his balance and he would tumble. He had tried to put his growing desire on ice, an act that apparently fooled Jane very nicely. He wished he could fool himself as well. He thanked the Lord that these past two days he had been away from the house—away from Jane, and he prayed for a miracle cure from this madness.

His life had no room for the complication of Jane Alexander. Even if they were suited—which they most certainly were not—he'd done nothing but cause her pain from the moment he'd stepped into her life. She detested him. If she hadn't before, she certainly must now.

Charles could win back his throne more easily than Matthew Hawkins could win the affection of Jane Alexander. The prince might lose his head in the bargain, just as his father had. What could he himself lose, Hawk wondered, if he was so foolish as to battle for a Puritan widow who regarded him as scarcely one step up from the Devil himself?

The prize most certainly would not be worth the risk, Hawk tried to persuade himself, even if the prize were attainable.

As their coach rolled into the Dutch countryside, Jane was glad to leave The Hague behind, glad especially to see the last of the Kipdorp residence. She didn't mind being treated as a servant, but the household's cold attitude of distrust and contempt made her feel so lonely and lost she could almost not bear it. Yet they had taken their manner toward her from Hawk, so she couldn't very well blame the Kipdorps for their rudeness. She was glad to depart their company, however, and glad to be out of the city. Here in their coach she had only Hawk to deal with—a difficult task in itself.

Holland was a strange land, a place of swamps, canals, windmills, and—just as strange—Calvinists. According to Grandmother Margaret, the followers of Calvin, though not quite as bad as papists, wore horns and forked tails. Jane smiled when she imagined what her grandmother would have thought of the Kipdorps—not only Calvinists but friends with a Stuart princess as well. Her smile faded as she wondered when or if she would ever see Grandmother Margaret again.

The Dutch countryside did not present its best face as their coach slogged its way southward toward the Rhine. Wet, gray meadows and orchards blended into gray fog which rose into low-hanging gray clouds. The air itself seemed gray—damp and heavy with a sharp south wind that drove spatters of cold rain before it. On the driver's box of the coach, Ned kept up a steady stream of imaginative cursing at his team of horses, the weather, and the mud that made their progress so slow.

Inside the coach Jane, Hawk, and Gideon rode in much more comfort than Ned. The vehicle that Hawk had purchased possessed the uncommon luxury of springs, the seats were well upholstered in soft leather, and several lap robes kept the cold at bay. Still, the interior of the coach was not what Jane would call comfortable, not with Hawk sitting across from her and Gideon, his face looking as though it had been carved from stone. All in all, the atmosphere in the coach was every bit as inviting as the weather outside.

The morning dragged on. The coach slipped and slid its way south, Ned continued his nonstop cursing, and Hawk and Jane sat in frozen silence. Even Gideon was silent—a rare state for him. He glanced nervously from Hawk to Jane, watching their carefully blank faces with growing tension. Once he channeled his restlessness into his feet, which commenced to thump against the seat in cadence to Ned's cursing, but a stern look from Hawk stilled Giddy's feet and honed a sharper edge on the tense lines of his face. His mouth twitched, fingers drummed, ankles crossed and uncrossed while his eyes rested first on his father, then Jane, and finally took refuge in staring at the floorboards of the coach.

"When are we going to get where we're going?" he asked petulantly.

"In two or three days," Hawk answered. "It depends on the roads."

"Can I ride up front with Ned?"

"Ned has enough problems without having you on the box beside him."

"I wouldn't be any trouble."

"You can stay back here." Hawk sighed impatiently.

"I'm bored," Giddy informed him.

"We brought some books to entertain you."

"I can't read when my eyes are jiggling."

"We brought *The Taming of the Shrew*," Hawk said. "You liked that play very much when you were younger."

Gideon screwed up his face and wrinkled his nose. Beside him, Jane stifled a smile. So much for Shakespeare, her look shot at Hawk.

"How did you escape?" Gideon asked Hawk suddenly. "Why weren't you hanged like all the other rebels?" His tone implied that Hawk certainly should have been hanged.

"I was never sentenced to hang," Hawk explained with sorely tried patience. "I was to be sent to the island of Barbados as a slave. I ran away before that could happen."

"Did you kill anyone when you escaped?"

Hawk's face grew grim as he remembered the guards who had beaten to death a sick and helpless prisoner, then tried to do the same to him, who was neither sick nor helpless. "Yes, Gideon, I killed one of the guards."

Gideon frowned. "Aunt Jane told me that killing, lying, cursing, stealing, and being lazy are wrong, along with a lot of other stuff I don't remember."

"She's right. Killing is wrong. But sometimes it can't be helped."

"I think you're going to hell," Giddy said, his eyes bright with challenge.

"Gideon!" Jane chided. "That's enough!"

"I want to go back to England," the boy insisted. He regarded Jane truculently. "Will you take me back?"

"That's enough, Giddy," she repeated. "Apologize to your father."

He stuck out his lower lip.

"Disrespect to your father is also on that list of things that are wrong. Now, apologize."

"You mean he's not going to hell?"

"He has as much chance of not going to hell as you or I do. And you should always address your father with respect."

"You don't!" Giddy accused Jane. "I heard you yelling at him when we were on the ship. Everyone could hear."

Hawk sent a how-are-you-going-to-get-out-of-this-one? smile in Jane's direction. She accepted the challenge smugly.

"Well, Gideon, Master Hawkins is not *my* father, is he? So I can be disrespectful whenever I choose."

"What is he then?" Giddy asked resentfully.

"He's . . . he's . . ."

"I'm her employer," Hawk provided. "I've hired Jane as your governess."

Gideon's looked at Jane as though she'd suddenly become a stranger.

"I thought you wanted to take me back!"

"Gideon . . ." Jane was at a loss to explain the complications. She tried to take Gideon's hand, but he snatched it away. Out of the corner of her eye she saw a wry smile of sympathy on Hawk's face.

"All the time you've been on *his* side when I thought you were on mine!"

"Gideon, there aren't any sides. We both want what's best for you."

Gideon's face hardened in distrust as he turned away, his little spine stiff as a rod and his shoulders set in a square of defiance.

The rest of the morning went no better. Gideon remained stubbornly uncommunicative and sulky. Hawk sat on his side of the coach wrapped in his own world, gazing silently out the window as if Jane and Gideon didn't exist, and Jane sank into a mood that rivaled the weather for gloom.

They stopped for the midday meal in a small farming village that boasted a tavern, ordering cheese, bread, and cold mutton, buttermilk for Jane, ale for Hawk, and small beer for Giddy, who interrupted his sulk long enough to be delighted with the drink that Jane had never allowed. The tavern was surprisingly clean, and though the tavern keeper and his wife spoke no English, Hawk surprised Jane by speaking fluent Dutch.

As they walked back to the coach, Hawk stopped to consider a black brute of a horse snubbed to a post in front of the tavern. The beast wore only a halter—no saddle or bridle. When Hawk stopped beside it the horse rolled its eyes toward the man in a manner that made Jane wonder if anyone could get close enough to saddle the creature. Ignoring the animal's laid-back ears, Hawk ran an appreciative hand down the sleek neck. The horse snorted in high temper, and a small smile relieved the taut line of Hawk's mouth.

"You and Gideon get in the coach. I have a small bit of business to attend." He returned to the tavern and, a moment later, reappeared with a young farmer who'd sat a few tables away from them.

They entered a lively conversation in Dutch, gesturing to the horse and to each other. The farmer stood back, pulled at his chin, and regarded Hawk with a canny look in his eye. He shot out a single word. Hawk smiled and countered with another. Then they both spoke at the same time, gesturing and shaking their heads in mock disgust.

It was obvious to Jane that Hawk was bargaining for the horse, though why anyone would want such a beast she didn't know.

"Did you get it?" she asked Hawk when he came to the coach.

"Aye," he said with satisfaction. "At a bargain. He's been under saddle once or twice, but the boy's been trying to break him to pull. Brought him into the village to get him fitted out with a harness. Any fool should be able to see that a creature like that wasn't born to pull a cart! Look at his lines and how he sets his head! There's good stock in his background."

"Couldn't you have gotten a better horse in Antwerp?"

He grinned, for a moment looking once again like the roguish Hawk who had invaded her house in London. "I mean to ride him to Antwerp!"

"You jest! That horse looks as though he eats people rather than carries them."

"He'll settle down once he learns who his master is." He slanted her a mocking smile. "Horses are a lot like women that way. And children."

Jane stiffened. "From the look of the beast I'd guess you two are well suited. May you both break your fool necks trying to decide who is the most unruly!"

"Is Master Hawkins going to break his neck?" Giddy asked hopefully when Jane settled back against the squabs.

"No, Gideon." She sighed in exasperation. "I was just letting angry words run away with my mouth."

"Oh," he said in a disappointed voice.

The tavern keeper sold Hawk an old bridle, saddle, and a martingale to keep the horse from throwing its head— though it certainly wouldn't prevent the beast from throwing Hawk when he tried to get on. The few customers in the tavern left their meals to cool and their drinks to grow warm for the entertainment of watching Hawk go flying.

They were disappointed, however. The black brute swung its mouth around for a chunk of Hawk's shoulder when he tightened the saddle cinch, but Hawk dodged its teeth with agile speed. A few futile bucks once Hawk was aboard and the horse settled down to surly acquiescence, but the gleam in its eye gave Jane hope the animal was saving some for later. She for one wouldn't mind seeing Hawk get dumped on his backside in the mud.

They resumed their journey with Ned still on the driver's box, Jane and Gideon in the coach, and Hawk astride his snorting volcano of a horse. The atmosphere inside the coach was definitely lighter without Hawk, Jane was relieved to note. She herself was less tense, and Gideon relaxed enough to exclaim on the beast that Hawk had purchased.

"He's big, isn't he! Do you suppose Master Hawkins would let me ride him?"

"I don't think so," Jane told him, praying fervently her words were true.

"I can see red inside his nostrils!" Giddy chortled. "He's a real horse from hell!"

Jane raised one brow. "I think you're much too occupied with hell, young man."

Gideon shrugged. "Master Peabody talked about hell a lot."

"Then I think perhaps it's a good thing you won't be seeing Master Peabody again. When are you going to start calling Master Hawkins Father, as he deserves?"

Gideon's expression returned to the morning's truculence. "I hope he gets thrown off that horse."

"Gideon!"

He avoided Jane's eyes and sank back into sulking. Jane sighed and resigned herself to a very long afternoon.

As the hours passed Hawk managed to stay atop his mount, though not through the horse's lack of effort to unseat him. Observing from the window of the coach, Jane noted Hawk's look of enjoyment at every skirmish with the beast. The horse's antipathy, she guessed, was much easier to conquer than his son's.

She wondered at her sympathy for the man. His feelings and moods seemed to be a part of her, so much so that his hurt seemed to pile up on top of her own. He deserved her hatred; heaven knew he had done enough to earn it. But the fact was she didn't hate him, not for taking Gideon, not even for dragging her with him and disrupting her life. Jane hated the change in him since they had left England, and she despised herself for still feeling weak-kneed and fluttery when he was near. She hated Hawk's betrayal, his arrogance, his dishonesty, and the savagery that lurked so close to the surface. But she couldn't hate *him*.

Something drew them together—something more than Gideon, more, even, than the unholy and unsanctified desire that invaded her dreams and even her waking thoughts. Hawk felt it too, Jane was certain.

Jane guiltily admitted that she harbored a very inappropriate affection for Matthew Hawkins. Such an attachment was disaster, and could bring only unhappiness. She had been taught from childhood that when it came to men, a woman should love only where given permission to love. Anything else was not only a sin, it was a calamity. Jane didn't mean to be sinful in this matter. She would gladly change her feelings if she could. The problem was that she didn't know how.

She looked across at Gideon, whose mouth was curved into a stiff little bow of displeasure. Would any of them emerge from this adventure with what they wanted?

Gideon lay on his pallet listening to the snores of the men in the room. There were five of them, and all of them snored. Even his father snored. Fighting with the big black horse had tired him so that he had fallen asleep almost as soon as he lay down upon his pallet beside Giddy's.

The inn was crowded. Gideon had never before slept in a room with so many people. Aunt Jane's room was on the other side of the inn, and even she had to share her room with other women. Gideon would rather have slept with Jane, even with the women there to disturb them. He didn't like sleeping beside his father.

Gideon looked over at Hawk, who slept on his side, his head pillowed on one arm. Sons were supposed to look like their fathers, but he couldn't see himself in Hawk, and he could see his father clearly by the light of the single candle that still burned in the room. Hawk's cheeks were stubbly, his nose much bigger than the mere button that decorated Giddy's face. His brows were dark and heavy, his jaw square and aggressive. The hair on his chest was heavy also—almost a solid mat of black covered his body, narrowing across his stomach and disappearing under the blanket that hid him from the hips down. Matthew Hawkins wasn't at all refined as a real gentleman should be. He had too much hair and too many muscles. Gideon wondered if he would look like his father when he grew up. He hoped not.

He turned on his pallet so that he faced away from Hawk. He didn't want to look at him. He didn't want to be in this room, in this inn, or in this country. The air smelled different here than in England. It was colder and wetter. The people spoke a strange language and he never knew what anyone was saying. The food wasn't as good here nor the people as friendly.

Gideon had never felt so alone in his life. Jane worked for his father. Probably she didn't love him anymore. Maybe she never had. Master Hawkins seemed to be angry even when he was quiet. His father certainly didn't love him. Gideon didn't understand why he had come back for him after such a long time.

Tears dribbled down Gideon's cheeks onto the dirty pallet. Crying was silly—something that girls like Melissa Winford did all the time. Gideon knew he shouldn't cry, but somehow he couldn't stop the tears. He wanted to go back to England. He wanted his life to be what it had been just a very short time ago, when Aunt Jane's gentle, unchanging love was the cornerstone of his safety, when his father was a vague figure of the past. He didn't like the strong, overbearing, surly man who was his father, and he didn't quite trust this new Jane who was his "governess." The old Jane had always been very certain of what to say and what to do. The new Jane was not the rock he had come to depend upon. He sensed uncertainty in her voice, unhappiness in her face, and even fear in the way she looked at his father. Worst of all, she sided too often with Master Hawkins when she should be siding with Gideon.

A new flood of tears coursed down his face onto the thin straw mattress. How he wanted things to be as he had known them before! He would even mind Grandmother Margaret if he could get back to England. If he could get back to England . . .

Gideon's heart began to thump so loudly he feared his father would hear. Why not go back to England? He could make Jane sorry she had changed. He could make his father sorry he was so angry all the time. Ned would take him back. Ned was his friend, and the little man knew all the captains of all the ships that could take him back to England, Giddy was sure.

He would stay with Aunt Sarah and Thomas, Trevor, and

George. He would even be nice to Deidre and—he cringed mentally—Melissa.

His mind set, Gideon rolled carefully off his pallet and stood up. He donned the shirt, breeches, doublet, and cloak Hawk had purchased for him at The Hague, then picked up his boots and the stub of the candle and stole silently toward the door, hesitating at each step to make sure he made no sound. Anxious, breathing hard, heart thumping, he tiptoed down the stairs. No one was about. Giddy smiled, beginning to feel better by the minute.

The stable was warm and musty with the smell of horses and leather, but Ned was nowhere to be seen. Gideon raised his little candle high and looked around. For a few moments he was at a loss; he knew Ned slept in the stable with the servants. Then he saw the opening to the hayloft. It was shut. Giddy looked around for a ladder but couldn't find one.

He scowled for a moment. Ned was beyond his reach, and if he called to wake him, likely the whole inn would wake also. Gideon squared his thin shoulders. He would simply leave by himself. He didn't really need Ned or anyone else. He was big for his age, and bright. Jane had often told him so. A boy as big and bright as he ought to be able to get to England without help. He would show them all—make them all sorry they had treated him badly.

Gideon decided that walking back to England would take too long. He would borrow his father's new horse. Back at Three Oaks he'd ridden almost every day with Thomas, Trevor, and George. Surely one horse was much like another.

He fetched a bridle and saddle from the tack room and dumped them outside the black horse's stall. The big brute snorted and rolled his eyes as Gideon peeked through the slats.

Slowly sliding back the latch, Giddy gathered his courage.

16

"Jane! Wake up!"

The demand scarcely reached Jane through a heavy fog of sleep.

"Wake up!"

She stirred and mumbled, but the startled squawk of the woman sleeping next to her brought her fully awake, her ears ringing. At first she thought she was still dreaming, for Hawk's face was poised above hers, his face etched into grim lines by the flickering light of the candle beside the bed.

'What . . . ?" she began, confused.

Her question was interrupted by another squawk. Both women with whom she shared a bed were now awake, babbling wildly in Dutch and clutching the blankets to their chins.

"What are you doing here?" Jane finally gained her senses. "You can't walk in on—"

"Gideon's gone," he said. The words cut off her complaint like a knife.

"Gideon's gone?" she asked in a panicky voice. "Where? How?"

"He slipped out while I was sleeping. I woke to find his pallet empty. I searched the whole inn and discovered"—

he paused, fighting down the panic in his own voice—"the black is gone."

Jane's eye grew wide. "Your horse?"

"Exactly."

For a moment their eyes met. The complaints of the Dutch women faded into the background as Jane joined Hawk in his despair.

"I'm going after him. I want you to stay in the taproom in case he returns on his own."

"Of course."

"I'll meet you downstairs."

"I'll be right down."

Before he left Hawk reached for her hand and gave it a comforting squeeze, a gentle gesture that almost broke Jane's fragile control and brought her to tears. Then he spoke a few words in Dutch explaining the situation to the two indignant matrons whose dignity his invasion had offended. Their complaints immediately changed to sympathetic wails—not much of an improvement as far as Jane was concerned.

When Jane descended to the inn's taproom, it seemed the whole inn had been roused, even though the night was still fully dark. Borst, the innkeeper, his plump, fair-haired wife, and two strapping sons were all there. Four men guests were gathered around Hawk, gesticulating and admonishing in Dutch, and the wives of two of the men—Jane's bed companions—followed closely behind Jane down the stairway.

The innkeeper's wife—Katarina, she had bade Jane call her when they met—greeted Jane with a sympathetic pat on the arm. She caught Jane's look of question toward the knot of men.

"They try to convince Lord Chester not to go till dawn,"

she said in heavily accented English. "When sun rises they will help search for boy, but now, in dark and fog . . ." She shook her head sadly. "Bogs are very bad. Men who live here all their lives will not ride out in dark."

Jane's heart skipped a beat. The situation was even worse than she'd feared, if that was possible. Gideon was alone on a vicious beast of a horse in the dead of night. And now Katarina told her the earth itself might swallow the boy.

Hawk slammed his fist on a table to demand silence. He flung out a demand in Dutch.

"Ah!" Katarina exclaimed with a shake of her head. "He will go anyway. He asks men to sell him a horse."

Silence was his answer. Hawk spoke again.

"He offers much money," Katarina translated.

This time Hawk got what he wanted from a portly, bejowled fellow who had been one of the most vociferous in his warnings. He uttered two succinct syllables—a higher price, Jane guessed.

Hawk agreed. They shook hands while the other men shook their heads at what they must have considered idiocy. One spat into the straw upon the floor.

"A brave man," Katarina ventured, her soft brown eyes worried, "but he should wait."

Hawk spoke a few final words with the man who had sold him the horse, then walked over to Jane and drew her away from her companion. "Stay here in case Gideon comes back on his own."

Her throat closed; she couldn't answer.

"You could run away while I'm gone. I doubt Ned would stop you. You could find your way back to England." He gave her a long look. "But I know you won't."

"I'll be here. Take Ned with you."

Hawk shook his head. "I was lucky to get *one* saddle horse. Besides, I wouldn't leave you here without protection."

He touched her cheek, and for a moment Jane thought wildly that he was going to kiss her right here in front of all the gaping inn patrons. He merely smiled, however, his lips tight with worry. "Have the innkeeper start the kitchen fires and heat water. Giddy's going to be cold when I get him back here."

"All right." Jane's voice was a mere whisper.

"I *will* bring him back, Jane."

"I believe you."

Their eyes met without the reserve that had grown up between them, and the determination in his gaze reassured Jane against all the demands of logic.

When Hawk left, Jane felt suddenly empty. As he opened the door and walked into the night, the fog seemed to curl around him like grasping tentacles.

Katarina was immediately at her side, patting her hand and guiding her to a table to sit. "I start fires," the plump little matron told her. "Bring tea, warm milk?"

"Warm milk would be nice," Jane said.

A few minutes later Ned came into the taproom, scraping the mud from his boots at the entrance and shaking the moisture from his wool cloak. He spied Jane immediately and came to sit beside her. "Thought the boy 'ad a better 'ead on 'is shoulders than to do somethin' like this."

Jane sighed miserably. "I knew he was unhappy. I didn't know he was this unhappy."

" 'Awk'll bring 'im back, and I'll wager Giddy won't be sittin' on 'is backside fer a couple o' days when "Awk's finished teachin' 'im a thing or two."

Katarina brought warm milk and a promise of bread soon to be out of the oven.

"What are those gentlemen saying?" Jane asked tensely as the plump woman sat down at the table.

Katarina clucked sympathetically. "They are old fellows who are only good for sitting in front of a fire drinking ale. You should not listen to them."

"What do they say?" Jane insisted.

The little matron shrugged. "They say boy has no chance in bogs at night, no more than father. You are boy's nurse?" she asked.

Jane hesitated. "Yes. I'm his governess."

"Fond of boy, I can see. Maybe father will find. Soon it will be dawn."

Ned snorted at the pretense. "Sometimes I think 'Awk ain't got no better 'ead on 'im than 'is boy. I'm goin' back to the stable. Don't you worry none, Mistress Jane. If 'Awk's not back in good time, I'll 'op on one of those sloggin' miserable carriage 'orses and go after 'im. They might not be 'igh-steppin' strutters, but I'd wager they're better in this country than that 'igh-bred black beast that Giddy's on."

Jane merely nodded and smiled, knowing Ned was trying to comfort her. The carriage horses weren't even broken to saddle, though she had no doubt plucky Ned would try to do exactly as he'd said if Hawk didn't come back. If Hawk didn't come back . . . The thought swelled painfully in her mind, and she couldn't push it away.

"Fond of man also?" Katarina inquired with a chuckle. Jane's expression brought a smile of approval on Katarina's broad face. "Good man. Brave. Handsome. Rich?"

"No . . . yes . . . I don't know. Probably."

The minutes ticked on into hours, and hours stretched

into eons. Hawk didn't return. Slowly Jane faced the prospect that she was losing not only Gideon but Hawk as well. She'd never thought that losing Hawk—or getting rid of him, which had been the slant of her usual thoughts—would be painful. But it was. He'd become a part of her life, a burden to bear but often a blessing as well. His provoking smile, mocking words, the way his wide mouth twitched up at the corner when he was being particularly irritating, the light in his eyes when he teased her, the hunger he somehow infected her with—all that was but a small part of him. He was devil and angel at the same time, savage, gentle, charming, crude, temptor, savior. Enigmatic scoundrel that he was, he had gained a grasp on her heart just as surely as his son. The loss of either one of them would rend that fragile organ into pieces.

Dawn came, a wet, gray forecast of another sullen day. Hawk did not appear. Katarina served a breakfast of cheese, warm, crusty bread, cold ham, ale, and milk. The other guests shook their heads at the night's tragedy and prepared to leave. The women who had shared Jane's bed gave her sympathetic nods and a few soft words in Dutch that Jane didn't understand. Katarina sat with her and tried to make her eat. Ned stomped in once or twice, scowled, muttered a few curses, and left again. Jane sank into despair.

It seemed that anything she came to love in this life was snatched away. Jane's father would have told her that God had taken Hawk and Giddy from her because they were tempting her from the True Path, as he called it. She could almost hear his solemn voice in her head, telling her that the soul's health was far more important than human joy, or love, or longing. As a young girl she had always thought her father right, and it was tempting to fall back into the habit of blaming all her misfortunes on her own sins. But now she couldn't quite accept that premise.

Surely, she reasoned desperately, God must love Hawk and Gideon as much—even more, in fact—than she did. Perhaps she had strayed from what was right, but God wouldn't punish them for her sins.

"Eat," Katarina urged. "You must eat! You are too thin!"

Jane looked at the hot bread the matron was trying to tempt her with. "Later," she told her. "I'll eat when they return."

She saw the sadness and doubt in Katarina's eyes, and wondered how long she should wait before sending Ned to look for bodies. Her very soul cringed; a lead weight settled down upon her heart.

Jane rose and went to the window. The fog was rising a bit, the day's light brightening to a softer shade of gray. *Send them back to me,* she prayed silently.

If she had had money, she would have pledged it to the church for their safety, but she didn't have enough to matter. She would have promised her soul, but that, she hoped, already belonged to the One she petitioned.

Bring them back because I love them so much, she pleaded. *Both of them. Please.*

An hour past dawn her prayers were answered when Hawk returned with a soaked, grimy, half-frozen and unconscious Gideon. Hawk was in little better condition than his son. Both were covered with evil-smelling mud and were chilled to the bone.

"He veered off the road into a bog," Hawk told her as he lowered Gideon from the saddle into Ned's waiting arms. "The horse panicked and threw him. No sign of the beast. Giddy's leg is hurt. Can't walk, but he crawled a ways after he was thrown."

Jane anxiously divided her attention between Gideon and his father. "Are you all right?" she asked Hawk.

Hawk practically fell out of the saddle. "Went swimming in some mud to get . . . to get Gideon out. I'll be all right." A stableboy led the horse away and Hawk swayed without the animal's body to lean upon.

" 'Ere now!" Ned objected. "Don't be fallin' on yer duff in the middle of the yard!"

"I'm not falling on anything," Hawk objected blearily. He did allow the innkeeper to half support him as they walked into the taproom, though.

"Ye're a stinkin' mess," Ned commented.

"He's hero!" Katarina exclaimed—in English for Jane's benefit. Her husband added his own commendation in Dutch, nodding his head in approval.

The innkeeper's sons found themselves chased out of their room by their parents so Gideon could have a bed in a private chamber. Ned and Borst carried hot water upstairs to bathe the unconscious boy while Hawk and Jane stripped Gideon of his wet clothing. Katarina hovered around the bed like a plump, nervous hen.

" 'E's a tough little tyke," Ned told Jane. " 'E'll be right as rain in a while."

Ned's voice, Jane noted, was not nearly as certain as his words.

They bathed Gideon in warm water, then bundled him in blankets. His face began to show some color, but not enough to comfort Jane.

"His leg's not broken," Hawk told her, "but it's twisted good. He won't be walking on it for a while."

"Walking may be beside the point!" Jane snapped, fear

giving a sharp edge to her words. "Just please let him live!" She looked up at Hawk and was hit by his haggard weariness. "Oh, Matthew! I'm sorry! Of course he'll live!"

Hawk raised his eyes and their gazes met over Gideon's blanket-wrapped little body. Both knew that the certainty of her assurance was a lie.

"Look at you!" Jane chided Hawk in a resolutely efficient tone. "You're as cold and slimy as your son. Go clean yourself up and get some sleep."

"I'll stay."

"No, you won't! Do you think I want two sick men on my hands?" Her voice rose to near hysteria, and Hawk reached across Gideon's body and took her hands, squeezing gently.

"All right. You're right, as usual."

"Poor man!" Katarina gave a motherly cluck as she took Hawk in hand. "You need bath and sleep also, no? We will find a place where you can sleep well. Come with me."

"I'll sit with Giddy," Jane promised as Katarina propelled Hawk toward the door. "I won't leave him."

"I know."

She wouldn't leave Hawk either. They both knew it.

All through the morning Gideon lay as one floating in the borderlands of death, his breathing shallow, his color pale. Katarina brought hot soup up to the room, and together she and Jane managed to get some down Gideon's throat.

"It will warm him inside," Katarina said hopefully. "Beautiful child." She brushed back a lock of his hair. "My son Hans looked like this. Wild like this, too."

In the afternoon Jane was joined by Hawk in the vigil. Having bathed and slept for several hours in the rarely used garret room Katarina had cleaned for his use, he had recovered well enough from the morning's ordeal, but when he looked at his son lying deathly still on the bed, his face grew grim.

"He hasn't changed all morning," Jane told Hawk as he pulled a chair by the bed to sit beside her. "He just lies there as though he were . . . were . . ."

Hawk didn't let her finish the thought. "I can't lose him now. God wouldn't be so cruel. Gideon *will* wake up."

Jane heard the command in Hawk's voice. He was a strong man, accustomed to the power that came from strength. He fought for what he wanted with cunning, courage, and sheer muscle if he must. But here he faced a situation that he couldn't fight; he could only watch, pray, and hope. Jane was more used to such an ordeal. For all her heartache, she realized that Hawk suffered even more than she.

Hawk got up, crossed to the window, and gently brought his doubled fist against the window frame, a blow in slow motion. Restrained as the gesture was, Jane could feel the leashed violence in his clenched fist and the pain in his eyes as he gazed out upon the afternoon. The fog had lifted, leaving behind a brilliant blue sky. Yellow sunlight streamed through the window, patterning the floor in brightness. The fairness of the day somehow seemed cruel, given the circumstances.

"If I could take back my every act that led to this, I would," he said quietly. "If I could move back in time, I would leave Gideon with you, where he was happy. I would depart from his life, let him think his father a dead traitor. Anything . . ."

"Matthew . . ."

"But I can't!" His voice rose with frustration. "I can't. God, how I wish I could!"

Drawn by his pain, Jane went to him and laid her hand lightly upon his arm. "None of this is your fault, Matthew. If you hadn't ridden out and risked your own life, Gideon would most certainly be dead right now. You did all any man could, and more than most would have."

"If I hadn't taken him away, none of this would have happened!"

"You mustn't shoulder the blame where there is none," Jane said gently. "You were . . . were right in taking Gideon." Her voice faltered with the pain of the admission, but she continued with determined strength. "You're his father, and you were right in saying he belonged with you. In your place I would have done the same thing."

"Would you?" he asked sarcastically. "Would you have been so selfish?"

Jane sighed. She clasped her arms across her chest, as if by folding in upon herself she could lessen the memories that rose to the surface and added their bitter anguish to today's pain. "When my Joshua died of pneumonia, every day getting weaker and paler until at last he faded into death, I would have followed him through death's door and snatched him back from God Himself if I could have. God forgive me, but I would do the same for Gideon. So I can't blame you for taking him back from me, can I?" Her voice broke, and the tears that had been gathering all morning flooded into her eyes. No longer able to control her sobs, she turned away and covered her face with her hands.

Hawk pulled her into his arms, turning her and cradling her against the formidable bulwark of his chest. "Jane, love, don't cry."

His murmured comfort made her weep all the harder, but she didn't resist the comfort of his embrace. The muscles of his chest flexed against her cheek as he folded her closer, his arms like a steel cage that could keep her safe from grief. Finally her sobs abated. Against all reason, the warmth of Hawk's nearness soothed the pain. The feel of him, hard and yet supple; the smell of him, soap, soft linen, wet now from her tears, sharpened by the masculine aroma that was as distinct as he himself; the sweet warmth of his breath in her hair—all this came together to make her want to burrow more deeply into his embrace and hide from grief, death, and the world itself. For a moment she let herself be lulled by his comfort. Then self-control reasserted itself. Jane forced herself to draw back, ashamed of putting on such a childish display. "I'm sorry," she murmured. "I'm so sorry."

He picked up one of the damp towels hanging from the bathtub and dabbed at her tears. "There's nothing for you to be sorry about."

"I'm usually not such . . . such a watering pot."

He shook his head, looked at Gideon, then back at Jane with and odd sort of resignation in his expression. "What is to become of us, Jane Alexander? We are bonded by more than my son."

Jane grew very still, so still she could hear her own heartbeat. Pretending that she didn't know his meaning would be useless and hypocritical. She knew very well. "Nothing will become of us, Matthew. We are from different worlds and want different things."

"Do we?" he asked softly.

The longing in his voice almost broke Jane's resolve. She tried to remind herself that following one's heart instead of one's head almost always brought disaster. In the scheme of this world, Hawk was not for her, nor she for him.

"We do," she replied resolutely. "When it is safe to return to England"—she smiled wryly—"when your esteemed cousin wins his throne, we will go back to our separate homes and continue with our separate lives. Whatever there is between us will fade, and Gideon will be where he belongs—with you. I realize now that he is your son, not mine. You love him as much as I and with much more right."

She felt his eyes devour her, as if in this moment of rare honesty between them he would burn her face into his memory, tear streaks, puffy eyes and all. One part of her wanted to walk back into his embrace, yield to temptation and the emotions of the moment, surrender to the overpowering magnetism of his masculinity, his strength, his sexuality. He truly was the Devil's own lure.

"Are you sure you want to stay in your world?" His voice, for all its softness, held a bitter edge. "You're a butterfly trapped in the mold of a moth, with a spirit much too fine to be shackled by such a drab existence."

Jane shook her head and smiled. "How fanciful you are. And how impractical. No matter what I feel for you, Matthew, I could no more live in your world than you could live in mine. You know that's true. If I'm trapped in the mold of a moth, as you say, then it's because that is what I am."

He didn't answer. For a moment they simply looked at each other, leaving much unsaid, knowing the impossibility of what they desired but somehow wanting it anyway. Any more words spoken on the subject would only lead to pain.

All through that night and the next day Hawk and Jane sat together, seldom speaking, watching Gideon's pale little form and carefully avoiding any further gestures or words that might be interpreted as intimacy. They shared the common ground of their grief and worry, but in all else they tacitly agreed to maintain separate camps. Katarina brought meals regularly, and just as regularly removed the scarcely touched food. Ned came in every few hours, ostensibly to check on Gideon but in reality to check on all three. He scolded Jane for not eating and growled at Hawk for not making her eat. One one visit he pulled Hawk to the corner of the room and hissed in his ear.

"Mistress Jane's a woman, an' I wouldn't expect 'er to 'ave enough sense to keep 'erself goin' properlike. But ye bein' a man, ye oughta be smarter'n that. Ye oughta stuff some food down 'er face, an' yer own as well!"

"Ned, Gideon is our main concern right now—"

"Well 'e shouldn't be!" Ned interrupted. "Young Giddy's gonna be all right. 'E's 'is father's son, an' I seed 'is old man pull through a lot worse than this a few years back."

"Ned . . ."

"Ye oughta be payin' more mind to Mistress Jane," Ned advised. "Ye brought the boy back and now ye got 'er right where she can 'ardly resist ye—if I know anything about women. And I do, ye know. They love 'eroes. Ever' one of 'em."

Jane's attention had turned their way. Hawk raised a brow. "Can we talk about this later?"

Ned puckered to spit on Katarina's clean floor, then thought better of it. Instead he gave a disgusted snort. "Sometimes I wonder about ye, 'Awk. Ye wouldn't recognize the angel o' good fortune if 'e came up an' spit in yer eye."

Jane questioned Hawk as Ned stumped out. "Were you two arguing?"

"Not really," Hawk told her. "It's just that Ned sometimes thinks he's my mother instead of my friend. He's saved my life more than once. I suppose that gives him a proprietary interest."

"I vow he's the oddest person I've ever met," Jane commented. "But strangely enough, I like him."

Hawk smiled. "He likes you, too. He thinks any woman with the wits to see through his bluster deserves a medal."

Jane fell silent. Her attention never wandered for more than a few moments from Gideon. She gently brushed his hair back from his brow. "I think his color is slightly better. Do you?"

"Yes," Hawk agreed. "His color's better than yours. I think you should eat something."

"I'll eat later."

"You'll be sick later. And as a wise woman once said to me—do you think I want two sick patients on my hands?"

Jane sighed, but she agreed. "All right, I'll eat if you're determined to bully me into it." Her tone was resolutely cheerful, but her eyes slid away from the warmth she saw in his expression.

As midnight came and went, Jane lost the battle with exhaustion and fell asleep in her chair, one hand holding Gideon's. Hawk gently picked her up and laid her down upon the bed beside his son. Even in sleep she wouldn't let go of the boy's hand. For a moment he watched them, woman and child. Much as Jane had done earlier for Gideon, Hawk tenderly brushed back a lock of Jane's golden hair. She stirred slightly and smiled, and his body tightened with a longing that had little to do with sexual desire. In its own way, his obsession with Jane had become equal to his obsession with winning back his child. Neither battle was going his way.

Hawk watched Jane so intently that a moment passed

before he realized that Gideon's eyes were open and staring at him.

"Master Hawkins?"

"Gideon!"

"Where am I?"

Hawk took Giddy's face in his hands, finding it difficult to believe that his son had actually spoken. "You're in the inn, with Jane and me. How do you feel?"

"Hungry."

"Gideon?" Jane woke and pushed herself up onto her elbows, shaking her head to clear the sleep from her brain. "Gideon! You're awake!"

"I'm hungry," Giddy repeated.

"He must be fine!" Hawk exulted. "He's hungry! Ned! Katarina!" he called.

Even though it was the middle of the night, Katarina and Borst both rushed in with smiles on their faces. Behind them Ned clumped up the stairs.

"He's hungry!" Hawk and Jane said together, then laughed.

"Then I will bring food!" Katarina replied. "Oh what a fine boy!"

The crowd of them watched Gideon eat as though he were the first boy to ever consume food. He accepted their attention as his due, but when finished, he pointedly asked: "Is there enough time for me to go back to sleep before we leave? I'm tired."

"Certainly there is," Hawk said, his voice restrained lest he choke on the emotions that tightened his throat. "There's plenty of time for you to rest."

"This is very strange," Gideon confided to Jane as Ned, Katarina, and Borst filed out, chattering with happy relief.

"Why are we having dinner in bed? It's the middle of the night!"

"You've been sick," Jane said gently, sitting down on the bed beside him. "Everyone is very happy to see you well enough to eat."

"Oh," Giddy said with aplomb. "I don't remember being sick. But I had a nightmare, Aunt Jane. I dreamed I was riding Master Hawkins's mean horse and he threw me into an awful swamp."

"That wasn't a dream, Gideon," Hawk said, looking at his son from the foot of the bed.

"That really happened," Jane confirmed. "Your father risked his life to bring you back safely, Gideon."

Giddy looked at Hawk thoughtfully. "I suppose I was an awful lot of trouble," he finally said.

"You were," Hawk agreed.

"Are you angry because I took your horse?"

"We can talk about that later."

A tension built up between the boy and the man as they continued to look at each other. After a few moments of silence, Gideon grimaced, but his eyes never wavered from Hawk's.

"I wouldn't have wanted to stay in that cold swamp," he said. "Thank you for bringing me back."

A smile twitched at Hawk's mouth. "You're welcome, Gideon. That's what fathers are for."

Gideon broke their gaze and ducked his head. Then he looked at Jane. "I've got some things I want to think about, but I'm too tired to think right now. Can I go back to sleep?"

"Of course you may." Jane's voice was hoarse with tears.

"Will you leave the candle burning?"

"Yes."

Gideon sank back into sleep almost before Jane could tuck the blankets around him. For a moment she braced herself on the bed, her breaths a labored effort to keep from weeping with relief and happiness. Hawk moved around behind her, took her shoulders, and turned her into his embrace. The last rein on her control snapped. She laughed and wept at the same time.

"He's all right," Hawk whispered. "We haven't lost him."

Jane couldn't reply. She merely nodded her head and accepted his handkerchief. Instead of attending to her own tears, she dabbed at the streams that coursed down Hawk's face.

"We're a mess." She laughed between sobs. Her hand froze as his gaze locked with hers.

Exhaustion had robbed her of the will to fight the beckoning she saw in his eyes, elsewise she surely would have fled. Suddenly nothing seemed so important as the passion between them, here and now. Yesterday was gone. Tomorrow didn't matter. After sharing their grief, pain, and now their joy, sharing a measure more seemed only right and natural.

"Jane."

From his lips her name seemed no longer plain, and when he lowered his mouth to hers she closed her eyes and let herself be consumed by the joining of their desires.

Hawk felt her surrender with both exultation and odd regret. He was past the point of playing the gentleman. "Forgive me," he whispered almost silently against her hair, then lifted her into his arms to carry her to his isolated little room in the garret.

17

The garret chamber Katarina had allotted to Hawk's use was small and rather crude, cruder even than the other rooms in the inn, for this one was generally not used. But if only one candle lighted their way, if the bed was lumpy and scarcely big enough for one, much less two, and if no fireplace eased the cold, they took no note. Their souls and bodies were focused on each other, and nothing outside themselves mattered.

Hawk laid Jane gently on the bed and followed her down onto the mattress. Space between them was the enemy, and he banished it, pulling her close until their bodies fitted together so neatly they might have been made for lying together. His hands enveloped her face as he marked each feature with a tender kiss—one closed eyelid, then the other, the pertly tilted nose, and then her mouth. On that he lavished a wealth of attention. First he brushed lightly, lips upon lips, as a butterfly might test the wind with its wings. When Jane sighed beneath the gentle caress and parted her lips, Hawk delved deeper, teasing with his tongue, urging her mouth to open to his and receive the tender invasion. She surrendered eagerly, and Hawk felt his careful restraint slip as mouths and bodies both molded together. He ached to rip away the clothing that separated them, to feel her naked flesh rubbing against his own, to feel her warmth receive and close around him, to spend his burning desire deep within her willing body while he watched the knowledge of his possession light her eyes. He ached, oh, how he ached!

Rather than yield to an explosion of passion, though, Hawk pulled gently back. Jane's mouth was red and sweetly swollen from his kiss, her eyes warm as they returned his gaze with no hint of coyness.

"Matthew . . ." Her voice was like a caress.

"I don't want to frighten you, my love."

She smiled. The smile of an angel, he thought. "No, Matthew. You could never frighten me."

Jane was very aware of what she did. She was no innocent who had never been with a man, though the feelings that washed through her at Hawk's touch, his look, the sound of his voice, were nothing like what she had felt for her husband. She had never before experienced the wild abandonment of reason, the sweet, tormenting tension that coiled within her, the ache of desire that made her want to cling to Hawk until their bodies merged into one flesh. Their joining was wrong and sinful. Jane didn't care. Her conscience seemed to watch from a distance and shake its head in reproof. She didn't care about that either. The only thing she cared about was stealing a moment of bright passion to ease the ache that had gnawed at her since she had first seen Matthew Hawkins leaning over her with his wicked smile and devilish gleaming eyes.

She touched the cheek that was so close above her face, ran a finger down the scar that gave him such a dangerous look, brushed against the mouth that was made for seduction. "I want you so much, Matthew. Please take what I offer."

"Said the lamb to the wolf." Hawk playfully bit the finger that strayed too close to his mouth. He kissed her palm. "Such a feast you are, my lovely Jane. I'm tempted to glut myself with you, gorge until I exhaust myself with my own passion. But I won't. This feast is best enjoyed slowly, piece by lovely piece, until the very last inch of our flesh is weary and satiated with glory."

Jane had certainly never thought about the act of joining in such terms, but for this night, at least, she had given herself into Hawk's care, and she trusted him.

Hawk removed her clothing piece by piece, as if unwrapping a much sought after gift and deliberately prolonging the pleasure. Her coif he cast aside. Loosening her hair and combing his fingers through the heavy mass, he murmured: "You should never wear such things, my glorious Jane. You have the hair of an angel." His fingers massaged in tiny circles on her scalp until she arched toward him in ecstasy. "You are so easy to please," he chuckled.

He attacked her bodice next, patiently unfastening the lacings which pulled it tight. Slowly he eased it off, leaving only the fragile chemise covering her breasts. He watched the rosy nipples beneath the thin fabric pucker and grow erect under his gaze, then brushed the rising peaks with his thumb. At Jane's gasp of pleasure he put his hands beneath her back and forced her breasts up to meet his mouth. He suckled and licked at the tempting mounds, leaving her chemise wet and clinging to each breast.

"Please," Jane gasped. "You make me lose . . . lose myself."

"I mean to," he admitted hoarsely. "Let go, my love. I will catch you."

He unlaced her whalebone corset and tossed it aside, then peeled down the chemise and continued his rapt ministrations on her naked flesh while she grasped his shoulders desperately. It seemed to Jane as if Hawk's strength was the only thing that still anchored her to the world around them.

By the time Hawk unfastened the tabs of her skirts and slid them over her hips Jane felt drugged, unable to resist the pleasure that swept over her in wave upon wave. His hands explored the contours of her thighs and buttocks through her cotton drawers. She struggled to rid herself of this last piece of her clothing, but he gently took her hands and imprisoned them above her head.

"Slowly, my lovely Jane." He bent to kiss each breast as his hand dipped between her legs and caressed where her desire had moistened the heavy cotton. "All things in good time." She pressed against his hand as a jolt of lightning-like pleasure rippled up from his touch. Her body seemed to convulse in shock waves of ecstasy. Stunned, Jane closed her eyes and let the rapturous tide pull her out to sea. When she opened them, Hawk smiled at her—a wicked, devilish smile that caught at her breath and made the pleasure start again.

"You are surely the loveliest creation ever wrought," he said softly.

Her wool stockings were the next to go. He peeled them down and laid kisses along the newly exposed flesh. "Such plain things to hide these pretty legs." He kissed her ankles, then each toe, massaged her calves, her thighs, nipped playfully at the triangle of curls covering her Venus's mound. Jane moaned as he curled his hands under her buttocks and forced her up against his mouth. He bit her, not hard enough to hurt, but certainly more than a playful nip. "I could devour you," he murmured. "The wolf feasting on the lamb."

Jane tangled her hands into his hair. "Please," she begged, though she knew not whether she pleaded for him to retreat or advance. If he stopped she would surely die. If he continued he would drag her further into an ecstatic but fearful land where she might drown in a sea of sensuality.

"My lovely, lovely Jane." He devoured her naked body with his eyes—full breasts still rosy from his attention, narrow waist, firm thighs, and a moistness between them that bore witness to her passion. He fought the urge to end the game now, to bury himself where those wet curls invited and carry them both to completion. But he'd promised her a slow feast, and only the first courses had been served.

With jerky motions he stripped off his doublet. She raised one knee and gazed at him languorously, sorely trying his control. "Have you never learned to undress a man?" he challenged her.

She smiled, all remnants of shyness burned away by the desire he saw lighting her eyes. "No," she answered. "But I'll learn."

She rose to her knees with fluid grace. The candlelight shadowed the curve of her breasts and the valley between her legs, making them dark mysteries even more inviting to explore. Hawk girded himself with iron control.

"Like so?" She teased him as he had teased her, slowly unbuttoning his shirt and sliding her warm hands inside to tantalize his hard masculine nipples. Every hair on his body stood erect as she explored along his ribs, smoothed across his breasts, measured the breadth of his shoulders, and traveled the ridges of his back. When her seeking hands found his navel and dipped below the waistband of his breeches, he almost lost his precarious control of himself.

"This feast grows too long," he choked out. He swung

himself from the bed and stood to loosen his breeches, which were beginning to cause him pain. Not to be denied her lesson, Jane slipped off the bed and stood behind him, her hands following his as he unlaced the breeches and pushed them down off his hips. She molded herself to him, her breasts pressed to his back, her hands roaming his chest. She felt the muscles of his abdomen contract sharply as her hands followed the mat of body hair that arrowed down from his navel. He caught at her wrists, then wrapped her fingers around the organ which stood so proudly erect—velvet over hot steel.

Jane felt her body turn to warm syrup. She pressed more tightly against him, needing his support to stand. She hadn't known the male organ could be this huge, this hard. The feel of him filling her hands didn't frighten her. She wanted nothing more than to have him inside her, even if he should split her asunder. Reason, modesty, sanity itself had flown. Only Hawk was left inside her mind.

Unable to help himself, Hawk moved himself within her fingers. The world had narrowed down to focus on one thing, and one thing only. A will of iron enabled him to stop, to slowly breathe, to restrain the explosion. Gently he removed himself from her grasp and turned. Jane was still as a statue, her eyes stunned, her lips moist and parted. "You're a fast learner," he said hoarsely, "and a damned genius at sending a man over the edge. Come here."

They sank together on the bed. Hawk could wait no longer for the main course. Jane's thighs opened eagerly to receive him; her hand grasped him and urged him home, but he needed no help as he plunged into her wet and welcome sheath. She was tight as a virgin, and her small gasp of pain attested to her long celibacy, but Hawk was beyond gentleness, and Jane didn't need it. She wrapped her legs around his hips and moved with his powerful thrusts. Her hands scraped at his back and shoulders and reached down between his legs to gently cup his turgid, desire-swollen testicles, as if to urge him to even more power. It did. With an animal growl he plunged deeper still, grasping her buttocks and imprisoning her tightly against him as he exploded within her. She felt the mighty pulses of his ecstasy and her body answered with a convulsion of joy. She soared on a warm bright wave of delight, spiraling up in a dizzy ascent. The world spun, Hawk at its center, his hard body the core of all creation. For a moment of pure heaven Jane floated, aware of only Hawk and herself melting together. Then she began to fall, slowly, gently, drowning in her own senses. Everything melted into warm, welcoming black. . . .

"Welcome back," Hawk said an eternity later.

Jane closed her eyes again and enjoyed the feel of him still inside her, the brush of his chest hair against her breasts, his weight pressed against her hips.

"You left me for a moment," he said.

"I fainted?" she asked, her words scarcely a whisper. Her brows puckered in disbelief. "Surely not."

"Surely yes." He smiled, looking as proud of himself as a strutting cock.

"Don't," she said as he started to ease off her.

"Greedy woman," he chuckled. "You've wrung me dry, I fear."

She ought to be ashamed and embarrassed, Jane mused sleepily, but she wasn't. "Greedy, indeed," she agreed. "I just learned that I've starved all my life, and now I'm greedy."

"You never need starve again," he assured her softly. He

brushed a stray lock of hair from her face, and before his hand left her cheek she was fast asleep.

For a moment Hawk contented himself with just looking at her in the dim candlelight, savoring the rose blush of her skin, the delicate sweep of thick honey lashes against her cheeks, the contented smile that curved her lips. She was as peaceful and contented in her sleep as a kitten with a full tummy. Lulled by exhaustion and satiation, her mind floated blissfully in the serene sleep of unremembered dreams. There would be no room tonight for anything but joy, wonder, and love.

Love—fearful word. Hawk did not deceive himself that Jane had given the gift of herself out of anything but love. Angels seldom fell from their pedestals for anything less. As for himself, he wasn't certain what he felt. Love was a word for poets, playwrights, and women. Even before his fall he'd contented himself with milder emotions—except regarding his son. Now Jane Alexander burst through the boundaries of his heart and demonstrated that sex could go beyond lust, affection beyond simple warmth. He'd thought once he'd satisfied himself with her body he'd be content. But he wasn't. Possession made him want her even more. Was that love? Hawk didn't know.

Jane sighed in her sleep. Her lips parted and she smiled. Hawk wanted to kiss her again, to cover that soft mouth with his own. He didn't, knowing she needed to rest. In the morning she would doubtless feel the pain of her fall from that almighty pedestal.

A prick of conscience dimmed the glow of his male satisfaction. How callously he had once tried to seduce Jane and rob the Puritans of one of their virtuous flock. Then how nobly he had vowed not to touch her. The vow hadn't been worth much, Hawk mused guiltily. Let the woman drop her guard but once and he had her in bed before she could come to her senses.

He should have been ashamed of himself, but he wasn't. How could one regret opening a new vista of feeling, a new chance at happiness? Damn the consequences. He didn't know quite what he felt for Jane Alexander, but he wanted to hold on to the feeling, whatever it was.

Careful not to wake her, Hawk settled down on his side and drew Jane gently into the curve of his body. She had surrendered more than she knew, Hawk reflected, for now he'd tasted the nectar of her love, his poor delinquent honor didn't have a chance of protecting her from him. Damned if he wouldn't protect her from everything else in the world, though. He didn't know how, but he would, Hawk vowed.

A narrow shaft of sunlight slanted through the shutters and hit Jane in the eyes. She blinked awake, looked groggily around the room, and tried to remember where she was. The cobwebs of sleep faded slowly. Gideon was much better, she remembered. Smiling, she relaxed back against the thin pillow, then recalled the celebration that had followed. In near panic, she looked to the other side of the rumpled bed. She was alone. Surely she'd been alone all night, dreaming of forbidden pleasures that still clung to her mind!

Jane's first movement to get out of bed convinced her the interlude with Hawk hadn't been a dream. She groaned and fell back into bed. Some delicate parts of her were very sore, and the undeniable reality of her sin made her conscience smart even more painfully than her tender flesh. She didn't question how she could have done such a thing. The sin had been stalking her ever since Matthew Hawkins had stormed into her life. Her strength had not been equal to the task of fighting it off.

Sighing, she rose, grimacing as she moved. Her clothes hung neatly from the room's one chair—Hawk's work, no doubt. Jane blushed to remember how they had been discarded the night before. Her husband had always preferred that she disrobe in privacy and wait for him in their bed. With him the act of joining had been quick, efficient, tolerated but seldom enjoyed. Jane had simply lain still and allowed her husband to do what he deemed necessary.

How different the act had been with Hawk. Remembering how she herself had eagerly participated in their mating, Jane felt a strange warmth spread from between her legs. She closed her eyes and willed the feeling to fade. Such things were not right even within the bounds of holy matrimony, and without marriage, surely they were mortal sin.

In one corner of the room stood a bucket of water and a towel—another of Hawk's touches, Jane acknowledged, for such amenities were seldom provided by an inn such as this one. Unmindful that the water was cold, she washed the gritty feeling from her skin, paying particular attention to her thighs and the tender spot between. Again she could imagine Hawk's touch, his playful teasing, his skillful coaxing her into a world where only he and she and their desire existed. A rebellious thought reared up against the prick of conscience. How could anything so lovely be sinful?

Washed and dressed, her hair pulled back into a severe bun and properly covered with her coif, Jane made the bed, straightened the one chair, wiped spilled drops from around the washbucket, and sought any other excuse to keep her in the room. She longed to be out and see Gideon, but she dreaded an encounter with Hawk. What must he think of her, prattling endlessly about virtue, then falling into his arms like some doxy seeking his favors! She was a hypocrite, and a slut into the bargain.

Jane opened the shutters and turned her face to the sunlight, breathing deeply to rein in her emotions. She almost had to laugh at her dilemma. Jane Elizabeth Stratford Alexander, the rock of propriety who was the pride of her family and church, had finally slipped from the altar of her exalted virtue. Nor was it a little slip. She had plummeted. Worst of all, she couldn't say that if she were given a second chance, she would act at all differently. Exhausted and worn as she'd been, Jane had known exactly what she was doing when she surrendered herself to Matthew Hawkins.

Closing her eyes, Jane sought inside herself for the woman she had been the night before. The wanton creature was there, Jane knew, and a nudge from Hawk would surely wake her again.

"Good morning, slugabed. Or should I say good afternoon?"

Jane's heart jumped at the sound of Hawk's cheerful voice. She stared resolutely out the window, unable to face him, unprepared for what he might say. "How is Gideon?" she asked lamely.

"Well enough to be eating his way through Borst's larder," Hawk told her with a laugh. "And how are you?"

His hand fell gently on her shoulder, and a warmth that rivaled the sunlight spread through her traitorous body. "I'm well," she assured him.

He turned her around. The look in his eyes made Jane's breath catch in her throat. It was the look of a man who has possessed a woman and now considers that woman his own. She had never seen such a thing before, but her woman's instinct recognized it for what it was.

"You should never wear this." He untied the ribbons beneath her chin and removed her coif. "I like the way the sunlight glistens on your hair. Why would you hide such beauty?"

"I've told you before that I'm a plain woman. That is my choice." Her voice had a sharper edge than she intended.

"My dear," Hawk said cheerfully, "were you to drape yourself in a black sack from head to toe, you still would not be plain, choice or not. I fear you were designed to be beautiful—from head to toe."

A blush stained her cheeks as she took the coif from his hands and placed it back upon her head. Hawk's large hands captured hers before she could tie the ribbons. "I see your Puritan conscience has been awakened by the sunlight."

She tried to turn away, but he held her fast.

"Jane. My beautiful, virtuous Jane. Do you really think such happiness as we shared last night could be sin?"

She gathered the courage to meet his challenging gaze, but she had no answer either for him or herself.

"My love, nothing is as absolute as the clergy make it, whether they be of your church, or mine, or the Pope himself. Think of all the godly men in the Bible who not only had more than one wife, but numerous concubines. Were those women all sinners? Were their men sinners? God didn't seem to think so then."

Jane felt herself close to tears, as much for the gentleness of Hawk's voice as her own self-condemnation. "Matthew, that was long ago in a different land. This is now, here."

She didn't resist as he brought her captured hands against his chest and held them there.

"I've been taught all my life that the pleasures we took should be shared only between those bound together before God," she continued. "Otherwise they are corrupt and lead to damnation."

Hawk shook his head. "If that is true, then God will have very little company in heaven."

She smiled wryly. "Strait is the gate . . . and few there be who find it."

"Dammit!" He released her hands as she drew them back. "I'm sorry. I'm not in the mood for Bible quotations."

Jane turned away and stared once more out the window. "The fault is mostly mine. I am the one who violated my conscience."

"And I suppose you think I have no conscience to violate."

"That's not what I think," she denied calmly.

"The responsibility is mine. I violated my oath to you, if not my conscience. I seduced you even though you made it plain many times you wanted no part of me."

She turned to face him, a self-deprecating smile gentling the sorrow of her expression. "If I remember correctly, I made it very plain last night that I wanted every part of you."

Hawk chuckled, his vexation diffused. "Always my honest Jane. You cannot spare even yourself the rigor of your honesty."

"Why should I?" she asked. "You didn't force me, Matthew, or even lure me to a destination I didn't know." That last was not strictly true, Jane acknowledged to herself. Their destination had been quite different from what she imagined, and all the moralizing of her conscience could not make her sorry she had followed him there.

"Did you know where we were going, Jane?"

He read her mind much too easily. "I was not a maiden," she said obliquely. "I knew what I was about."

"Not a maiden," Hawk repeated. "But certainly a virtuous woman. No man with pretentions to being a gentleman goes about debauching virtuous women—tarnishing the halos of angels."

"I'm surely not an angel, Matthew, as you should well know. And I have my doubts about your being a gentleman."

He laughed. "I see you've recovered your sharp tongue."

She acknowledged the barb with a smile. " 'Tis one thing I fear I will never lose, no matter what else I am stripped of."

Hawk suddenly grew serious. "You obviously believe you've been stripped of your honor."

Jane's smile faded.

"My dear little Puritan Jane, since I can't convince you of your innocence, perhaps I can restore some of what I took from you by offering marriage."

Jane's heart nearly stopped, then proceeded to race at an alarming rate. "You jest."

"Not at all."

" 'Tis impossible."

He raised a devilish brow. " 'It is better to marry than to burn.' You see, my love, I also can quote the Bible to my advantage."

"No." Jane hid her flaming cheeks with her hands. "Such a thing would be wrong. Very wrong."

"Tsk, tsk." His voice was confident now, the voice of a conqueror who realizes victory is near. "If you will but listen to that overactive conscience of yours, it would tell you that you have no choice. Especially since we're going to be together for an unknown length of time, and I have no such honorable intentions of denying myself the pleasure of bedding you whenever the opportunity arises. My sweet lady, I fear you are addicting. Once tasted . . ."

He advanced upon her. She backed away, her eyes wide, until the wall was at her back.

"Angel you may be," he said softly, "but I flatter myself that you cannot long resist the power of my seduction. I think that has already been well demonstrated."

He demonstrated again, caging her in his arms and kissing her with a gentle fervor that set her senses spinning. His tongue demanded response, and Jane obeyed, surrendering to his invasion and melting against him as her blood turned to warm, sweet syrup. She couldn't fight herself and him as well. When he released her, she clung to him until the world stopped spinning. His own breathing was as rapid as her own, she noted, and the hands that circled her waist held a tension that vibrated through both their bodies.

"This is wrong," she said to herself as much as Hawk. "Marriage is for people from similar backgrounds with similar beliefs. Marriage is for those who think alike, want the same things—"

"And for all others whom a careless fate throws together," Hawk added, a hint of irony in his voice. "Think on the bright side, my love. Now Gideon will truly be your son."

They were married that evening by a Calvinist clergyman who rode seven miles for the privilege of presiding at the union of the English Earl of Chester and his bride. In attendance were Ned, Borst, Katarina, Gideon, and a sprinkling of curious inn guests. Ned gloated and told the groom in no uncertain terms that he had seen the worth in Jane Alexander long before Hawk had removed his own blinders. "About time ye gave the lass 'er due," Ned complained happily. "Took long enough about it, ye did!"

Gideon received news of the impending nuptials with equal amounts of confusion and joy. He'd had the whole day to think about Master Hawkins's pulling him out of the bog, he told Jane, and had decided that the man was acceptable father material after all. "But I want to call him Hawk, as Ned does," he informed Jane as she waited in her room for the arrival of the clergyman. "Do you think he would mind?"

"I think he would rather you call him Father," Jane said gently. "But why don't you ask him?"

"I suppose I could. Will you really be my mother when you marry Master Hawkins? Is that why you're going to wed him?"

"No, Gideon." Jane couldn't lie, even then. "That's not why I'm marrying him. But becoming your mother is certainly very important to me."

"Shall I call you Mother, or Aunt Jane?"

"Which would you prefer?"

"I want to call you Mother."

Jane's voice caught. "Then Mother it shall be."

Gideon accepted her hug and bounced out of the room in search of Ned, who would surely want to know that Gideon had a new mother. Even his twisted ankle couldn't restrain him.

The clergyman arrived. Ned, in the absence of Jane's father, escorted her down to the taproom. Katarina hugged the bride and wept for the romance of it all. Borst gave

Hawk a hearty clap on the shoulder that might have knocked a smaller man from his feet, and Gideon handed Jane a small wreath of evergreens to put on her head.

"There ain't no flowers," he explained dolefully.

"These are beautiful," Jane assured him.

She stood beside Hawk while the clergyman read the ceremony from his book, feeling as though she had wandered into a dream from which she might wake at any moment. The setting was not right for a wedding, the language the clergyman spoke was foreign, and the man beside her was the furthest thing possible from her notion of a proper husband. Oddly enough, though, she couldn't decide if she was having a dream or a nightmare, or if she wanted to wake at all. One part of her knew this marriage was a dreadful mistake. Another part knew that even without the wedding, she would never be free of Matthew Hawkins. He had become too entwined in her heart.

Hawk could feel Jane's tension as the clergyman droned on. He wondered just where he'd found the stupid nobility that had prodded him to propose—not only to propose but to talk a reluctant Jane into accepting his proposal. He'd bedded any number of women without wedding them, both noble and common. Granted, Jane was different. He owed her protection and succor. But a wedding? She'd not demanded it. In fact she'd offered to take responsibility for their liaison on her own slight but square shoulders. He couldn't blame her for this mess.

On the other hand, though the last thing he needed right now was a wife, he could have done much worse than Jane Alexander. He was fond of her, respected her, and Gideon loved her dearly. She was beautiful, sensible about most things, and set him afire in bed. On objective assessment, he might come out ahead in the bargain.

Love, of course, had very little to do with his situation. Hawk was much too practical a man to be swayed by such a thing, or even admit that it existed.

In difficult English, the clergyman asked Jane if she would take Matthew Hawkins as her husband. Hawk clasped her hand and squeezed it gently. She answered in a clear, steady voice that she would. He asked Hawk the same question in Dutch, seeming relieved not to have to struggle with the unfamiliar words. Hawk answered immediately in a confident tone. He would.

The clergyman snapped his book closed, made his last pronouncement and smiled broadly. Jane assumed she had just been declared the wife of Matthew Hawkins. Hawk turned her toward him and grinned wickedly. "Welcome to my life, Jane Hawkins," he whispered against her lips right before his mouth brushed hers with a chaste kiss. Their small audience cheered.

Borst and Katarina hosted a gala celebration for their guests that night and claimed credit for themselves in the romantic match between Lord Chester and his son's pretty governess. They recounted to one and all the dramatic events that led up to the wedding, and Gideon basked in the attention that was showered upon him as the catalyst of the drama. Ned had his eye on the local village girl who had come in to help Katarina serve and clean, but he promised to keep an equally watchful eye on Gideon when Hawk retired with Jane up the stairs.

Once back in their little garret room, Jane felt like a puppet whose strings have been cut. The nervous energy that had kept her going all day suddenly left. She leaned on the window frame and stared out into the night. "We are married," she said softly to herself. "I don't believe it."

"We are married," Hawk confirmed. He came up behind

her and began to massage her tired shoulders. "Well you may believe it."

"I don't feel married," she commented. "I couldn't understand a word that little man said."

"You'll feel very married before the night is out. I promise."

The desire that flared in his voice was unmistakable. Jane thought of the night ahead with misgivings. She chastised herself for sinful worldliness as she recognized her own fear that the magic that had passed between them the night before would never come again. Men were not so passionate with their wedded wives, and wives were certainly expected to be modest with their husbands. She turned to him.

"Matthew," she began, her voice full of doubt, "the things we did last night—surely decent married people do not . . . do not . . ."

He laughed and began to work at the laces of her bodice. "That and more, my love. I assure you."

"My husband never—"

"*I* am your husband, Jane Hawkins. And I will do with my wife whatever I please." He raised one brow in a devilish arch. "And whatever pleases her, as well."

"But proper behavior between married people—"

"There is no proper behavior between married people," he insisted. "Every square inch of you is mine." He removed her bodice, extracting her arms from the sleeves as though she were a child. His hand cupped one of her breasts and teased the nipple through her thin chemise. "This is mine." He moved to the other breast. "And this is mine. And this . . ."

He covered her mouth with his, demanded gently that

she open to his caress. With one hand he held her, with the other he began to strip off his own clothing.

"I ache for you, Jane," he whispered against her lips. "I've ached for hours. It's a wonder these poor breeches didn't burst before Borst finished his toasting."

"Matthew!"

"It's the truth. But now I've all night to soothe that ache."

Hastily and expertly he removed her skirt, petticoats, corset, and stockings. When he reached for the lacings on his breeches Jane could see that he'd told nothing less than the truth.

"Come here, Jane," he said with a smile. "I want to make love to my wife."

Weak with desire herself, awed at the sight of him standing boldly naked and aroused before her, she walked into his arms. His hands, warm, hard, and sure, traveled down her back to grasp her buttocks and press her close. His fingers dipped into the cleft between her legs.

"Ah," he sighed in an oddly tense voice. "You're wet for me, Jane."

She buried her face against his chest, embarrassed at her own arousal. Her husband—her *first* husband—had surely never even thought about such mortifyingly intimate details.

"Plenty of time for the bed later." He sat upon the chair and pulled her down with her legs straddling his body. Before Jane knew what was happening he was inside her, thrusting his hips up to plunge deeper and uttering a low growl of satisfaction.

She cried out first in alarm, then her cries became much different in nature as he held her tightly to him and thrust again and again. Her senses whirled in a dizzying spiral, like flames dancing in a chaotic wind. She moved with him, harmonizing with his motion, his hands grasping her hips to help her keep the ancient rhythm. But she needed little help. She was no longer a separate being, but moved to his command.

Hawk's climax came rapidly. Jane felt herself explode around him, her world going black except for—almost seen —the glowing embers of his offering as it burned its way inside her. She collapsed against him, as spent as he, and felt his chuckle tickle her ear.

"Can you take a lifetime of this, my love?"

She couldn't answer. His arms shifted. Their position suddenly seemed awkward. As he slid from her body, he rose and managed to lift her in his arms.

"To bed," he told her.

"To sleep." She inhaled the musky warmth of their love-making.

"Not for long, my love. Not for long. The wolf still hungers."

The lamb seemed not at all afraid, nuzzling against him as he sank with her upon the mattress. Hawk felt sleep claim her and then come for him as well. He drifted off, more at peace than he had been in years, wondering at how hard it was to hold on to his doubts while holding Jane in his arms.

18

Antwerp was a patient recovering from a near-fatal disease —religion. So Master Wegg, Giddy's new tutor, informed Hawk and Jane as they stood together on the balcony overlooking the garden of their rented house in the New Town section of the city. Beyond the wall of the garden they could see the prominences of Easterling House and, farther in the distance to the south, the great bell tower and steeples of the city's patron, the Church of Our Lady.

Master Wegg was something of an expert on the misfortunes that had befallen his beloved city. During the two weeks since their arrival, while Hawk was busy with Charles's courtiers, Master Wegg had taken Jane and Gideon on numerous tours. Giddy had been interested enough to be on his best behavior, and Jane had thought the city beautiful and fascinating, in spite of Master Wegg's laments that this queen of all European cities had been murdered during the religious wars. Antwerp, he told her, was the center of resistance to the Spaniards during the last century. Fifty years ago the city had been a busy center of commerce, thronged by scholars, artists, musicians, merchants, home to the great printing house of Plantin. Goods from all over the world had landed on the docks of the Scheldt River, which gave Antwerp access to the sea, and left by way of the great canal that connected Antwerp to Brussels and the rest of Europe. The Spaniards ended all that when they sacked the city and blocked the Scheldt. Violence between Catholics and Protestants had destroyed any remnants of the great center of art and commerce, leaving the city in the throes of deadly depression.

"We are rebuilding now," the tutor had told Jane one afternoon as they viewed the massive edifice of the Duke of Alva's castle, which had been torn down, rebuilt, then pulled down again during the recurring violence. "But Antwerp will never be what it once was. Wars kill cities, you see, as well as people."

"Your city is still very beautiful," Jane commented. She was amazed at the trees to be found lining almost every street. Unlike London, most of the streets were paved, and the homes that lined the streets were solidly built of brick with tile roofs and ornamental wooden porticoes. The numerous canals that interlaced throughout the city fascinated her. Antwerp boasted seventy-four bridges, Master Wegg told her, including the structures that crossed the moat outside the city wall.

Master Wegg was right about the city's lack in vigor, however. The marketplaces and docks were nearly empty of commerce, and not many people were seen on the streets. But Jane could picture what Antwerp had been like in the city's heydey. From Master Wegg's imaginative descriptions she could almost hear the calls of the vendors in the marketplaces, the raucous shouts of the stevedores unloading the ships that traveled the Scheldt from the sea, the endless tolling of church bells. What a crime that men had destroyed themselves and their city fighting over a God Who loved peace.

"Antwerp is an interesting city," Hawk commented as

they came in from the balcony to what Jane called the sun room. "I regret that I don't have the time learn more of it."

"Your wife and son have been most gratifyingly attentive on our tours, Lord Chester."

"I hope Gideon has been as attentive to his other lessons."

"He is an extremely bright and winning child, my lord."

"He also can be a little imp of the Devil." Over Master Wegg's shoulder Hawk slanted a devilish brow at Jane, and she smiled. If Gideon was an imp of the Devil, there was no doubt about the Devil in his sire. "Speaking of the little imp," Hawk continued, "I believe he awaits you in the library."

The tutor brightened. "Today we study the great Roman orators," he told them. Master Gideon's Latin is improving nicely."

"Glad to hear it. My lady and I will be going out for a few hours, so I hope you can keep him occupied until we return."

"We're going out?" Jane asked after the tutor had left to join Gideon. "I was hoping to have some peaceful time alone with you at home. You are here so seldom."

"You'll enjoy this even more. I promise. Get your cloak like a good girl."

"I've been meaning to talk to you about Master Wegg," Jane said as they descended to the main floor.

"Don't you like him?"

"Oh, yes. Very much. But he is very . . . worldly, don't you think? A boy with Gideon's spirit needs to learn more of . . . of . . ."

"Virtue and righteousness," he finished for her, smiling wryly. "My dear, what you call worldly is commonly thought upon as sophistication. And what Gideon needs to know of virtue and righteousness he can learn from you."

Jane winced, but taking offense at Hawk's words was difficult when they were accompanied by the light she saw in his eyes. He leaned over and pecked at her lips, a fond gesture that quickly escalated into a fierce and possessive kiss.

"You're right," he breathed when he released her. "I've been neglecting you. I think we can find several hours this evening to remedy that."

Hawk's planned outing was to an exclusive modiste. When he stopped their carriage in front of Madame Fourier's shop and announced that his wife needed a new wardrobe, Jane objected strongly.

"What I have will do very nicely. You needn't be spending your money on such frivolities."

"May I remind you we have an audience with the King in two days. Do you intend to go in your festive gray wool? 'Twould draw all eyes to you, a countess dressed like a governess."

Jane suffered a pang of resentment. She did not consider herself a countess, nor did she consider Charles a king. Though he had been crowned in Scotland, that hardly counted; he certainly had not been crowned in England. But to say as much to Hawk would only bring on a useless argument, for Charles's cause had become her husband's life, as if helping to restore the monarchy would settle his account with the Puritans he hated.

"I suppose one or two things for occasions that I can't avoid."

One or two things was not what Hawk had in mind, however. The modiste was delighted and Jane dismayed by the number of fashionable gowns, petticoats, shoes, cloaks, hats, gloves, and even intimate wear that he ordered.

"I have no need for all of this!" she insisted.

Hawk merely smiled. "Indulge me, my love. I've never had a woman so beautiful to spend money upon."

He insisted on supervising the fitting himself, and Jane had to admit that his taste was impeccable. In all honesty she conceded that the bright colors were fetching to the eye, and the fine undergarments were very much softer than the coarse cotton she had always worn.

"The colors are very fetching," Hawk agreed with a sparkle in his eye. "But not half as fetching as you are."

Madame Fourier had gone to fetch more patterns, and Hawk was quick to take advantage of the modiste's absence in exploiting Jane's half-dressed disarray. He backed her against a wall and kissed her soundly while he pressed against her and left no doubt as to his need.

"Hawk! Don't! What if—"

He stopped her objection with another kiss.

"You're mad!" she said as he came up for breath.

"Not mad. Merely frustrated. You're right. We should have stayed home and gone to bed."

"That's not what I meant by spending peaceful time at home!"

Hawked grinned all too knowingly. "Yes, it was. Don't fret, my love. Even angels are permitted to lust after their husbands."

If Madame Fourier took note of Jane's rosy blush when she returned, she didn't speak of it. After all, Madame was French.

When they returned to the house in New Town, Hawk told the housekeeper that the countess and he required privacy and pulled Jane up to their third-story bedchamber.

"Matthew!" Jane admonished halfheartedly. "In broad daylight?"

"Anytime I can get you alone."

He confirmed his words by expertly ridding her of the burden of her clothing, then doing the same for himself. For all Jane's pious objections she was as eager as he. No preliminaries were needed, and when Hawk eased her down upon their bed and found her wet and ready to receive him, he plunged home with an eagerness that bordered on desperation. "Oh, God!" he moaned. "It's been too long."

Jane paid no mind to his blasphemy as she closed her eyes and rocked on the waves of their passion. Those moments when Hawk was inside her were the only times when she felt completely sane. She welcomed his driving thrusts with quiet moans of ecstasy, and would have cried out in joy at the splendor of their climax had Hawk not clamped a discreet hand over her mouth.

"Would you have the staff think I beat you?" he asked with a wicked twinkle in his eye once they had both resumed a semblance of normal breathing.

"You are absolutely corrupting me," she retorted, but her smile took the sting from the words.

"A little corruption won't hurt you, my love," he said teasingly. "As long as you're only corrupt with me." Suddenly he sobered. "It's fortunate you're a married woman, Lady Chester, or Charles would be after you in a trice once he saw you. He might anyway."

"Don't be ridiculous," Jane admonished him.

"You are much too innocent for your own good." He shifted his weight off her and appreciatively ran a hand over her breast, lingering there while his thumb played with her nipple. "Charles is notorious with women. You are to be cautious around him."

"I am cautious around all men. I should have been more cautious around you."

He smiled down at her. His hand parted her legs and dipped into the valley between. "Obviously. You see what can happen?"

She closed her eyes as her breath caught.

"Neither will Charles be happy to learn you are the widow of a man who ranked high in the army that drove him from his country and executed his father. You are not to tell him you are a Puritan, nor tell him of your past."

She opened her eyes. His hand had stopped its caress and his face was grimly serious. "Matthew, you can't ask me to lie. Is what I am so distasteful to you?"

"What you are is goodness itself, my love. But a king—even a dispossessed one—is a powerful man, and sometimes dishonesty is the price of survival in this world."

He tried to ease the hurt he'd dealt with a kiss. The kiss led to much more as he rolled atop her and pressed his thigh between her legs in a sensuous, teasing caress. But even as her senses fled before the storm of desire, Jane had a brief thought for the labyrinth of deceit and falsehood into which she was rapidly falling. One of her father's stern sermons painted religion as a rock to which the righteous cling in a stormy sea of unhappiness and sin. For a brief, panicky moment she pictured herself swept free of that rock and sinking deeper into the dreaded chaotic flood.

Then Hawk lifted her to meet his thrust as he plunged into her body. She clung to him, half in passion, half in desperation. He was her rock. He was her anchor. The world could not engulf her as long as he defended her.

Flawed champion he might be, but he was still stronger than she.

February 27, 1659—Antwerp
My dearest Sarah,

I hope my last letter did not distress you overmuch. I pray that you will reply soon, even if in anger, for my greatest fear is that you so despise me now that you have cut me off completely from your affection. I do not expect you to understand what I did. I myself scarcely understand my behavior. My only hope is that proving a good wife to Matthew Hawkins will somehow expiate my foolishness.

You and Geoffrey and your children are constantly in my mind. The social whirl among Charles's courtiers is never-ending, and Matthew and I see a great number of people. None of them, however, can truly be called friends, and with none can I share the common spiritual and intellectual ground that you and I walked together so often. Matthew has been very kind to me, but he is frequently absent on business for Charles. Sometimes he travels with the Prince, who with his chief courtiers bounces between Antwerp, Brussels, Bruges, and Ghent. Though Matthew tells me little, I believe he also plays the diplomat for Charles with the House of Orange in Holland and also with the governments of Flanders and Spain. I suspect that his activities put him in some danger, and I am almost afraid to question him too closely for fear of learning something I would rather not know.

Matthew and I were granted quite a long audience with Charles. Everyone here, of course, refers to the exiled Prince as King of England, even considering that is a fact far from accomplished. Much to my surprise the

Prince showed every sign of poverty—his courtiers for the most part dress more grandly than he, though he is quite a handsome man and has a regal bearing fit for any king, I must admit. Charles is rumored (here, dear sister, as well as in England) to be a wastrel and a rake. Nevertheless, he impressed me as an intelligent man who is skilled in manipulating others. I believe those in England who would keep him from his father's throne underestimate the Prince. Cynical and debauched he may be, but also determined and bitter.

On a more cheerful subject, Gideon is thriving. He is forging a respectful and affectionate relationship with his father that I suspect is tinged with hero-worship. There were times on the trip from England that I thought father and son would never be anything but antagonists. Matthew was able to find Gideon an excellent tutor, a very likable and intelligent young man whom Giddy adores. In this Spanish-dominated land, we were very lucky to find a tutor who is not a papist. Matthew himself is teaching his son swordsmanship, and his skill exceeds that of many of the instructors in the city, I suspect. I hope that skill is sufficient to keep him safe on the missions he undertakes for Charles. I cannot tell you how strange it feels—after so many years thinking of royalists as our enemy—suddenly wishing them success, at least where my husband is involved.

I wish you could see the lovely house we have rented in the New Town section of Antwerp. Like many houses in the city, it is built all of brick with a beautiful tile roof. Though it has very narrow hallways and steep stairs to the three levels, it is a very cheerful place. The ceilings are painted with most improbable pastoral scenes, the walls are hung with beautiful tapestries, and windows of colored glass admit a rainbow of color. With your love of bright colors, you would very much like this place, I believe.

I wish I knew when we will be together again, dear Sarah. You will scarcely recognize me, I think. On Matthew's insistence, I dress in the fashion of the other ladies in our little group of English exiles, though I am not yet so corrupted that I spend the hours devoted to vanity which many of the ladies do. You will laugh to hear about the remedies they use to combat nature—dog urine as a beautifier for the skin, and the fumes of powdered myrrh sprinkled with white wine and heated on an iron plate to smooth wrinkles. And, of course, any blemish which cannot be removed by such odious means is covered with an elaborate patch. One royalist lady of my slight acquaintance appeared with a patch fashioned after a horse and carriage. It was very much admired by the other ladies.

Though I do not yet stoop to such artifices, I admit to discovering within myself a love for beautiful clothes and laughter. My true nature, I fear, is not very sober or proper, and I'm sure I don't approve of the change in myself. Yet I admit to being happy, despite the circumstances. Is there sin in that?

I have written my late husband's solicitor in London and asked him to arrange for the house on Great Queen Street to be closed, as I have no idea when I may return. Until I do return, dear sister, please let me know that I am still in your heart, as you and your family are in mine.

Your loving sister—

The year rolled on into spring. The exiled Earl of Chester's household rounded out into a butler, housekeeper, cook, scullery maid, gardener, and groom. When Jane questioned her husband on how they were to finance such luxury, he told her with an unrepentant grin that not all of his ill-gotten gains had gone into Charles's pockets, besides which he still held lands in Flanders and France that Cromwell had been unable to touch, and the income from those lands was considerable.

"Did you think you married into poverty, my love?" Hawk asked in a joking tone.

"Obviously I had no idea what I was marrying into," Jane said doubtfully.

"You'll get use to it," he told her, grinning. "Someday you might even get used to me."

Ned held a unique position in the household, neither servant nor family, and was very content with that, he told them. He came and went, bullied the servants, flirted outrageously with the cook and scullery maid, and generally made a nuisance of himself. Sometimes they didn't see him for days, but when Hawk was absent on one of his trips for Charles, Ned always stayed close by to keep a watchful eye on Jane and Gideon. Jane was still not quite sure whether the little man was protector or gaoler.

Hawk's trips away from Antwerp were short but frequent and grew more frequent as the year grew older. When he was gone, Gideon complained sharply of his absence, sulked, and drove both Jane and Master Wegg to distraction. All Jane's Puritan teachings of the last three years fell by the wayside as the boy imitated his cavalier father in dress, speech, mannerisms, and occasional arrogance. Hawk's talent for mischief he had always shared.

Jane battled pangs of jealousy as she saw Giddy's attachment drift from her to his father. Such a change was right and natural, she scolded herself, but she couldn't help feeling more and more isolated in a world that wasn't hers. She was truly content only when she was in Hawk's embrace. When her husband made love to her, possessed her with his splendid body, or even lay with her in his strong arms, then Jane's world sailed on an even keel in spite of the storms gathering around her. Even in those moments, however, she sometimes felt walled off from a part of him —some driving, intense, frightening part she didn't understand and never had. Nor did she have hopes that she ever would.

In May, with spring in full bloom, the Earl of Chester and his countess hosted a small social gathering in their garden. Hawk assured Jane the affair would be small, but she still panicked at the knowledge that Charles and his chief courtiers would be attending.

"I have no experience as a hostess!" she objected. "I know the lack does not befit the wife of a man in your position, but there it is."

"You'll do fine." Hawk gave her a fond kiss on the cheek, as a parent might comfort a child, Jane thought sourly. "Charles is in no position to quibble about the quality of food or entertainment. The way things are going, with the Duke of Buckingham slandering his character in England and his cavaliers behaving like spoiled children all over Europe, Charles will be grateful simply to see some friendly faces."

Nevertheless, Jane bustled from kitchen to garden to freshly cleaned guest rooms in a rare panic hours before her guests arrived. She felt entirely inadequate to the task assigned her, and hated the feeling. Rarely in her life had she felt inadequate to anything.

Ned lounged in the kitchen, sampling the delicacies the cook had prepared for the exalted company and eyeing the cook as if she herself were part of the feast. He regarded Jane's comings and goings with wry amusement.

" 'Old on to yer feathers," he advised her as she checked the menu for the third time in the same hour. He grinned at the cook, a doe-eyed, softly rounded young woman frequently prone to fits of giggling whenever Ned was near. "Lovely Greta 'ere 'as everything under 'er thumb. She won't let ye down, mistress."

Greta giggled and blushed on cue.

"Yes, of course." Jane tried to sound confident.

"An' that butler fellow Stanworth. Couldn't no one be more official looking than 'im. 'E'll impress the pants offa the King and 'is gents."

Jane sighed and sank down onto a stool. "I don't think I even care."

Ned chuckled. "Greta, me love, bring yer mistress a sip o' that good wine. I think she needs it."

The gathering was a success in spite of Jane's worries. Charles was a gracious guest who eschewed formality and had little use for the reverential treatment that kings and aspiring kings usually require. He was quieter and more sober than his courtiers, Jane noted to his credit, and possessed a charm that he could turn on and off at will. Against her will she found herself liking him and pitying him at the same time.

"Very fine place you have here," Charles complimented her, strolling to where she stood under a linden tree watching over the specially hired staff that Stanworth had assembled to serve the guests. "You're a lovely hostess, my lady."

"Thank you, Your . . . Majesty."

The would-be King of England gave her a sharp look at

her unintentional hesitation over his title. Then he smiled disarmingly. "Damned if a mystery doesn't intrigue me, especially where a beautiful woman's concerned. Can't get that husband of yours to say where he found you, you know." His mouth quirked in a self-deprecating grin. "No doubt he wishes to protect your sisters at home from my well-known lecherous clutches—if they are as beautiful as you."

Jane felt Hawk's gaze from across the room and remembered his warning about the King's wandering eye.

"My only sister is married with five children, Your Majesty, and though she is dear to me, I doubt you would find her to your taste."

"Ho!" Charles declared. "An honest woman." He raised his glass to toast her. "I like you, my lady. You do not simper and require the flattery that most females cannot live without. Neither do you indulge in useless flattery, even to your King." He gave her a shrewd look. "If I guess correctly—and I usually do with women—I would say you do not like me much."

Jane was curious at her own lack of fear. "Your guess is wrong, sire. I think I do like you, though I rather surprise myself that I do."

Charles smiled slowly. "I perceive that such words from your lovely mouth, my Lady Chester, are worth a hundred compliments from mouths less straightforward. I hope your husband appreciates the treasure he has in his wife."

For a moment Jane detected genuine sadness through Charles's cynical facade, and she remembered that he'd recently been refused the hand of Princess Henriette Catherine of Orange. She wondered if he loved the Princess, then chided herself for naïveté. In Charles's world—even in Hawk's—husbands seldom loved their wives, and if they did, the affection was a fortunate happenstance which came after the marriage, not before.

Suddenly the King was all joviality again. "I trust we will see you and your good husband at the tennis outing that Viscount Henley is planning next month."

"I'm sure we will be there, Your Majesty."

"Splendid. Splendid."

As the King drifted away, Jane started into the house to see that Stanworth replenished the rapidly dwindling supply of wine, but she stopped as she spotted Hawk across the garden. The Countess of Woodford, Barbara Cressman, was clinging to his arm and any other part of him she could reach. Hawk looked not at all perturbed.

Ned materialized beside Jane, dressed in the same livery as the servants. "Don't mind that." His eyes followed her distressed gaze. "Fer all 'er fancy trappin's, she's a bigger slut than those what sells themselves in Southwark's stews. 'Awk's just being . . . diplo . . ."

"Diplomatic?"

"Right."

"Of course he is." Jane took a deep breath to combat the pain. The bright spring day suddenly seemed to grow cold.

"Ned, would you please find Stanworth and ask him to bring up more wine?"

"Now there's a task that's next to me 'eart."

Jane managed to give him a smile, but apparently her effort was not quite convincing.

"You all right, mistress?"

"I'm fine," Jane answered. "Off with you or the guests will be thirsty."

Only when he was gone did her eyes turn back to where Hawk and the countess had stood. They were nowhere to be seen. Jane frowned thoughtfully, but Hugh Cressman's voice intruded upon her contemplation.

"I see you've made a favorable impression on the King, Lady Chester."

Jane suppressed a shudder. She had met the fair-haired, florid Earl of Woodford on several previous occasions. He and his sultry countess were always present in the social whirl that centered on the King. "You would have to ask him," Jane replied with cool courtesy.

Woodford smiled slowly. "I would much rather talk with you."

More than once Jane had felt his pale blue eyes roving over her as though he were undressing her garment by garment. The fact that he did the same to any attractive woman made her feel no better. Tall and almost ascetically thin, he reminded her of nothing so much as a green stick-like insect she sometimes found on leaves in the garden—a species she particularly disliked. She wondered if he knew his wife was making a spectacle of herself hanging on Matthew Hawkins—or if he cared.

"I am quite busy at the moment, my lord. If you would excuse me."

"I'm not sure I will." His breath stank of strong spirits, his usually taut mouth was slack and rather moist. Jane guessed that a goodly part of their wine had disappeared down his throat. "Come now, my lady. You have servants to take care of your guests. Surely you deserve some time for . . . yourself."

Lord Woodford had maneuvered them behind a hedge like the expert that he was. He put his hand on her arm, his thumb blatantly brushing against her breast. Jane backed away and felt the prick of the hedge at her back.

"My lord! I insist that you behave or I shall call for assistance."

He tsked disparagingly. "Such beauty should not be wasted in prudery, my dear. One would think you were a Puritan." His hand slipped down to her waist and was joined by the other. Jane was ready to scream for help, no matter the humiliation and indignity of being found in such a situation, when the amorous earl was abruptly jerked off his feet.

"Trespassing on a man's property can sometimes result in distressing consequences, my lord." For a tense moment, Hawk dangled the startled earl with his jewel-encrusted shoes a few inches off the ground. Then he dropped him. Lord Woodford landed on his feet with very little grace. His arms flailed as he attempted to keep his balance.

"Matthew!" Jane cried.

"Are you hurt?"

"No." She retreated from the menace she saw in his expression, but his face softened as he reached out and touched her cheek. The anger was not for her. "Then get you gone, wife, and see to our guests."

She dared to glance toward Woodford, who had regained his balance and was regarding Hawk with alarm and indignation alternating in his expression, as if the man couldn't decide which reaction was appropriate.

"Matthew . . ." Jane sensed the violence so close to the limit of Hawk's control. Woodford was a powerful man, a favorite of Charles's. This wasn't Southwark where Hawk was king and violence was a way of life.

"Do as I say, Jane. His lordship and I need to have a private conversation."

Reluctantly, Jane left.

The Earl of Woodford was not seen again at that particular gathering, and friends of the earl who saw him in the next few days reported that the fellow sported a black eye and several nasty bruises from a riding accident, although just how one got a black eye from falling off a horse they couldn't say.

As spring rolled into summer, Jane rapidly grew tired of the constant cavalier amusements—horse racing, bird shooting, cockfighting, dancing, drinking, and by night games of whist, honours, French ruff, one-and-twenty, backgammon, and less innocent entertainments of flirting and private assignations to which husbands, wives, and all others seemed to turn a blind eye. She begged off many of the social engagements to stay home with Gideon, especially at times when Hawk was gone and couldn't accompany her. Jane, Gideon, Ned, and Master Wegg enjoyed quieter entertainments. They explored the grounds of Alva's castle, stood in awe at the huge Church of Our Lady, rode the canals in sturdy little boats paddled by Ned or Master Wegg, and walked along the white stone city wall with its terraced top of red brick. Jane found the people of Antwerp—conservative Spanish aristocrats, merchants, tradesmen, and workers—papists though most of them were, preferable to her own raucous countrymen who were guests here.

She did attend Viscount Henley's tennis outing, since she had promised the King. Being home, Hawk accompanied her, but Charles snatched him away for a conference almost the minute they arrived at the great roofed-over courtyard that Henley, who was quite well fixed, had built particularly to suit Charles's liking for the game of tennis.

Jane looked around and spotted Lord Woodford in the

company of his wife, for a change. His eyes met hers in a glance that was both challenging and resentful before his wife demanded his attention by tapping her fan upon his arm. Jane didn't understand why the man chased after every female who crossed his path. The countess alone seemed more than he could handle in the way of women.

Jane joined a bevy of ladies who were chatting around a table laid with little cakes, sweet tarts, custards, fresh fruit, and comfits. They bade her welcome, but the greetings rang with a sour note of feigned affection. In spite of her fashionable clothing and titled husband, in spite of her obedient silence about religion and politics, she was an outsider, and the ladies of Charles's exiled court sensed it even if the men didn't.

Jane took a pear and listened absently to the small talk that eddied around her. This was her husband's world, a world of plots and licentiousness. The ladies floated through the crowd with their low-cut bodices, ridiculous patches, ceruse-painted faces, and lips rouged with Spanish paper; the men prowled like wolves, plotting and maneuvering for power, worldly pleasure, empty honors, and status. How could anyone find happiness and peace in such a world? Suddenly Jane felt very lonely.

"My dear, don't look so low. Surely nothing is that bad."

Jane turned toward the unexpected voice. The widowed viscountess who had spoken was a lady she had seen but never formally met. Jane knew Lady Kesterling by reputation, for she was one of Charles's more notorious lovers. Well into her thirties, she nevertheless retained a youthful, elegant, unartificial beauty which made it easy for Jane to believe that the King was besotted with her, as rumor said.

"You should not give these harpies the satisfaction of your obvious distress, my dear Lady Chester. It only encourages them." The viscountess regarded Jane with a spark of sympathy in her eyes.

"I beg your pardon?"

"In our circle rumors always fly. A man has but to bid a lady good morning and the gossips will have him bedding her in no time." She inclined her head toward the gaggle of ladies around the table, who were laughing among themselves. "Just because rumors link your husband with the Countess of Woodford is no reason to be so down in the mouth."

"Oh!" Jane hadn't heard any such rumors, but then she'd been absent from many of the social gatherings where such vicious tales circulated. She remembered with a sudden painful stab how possessively the countess had clung to Hawk at the party she and Hawk had given just three weeks ago. "That . . . that isn't it at all, really. I was simply feeling a bit . . . out of sorts." Until now, Jane reflected. Now at least she had a concrete reason to be thoroughly depressed.

"Newly married as you are, I can understand why you might be upset. You doubtless still believe yourself in love with your husband. But that will pass, and you'll be much happier for it, I assure you. Besides, dear, *you* are Lord Chester's wife, after all. You have an assured place in his life, no matter how many mistresses he takes."

Jane was nonplussed. She wondered if the viscountess could really be as cynical as she seemed.

"If you want his attentions back, perhaps you should take a lover yourself. There isn't a man here who hasn't given you a second look, dear. Lord Woodford has made it clear that he finds you perfectly charming, and I can well attest that he treats his mistresses very generously."

"I . . . I . . ." How did one answer such an outrageous

statement? Jane wondered. "I thank you for your advice, my lady."

" 'Tis nothing, dear. Anyone can see you're a lamb in the wolves' den. You must be a wolf yourself, you know, or get served up for dinner."

The viscountess drifted on, elegant, sophisticated, bantering, and smiling as she went. Jane felt a tug of sympathy for the woman. Only a very bruised heart, she decided, could produce such cynicism. She wondered if being long in the company she now kept would give her a similar attitude.

She looked around for Hawk. He was nowhere to be found—still with Charles, Jane assured herself. Barbara Cressman was also nowhere to be found, and Lord Woodford was looking at Jane with hungry eyes.

Jane suddenly was hit with a longing so powerful that she had to fight the tears that welled in her eyes. She ached for her old sober, secure world, her drab but contented existence in England. Thaddeus Alexander had never given her the ecstasy that Hawk gave her, but neither had he caused such pain. Her father's rock-in-the-sea image rose again in her mind. She felt herself being swept further and further from her anchor, helpless to stop the inexorable pull of the tide. The blame lay with no one but herself, Jane acknowledged, for she was the one who had let go of the rock.

She wandered aimlessly away from the chattering ladies, unable to force herself to socialize, Lady Kesterling's words dragging like a lead weight at her heart. The burden would have to be borne, and Hawk would never hear a word of reproach from her. After all, Jane reminded herself, he had offered her marriage to save her respectability, but he had never said that he loved her. Nor had he promised to be faithful.

In fact Matthew Hawkins had promised her nothing but his name, and now Jane found that was not enough.

19

Hawk strolled through the Great Market Place opposite Antwerp's town hall and looked idly through the vendors' stalls. Ned idled along with him.

"D'ye think Greta might fancy this bauble?" Ned picked up an amber pendant from a stall selling chains, necklaces, brooches, and the like. "It matches 'er eyes."

Hawk snorted. "First I've heard of you noticing a woman's eyes. Usually you're more interested in what's below the neck."

"Some women're only worth what's below the neck. Some 're worth more."

"I think Greta would like the amber."

"Aye. That's my thought." Ned glanced at the vendor, who was busy with another customer, and a familiar crafty sparkle appeared in his eye.

Hawk lifted one brow.

"Child's play," Ned told him.

Hawk was ominously silent, and Ned squirmed.

"All right," Ned grumbled, and extracted several coins from the leather purse at his belt.

"Greta wouldn't approve of her gift being prigged," Hawk said with a smile.

"Never knew a woman yet to ask where a bauble comes

from." Ned cocked his head and drew his mouth into a wry smile. "But Greta might. Ye're right."

Hawk moved to the next stall, where silks, taffetas, and velvets were piled high. He fingered a blue silk moiré and thought of how fine the color would look on Jane. She would likely hit him if he demanded she have another gown made up. Only the day before she had claimed to feel like a peacock as he had helped her lace the bone-stiffened bodice of an emerald-green gown that had set off her hair to perfection. The heavy green skirt parted below the vee waist to display a lace-trimmed gold underskirt that matched the stomacher. Hawk had thought the ensemble quite becoming. Jane had pulled at the bodice and frowned her disapproval of the low décolletage that fetchingly emphasized the lush upper curves of her breasts. She covered the display with a fan-shaped ruff which Hawk promptly removed.

"It's already a much more modest gown than most of the ladies wear," he reminded her.

"I am not one of the other ladies!" she snapped.

"I wouldn't want you to be." He held the ruff out of her reach when she grabbed for it. "Did you not once promise to obey me, wife?"

She huffed in disgust and with a visible effort got herself in hand. "Very well." A hint of challenge still in her voice, she surrendered. As she left their chamber, she grabbed up a lacy shawl to drape across her shoulders and chest.

"A shawl looks rather strange in July!" he called after her.

She'd ignored him. Hawk smiled, remembering the look of triumph on her face.

"What're ye daydreamin' about?" Ned asked. " 'Tis a

good way to get yer pocket picked, as ye well oughta know."

Hawk merely grinned.

"Chester!" came a call from across the square. "Matthew Hawkins, Earl of Chester! I don't believe it!"

A stocky bear of a man came striding toward them, his arms outstretched in amazement. Ned reached for his knife, but Hawk stayed his companion's hand. His face broke into a huge smile. "Waltham! As I live and breathe!"

"That's what I don't believe!" Thomas Waltham laughed. "That you live and breathe! I'd heard rumors you were here, but I didn't believe my ears."

"You made good your escape at the same time I did?" Hawk asked.

"Aye—thanks to the confusion you created. I hid out for a while, then found passage to France. Lord, it's good to see you, my friend! All these years I thought you must've gotten caught. I should've known better."

"Ned, this is Sir Thomas Waltham, late of London. He's the rebellious, idealistic blackguard who sucked me into his troublesome wake and landed me in prison."

"Couldn't have happened to a more deserving man," Waltham said with a chuckle. "At least it got you off the fence and into the right camp."

"It got me several other things as well," Hawk told him, smiling wryly.

Ned and Waltham exchanged assessing looks. Waltham, in spite of the ribbon loops that trimmed his doublet and petticoat breeches, the lacy cannons that fell from his knee garters almost to the tops of his high-heeled shoes, and the delicate falls of lace at his wrists, had an air of confident strength and purpose that couldn't be missed.

"Have you come to join our little group in the Netherlands?" Hawk asked.

Waltham shook his head. "I only come and go. I'm at St. Germain with Queen Henrietta Maria." He grinned. "I am one of many who try to keep the seas smooth between Charles and his illustrious mother. By the way, Matthew, I've seen your cousin Ormonde. He believes you dead, you know. You really should tell him otherwise."

"You may tell him for me. He's always fancied my lands in France. I'm surprised he's not tried to claim them."

" 'Oo's this fellow Ormonde what's priggin' yer land?" Ned asked.

"My mother's cousin who lives in France," Hawk replied. "We've never gotten on well." At the thought of Ormonde, Hawk wondered suddenly how he ever could have thought his French cousin would be better to Gideon than Jane would be.

"St. Germain is also in France," Waltham informed Ned. "King Charles's Queen took refuge there during the civil war some years ago."

"Fancy that." Ned yawned.

"Does the Queen still plot to marry Charles to La Grande Mademoiselle?" Hawk asked Waltham.

"She will never give up hope of that one."

"La Grande Mademoiselle is the daughter of the most powerful Gaston d'Orléans," Hawk explained. "She is the Queen's niece."

"Aye," Waltham continued. "And she has enough money to buy half the kingdoms in Europe! More than enough to buy Charles an army to throw at the Roundheads. But Charles hasn't played the simpering lover well enough, and she'll have no part of him."

Ned snorted. "Charlie oughta take lessons from me. I'd

teach him 'ow ta 'andle a woman." He patted his pocket where the gift for Greta lay. "If ye're gonna jabber about yer politics, 'Awk, I'll be on me way back home." He winked. "Greta might need some 'elp with 'er cookin'."

"Interesting fellow," Waltham said as Ned left. "What did he call you? Hawk?"

"It's a long story," Hawk told him.

"That I'd wager."

They strolled together down the row of stalls, stopping occasionally to examine the merchandise.

"How is my cousin Ormonde?" Hawk inquired.

"I saw him Christmastime. He is growing old, as are we all. And how fares your young son?"

"Gideon is well."

"I'm anxious to hear the story of your escape, my friend. See what adventures I precipitated for you on that night I sought refuge in your house. I vow you should be grateful to me for stirring up the dull existence you called a life."

Hawk chuckled. "I'll have you know that I quite enjoyed what you so contemptuously name a dull existence."

"But now, my friend!" Waltham laughed. "How much more fully you live! Rumor has it that you've Charles's ear, a beauteous wife on one hand, and the ever-seductive Barbara pursuing you on the other. What man could ask for more? Power and beauty both!"

"Rumor exaggerates. No man has Charles's ear except Charles himself." Hawk flipped a coin to a fruit vendor and picked up a peach.

"And the wife?" Waltham raised an inquiring brow.

Hawk grinned, tossing the peach into the air and catching it with a flourish. "More beautiful than you could imagine."

"Ha! I knew it! You have always had the women flocking

around you like flies around honey, and now look at you! The mere mention of your wife brings passion to your voice, and still you have time for the Countess of the Bedchamber. Admirable, my friend! Admirable!"

"Countess of the Bedchamber, eh?" Hawk chuckled. "An apt title for Barbara. Though I'll wager it wasn't Hugh who awarded her the accolade."

Waltham's eyes gleamed appreciatively. "A woman generous with her favors, as you have had happy occasion to learn, I'm sure. Even the Queen knows of the beauteous Barbara and fears she will get her hooks into Charles as Lucy Walters did years ago. But now"—he grinned wickedly—"I shall tell Her Majesty that you are doing her the service of keeping the lady in question out of Charles's bed."

Irritation flashed in Hawk's eyes. "You may tell the Queen whatever you wish, but don't assign Barbara Cressman to *my* keeping. The woman's little more than a slut, and I haven't the time to give attention even to my wife, much less a mistress."

"Ho!" Waltham threw up his arms in mock alarm. "So fierce! I remember a time when the Earl of Chester did not have such a harsh opinion of such women as the lovely Barbara."

"Perhaps some of my wife has rubbed off on me. Jane has some rather . . . Puritanical notions."

"A miserable trait for a wife," Waltham said sympathetically.

"She is worth it, I assure you."

Waltham sent Hawk a tragic look from beneath lowered brows. "My dear man! You have not fallen in love with your wife! How unfortunate! How unfashionable!"

Hawk laughed, but an edge sharpened his laughter. "My

marriage was a matter of necessity, my friend. Jane is a remarkable woman who inspires in me a great deal of admiration and respect. Not love."

"And passion?" Waltham asked with meaningfully arched brows.

"That also," Hawk admitted with a smile.

"What a shame! You are in a very bad way, Matthew, for what else is true love but the wedding of passion to respect, eh?"

Hawk laughed as they walked together down the row of stalls. "You should return to France where they give such flimsy ideas credit!"

They chatted of other things—Hawk's cousin in France, Charles's campaign to win the throne, the Queen's ever present attempts to manipulate her son—but Hawk's mind drifted from the conversation. The followers of the English court flirted and fornicated with abandon. Lust was very much in fashion, love a notion left to poets and playwrights. Hawk didn't love Jane, of course. He had given her his name and his protection; he also gave her tenderness, affection, and a faithfulness few other men gave their wives—a woman as gentle as his Jane needed such things from a man. But love her?

Hawk had no time for such sentiment. He gave Jane what he could, but love carried with it the concern not only for a woman's welfare but her happiness as well. From the first he had sensed Jane's unease with this life into which he had dragged her. Something inside him wanted to comfort her and find a compromise for both of them that would not require such sacrifice of her precious principles, but he had no time for such maunderings right now. England and Charles were precariously balanced at a pivotal point that would determine their future, and his and Jane's right along with it. Hawk had a small part to play in swinging the balance in the King's favor. If he was coming down with the disease called love, the illness would have to wait on the fruition of Charles's schemes.

Not that Jane didn't deserve better of him. She put a great deal of painful effort into playing the role that he required of her, all because she believed a wife's duty to her husband was obedience—one Puritan notion that suited Hawk's purposes very well. She was a willing and passionate lover, a good mother to his child, and the only stable part of his life. The realization of his dependency almost frightened Hawk. He had come to count on Jane's quiet welcome and her imperturbable calm. She was an island of peace in a sea churning with storms, a woman who could make him forget the day's trials with a mere touch—and renew him with that current of passion that flowed beneath the surface of her prim demeanor. Even now he could feel the ache for her in his soul as well as his loins.

"Lord Chester! My lord!" Another voice interrupted Waltham's steady flow of gossip and cut across Hawk's musings as the aging Sir Victor Cotswell urged his mount through the crowded market square. He nodded to Waltham as he caught his breath. A worried frown made his face even more gray than usual. "My lord. I bring the King's summons. We've news from England."

"What news!" Hawk demanded.

"The revolution is at hand, my lord, and Charles is bound for Calais to await his victorious return to his kingdom."

"Why does it have to be you who goes?" Jane asked. She paced the floor of their bedchamber, her long cambric night rail billowing out behind her. Even the thick Turkish carpet could not completely muffle the angry rhythm of her strides. "Haven't you suffered enough already from your connection to Charles?"

"I'm not the only man going," Hawk told her patiently. "Every cavalier who can hold a sword is headed to England."

"But 'tis you whom Charles ordered to organize the effort, you who will be out in front when your little band rides to meet Parliament's Colonel Lambert!"

Hawk stopped her pacing by reaching and taking her by the shoulders. Irritated, she struggled to rid herself of his grasp, but his hold was relentless as well as gentle. "Jane, I assure you we'll be a very minor part of the action."

"I don't believe you!" she shot back. "You lie as easily as you breathe!"

Hawk chuckled. "I guess I can't deny that."

Jane refused to be diverted from her subject. "The royalist uprising four years ago cost you dearly. It took your home, your son, your way of life, almost your life itself. What will you lose in this one?"

"My love, I didn't even fight in that rebellion."

"But you suffered anyway, and not having learned your lesson, you *will* fight in this one."

"Aye," he agreed resolutely. "Charles needs a direct liaison with the rebels in England. I will go for him because he asked me, not because he commanded me. And I will lead those of my fellow exiles who wish to stop languishing in a foreign land and fight for their own."

"Then you are twice a fool!"

"Only God and history will decide that."

Jane wrenched free from his grasp and turned her back.

"By then it will be too late to change your course, won't it?" she said bitterly.

"Don't turn away from me." He took her arm and gently forced her to face him. "Jane, I don't want to go. I don't want to leave Gideon, or you, but sometimes a man has little choice. This rebellion will happen—is happening!— whether or not you want it to. The English people are clamoring for restoration of the monarchy. Charles's victory is inevitable; you must accept the fact that Puritan rule is rapidly coming to an end."

Jane exploded. "Do you think *that* is what I worry about, you great idiot?" Tears overflowed her eyes and dribbled down her cheeks. "You think I worry about the power of my church while you ride off to get yourself skewered or your head blown off?"

"Tch! You have a temper after all, my love. I didn't mean it to sound that way." He drew her against his chest and ran a soothing hand over her freshly brushed hair, then slipped his hand under the golden mass to massage the vexed tension from the muscles of her shoulders. "Besides"—he chuckled, and Jane could hear the deep rumble within his chest—"there was a time not long ago when you might have blown my head off yourself if you could have managed the deed."

She pushed away from him, not seeing any reason for humor.

"It's true," he insisted with a grin, then surprised her with a quick kiss. "Don't send me away with the memory of this frown." He traced the lowered line of her fine brows with one finger.

Jane resisted his cajolery and pulled back from his light caress. She was too angry to allow his wooing. He had robbed her of all she had and put himself—his passion, laughter, kindness, his provoking, impossible bantering—in its place. Now he would take even that.

"You're a fool!" she insisted. "You're going to get yourself hanged, drawn and quartered, or sold into slavery, and you will not have my blessing for such a thing!"

"That won't happen. I promise."

"Your promises are not worth the breath taken to utter them!"

"I'll be back"—he grinned wickedly—"if only to hear your sweet tongue continue to speak my praises. I don't ask your blessing, but I crave a warmer good-bye than such a glare."

"You'll get nothing from me!"

His grin softened to a sensuous smile full of male confidence. "You think not?"

"Stay away from me, you oaf!" She retreated from his advance.

"What kind of a wife calls her husband an oaf?"

"An angry one!" Her back hit the wall. She held out a stiff arm to ward him off. "Don't touch me, Matthew! I'm in no mood for your games!"

He chuckled with the deep, rich, resonance of building desire. "Are they only *my* games, Jane?"

Her arm collapsed as it met the advancing wall of his chest. He pressed forward until she was caged by his arms on either side of her. Hawk leaned forward for a victory kiss, but Jane ducked beneath his arm and ran toward the door.

"Why, you little imp!" He sprinted to reach the door before she did and deflected her hand just as she reached for the latch. "No, you don't!"

"I do not choose to stay in this room with you tonight!"

"Well, I choose that you do!"

"Would you assault your own wife?"

He shook his head, a sparkle of fond memory in his eye. "I won't have to, my love. We've been through this before, you know. The first time you almost got yourself very thoroughly loved in a pile of hay. We could always go to the stable and try to complete that interrupted performance."

She colored, amazed that even now Hawk could make her blush. "You're irredeemable!"

"Probably. I'm also very hot for my wife."

"Then cool off," she suggested primly.

"I mean to."

"No, Matthew! I'm really not in charity with you tonight."

"I can change that," he said confidently, advancing once again. Before she could play coy, he lunged, grabbed her around the waist, and carried both of them to the plush carpet on the floor, rolling quickly so he pinned her down with the weight of his body. Pressing his advantage, he kissed her soundly, then again.

"Surrender?" he asked with a chuckle.

"Certainly not!"

He kissed her again, this time forcing her mouth to yield beneath his, thrusting with his tongue in mock possession. Jane felt a traitorous warmth steal into her veins and diffuse her anger. Her mouth softened; her tongue fenced with his. The hard length of his arousal pressed against her and started the familiar ache between her legs.

"Surrender?" he repeated, his lips still touching hers.

"Perhaps." Jane sighed as his fingers traced a line down her throat, slid along the line of her collarbone, then tantalizingly began to unfasten the buttons of her night rail. "Perhaps we should go to bed," she suggested softly.

Hawk shook his head, parted the front of her gown and

took one nipple lightly in his teeth. She gasped. His hands cupped her breast and forced it up to meet his mouth. When he released her, Jane looked up and saw her own need reflected in his eyes.

"I'm not letting you up to get into bed or go any other place. You can stay right here under me. The floor will do for now, I think. Later we'll try for a repeat performance in bed."

"Matthew . . . !" Surely being taken like an animal on the floor was every bit as vulgar as being taken in a pile of hay.

"Are you pleading for mercy?" He teased the other breast with his tongue and lips while he pulled her night rail up above her hips. The muscled bulk of his thigh intruded between hers, the material of his breeches rubbing intimately against her naked flesh.

"Oh, Matthew!" She arched against the pressure, unable to lie still.

"No quarter," he declared hoarsely. "God, but you drive me wild!" He shifted to unbutton his breeches and release the beast which now ruled him. With the clothing still around his hips he plunged into her moist and welcoming warmth. Jane rose to meet him with a cry, giddy with sensual joy at the feel of him filling her, stretching her, penetrating to the very depth of her being in a way that was much more than just physical. He thrust rapidly, deeply, almost desperately, his control slipping as her muscles tightened around him in climax. With an animal growl he stiffened, held her hips immovable against his, and then slowly resumed his labored breathing. He wrapped her in his arms and took her with him as he rolled to his side.

For a moment they simply lay together. Jane listened to Hawk's breathing as it gradually quieted. Their heartbeats pounded together, slowing in a mated rhythm. She could smell the musk of their passion, feel the sheen of sweat that moistened both their bodies. The silk of his shirt tickled her nose; his breeches still rubbed against her bare leg.

"You didn't even bother to undress," she said in gentle reproof.

He chuckled. "I was in a hurry." He kissed her nose. "I don't get to lie with you often enough to take the edge off my hunger."

"I think it is really quite vulgar of you to take your wife upon the floor. No decorum at all." A sparkle of mischief lighted her eyes.

He propped himself up on his elbows and regarded her innocently. "You're quite right, you know. I fear I must atone for the insult and prove to you that I'm not always such a vulgar fellow."

"Indeed?"

"Yes, indeed!" In one fluid motion he rolled over, pulled up his breeches, and stood. He offered a hand to assist her. When she took it, he swept her up onto her feet and farther—up into his arms.

"What are you doing?"

His smile would have shamed the Devil. "Showing you that I know how to take my wife with all proper decorum." He set her down upon their bed, modestly tucked the covers around her chin, and began to remove his clothing. "Convenient that I'm already undone," he commented blithely. "I find that I'm getting in a hurry again."

Jane smiled. "You're making fun of me."

"Aye." His voice was warm and set her nerves atingle once again. She threw back the covers, got to her knees, and helped him unbutton his shirt. "You're my favorite lady to make fun of. There aren't any others. I want you to know that."

Her smile faded a bit. "I never asked you if there were."

"I just wanted you to know. I wouldn't lie about such a thing."

"Then let's not talk about it." She effectively ended the conversation by slipping his breeches down from his hips and deliberately, seductively letting her hands slide across the organ that was again growing hard. "Are you coming to bed?" she whispered.

Hawk's suddenly quickened breathing hardly allowed him to answer. "To bed, nay. I'm coming to my wife."

He sat down and pulled off his boots. Scarcely had they hit the floor than his breeches were flung on top of them.

As he turned, Jane met his gaze boldly, still on her knees. She remained immobile while he lifted her night rail over her head and slowly scorched her with his eyes. "You should sleep as you once did, without a stitch. 'Tis a sin to deprive your husband of sleeping beside such beauty."

" 'Tisn't proper." A tease of a little smile lifted her lips.

"In my house I will say what is proper." On his knees in front of her, he reached out to run his hand over her breast, her ribs, the indentation of her waist, and down her hip in an almost reverent gesture. "Anything between us is proper, my beautiful Jane. In bed, on the floor, on the damned kitchen table. Anything. Anywhere."

Jane's pulse raced even faster when Hawk slipped his hand between her thighs to feel the warm creaminess of the desire he aroused in her.

"You're more a woman than even you believe. You're more than any man has a right to be given."

She melted onto the sheets as he gently pushed her

back. "Let's see if we can make love properly this time," he suggested in a throaty whisper as he followed her down.

Several hours passed before Jane realized that she'd been adroitly diverted from her argument. She'd been maneuvered into surrender by the oldest battle tactics in the world, and now she had neither the heart nor the energy to be angry. Hawk lay beside her, his chin resting on the top of her head, his arm across her waist, one leg pinning hers. The bedclothes were tangled around them, leaving most of their bare flesh exposed to the air, but Jane needed no covers. Still warm from their lovemaking, both inside and out, she was content to lie in Hawk's embrace, feel the tickle of his breath in her hair, smell the heady male scent of his closeness, and revel in the touch of his flesh on hers. Soon this pleasure would be taken from her.

A sharp pang of loss shattered her serenity. Before Hawk had thrust himself into her heart, Jane had been blissfully independent, her life a calm plateau. Now she danced to Hawk's tune, not because he forced her, but because her heart and very soul had become entwined with his. He had dragged her off her plateau and galloped with her over high peaks and abysmal valleys, careening around turns she couldn't foresee. They were linked in an emotional dependency that was frightening. Now after dragging her into this world and sealing her to him in an unbreakable bond, he would ride off and risk everything for a displaced king—and for revenge. If he got himself killed, she would never forgive him.

He stirred against her and placed a kiss on her hair. His hand woke to make lazy circles on her stomach.

"When will you leave?" she asked quietly.

Hawk looked toward the window, where dawn was beginning to tinge the shutters with a rosy hue. "This morning," he answered.

"When will you return?"

He was silent.

"You will come back," she prompted.

"Of course. I don't know just when, though. With luck, a fortnight or so."

Without luck, Jane amended silently, he wouldn't come back at all. Her heart ached with the knowledge of how much she loved this man, irreverent and unrepentant as he was. The resurrection of her heart that had started with the son reached its culmination in the father. She wanted to cling to him so he couldn't leave her. Instead, she merely touched one finger to his chin and smiled.

"I will come back, Jane." He captured her finger and folded it with the rest of her hand in his much larger one. "This time I don't lie."

With the King in Calais and many of the cavaliers crossing to England to fight for the throne, the life went out of the royalist circles throughout the Spanish Netherlands. Jane felt that the life had gone out of her as well. Even the joy of having Gideon close was not comfort enough to assuage her fear that something was about to go wrong. Gideon himself was more than usually gloomy at his father's absence. He seemed to sense there was a danger in this trip that had not been present in the others.

Fortunately, Jane had plenty to do besides worry. She sat in on many of Gideon's sessions with Master Wegg and accompanied their outings. Together with the housekeeper and butler she planned and supervised a thorough cleaning of their New Town residence. She even accepted invitations to a boating picnic and an informal supper with several of the royalist ladies who had been left behind by their men as she had. The chief organizer of these occasions was the notorious Lady Kesterling, who seemed to genuinely miss the King, Jane noted. Much to Jane's surprise, the ladies were much more amiable away from the furious social whirl that followed Charles. Lady Kesterling was as coolly cynical as always, but for some reason of her own she was kind to Jane, and the other ladies followed her lead. Their picnic, in spite of the baskets of sumptuous food and the gaily decorated barge that floated them down the Scheldt, was a quiet affair, as was the supper followed by card games a week later. All were waiting, half hopeful, half fearful, for news from England, which did not come. None were in the mood for gaiety.

Ned was the only person who seemed to have no worries. He stayed at the house most nights, saying he had to keep an eye on things since Hawk was gone. During the day he pursued his own schemes—honest schemes, he assured Jane. Jane didn't believe him, of course.

"Why didn't you go with Hawk?" she asked him one day when she and Ned took Gideon to the horse market by Red Gate in the city wall. Master Wegg had taken a much needed holiday, and Gideon had begged so to look at the horses that Jane had drafted Ned as escort.

Ned snorted. "I'm not barmy enough to put my life on the block for some fellow what wants t'be king. I leave that to the 'igh-blooded gents like 'Awk. Besides, 'oo'd look after ye and the boy?" He cast one of his strange, twisted smiles toward Gideon, who was a few feet off wistfully admiring the meat pies that a vendor was selling out of a cart.

Jane followed the direction of his smile. "He's more interested in the pies than the horses." Her eyes rested on

Gideon, but her thoughts drifted far away, with a "high-blooded gent" who was barmy enough to fight for Charles.

"Don't be thinkin' like that, mistress," Ned warned.

She shook her head sadly. "Like what?"

"I can see clear through that 'ead o' yours. Don't ye be worryin' so. 'Awk'll be back."

"Can I have a meat pie?" Giddy interrupted.

"I thought you wanted to see the horses," Jane said.

"I do. But I look at them better when my stomach isn't rumbling."

"Indeed?"

The boy grinned at her.

Jane grinned back and handed him a coin.

"Father said he would buy me a horse of my own soon. Did you hear him?"

"Yes, I did."

"Can I have one of these?"

"We'll have to wait until your father returns."

"Oh." Giddy looked at his coin and his mind turned again to food. He trotted off toward the meat pies.

Jane's smile faded. "How can you be so sure that Matthew will be back?" she asked Ned. "You yourself said all those men fighting for the King are putting their lives on the block."

" 'Cause 'Awk's a tough one." He puffed himself up proudly. "I taught 'im ever'thin' I knows about fists and knives, mistress, and 'e's more'n a fair 'and with a sword and on a 'orse. Lotta those other gents 'ave gone ta fat, but not 'Awk. 'E's all muscle and bone, and if need be, 'e can be quick as a rat and slippery as a sea snake."

It wasn't a very flattering picture of her husband, but Jane did find some comfort in Ned's words.

"Good afternoon, Lady Chester."

Jane started at the sound of Hugh Cressman's voice, and she turned to find him smiling at her. Beside him stood his wife, Barbara, who regarded Jane with the superior satisfaction of one cat that has just snatched the cream from another. Jane tried to achieve a cordial expression. If Lord Woodford chose to ignore the debacle of the garden party where Jane had last seen him, Jane supposed she could put up a pretense as well. Beside her, Ned stiffened. She cautioned him with a sideways look.

"I'm surprised to find you here rather than in England," she said to Woodford.

"Some of us must be willing to sacrifice glory for practicality, my lady. I remain here as liaison with the Spanish government."

"Is there any news?" Jane asked anxiously.

Woodford shrugged. "There has been some heavy fighting. Colonel Lambert met our men with a considerable force, I understand." His cold blue eyes seemed to soften in sympathy for her obvious worry. "If I hear anything, my lady, I will be sure that you are apprised of the news."

"Thank you."

Suddenly uneasy, she called to Gideon as the earl and his wife moved on.

"That's a bucket 'o slime if I ever saw one," Ned muttered. "The both of 'em."

"Aye," Jane had to agree. "But mind your manners, Ned. The man's an earl."

"I'll mind me manners as long as 'e minds 'is."

Late that night, however, the earl forgot to mind his manners.

As her household slept, Jane curled up on a brocade-upholstered settee in the library and read, a quite common midnight occupation since Hawk had left her bed empty and her mind too restless to sleep. She had found quite a bit of merit in Shakespeare, a discovery she would certainly never admit to Hawk. A cool breeze drifted through the open window, relieving the late July heat that was oppressive even at night. Jane lifted the mass of hair from her neck and plucked her dressing robe away from her breasts to let the breeze play over her skin.

A faint knock sounded at the front entrance. She cocked her head to listen. It came again. Her heart started to race. Who would be calling at this time of night except someone with urgent news from England?

Without a thought she wrapped her robe modestly around her and ran to the front hall. A cautious peek out the window revealed Hugh Cressman on the stoop. His horse stood behind him, its head sagging wearily. The earl also slumped in a tired pose, as if he'd been all night riding the rounds to give his news.

Jane threw the door open, heart pounding, fearing the worst and hoping for the best. "Lord Woodford!"

"My lady!"

Fumes of liquor assaulted her. The earl wasn't weary, he was drunk. He pushed across the threshold before she could close the door.

"My dear Lady Chester," he slurred.

20

⚜ ⚜

"You're drunk!" Jane said accusingly as the earl closed the door behind him and leaned heavily back upon it.

"I've a right to be drunk. 'Tis women like you"—he pointed an accusing finger—"that drive a man to lose his senses in liquor. No better than a damned Puritan with your silly airs of a virtuous wife. Ain't no such"—he hiccoughed, blinked, then started again. "Ain't no such thing as a virtuous wife. I oughta know."

"Perhaps there are as many virtuous wives as faithful husbands, Lord Woodford. You've little right to expect virtue from your wife if you have none yourself!"

"A lecture!" He guffawed. "Shoulda known that's what you'd give me! Don't you know how to give anything else, m'lady? Ain't that stalwart husband o' yours here often enough to soften up what's between your legs?"

Jane felt the blood drain from her face. "Get out!" she ordered coldly.

Woodford pushed himself away from the door and wove his way toward Jane, who was clutching the stair banister, white-knuckled with fury. "Why should I?" he asked. "Your husband ain't here. Trusting fellow to leave a little mouse like you unguarded with all us cats around."

"Get out!" Jane backed a step for every one that Woodford advanced.

"Nay, m'lady."

He seemed to grow less drunk and more menacing by the second. Jane felt her first real stab of fear. "This is madness! Leave me be!"

Woodford laughed. "Not before we have a li'l fun, m'lady. You'll be crooning like a bitch in heat, an' movin' yer li'l tail just as hard. Yer gonna be wet an' pantin' and beggin' fer more, 'cause I've got a cock like a bull's and I rut like a damned stallion. You'll see."

Jane backed through the double doors into the small family parlor, her stomach churning from both fear and disgust. Desperately she looked around the room for a weapon to hold off the drunken earl. Her eyes lighted upon an iron poker beside the fireplace and she angled toward it. Woodford followed, slowly stalking, seeming to enjoy this prelude to his victory.

"You won't get away with this," she warned him. "I'm not alone. The servants—"

"Sleep in the attic, where I doubt they'd hear a bevy of whores screaming out their mating cries—as you soon will be, m'dear."

Only a few feet separated Jane from her goal. "The groom—"

"Sleeps in the carriage house with your loyal Master Crow—a fact I made sure of."

Woodford's face was flushed. Sweat glistened on his skin. Jane could almost smell his lust.

"I'm gonna take you on the floor, with yer li'l backside bouncin' against the rug—then on the settee, then"—he glanced through the door into the morning room—"then in there on the table, a li'l late-night feast, eh? I'll wager yer tasty enough." He reached for the fastenings of his breeches.

"None of that!" Jane reached behind her, grasped the poker, and swung it out in front of her like a sword. "Now get out."

Woodford lurched to a halt, swaying. "Why, you li'l bitch," he said with a woozy smile. "I think you must be punished f'yer impo . . . impudence."

"Get out!"

With no warning he lunged for her. Jane swung the poker; it hit Woodford's shoulder with a meaty thud, but he merely laughed. She swung again; he grabbed her wrist and twisted hard. With a cry she let go of her weapon and it clanged to the floor.

"Bitch!" He twisted her arm again, then slapped her. "Bitch! I'll teach you some manners!"

Jane choked on her own scream as he hit her again.

"I was going to be nice. But you don't deserve nice, you high-and-mighty bitch. Now I'm going to hurt you."

He slammed her up against the wall; her head hit the plaster and her senses reeled. "You would've liked this," he snarled, cupping a breast with one hand while the other pinned her in place. "But this . . ." He pinched her nipple hard, then slapped her when she cried out. "Bitch! I'm going to ride you tonight like you've never been ridden!"

Jane struggled feebly as he pushed her to the floor and pulled her night rail up over her hips, but the world spun from his blows and the strength had left her limbs. When he stood to pull down his breeches she tried to get up, but he casually kicked her in the side. She rolled up into a helpless little ball of pain.

"Look here, bitch! I've got a big present for you." He knelt beside her, crading his turgid organ and caressing himself as he gloated over her helplessness. She kicked out at him. He barely deflected the blow with his thigh.

"Vicious creature. We'll have no more of that!" He grabbed her shoulder and hip and flipped her onto her stomach. Face ground into the carpet by the pressure of his hand, Jane could scarcely breathe. With the other hand he gave her buttocks a cruel pinch. "That's for the kick." She felt him press the head of his swollen organ between her legs, and she screamed futilely into the rug. Woodford laughed. "This is for—"

A shriek echoed in Jane's head, and suddenly she was free of Woodford's grasp. A moment passed before she realized the shriek had not been her own.

"Get off her! You're hurting my mother! Get off!"

"No! Gideon!" Jane scrambled for the poker as Gideon flew at Hugh Cressman with nightshirt billowing and little fists flying. "No! Don't hurt him!"

The drunken earl picked the boy up and tossed him aside as a terrier might fling a rat. Gideon slammed against the wall and crumpled into a limp pile of awkwardly sprawled arms and legs.

"No! Gideon, no!" Jane crawled toward the unconscious boy, but Woodford grabbed her ankle and hauled her back toward him. She kicked out and flailed at him with her fists. He merely laughed, grabbed her thighs in a bruising grip, and forced them apart.

"I wouldn't, yer lordship, lessen ye want yer cock lopped off an' stuffed down yer throat."

Woodford froze, feeling a knife at the back of his neck.

"Go see to the boy, Mistress Jane."

With a little cry Jane flung herself away from the earl, who stayed perfectly still while Ned moved around in front of him. The knife slid along Woodford's neck in cold caress.

"Is Giddy all right?" Ned asked Jane, never taking his eyes from Woodford.

"He's bruised, but he's coming awake. Gideon," Jane pleaded, "can you hear me?"

"Mother?" The boy's answer was scarcely audible, but Jane wept in relief.

"Lucky you," Ned said to Woodford. "If you'd hurt him bad or dirtied the mistress with that little cock o' yours, I woulda killed you slow. Since you didn't, I'll slice yer throat quick an' clean. Mistress, take the boy back to 'is bed and stay with 'im."

"Ned, no! You can't!"

"Take the boy an' leave, my lady."

Jane crouched on the floor and hugged Gideon to her, but she refused to leave. "Ned, he's an earl. I don't mind what happens to him, but I do have a care for you."

"She's right," Woodford confirmed in a shaky voice. "You'll be hanged and gutted and left for the birds to peck at."

"You won't be here to enjoy it," Ned said calmly.

"Ned, please! You mustn't. You'd be found out. The whole town would know what happened, and I'd be . . . I'd be . . ."

" 'Twasn't yer fault, mistress."

" 'Tis always the woman's fault," Woodford sneered.

Ned pricked the earl's throat with the tip of the knife. "Say ye're sorry, yer lordship." Blood ran down Woodford's throat into his collar.

"I'm s-sorry," he gasped.

"Say ye're an ass with a cock like a worm."

Woodford turned white as the knife pressed deeper. "I'm an ass with—"

"Ned! Please just make him leave."

"Let me kill him, mistress. If me nose fer trouble 'adn't told me somethin' was wrong in the 'ouse, you woulda been on the floor with this bastard's butt achurnin' above ye, and young Giddy—"

"Just get him out of here!" she choked out.

"As ye wish." He growled at the cowering Woodford. "If ye ever even look at Lady Chester again, I'll cut yer cock off and stuff it down yer throat till ye choke on it, yer lordship. Remember that."

While Ned pushed Woodford out the door, Jane helped Gideon to his feet. Together they headed for the stairs.

"I can walk!" the boy protested as Jane helped him up the steps. "Did that man hurt you, Mother? Why was he here?"

Jane suddenly found herself leaning on Gideon instead of helping him. She felt as though all the blood had drained from her body. The world spun, and Gideon's voice echoed in the far distance, shouting her name, but she couldn't answer. Slowly she slipped down to crumple against the banister.

Jane woke to the sight of the housekeeper's plump, rosy face hovering above hers, her starched white coif bright in the morning sun that streamed through the windows. "Here we are, my lady," Mistress Weston chirped. "Awake, are we? Here's what'll make you feel the thing." She waved a bowl of something aromatic under Jane's nose. "Greta cooked up some nice broth to be especially easy on your delicate constitution."

"Where am I?"

"Why, in your own bed, my lady. You had a bit of a fainting spell."

Jane closed her eyes as it all came back—Hugh Cressman, Ned, Gideon. "Gideon?"

"Master Gideon took a few bruises, my lady, but he's quite all right. Ned has sent for a physician to look at the both of you, however. 'Twas a nasty fall you took."

"Fall?" Jane said, feeling stupid.

"Ned told us he saw you and Master Giddy land in a heap at the bottom of the stairs early this morning. You must have fainted and sent the both of you tumbling. As I've said many times to Stanworth, that staircase is much too narrow. It's dangerous, it is. And now look what's happened."

"Yes," Jane whispered. "I remember." Ned had not told them, Jane thought with relief. She must remember to caution him about telling Hawk. She couldn't imagine how her husband would react to such a thing, and she didn't want to find out.

"Here, let me prop you up so you can drink your broth." Mistress Weston plumped the pillows and helped Jane to sit up. Then she pulled a chair beside the bed and sat down with a rustle of stiff petticoats and starched apron. "Are you feeling more the thing, my lady?"

"Yes, of course," she assured the housekeeper, though the truth was that every inch of her ached from Woodford's blows. "How silly of me to faint like that."

" 'Tis not so surprising, my lady. Women with child are expected to be delicate."

Jane gave the housekeeper a puzzled look. "I'm not with child."

"Tsk," Mistress Weston chided. "What else would stop

your courses for the last two months, my lady? I've seen no bloody linen from you in that time."

" 'Tis impossible." Hope flooded Jane's voice in spite of her denial. "My first child ruined me for conceiving. The physician told me."

"Aye, and that shows you how much men know about the getting of babies." She smoothed the bedclothes then patted Jane's hand with motherly affection. "They should leave the birthing and rearing of young ones to us women, I say. Now drink up this broth, dear, and I'll have Greta heat you some more. You'll need your strength."

Jane obediently emptied the bowl that the housekeeper handed her.

"You must rest the entire day," Mistress Weston ordered. "Nay"—the housekeeper denied the protest in Jane's eyes—"I know you're not one who abides pampering, my lady, but you must think of the little one inside. He's taken quite a tumble today, and he needs his rest."

Jane lay back against the pillows once Mistress Weston had left. She closed her eyes and let her thoughts turn inward to investigate the wondrous possibility that the housekeeper might be right. Might God in His mercy have granted her another child of her own? She scarcely dared to hope for such a miracle. For so many years she had accepted her barrenness as one of life's crosses. She pressed a hand to her flat stomach and willed there to be life inside. "Please," she prayed softly. "Please."

The physician that Ned had summoned confirmed Mistress Weston's diagnosis. "Nasty bruises," he remarked of the purpling discolorations on Jane's ribs, buttocks, and face. His English was only slightly accented, as he'd spent several years studying at Oxford, he told her during his examination. "But nothing's broken. This other ailment you should be rid of in another seven months or so," he told her with a twinkle.

Jane beamed in joyous amazement, and the doctor answered with a smile of his own. "Just don't be tumbling down any more staircases, Lady Chester. 'Tis a miracle you didn't lose the babe."

The babe. Babe. It rang through her mind like the pealing of a bell. "Are you absolutely sure I'm . . . with child?"

"As sure as I can be at this stage. You've all the symptoms."

"After the birth of my first child, the physician told me I could never again conceive."

The doctor shrugged philosophically. "Sometimes Mother Nature fools us, my lady. How dull life would be if we knew all her secrets. You seem in the peak of health and well able to carry the child to term. If you have any complaints or problems you should contact me, though. No sense in taking chances."

"I will. You're sure Gideon's quite all right?"

The physician had reassured her when he'd first come into her room, but he didn't seem to mind repeating himself. "Quite sure, my lady. Boys his age don't fall, they bounce. He's a sturdy lad."

When the physician left, Jane lay back and closed her eyes to savor the feeling of life growing within her. She thanked God for His bountiful mercy and Hawk for the gift of his child, hoping her husband would be pleased. Would Hawk love this child as much as he loved Gideon, or would he find a growing family a burden? How would she tell him the news? Words and phrases ran through her mind, none satisfactory. The words, time, and place had to be just right. One did not just casually let drop news of such a miracle. The telling had to be momentous—and planned.

Her thoughts took a dark turn as she remembered that Hawk was in battle. She might never get the chance to tell him he was to be a father once again. Just one more miracle, she prayed. If Hawk could come back to her safely, she would never ask for another.

A timid knock preceded Gideon as he peeked around the door. "Can I come in?"

"Of course you may. There's no one I'd rather see."

When he came to her bedside, he looked at her with a long face. "Did that man hurt you, Mother?"

"No, Gideon, he didn't hurt me." She reached out to brush his hair back from the cut on his forehead, but stopped herself. The cut looked much too sore to touch. "Your poor head," she said with sympathy.

"It's fine," Gideon assured her.

"And your shoulder?" She gently touched the sling the doctor had wound around his pulled shoulder and arm.

"It's fine." He lowered his eyes. "I'm sorry. I was going to rescue you, but I didn't do so well."

"You were very brave," Jane told him. "I'm proud of you."

Tears dribbled down the boy's cheeks. "I should've fetched my sword and stabbed him. He was hurting you. Why was he hurting you?"

She dabbed at his tears with the corner of the sheet. "I don't know why people hurt other people, my love. But I'm glad you didn't stab him. You are much too young to have to do such a dreadful thing."

"I would've," he insisted.

"I know."

"Why didn't Ned kill him?"

"Ned didn't have the right to take his life," Jane explained.

"Would Ned have gotten into trouble?"

"Dreadful trouble."

"I wish Ned had killed him," Gideon insisted, his face suddenly losing its childishness. He sniffed back his tears and took Jane's hand in his. "Next time I'll remember to bring my sword."

Jane squeezed his hand. "Let's hope there won't be a next time, shall we?"

Gideon still looked determined. Jane sighed, hating to involve him in deception, but not knowing how to avoid it.

"I think we should tell your father that we both took our bruises in a fall down the stairs, Gideon. 'Tis the story Ned told the servants, and we should let everybody believe it's the truth."

"Why?"

"Because your father would be very upset by the truth; he would be very sad to know we were subjected to such a thing, and perhaps very angry. Besides, if the servants learned of what happened, I would be shamed before them all."

"You said it was wrong to lie."

"Yes, I did." Jane closed her eyes in misery. She hated the words that were about to leave her mouth. "I suppose we're doing wrong to prevent a greater wrong. Sometimes that happens."

Giddy screwed up his tear-streaked face. "I don't understand. We'll get in trouble with God."

Jane couldn't think of anything wise to say. "Someday you'll understand. I wish you never had to understand things like this, but someday you will."

When he left Jane wept. The longer she stayed in this

world, the more tightly woven became the net of deception and falsehood that enveloped her. Now Gideon was dragged into the net, and soon . . . Jane pressed her hand against her belly, grieving that the precious burden she carried must be born and raised in such a world. She thought of her own childhood in London. Her parents had been rigid and strict, and she'd been raised with the stern reality of sin and punishment constantly held before her. But she'd never been confused about right and wrong. She'd never been subjected to the sight of violence or talk of debauchery.

What would her own children remember of their childhoods?

Eight days later Hawk returned to Antwerp, thinner, exhausted, but unhurt. Parliament's Colonel Lambert had beaten back the royalists with ease, he revealed bitterly as he shed his filthy clothing on the floor of their bedchamber. The fire of revolution they had hoped to kindle in favor of the King sputtered and died before igniting; the common people who cried for the return of the monarchy were not willing to risk their lives to ensure Charles's victory. All the blood was spilled for nothing.

Jane held back a retort that the spilling of blood seldom was an answer to anything. She was too grateful to have him back.

"Is your revolution over, then?" she asked hopefully.

"Nay. It will not be over as long as Charles is alive." His words were bitter, but when he looked at her the anger went out of his face. "You are truly a sight worth coming home to, Jane."

"And you are a sight that could scare the life out of anyone," she declared with a smile. His face was bronzed as a barbarian's, his sable hair scraggly and unkempt, but as her gaze traveled over his bare chest and half-unlaced breeches, Jane felt the familiar warmth rise from the pit of her belly, despite the dirt and sweat. He might look like a barbarian and at times act the rogue, but he was her barbarian rogue, and she loved him.

"I'll take my welcome-home kiss," he said, holding out an arm.

"Nay!" she teased and leapt out of his reach. "Not until you've bathed."

"When I've bathed I'll take a more complete welcome home."

She danced away from him, her skirts swishing in saucy invitation.

"Too filthy for you am I, wife? We'll see about that." He trapped her against a wall and pinned her in the cage of his steel-thewed arms. "I'll be a thoughtful husband and not get you dirty." He touched her only with his mouth, carefully holding his body away from her while he took his kiss. His tongue thrust past her lips hungrily, gently ravaging her mouth until Jane felt herself melt. Heedless of filth, she wrapped her arms about his bare torso and molded herself against him. His arms dropped around her and pulled her closer. The swell of his erection prodded insistently at her belly.

"Now you're filthy too," he whispered in her ear. "I think we both should bathe."

Before she could answer he began to unlace her stomacher. Jane longed to help him, and then remembered the bruises that would be revealed if she stood before him naked. "There's only room for one in the tub!"

"We'll make do," he answered with a grin.

"No, Matthew. Really."

"Don't be coy, my love. I've been too long without you."

His hands ripped at her bodice and tore it away along with her corset. Deftly he unfastened the tabs of her skirt and pushed it down to pool around her ankles. "Lord, but you're beautiful! Come here."

Jane knew resistence was useless when he pulled her against him and peeled down her chemise so that her bare breasts rested against his chest. Her nipples hardened to taut nubbins as he lowered himself slowly to kneel before her, spreading kisses across her throat and her breasts as he worked his way down. On his knees, eyes closed in bliss, his lips worshiped her navel and sent streamers of pure fire straight to her loins. Hawk spread his hands across her buttocks and pressed her hard against his mouth. She gasped in startled pain as his hand spread across the spot where Woodford had so cruelly pinched her.

Hawk froze. He opened his eyes right on a level with the ugly yellow-green remnant of Woodford's kick to her ribs. "What's this?"

"I . . . fell."

He didn't answer, merely ran a gentle hand over the bruise. "What else did you hurt?" he asked in an ominously quiet voice.

"My . . ."

"Backside?" he supplied with a wry twist to his mouth.

"Yes."

"Turn around." He peeled away the rest of her clothing and examined the marks on her buttocks, then turned her around to face him. "Your face as well, I see now when I look closely. I wondered why you had suddenly adopted the fashion of wearing powder. That must have been quite a feat, falling so that your ribs, backside, and face all got knocked about."

"Yes," Jane agreed hesitantly. "It was quite a fall—down the stairs. And I fear I took Gideon with me. He has a pulled shoulder and a cut head."

"How clumsy of you."

"Very clumsy."

Again Hawk was ominously quiet, with an air of waiting that set Jane's nerves on end. Uneasy, she stepped out of the pool of her skirts and petticoats and went to the wardrobe to fetch her dressing gown.

"Your water's getting cold," she reminded Hawk.

He gave no answer, simply got to his feet and leaned against the pillar of the bed canopy, his chest bare, his breeches half unlaced. He folded his arms across his naked chest and waited, looking at her with dangerous calm.

"Matthew! I thought you wanted a bath. Are you waiting for something?"

"Yes," he answered quietly. "I'm waiting for you to tell me the truth about those bruises."

"I told you that I fell!"

"You've no talent for lying, Jane."

"I . . . I . . ."

"You didn't get those bruises in a fall. Especially the ones on your face. Come here." He didn't wait for her to obey, but reached out and pulled her over to the tub, where he dipped a washcloth in the warm water and proceeded to clean every trace of powder from her face. "I imagine when those were fresh they were quite something to see. What happened?"

Jane sighed. Hawk was right. She was sadly inadequate as a liar. "I had a bit of a misunderstanding with a gentleman."

Hawk translated that. "You were attacked."

"He was drunk."

"Did he rape you?"

Shame heated Jane's face. She shed his loose grasp and sat down heavily upon the bed. "That was his intention, but Ned drove him away. Gideon tried to rescue me and was hurt in the attempt." Tears welled up in her eyes. During the last week she'd not known whether to cry for the pain of her violation and Gideon's trauma or rejoice in the knowledge that she carried Hawk's child. She'd done a little of both. Now the terror and humiliation of Woodford's attack raged to the surface of her tender emotions. Tears welled in her eyes. She hid her face in her hands and let the tears flow.

Hawk sat down beside her, took her into his arms, and turned her face into the comforting wall of his chest.

"I'm sorry," she sobbed. "I didn't invite . . ."

"Jane," he chided gently, rocking her back and forth as though she were a hurt child, "surely you can't believe that I think any shred of blame attaches to you. What kind of villain do you think I am?" At her renewed wailing he sighed. "Aye, well, we both know what kind of villain I am, don't we?"

She pushed away from him, and he handed her the washcloth to wipe her face. "I'm sorry, Matthew. I'm acting like a silly child. I don't know what came over me."

"Jane." He took her chin in his hands and forced her to look at him. "Do you remember once I told you that the only true dishonor comes from within ourselves?"

She nodded, sniffing back tears.

"Then you have nothing to be ashamed of, do you? The entire fault lies with your attacker, and I will see that he pays dearly for his sins. Who was this brute who dared to lay a hand upon you and my son?"

Jane bit her lip.

"If you don't tell me, I'll have it from Ned or Gideon. So there's no help for the truth, is there?"

"Hugh Cressman," Jane told him reluctantly.

Hawk's eyes hardened. Jane read the promise of violence in their depths.

"Matthew, no. Please stay away from him. The whole thing is over."

"You needn't worry I'll creep up behind him and slit his throat," Hawk said grimly. "I'll give the bastard a chance to defend his honor with a fair duel."

"No, please!" She took his hands in hers—his were warm and dry, hers cold as ice. "Charles would never forgive you if you killed Woodford. You know he despises dueling!"

He squeezed her hands and smiled wolfishly. "I've no intention of killing the villain; I want him to live to regret what he did to you."

"Oh, Matthew. Responding to evil with another evil doesn't make things right!"

"But it makes a man feel a hell of a lot better," Hawk replied grimly.

Jane rose and paced the floor. Fear drove away her tears and left a lump of icy fear that lodged in her chest where her heart should have been. She could feel Hawk's eyes upon her. "What if Woodford kills you?" she asked quietly.

"He won't," Hawk assured her.

She heard the implacable determination in his voice. All that she had feared had come to pass. Because of her, Hawk would do violence, would endanger himself and his standing with the King. She wouldn't have that on her conscience along with everything else that weighed it down. Jane pulled out her last weapon, one she was loath to use.

"I think Lady Woodford will not be pleased if you create

a scandal with her husband. She is very sensitive about being made to look a fool, I've heard, and she values Lord Woodford for the position he gives her if for nothing else."

Hawk was silent for a moment, and Jane's heart ached as she imagined him weighing the beautiful Barbara's reaction much more heavily than he had weighed hers. "What does Hugh's wife have to do with this?" he finally asked.

Jane turned away without answering, and his question seemed to hang in the air between them.

"Answer me," he demanded.

"You and she are friends of a sort. Would you do her the grief of harming her husband?"

"Lady Woodford and I are not friends, Jane. If she wants to keep her husband in one piece, then she'd best keep him from attacking other men's wives." Hawk came to stand behind her. "He'll not bother you again, Jane. I promise." He circled her with his arms and she turned to look up into his face.

"I would rather have your promise to leave him alone."

"I can't give you that. We live in the midst of a wolf pack, and a man sometimes has to fight to maintain his position. If I ignored what Woodford did, that would signal others that I didn't care enough for you to protect you against the pack. And I do care." He chuckled. "Don't worry your soft heart about Barbara. That woman can very well take care of herself."

Jane could have argued on forever, but she didn't. She was tired and defeated, and Hawk's arms were a welcome haven. She closed her eyes and let him pull her against him.

"The bath water's lukewarm by now, but I think we could heat it up," Hawk suggested.

Jane didn't protest as he pushed her dressing robe to the

floor and stood warming her with his appreciative gaze. He reached out to touch the bruise along her ribs.

"How did he do this?"

"He kicked me," Jane said dully.

Hawk didn't comment, but his mouth drew into a grim line. Jane didn't want to think about it anymore.

They bathed each other, and Jane was almost able to forget about Hugh Cressman as she scrubbed Hawk's splendid body with soap-slippery hands. When he did the same for her, she felt her tension slowly yield to a rapturous lethargy. When he had her stand so he could wash her lower parts, his hands drawing soapy circles on her belly, massaging the taut muscles of her legs, then finally lingering between her thighs, she thought she would simply dissolve into the warm water. He stood to pour the rinse water over her, then pulled her against the wet length of him, her back to his chest. His arousal pressed insistently into the small of her back.

Hawk lifted her hair and kissed the nape of her neck. "Come to bed," he invited, his voice taut with desire.

She laughed. "We're still wet."

Before Jane could protest, he lifted her into his arms, stepped quickly from the tub, and deposited her on the bed. She saw the fire in his eyes as he lowered himself to cover her with his body. "It's been much too long," she whispered as he kissed her breasts and his fingers stroked gently between her legs. She found him and urged him home, needing nothing so much as the comfort of having him inside her.

He laughed, his breath warm and sweet in her ear. "And I thought *I* was impatient!"

Jane gasped with pleasure as he filled her with his own

hungry flesh. His thrusts were powerful and rapid, driving them quickly to ecstatic release. She clung to him and let the warm flood of rapture sweep her away. But tonight the rapture carried with it a hint of despair.

21

Hawk wasted no time in demanding satisfaction, and Woodford didn't bother with denials. He seemed as eager as Hawk to fight. The contest of honor was arranged two days hence, to take place in a grove of linden trees outside the city walls, well out of the notice of Charles, who detested dueling. Even though the King was presently in Bruges, there was always the chance he might return unexpectedly to Antwerp.

Hawk chose as a second Sir Thomas Waltham, who was once again visiting Antwerp on behalf of Henrietta Maria. They arrived at the grove well before the appointed hour so Hawk could limber up his sword arm. Woodford had chosen swords as weapons. Hawk was grimly confident. There were men aplenty who could stand against him with a sword and win, but he suspected Hugh Cressman wasn't one of them. Hawk's blood was hot to fight. The thought of Woodford's laying hands on his Jane was a poison which could be expunged only by the villain's humiliation. The insult ate at his gut, demanding a catharsis of violence. Had the attack been aimed at him, Hawk might have let Charles take care of disciplining the culprit, but an attack on Jane . . . that was a different matter entirely. A man had a right to protect his wife, and even Charles would not make Hawk stay his hand.

Hawk knew that part of the anger that burned in his blood was directed at himself for dragging Jane into this nest of debauched scoundrels. He'd watched her cheerful innocence erode, day by day, week by week. Time and again he'd been forced to leave her alone in a world where she didn't belong, and now not only her happiness but her safety was attacked. Hawk was almost as angry at himself as he was at Woodford—angrier still because he didn't know how to solve the problem.

The morning of the duel was shrouded in heavy fog. When Woodford's coach arrived at the linden grove, it was a mere shadow among the trees, and the men who emerged from it gray and ethereal in the mist. The figures took on substance as they walked toward the clearing where Hawk and Waltham waited—Woodford a tall, menacing stick of a man, his companion shorter and rounder, scrambling to keep up with the earl's long stride.

Woodford was dressed as for a social occasion. The plumes on his hat and ribbon loops adorning his doublet and breeches hung limply in the fog, and the starched lace of his falling-band collar lay wilted about his shoulders, but the immaculate shine of his boots gleamed through the grass and the careful pleating of his full breeches defied the dampness. Likewise the morning's gloom did not subdue the eager light in his eye. His second, Sir Hubert Rowley, was dressed more plainly, as befitted his lower rank, but he also boasted the confident air of one who knows he is on the winning team.

"Morning, Chester," Woodford greeted Hawk. The earl's eyes ran contemptuously over Hawk's practical leather buff coat, close-fitting breeches, and plain knee-high buskins.

Hawk smiled at Woodford's expression. "I didn't want to get your blood on my best, Lord Woodford."

"Or *your* blood either, I'd wager." Woodford doffed his gloves, his manner as relaxed as if he were simply out for a morning's stroll. "I must say, Chester, this is a lot of bother over a woman."

"*This* woman happens to be my wife. You may treat other men's wives as you please, Woodford, but when you lay a hand on mine, you pay for the crime."

"Crime, is it? My, you are upset. But I suppose the lovely Jane is probably worth being upset over." He pulled at his chin thoughtfully, making his long face even longer. "Such a woman as she might even be worth fighting for."

"When this contest is over, you may think the price too high," Hawk warned.

"Don't be concerned for me, my lord. I'm no novice at dueling, and I've never yet been bested."

"Knowing the lot you run with, Woodford, I doubt you've truly been tested."

Woodford flushed. "We shall soon see, won't we? I think you've been lording it over the gutter scum of London too long, my lord. You've no doubt forgotten what it's like to fight a real man. I won't mind taking you down a peg or two before I run you through. And of course"—he gave Hawk a predatory grin—"I will be honored to comfort your unhappy widow in her loss. You shouldn't worry on that score, Chester."

"Let's see if your sword arm is as powerful as your boasting," Hawk suggested with a grim smile.

"By all means," Woodford agreed. "Let us be on about

this business. I have a breakfast engagement that I mustn't keep waiting. Sir Hubert, the weapons, please."

Sir Hubert presented an ornate wooden case in which two gleaming foils lay cushioned in a crimson velvet lining. The flimsy swords were much lighter weapons than those Hawk was accustomed to wielding, but quite deadly all the same.

"Since I am providing the weapons, Chester, you may have first choice. They are both equally well balanced and flexible. You may take my word on it."

Hawk tested both weapons and found that Woodford told the truth. He selected one, examined the tip, flexed the blade, then handed it to Waltham to examine. Sir Thomas nodded approval.

"Have you chosen, then?" Woodford asked politely.

"This one will do," Hawk said.

Woodford picked up the other blade and cut the air in a deadly slice. "Are you quite ready?"

Hawk nodded. The seconds retired to a discreet distance, and Sir Hubert called "*En garde*, gentlemen."

Woodford's cockiness diminished rapidly after the first engagement of blades. Hawk easily countered Woodford's first attack and followed with a thrust that cut through the earl's defenses and pinked his shoulder.

"Can you do no better than that?" Hawk taunted, enjoying the surprise on the other man's face. "Perhaps your skill lies only in attacking women."

"I don't know what your charming lady wife told you, Chester, but I seldom need to attack women. I merely accept their eager invitations." He raised his blade to parry Hawk's thrust—too late. Both shoulders now trickled blood down the gold-embroidered front of his doublet. He returned the attack with a vengeance, but his steel slithered off Hawk's and thrust far wide of its mark.

"You shouldn't speak lies of a lady," Hawk warned him calmly. "Such ill manners only worsen your punishment."

They fought on, no longer wasting breath in the exchange of insults. Woodford's face took on a pallor that matched the colorless morning as time and time again his blade was thrust aside and Hawk's hungry steel came in to bite him. After ten long minutes he bled from more than half a dozen cuts, none of them serious, but all of them delivered with an ease that let the earl know that Hawk was playing with him as a wolf might cruelly play with a rabbit before satisfying its deadly appetite.

Hawk derived a great deal of satisfaction from seeing sweat start to glisten on Woodford's face and fear light his eyes. Humiliation was a far better revenge than murder, and he'd been fed enough humiliation over the last few years to know well how to dish it out himself. He aimed a slice at the earl's chest that neatly ripped open Woodford's doublet and set crimson to welling out of the cut.

"My compliments on the quality of your weapons, my lord. This tip is sharp enough to pierce bone, I do believe."

Woodford had no breath for a retort. His face was flushed and glistened with sweat. A cut above his left brow welled scarlet that streaked from temple to jaw.

"I'm not going to kill you . . . today," Hawk told him in an affable voice. "But I'm going to hurt you much worse than you hurt my wife."

"It wasn't my fault!" Woodford panted. "She teased me, the bitch!" He desperately parried a thrust aimed at his groin, and his eyes widened with panic as he realized the full extent of Hawk's intended punishment. "She lured me on, Chester! God, man! Why else would I have gone to your house at midnight? Why else would she have let me in?"

"Because you're a pox-brained bastard, and she's an innocent who's not yet learned to mistrust every face she sees and every word she hears. But she's learning, partly thanks to you!" Hawk's blade sliced low and fast and left a trail of blood angling across the crotch of Woodford's neatly pleated breeches. The earl screamed and doubled over in pain.

Hawk saluted with his crimsoned foil, grim satisfaction twisting his mouth into an unpleasant smile. "Consider your life a gift from the woman you abused. The only reason I don't end your wretched existence is to avoid offending my wife's tender sensibilities. But if you ever so much as look her way again, I'll hang you out for the vultures."

Woodford's screams trailed off into piteous whines. Blood trickled down his thighs. Hawk grinned wolfishly and flicked his blade toward the earl's injured privates. "At least you won't be offending women with that thing anytime soon."

"You bastard!" Woodford managed to moan.

Sir Hubert walked forward and took the blade from Hawk's hand. " 'Twas scarcely the act of an honorable gentleman, my lord. I cannot consider this duel well fought."

"It was fought well enough for my purposes," Hawk replied sharply. "And as for honor—do you hold that forcing oneself upon an unwilling and virtuous woman is an honorable deed, sir?"

Sir Hubert looked indignant. "No slur upon Lady Chester, my lord, but I've seldom known a woman to be either unwilling or virtuous, be they wed or not. A truly virtuous woman is a rare thing."

"Indeed she is," Hawk agreed. He sighed, then quoted,

more to himself than to Sir Hubert, " 'Her price is far above rubies.' " For a moment he let his thoughts wander to Jane. He remembered the tears she had shed in the misery of her shame, the bruises—still ugly and sore after all these days, and then Sir Hubert's smug expression came back into focus. "My wife is one of that rare breed of virtuous women, Sir Hubert, and any man who sullies her reputation or even mentions her name in connection with this affair will feel the bite of my blade. Do I make myself clear?"

Sir Hubert retreated a step at the ferocity of Hawk's tone. "You'll hear no insults from me, my lord."

"Or from him either, I'm guessing." Thomas Waltham nodded toward Woodford as he strolled up and handed Hawk his own sword. Sir Thomas walked a bit stiffly in sympathy with the earl's agony. "Remind me never to cross you, my friend. Your notion of justice is quite poetic. Should we perhaps haul your victim to a physician before he is permanently impaired?"

"Let Sir Hubert take him. Or perhaps there is one here." For the first time he noticed the dim form of two mounted figures behind his coach. "Did you engage a physician to attend the contest, Sir Hubert?"

"No, my lord."

"Then perhaps we should ascertain just who has been our audience this morning."

Sitting like a statue upon her horse, Jane watched Hawk approach. Mounted next to her, Ned shifted uneasily. "We're in fer it now, mistress."

She knew the moment that Hawk recognized her through the fog. Disbelief, then anger tightened his face, but she could feel neither remorse nor dismay. Her senses were sickened to the point of being numb. She had come out of fear for Hawk and a sense of guilt that she was the cause of the whole ugly affair, but she hadn't been prepared for the sight of two men trying to cut each other to pieces. Neither had she been prepared for the spectacle of her husband's calmly savaging his victim, then leaving him to scream and clutch at himself with bloody hands. Even though Woodford's screams had faded to whimpers, they still seemed to echo in her ears.

This was Hawk at his most savage, the man she'd glimpsed from time to time but hoped she'd never truly see. He existed alongside the man who'd saved her life with his gentle care, who'd risked his own life to save his son's, who'd stolen her heart and her body, then sacrificed himself to duty to make her sins right in the eyes of man and God. This grim-faced, narrow-eyed man who stalked toward her with blood on his hands and another man's agony staining his soul was her husband, the man she loved, but suddenly she felt that she didn't know him at all.

"What is the meaning of this?" Hawk growled, looking at Ned.

Ned grimaced. "She would come, 'Awk. She's a determined little lass, and I couldn't keep 'er in without tyin' 'er down."

"Then you should have tied her down, you fool!"

As Hawk turned to her, Jane's stomach clenched, but she met his angry scowl with chin held high.

"What the hell do you think you're doing?"

She let his cursing pass without remark. It seemed mild compared to the fury that burned in his eyes.

"Do you have any notion of the foolishness of your being here?" he demanded.

Jane answered calmly. His anger couldn't touch her; she

was already beyond feeling. "Did you expect me to cower at home while this iniquity took place because of me?"

"This did not take place because of you!"

"But I'm a part of it, am I not?" She looked toward Woodford, whom Sir Hubert was helping to his coach. "Why else would you have done what you did? I asked you not to kill him." Her voice broke momentarily, then she regained control. "I didn't think to ask you not to maim him. I had almost forgotten that you had such . . . such barbarism in you."

"All men are barbarians, rich, poor, gentleman, or peasant. That's something Cromwell taught me—and the merry inhabitants of London's dives and stews."

Hawk couldn't maintain his anger in the face of Jane's dejection. Grief set the rigid lines of her face and darkened the gray of her eyes.

"Woodford will recover, Jane. You needn't grieve for his fate. He got less than he deserved."

"I grieve for you, and for myself," Jane said softly.

Hawk flinched, both at the sorrow in her words and the stab of his own guilt. Now was probably not a good time to tell her that he must leave with Charles for an uninvited visit to Spain to solicit King Philip's assistance. Not a good time at all.

The sun-room glowed with the colorful beams of light that streamed through the stained-glass windows. Jane stood and watched the colors dance as the tree outside the window rustled in the breeze and alternately blocked and passed the sunlight. She would miss this room, with its bright colors, light, and cheer. She would miss the garden with its linden trees and carefully landscaped flower beds.

She would miss Antwerp, its canals, bridges, its old castle and soaring cathedral. Most of all, she would miss Hawk.

She stood still as Ned moved restlessly around the room, picking up a vase here and a candlestick there, as if weighing their value—a habit he'd still not lost. Every few moments his eyes strayed to her, and Jane could sense the disappointment in his gaze. No doubt he thought her disloyal and a quitter. Perhaps he was right.

"I am quite determined," she told him in a firm voice. "If you'll not help me, Ned, then I'll seek help elsewhere. But I will go."

Ned couldn't hurt her with his disgusted expression. Where her heart had once beat was now a hollow, empty shell devoid of feeling. One by one over the last few days she had locked her feelings away, for if she could feel, she would never be able to leave knowing that she might not see Hawk ever again. And she had to leave; no doubt remained in her mind.

Hawk had left to meet Charles the afternoon of his duel with the Earl of Woodford. Jane was not even granted a night to lie in his arms and convince herself that her husband was still the same man whose caress was so gentle— or assure herself that the tight, angry line of his mouth could still soften to the slow smile she loved so much.

Hawk had been gone a week, and it had taken all of that week for Jane to realize she must leave. She loved Hawk; she would always love him. But she could no longer stay where frivolity, immorality, deceit, malice, and violence were a way of life. Nor could she bear for Gideon and the child she carried to be raised in a world where innocence and honesty couldn't survive.

" 'Awk ain't gonna like you leavin'," Ned warned. "Why

don't you just wait until 'e gets back and 'ave a little wifely chat with 'im."

Because he would use her love against her and charm her into staying. Jane knew her own weakness all too well. "A chat isn't going to do any good, Ned. Hawk has a commitment to Charles that he feels he must honor. I have a commitment also."

" 'E's gonna be right mad at you takin' the boy."

"I'm not trying to take Gideon away from him. He can come to Giddy whenever he likes. But I think even Matthew realizes by now that his son will be better off in England with me."

"Could be 'e'll think ye're both better off with *'im*!"

"Then he can leave this nest of intrigue and immorality and join us." He wouldn't, Jane reflected sadly. He would be angry and sad at losing them—especially at losing Gideon. But he would never leave his king and his pursuit of what he had lost—even for Gideon, and Lady Woodford would be eager to comfort him. Jane tried to prevent the beautiful Barbara from intruding into her mind to cause even more grief, but the slut intruded anyway. Hawk had denied that he and Barbara were friends, but Jane had difficulty believing him. "There's no help for it," she told Ned in a sad voice. "I'll go with or without your help."

Ned glowered at her for a moment, but he'd learned long ago that his frowns, fierce as they might be, didn't impress Jane. She stood straight and met his gaze. "Then I suppose it'll be with my 'elp, mistress. You and 'Awk are both barmy fools. I tell you and I'll tell 'im as well. But least I can see ye safe so 'e can go to fetch ye."

Jane smiled, but the smile didn't reach her eyes as once it had. "Thank you, Ned. You're a good friend."

"Fools like ye need good friends," he grumbled. "I'll see

ye to Dunkirk. There's bound to be someone I know shippin' outta there, an' I'll see ye're fixed up. 'Awk'd want ye to go first class—so yer neck'll still be in one piece when 'e comes to wring it."

"I've the money to pay the passage," she told him. "My sister gave me a purse before I left to go chasing after the *Mary Catherine* that morning." That morning so long ago—when she'd had no idea of what awaited her. Tears welled into her eyes at the realization she would soon see Sarah and her children, Grandmother Margaret, good old stolid Geoffrey, the house on Great Queen Street—all things she'd thought were lost to her. Would regaining all those people and things compensate for the loss of Matthew Hawkins?

The journey to Dunkirk was uneventful. Mistress Weston—Millicent, she insisted Jane call her—came along as Jane's companion. Portly, silver-haired, and cheerful, the housekeeper was an effective antidote for Jane's depression. She filled Jane's silences with tales of her own small adventures growing up in Derbyshire—the two husbands she had outlived, her children, now grown and married with children of their own. Thirteen years ago she'd fled England with the royalist family she served—the same year that the youthful Prince Charles had at his doomed father's command fled Penzance for the Scilly Isles and begun his long years of exile. Millicent had always wanted to return but had never had the means.

Ned left them at Dunkirk in the care of a bluff and ruddy-faced merchant captain he knew from his sailing days. Jane offered to pay his passage if he wished to return to England, but Ned admitted the desire to return to his little cook. "I'd just go back to me old ways in London," he told her, "an' Greta don't like me 'abit of priggin' purses.

I've a mind to marry and turn 'onest." The admission came with a shamefaced flush.

"I think you'll make a very fine honest man," Jane said with a fond smile. "Greta is a lucky woman."

" 'Awk won't be 'appy about yer leavin'" were Ned's final words to Jane.

She wasn't happy about it either, nor was Gideon, who, quiet and rather withdrawn since Woodford's assault, had become even more subdued. But Jane was convinced she had chosen the lesser of two evils.

The crossing to England was comfortable and dull. The breezes were steady, the weather bright and warm. Millicent was an amiable companion, and Gideon was well behaved—much too well behaved. Jane was worried. Giddy hadn't objected when Jane told him they were going away for a while and Hawk was not coming with them. "Has Father gone off with the King again?" had been his only question. Then he had agreed in a voice that seemed to Jane much more worldly and mature than it ought to be. "I think it's time we went back to England. Father will come see us there."

Perhaps Hawk would come to see them in England, Jane thought hopefully, if only to see Gideon. She'd not had the chance to tell Hawk that he was soon to be a father again. The time had not been right, and, upset as she was, Jane hadn't found the words. What a surprise he would get if he returned to England. Perhaps knowing about the child would change his priorities. Once away from Charles and his circle, Hawk and Jane might find a place somewhere between his world and hers where they could both be content, where their children could grow up with his lust for life combined with her vision of what was right and good.

An impossible dream. But sea trips were the right place

for impossible dreams. Isolated from the hectic world, surrounded by the beauty of a calm ocean and blue skies, she could dream to her heart's content and not be jolted back to reality until stepping back onto dry land.

They arrived at Three Oaks unannounced, in a hired coach, tired, dirty, and travel worn. Sarah greeted them with cries of delight. Geoffrey was more subdued in his welcome than his wife; the requirements of dignity did not allow for such unrefined displays, and Geoffrey took his dignity very seriously, Jane remembered.

The children were with their tutor, but upon hearing Jane's voice in the parlor, all five of them trooped down the stairs in an undisciplined mob. When he saw them, Gideon's face shone brighter than it had in weeks, and Jane felt a burden lift from her heart.

Jane introduced Millicent Weston and Sarah generously offered the woman a place on her staff. "Don't go stealing her from me," Jane warned her sister. "Millicent has agreed to help me open the house in London. Without her I don't know what I'd do."

"But, Jane, surely you must stay with us! You can't consider leaving again!"

Geoffrey harrumphed into the conversation. "You ladies can discuss that later, I would think. I for one would like to hear what Jane has to say of her adventures."

"Yes, indeed!" Grandmother Margaret's voice rang from the top of the staircase. She descended slowly and regally, great-grandchildren scampering out of her way and Geoffrey and Sarah both watching her with apprehension. "Well, Jane, my girl. What have you to say for yourself?"

"I've a great deal to say for myself, Grandmother, if you'd care to listen."

Jane almost felt like laughing. This was the world she'd

always known—and yet it wasn't. Her grandmother was no longer an intimidating harridan who made her quail; she was merely a rigid old woman to be loved and pitied. Somehow, Sarah seemed but a child, though she was six years Jane's elder, and pompous Geoffrey was slightly ridiculous in his knightly dignity, not the worldly and sophisticated man Jane had once thought him.

Jane had changed from the girl who had so foolishly chased after the *Mary Catherine* at Billingsgate. She was glad of the change, she realized with some surprise. The time she'd been gone had aged her more than just a few months. Grief, frustration, passion, love—they had given her a new knowledge of her own strengths and weaknesses, and Jane supposed that in itself was wisdom of a sort. Hawk had shown her a different kind of paradise from the one she'd learned of in church—and a different kind of hell. She'd run from the second, and in doing so lost the first. How she prayed that she'd done the right thing!

"The stubborn little wench would've gone anyway, 'Awk! Did ye want me to let 'er and the boy to leave on their own an' be prey to thieves and cutthroats along the way?"

"No! I wanted you to keep her here, you miserable son of a whoremonger!"

Ned raised a bushy brow. "No need t'get personal about it. I did me best!"

Hawk paced the length of the room that Jane had named the sun-room, though no sun sent light through the colored windows on this cold and foggy December day. The dreary weather matched Hawk's mood. He was cold, his clothes travel stained and dirty, his body aching with weariness.

For three months Charles had tied him down to help

with the useless palavering with the Spanish. King Philip would not receive them. Neither would Mazarin, the true power in Spain. In the town of Fuenterrabia the Spanish nobility had fawned over Charles for weeks—no help for Charles's cause but balm for his battered ego. The endless receptions, balls, and hunting parties had only made Hawk impatient. He had itched to return to Jane. It was sin to need a woman so much, but Hawk had needed her, wanted her, missed her.

Release had finally come on November 8, when rumors that the English General Monk had declared for the monarchy sent Charles riding to France to see his mother in France. Hawk had risked the King's anger by asking to return to Antwerp. Commenting that such a pretty bride would make any man strain at the bit, Charles had winked and given him leave.

All for this! Jane had gone, taking Gideon with her. She'd left only a letter explaining her reasons. The little fool had gone back to England, straight into the lion's den. How could she have so completely ignored his warnings about Colbert? How could she have dismissed his love?

But then, he'd never told her that he loved her, had he? She'd been miserable, and he'd all but ignored her; frightened, and he'd not taken the time to comfort her; friendless, and he'd hardly spared a moment to spend with her.

"I'm as big a fool as she is," Hawk growled at Ned. "I should've seen this coming, and I left her with you of all people. She wound you right around her little finger, and it's not the first time."

Ned snorted unrepentantly. "Aye, I own she 'as a way o' doin' that. If ye'd have let her wind *you* a time or two, she might not've left. A wife needs to know she's got some influence with 'er husband."

"I suppose you're an expert on wives now that you've married your Greta."

"Aye," Ned claimed. "Wives and women. I knew a bit about 'em e'en before I tied the knot. But, ye bumblin' ass, ye know less about women than ye knew about knife fightin' afore I picked ye outta that alley in Southwark. Ye 'andled the lass all wrong, 'Awk. Ye'll 'ave to admit it."

"I'll be damned if she's going to get away with this. I'm going after her, and when I get her in my hands I'll . . ."

"Ye'll what?" Ned challenged him.

"I'll"—Hawk gusted out a sigh of frustration—"I'll make her sorry she ever left, damn her hide. Then I'll make sure she never leaves again."

Ned chuckled. "That's the lad! But didn't ye say ye're to meet the King in Brussels in a fortnight?"

"Hang the King."

"I imagine there's some what'd like to," Ned commented with a twisted grin.

Hawk stayed in Antwerp only long enough to rest his horse and get a night's sleep. He would do Jane no good if broke his neck on the road or arrived dead on his feet, though even a night's waiting chafed him. She might already have fallen to Colbert's hand. If the colonel saw her . . . Hawk tried to dismiss the chill of foreboding that shook him. Colbert wouldn't dare harm her; he would remember Hawk's promise of retribution and know from their years of association that Hawk would keep it. Colbert wouldn't dare touch her. If he did . . .

Hawk realized suddenly that Jane was his life. The politics of the powerful, his home, his titles, the King himself—nothing was as important as Jane and Gideon. Each ruled his heart in a very different way. Gideon had become an obsession when he was lost to Hawk, and now Jane, lost as well, became an obsession also.

Hawk cursed himself for ever leaving her and cursed her for leaving him. He wondered if he must always lose something before he realized how much it meant to him.

22

December 19, 1659—London

So much time has passed since I organized my thoughts and entered them herein that my pen must creak with disuse. When I am old and read these pages to remember the events of my life, no doubt I will chastise my younger self for this gap, but I will not have forgotten what transpired in those missing months—the adventures, good and bad; the hard lessons that taught me that love transcends barriers of class, religion, and even ideals; the creation of a precious child I never thought to be blessed with; and finally, the sad journey home. How could I forget?

After my time in Antwerp, London seems quite squalid with its muddy, unpaved streets and noxious smells. But now that I am once again established in the house on Great Queen Street, I feel that I have at last come home. Sarah and Grandmother accompanied us from Three Oaks and plan to remain until spring. I welcome their company as well as the presence of Millicent Weston, who has proved to be a jewel not only as a housekeeper but as a companion as well. She is a great comfort to me, being experienced in midwifery and having borne three healthy children of her own. Sarah is also a help, of course.

In truth, I've needed very little help so far. Though the child should be born in February, I carry him quite easily and have not yet become awkward or uncomfortable. Gideon looks forward to having a sister or brother. I have been concerned for him, for he has been remarkably quiet since we returned to England, and that is not like him. I believe he misses his father far more than he admits.

I have mixed feelings about coming home to London. Sarah expected me to remain at Three Oaks, but though she and her family made us very welcome, I felt like an interloper in my sister's home, a prodigal returning home after grievous sins. I must admit upon reflection, however, that I no longer consider my sins so grievous, and I have become very adept at ignoring Grandmother's admonitions to repent. Perhaps Hawk has infected me with his worldliness, but I grow quite weary of the constant examination of conscience and wailing over our shortcomings that the priests encourage. I have happier and more useful occupations for my time. Likewise, I refuse to discard the bright gowns that I brought with me from the Continent. Most of the wardrobe I left behind, for the clothing was, after all, my husband's property, not mine. But I enjoy those several that I kept. I remember how I protested when Matthew bought them, but I confess that even then I admired them. What a shame that I've had to spoil their high style by letting out the waistlines.

Geoffrey insists on providing funds for maintenance of my household until—as he phrases it—my husband returns to England to settle my affairs. I don't know what my future is to be. Matthew must hate me for leaving and taking Gideon, and I cannot expect him to forgive me after such an offense. I miss him dreadfully, I must admit. If he does pursue me, I fear facing his fury. Even more do I fear that he will take Gideon and the babe I will soon bear and leave me behind, as the law permits him to do. But, illogically, I still long to see him once again. I constantly question my decision to leave, but when I look at Gideon and feel the child growing inside me, I know that I could not have left them or myself in that place of violence and sin.

I fear that England's future is as uncertain as my own. Rumors abound that General Monk, who is in Scotland with the only part of the English Army that is not in disarray, has declared for the monarchy—a story I hesitate to credit because the general has in the past spoken so vehemently against the Stuarts. We also hear that the Prince (I have become accustomed once more to calling Charles "Prince" instead of "King," but I did make a few awkward slips when I first returned, nearly sending Grandmother into apoplexy) is visiting his mother in France. No doubt he waits like a lion to pounce upon poor disorganized England. I wonder if Matthew is with him and pray daily for my husband's safety.

Matthew would no doubt be satisfied to see the Puritan way of life dissolving in England. People clamor for Charles's return, though Parliament seems obdurate in refusing to listen. Many of Lord Cromwell's restrictions, though they are still in force, are blithely ignored. Tomorrow night Sarah and I are attending a private musical performance given by a friend of my late husband's. Such a thing would have been unheard of several years ago. Sarah labored long to persuade me to accompany her. I hesitate to go out because my condition has become quite obvious, even though I feel quite well. Grandmother, of course, disapproves heartily—both of the performance and of my attending. Perhaps that is why I finally told Sarah I would go. After all, it is a private performance—not quite the same as appearing in public.

The musical performance was like a trip back in time for Jane, for most of the guests were people she had known through Thaddeus Alexander—many of them army officers and their wives. They greeted her warmly, many remembering Colonel Alexander as a brave officer and fine man. Jane's condition made it obvious that she had remarried. She fielded questions about her husband by explaining tactfully that he was out of the country at the moment. When they assumed he was in Scotland with General Monk, she didn't bother to correct them.

Through the conversations that whirled around her she learned how conditions in the army had deteriorated since Cromwell's death. Morale was low, pay was tardy at best, and at worst, men and officers did not get paid at all. Most of the officers who had served with Thaddeus had returned to private life, and she sensed that the Puritan cause had lost its flavor with these men who had once been willing to kill and be killed for their principles.

The performance itself was less interesting than the socializing. Four ladies with more enthusiasm than talent presented two Italian madrigals by Monteverdi and an English madrigal by Wilbye. Then, accompanied by a harpsichord and a flute, they attempted a series of French *chansons*. Jane was relieved when two Italian musicians took their place and performed several fantasias written for the lyra viol. Their playing was splendid, and Jane's enjoyment was marred only by the uncomfortable feeling that someone's eyes rested upon her rather than on the performers.

Jane looked around with discreet glances but could see no one paying her undue attention. It wasn't until the social time after the performance that she recognized Colonel Colbert. Alarmed, her instinct was to immediately flee. Then she realized that of course it was too late. His eyes had been the ones fretting her during the performance.

Ramrod-straight as ever, Colbert made his way through the crowd and greeted her amiably. "Mistress Jane—or I suppose I should now address you as Lady Chester," he said quietly. "I heard of your marriage through my . . . ah . . . connections. Congratulations, my lady."

Jane looked around uneasily, but Colbert was nothing if not discreet. All were busy with their own conversations. "The title is unnecessary, Colonel. It is certainly not valid in England."

"We can hope that soon it will be," he replied, his thin mouth curved into a conspiratorial smile. "I am surprised to find you here, dear lady. I see your husband is not with you."

Jane felt a chill as she looked into his eyes. She'd not given him a thought in her painful decision to leave Antwerp. Later, when she had recalled that Hawk thought him a danger, she had comforted herself that Colbert would be in Scotland with General Monk. But he wasn't; he was standing right here in front of her, scrutinizing her in a way that made her skin crawl.

"Do you know where your husband is, my lady?"

"Matthew is with Charles," Jane replied uneasily, "so I imagine you know better than I exactly where he is."

"Perhaps," he admitted. "But, wherever he is, I wonder why you are not with him."

Jane sensed an ominous tone to Colbert's words. She decided to be forthright. "Colonel Colbert, Matthew told me of your concerns, and I would put them to rest. You need not fear my revealing your . . . connections with my husband."

He lifted a brow in surprise. "I never did have such a fear, my lady. Why should I?"

"I . . . that is, my husband—"

Colbert interrupted her with soft laughter. "What did the rogue tell you?"

"He simply said you thought I might compromise your safety."

"And then he told you that you must stay with him?" the colonel asked with a smile. "One must admire the scoundrel. No doubt he told you I villainously threatened your life if you were to return. Not very original, but then, the tale did get him what he wanted." He shot a meaningful look at Jane's swelling belly and chuckled.

Jane colored.

"Oh, don't be embarrassed, my dear. Hawk was very much taken with you, and a man must sometimes resort to subterfuge to gain the advantage with a woman, you know."

Right then Sarah came up to them. "Jane dear, I've just had the most interesting conversation with Lady Hopewell. I . . . oh!" She noticed Colbert, who had snapped to silence at Sarah's presence. "Am I intruding?"

"No, Sarah. Not at all. Let me present Colonel Colbert, a friend of"—she caught Colbert's stony look and almost bit her tongue—"Colonel Alexander's." She had almost identified him as a friend of Hawk's, which would have truly let the cat out of the bag. Perhaps the poor man should be concerned for his safety after all. "Colonel, may I introduce my sister, Lady Winford."

Colbert greeted her stiffly. "My pleasure."

"So pleased to meet you, Colonel Colbert. I did intrude —a frightful habit of mine, as my sister will tell you. Do please forgive me. I shan't talk your arm off—another habit, I fear. I shall just leave you two to reminisce, but we should leave shortly, Jane, so don't tarry overlong."

"I'm sorry," Jane said in quiet apology.

"No harm done." His eyes told Jane that he was very well aware of the slip she had almost made. "Did you say that your husband is with Charles?"

"Yes."

Pity flashed in his eyes. "Since you seem to be in fine spirits, I assume you've not gotten the news." His thin lips tightened. "Or perhaps you simply don't care."

"News?" Jane felt a stirring of alarm.

Colbert looked around them. The other guests were beginning to leave and file past them on their way to the door. "I fear this is a story that can't be told at a gathering such as this. Too many interested ears."

"Colonel Colbert! Has something happened to my husband?"

He shook his head at her, urging a more discreet voice. "I don't know," he said quietly. "I will tell you all that I do know, but not here, where we both may be overheard by those whose sympathies lie elsewhere. Meet me tomorrow at St. Paul's." He saw her start to answer, then hesitate. "It's a very public place, my lady. No need for you to fear for your reputation, or anything else. Perhaps together we can think of a way to help your rogue of a husband."

* * *

Hawk arrived in London on one of Geoffrey's fine saddle horses, cursing himself for the time he'd wasted going to Three Oaks. Every hour's delay chafed. The longer Jane was in London, the more likely she would fall afoul of Colbert.

At the house on Great Queen Street, Millicent opened the door to Hawk's pounding. "Lord Chester!" she exclaimed, then she stammered, "I . . . we . . ."

"It's all right, Mistress Weston. You may remove that bedeviled look from your face. I've come to talk to my wife, not throttle her."

She moved aside, wide-eyed, as he stepped through the door. "Where is my lady?"

"She's—"

"Not in!" Grandmother Margaret's voice cut sharply across the housekeeper's answer as the old woman stiffly descended the stairs. "So you've come," she shot at Hawk. "I was beginning to hope we'd seen the last of you. Have you returned to make trouble for my granddaughter?"

Hawk faced the old dragon with a mocking smile. "Your granddaughter is quite accomplished at making trouble for herself, Grandmother."

Margaret's mouth tightened into a lipless slash at the implied relationship.

"Now, ladies, where is my wife?"

"She's gone out to see—"

"Shut your mouth, Millicent! Mistress *Alexander's* whereabouts are none of this ruffian's business."

Hawk's mouth quirked up in a wry smile at the old lady's stubbornness. Millicent looked at him helplessly.

"Then I shall simply wait for . . . Mistress Hawkins," he told them, emphasizing the last name.

Margaret's face grew a furious red. "My granddaughter's

disgraceful marriage will never be acknowledged in *this* family, sir! You're the Devil incarnate—a scoundrel, rogue, cur, and villain."

"Thank you." He bowed sardonically. "I've been told much the same by your granddaughter, among others. But if I were your Devil incarnate, old woman, then you wouldn't be standing there to curse me. You'd have gone up in a poof of flame and sulphur even as you first opened your mouth." He threw her an insolent smile and strolled into the parlor. "I'll make myself comfortable here until my wife returns."

He had just seated himself in Colonel Alexander's favorite armchair by the fireplace when Gideon appeared at the top of the stairway. The boy bounced down the stairs with a gleeful shriek.

"You get back upstairs this minute!" Margaret snapped.

Giddy ignored the old woman and bounded into the parlor. "Father! I knew you'd come! I knew it! I heard a man's voice, and I knew it was you!"

Hawk rose from his chair and braced himself just in time for his son to attack him with a wild embrace. He gave Giddy a firm hug, then set him back at arm's length to look at him. "Have you been taking care of Jane?"

"Aye, sir! But she's been sad. We missed you awfully! Nothing was the same without you. There was nothing to smile or laugh about."

Hawk touched Giddy's cheek. "I missed you too, son. I didn't have anything to smile about either."

"Mother said you were in France, or maybe in Brussels!"

"She was wrong, wasn't she? I'm right here."

"I knew you would come! Do you want to meet my new tutor? He's awfully nice, and he doesn't talk about sinning all day."

"I'm glad to hear that," Hawk said with a smile. "I'll meet him later and he can tell me all what you've been doing. But right now I'd like to see your mother."

"She's out."

"Where?"

Margaret thundered like a sixty-gun man-of-war, "Be silent, Gideon! Come here at once!"

Giddy didn't flick an eyelash toward the old lady. "She went to meet a man named Colbert—because he knew something about you. Mother was very worried."

Hawk stiffened. "Where is she meeting him, Giddy?"

"I . . . I don't know."

He turned to look at Margaret. "Where is Jane meeting Colonel Colbert?"

Margaret's face was set in stone. Millicent stood in the parlor doorway and wrung her hands.

Hawk's fists clenched. His eyes turned to flint, but his voice was quiet, dropping heavily into the silence of the cold parlor. "Tell me where she is, or you'll lose her. You may have already lost her."

Margaret merely drew her mouth into a tighter line.

"Tell me!" Hawk demanded of the old woman. His voice was still low, but the undercurrent of anger made Gideon back away from the force of it. "Tell me or, by God, madam, I'll make your Devil incarnate look tame!"

"St. Paul's!" Millicent cried. She ignored Margaret's hiss of anger. "She told me before she left. She's meeting him in the nave at St. Paul's!"

Jane arrived at St. Paul's with dread sitting like a lead weight upon her stomach. Hawk must be in grievous trouble, elsewise Colbert wouldn't have spoken so gravely. She'd spent the whole night imagining terrible things that might have come to pass and therefore hadn't slept a wink. Sarah had advised her not to come. She didn't trust a man with such thin lips, she'd said illogically, and the remark had made Jane remember Hawk's warnings. Were his warnings about Colbert lies to keep her with him? Such a thing was just like Hawk.

The churchyard and nave both were loud and crowded, littered with beggars, merchants, apprentices, tradesmen, cutpurses, and even a nobleman or two. Geese were being sold at the entrance to the nave, and just across the grandly arched door two whores dangled their bait for a customer. The nave itself was dim and gray, cut through by slanting pillars of light that descended from the high windows. Everywhere were clots of people. An old woman sold chickens in the center aisle. On the steps to the altar five soldiers in stained and worn uniforms rolled dice. Stumbling drunkenly from pew to pew, a scarred man with one eye made his way through the crowd. Jane just caught the wink of a blade in his hand, and realized he'd cut a purse. She shivered and looked around for Colbert.

"My lady."

She turned. Colbert was behind her. He didn't look the military man today; his appearance was quite elegant—short-waisted doublet with the lower buttons unfastened to reveal a shirt of finest silk and lace, an elaborate falling-band collar of snowy white, ruffles of lace dripping from his wrists and knee garters, and a wide-brimmed hat of finest beaver, one side cocked up, the other side sporting two elegant ostrich plumes. In his boot was stuck a fine-tooled riding quirt with an ornate silver handle bearing what Jane assumed was a family crest. Altogether, he looked every inch the grand gentleman. Beside him Jane felt quite conspicuously plain in dark blue silk with a modest bertha concealing her neck and shoulders and the linen chaperon loosely falling about her head.

"You look lovely, my dear." Colbert made a leg and swept off his hat. "Shall we walk a ways? Perhaps you would feel more at ease in the yard. There's some prophet haranguing from the cross for the return of the King. That should make us both feel more the thing."

Jane gingerly laid her hand upon his gallantly offered arm. "If you don't mind, Colonel, I really mustn't linger long. What is it you have to tell me?"

"So straightforward and businesslike," Colbert complained. "Really, Lady Chester, if you are to take your place in Charles's court, you must learn to play the conversation game. Come, let us walk. Stuck to this spot we are much too conspicuous."

As they strolled up the aisle, Colbert neatly sidestepped a chicken that had escaped its cage. Jane brushed her skirts aside as a whore cackled and reached out to touch the silk of her gown. Beyond the whore the one-eyed cutpurse stared at them, his eye bright with calculation. Jane's unease grew. She didn't like the crowd, or Colonel Colbert. Sarah had been right; she shouldn't have come.

"I fear we are a bit conspicuous in any case, Colonel. Please, tell me what tidings you have. I dread to hear bad news, and yet I must know."

"How devoted you are to your husband. Or is it the King who concerns you so?" They reached the front of the nave and drifted to one side, near the colonnaded gallery where the crowd was thinner. He pulled the quirt from his boot and fiddled with the silver handle, which came off to reveal a sharp-pointed tip. "I noticed you were admiring this. I picked it up in France many years ago. Clever people, the French. Look at this tip—"

"Jane! Jane! Get away!"

Jane heard her name faintly above the bustle and noise of the crowd. She turned. The blood drained from her face; she thought she was dreaming.

Hawk's gut twisted with despair. He was too far away, and now Colbert was alerted, but there was no time for stealth. The quirt in Colbert's hand had a tip covered with the concentrated poison of the wolfsbane plant. A mere scratch would lead to nausea, loss of vision, paralysis, and, inevitably, death within a few hours. Hawk had seen the colonel use the same trick before. It was a neat way to do murder inconspicuously, with no blame attached. A lethal dose delivered by a scratch; the murderer leaves before the symptoms appear, and the victim becomes ill for no apparent reason and quickly dies.

"Jane! Get away from him! The quirt is poisoned!" Hawk was drawing stares, but he didn't care. The only eyes he cared about were Jane's, and even at this distance, pushing his way through the crowd, he could see them widen in surprise. Then she gave Colbert a frightened look and started to step away from him. The colonel was too quick for her. Cursing, he grabbed her arm and backed with her into the shadows beyond the columns. Hawk jabbed and pushed his way through the crowd to follow.

"Stay right there, damn you!" Colbert warned as Hawk grabbed at a column to stop his momentum. "Come closer, my friend, and your sweet wife dies." He breathed hard as he met Hawk's lethal stare, slowly regaining his cool demeanor. "Damned inconsiderate of you to show up at this particular moment. You've quite spoiled my careful plans."

Jane stood rigidly still, her eyes fixed upon Hawk.

"Touch her with that tip and you're a dead man, Colbert."

"So I would gather. That's a conclusion to this affair that certainly doesn't please me. But most likely if I let her go I'll be just as dead. I know you, Hawk. You're a vengeful man." His mouth stretched into a sinister grin. "I don't think you can kill me, but I think you'll try, whatever your lady's fate. So we have a stalemate, do we not?"

They were attracting a few stares, but not many. Hawk had heard it said more than once that murder could be done at St. Paul's and never noticed. Now he knew it was true. He carefully pushed himself away from the pillar. "There's no need for this, Colbert. Jane couldn't hurt you, even if she tried. Monk has declared for the monarchy and is on his way from Scotland. Charles has won. You'll be honored for your loyalty to the King, not hanged."

Colbert snorted. Jane closed her eyes fearfully. "If you believe Monk, then you're a fool. The man's an unpredictable bastard. He'll declare for Charles one day and the next he'll have the King's head on a stake if he attempts to set foot in England. It would be just like him to hang a few royalists to placate anyone uneasy over his shifting loyalties. And he particularly doesn't like spies. No, my friend. I can't afford to be exposed. Not even now."

Hawk's face tightened. "Jane wouldn't expose you."

"There isn't a woman alive who doesn't talk too much, including this one. She almost gave me away only last night. I warned you of her fate should she return, Hawk. Nothing has occurred to change my mind."

"I'll take her out of the country."

Colbert laughed. "I've seen how effective you are at keeping her under your thumb."

Hawk gauged the distance between him and Colbert,

wondering desperately if he could lunge for the colonel and knock him away before the bastard could harm Jane. The risk was great, but he didn't know what else to do.

Then a miracle happened. A disfigured but familiar face appeared in the shadows of the gallery behind and to one side of Colbert and Jane—One-Eye Carey, a vision from Hawk's ignoble past who might be the savior of his future. Hawk saw a spark of surprised recognition in the cutpurse's eyes. An ironic smile twisted Hawk's mouth. Bless Carey for being a conscientious cutpurse and following a wealthy-looking gull into the shadows of the nave. He hoped the rogue remembered their thieving days together as well as Hawk did.

"Now, Hawk," Colbert said. "I'm going to leave and take your lady with me. Make a move, my friend, and she dies. Once she and I stroll down the street a ways and you're out of sight, I'll let her go—provided you'll give your word to take her out of the country and stay there until you return with Charles. It's not a situation I'm happy with, but since you're set on having my hide for hers, I suppose I must relent."

Hawk saw the lie in Colbert's eyes; he was practiced enough at lying to recognize the look of falsehood when he saw it. The colonel would most likely kill Jane, then turn Hawk over to the authorities to protect his own neck.

"I'll take her out of the country," Hawk agreed.

Colbert started to move, dragging Jane along in casual but deadly embrace and tapping the deadly quirt against his boot. He grinned at Hawk. "We were a good team, Hawkins. It's a shame to end it because of a woman."

Hawk was silent. He shrugged almost imperceptibly and turned the palm of his left hand toward the retreating Colbert, praying that Carey was still watching and that the scoundrel remembered the signals they'd arranged between them when Hawk, Ned, and One-Eye Carey were a thieving trio in the crowds of St. Paul's.

"Don't come any closer," Colbert warned as Hawk took a step toward the retreating pair. Jane's face was stony, set in a determined effort at courage.

"It's all right, Jane," Hawk said quietly.

She threw him a desperate look, just as a lurching cutpurse wove his way from the colonnaded gallery and stumbled into Colbert and his victim.

"Sh . . . sorry, m'lord!"

Colbert snarled, but he hadn't time to launch a curse upon the miscreant, for the moment his attention was diverted Hawk lunged for the pair, pushed Jane away, and grabbed the wrist of the hand that held the quirt. With his other hand he neatly lifted Colbert's fat purse and tossed it to Carey. "My thanks, comrade."

Carey saluted and watched with interest as Hawk pushed Colbert into the shadows of a column. The two men struggled in a quiet contest of strength as Hawk slowly turned the deadly tip of the quirt toward Colbert.

"Matthew! No!" Jane pleaded. "Leave him to God."

The horrified note in her voice brought Hawk's fury under control. Colbert might deserve death, but Hawk couldn't afford to bring the authorities down upon his head. Nor would Jane ever look at him with anything but horror if he killed Colbert in cold blood. "I'll leave him to the Devil is more likely!" He tightened his hand around the colonel's wrist. Colbert's gasp accompanied the crack of bones, and the quirt dropped to the floor to be crushed beneath Hawk's boot.

"One-Eye!" Hawk called.

"Aye?" The cutpurse ambled from the safe corner from where he had watched the action.

"My lady suggests I leave this piece of silk-clad offal to God, but I think God might be too busy for such a trivial matter. Do you think your mates in Southwark might give Colonel Colbert the greeting he deserves?"

Carey's one eye lit with glee as he grasped Hawk's meaning. "We'd give 'im a merry welcome!"

"So I thought." Hawk smiled grimly, remembering his fate when he had stumbled into Southwark clad in silks and velvet.

Colbert slowly straightened, his face white with pain. "The Hawk's wings have been clipped," he sneered, lips curled in contempt. "And by a woman. You've no longer the stomach for blood."

"Aye," Hawk acknowledged cheerfully. "But my claws are still sharp, Colbert. If you manage to crawl out of Southwark, you may find out how sharp. But at least I've given you a chance to survive—if you're clever."

Tight-lipped, Colbert straightened his spine with military rigidity as One-Eye grasped his arm. The cutpurse's little knife flashed, then disappeared into the folds of the colonel's silk shirt.

Hawk grinned. "You've done me a great service today, One-Eye. I'm in your debt."

Carey's mouth twitched up as he patted the bulge of Colbert's purse. "No, me friend. I'm in your debt. 'Ow about a celebration of sausages and ale back at the Lion. Yer lidy too."

"Not today, One-Eye."

"Aye, then," Carey said with a grin. "I see you've got yer lidy to see to. I'll give yer greetin's to Moll. She'll be right pleased to 'ear ye ain't lost yer touch."

With a prod of the knife One-Eye urged his prisoner toward the nave door. "Thank'ee again, 'Awk."

Jane swayed, her eyes bright with tears she valiantly tried not to shed. Hawk gathered her against his chest, heedless of the ring of eyes that had turned their way. "I found you in time," he whispered. "Now I believe in miracles."

"Matthew." His name was fragile and soft on her lips.

Hawk turned her chin up to so that she met his eyes. "And I see now we've another miracle to thank God for." He gently moved her back and ran appreciative eyes over her ripe figure. "And to think I didn't even notice when I first saw you here with Colbert. Ah, Jane. My love." He pulled her back into his embrace.

She hid her face against Hawk's doublet. Her shoulders heaved under his stroking hands.

"Don't cry, love. It's over now."

"Oh, Matthew," she choked out. "I'm not crying. I can't stop laughing. You came. I can't believe you came."

He grinned wickedly. "Don't you believe in miracles?"

"I . . . oh, my!" She was seized by another paroxysm of laughter.

Hawk heard the hysteria in her voice. He shook her gently. "You should know by now that I don't relinquish something—or someone—who belongs to me." He wiped her streaming cheeks with a handkerchief.

"Is . . . is that why you came? We belong to you, Gideon and I."

"No." He brushed a stray lock of hair into her coif, and noted with amusement that the headpiece was no longer the plain linen cap she once had favored, but a lacy thing that scarcely concealed her golden glory. "I came because you—and Gideon—are the most important things in my world. I love you. You're my life."

A giggle became a sob. "Oh, Matthew, I . . ."

"You had better say that you love me, too. I came a long way to hear it."

"I do love you. I think I've loved you forever."

Hawk smiled. One brow rose into a devilish arch. "I think we should go home and talk about this in private."

When they got back to the house on Great Queen Street, Hawk directed Millicent to take Margaret shopping.

"Buy something to cheer yourself, Grandmother." He ignored the old lady's indignant sputtering. "Take Gideon, too."

Jane gave him a puzzled look. "Gideon doesn't need anything, Matthew. What are—"

His grin silenced her. A rosy blush crawled up her neck and into her cheeks.

"There's nothing that revives a woman like buying something, and Grandmother's going to need a lot of reviving when she learns how much I'm going to be around in the future," he told Millicent. "Besides, my wife and I need to be alone."

"Matthew, really!" Jane chided him as the housekeeper herded her charges out the door, Margaret glowering and Gideon grinning from ear to ear.

Hawk silenced her objections by kissing her with slow, languorous deliberation. "Is there a fire burning in the grate of your bedchamber?"

"Matthew!" She colored. "I'm as big as a barn."

"Don't worry." He nuzzled her neck, and she began to melt. "I'm very ingenious. We'll think of a way."

She pulled back from him, her eyes soft. "Husband, what are we to do with each other?"

He grinned. "Come up to the bedchamber and I'll think of something."

"Matthew! You know what I mean."

Sobering, he sighed. "Yes, my love, I know what you mean. I'll tell you what we will do with each other. We'll treat each other with kindness and tender care and live happily ever after." He saw disbelief in her eyes. "I'll even reform."

"You're lying again."

Hawk gave her a crooked smile. "Maybe. I suppose I'll always prefer Shakespeare to Matthew, Mark, Luke, and John. But I'll promise not to be a complete scoundrel—and I'll be a faithful husband to you and a good father to Gideon and . . ." He sent a meaningful glance toward her stomach.

Jane's eyes softened. "I suppose I can live with that."

He raised a brow in surprise at her lack of argument. "Are you going mellow on me, Jane?"

"Perhaps I've learned a little mellowing isn't such a bad thing."

Hawk touched her cheek with a finger. "We'll make do. I'll buy the property Geoffrey wants to sell in Kent. Then you can be close to Sarah." A sparkle of mischief lighted his eyes. "I'll become a gentleman farmer and boss my tenants about. We'll raise a passel of children and fine horses and create a paradise all our own. I'm halfway to paradise already, my love, just touching you."

"Only halfway?" Jane teased, her eyes falling to the swelling at his groin.

"Perhaps more than halfway," Hawk admitted with a grin. "Shall we go the rest of the way?"

Jane's mouth curved into a gentle smile. "I think so." She took the arm her husband offered and followed him up the stairs.

Epilogue

November 9, 1660—Crescent Park, Hampshire
Dearest Sarah,

 I do apologize for having let so much time pass without writing. You should not feel singled out by my neglect, however, for I've not written regularly in my journal, either. I've little enough time keeping track of Gideon and little Rachel Olivia, and Matthew, also, is very demanding of my attention.

 We are all well and happy. Gideon has settled in nicely with his new tutor. Hawk wouldn't dream of sending him off to school just yet, and neither would I. After all, Gideon has just regained his father; it would be cruel to send him away. Besides, we take such joy in watching him grow.

 Rachel Olivia gets more beautiful with every passing week. I believe I want ten more just like her. We've engaged a very competent nursemaid to preside over the nursery, but I insist on seeing to much of her care myself. It is not a chore, but a joy. Perhaps if God grants me a dozen babies I will willingly relinquish their care to a nurse, but I doubt it even then.

 Our continued happiness seems nothing less than a miracle to me. Who would have guessed that two such ill-suited people could find contentment in marriage? The King has been back in England for four months now and Matthew has shown no desire to go to court—except, of course, for a formal visit to thank His Majesty for restoring his titles and properties and granting him the new title of marquess. I remember well that day in May—Rachel Olivia's third-month celebration day—when we were all together at Three Oaks and the messenger from Lawrence Sheffield rode in with the news that Parliament had formally requested Charles's return to take the throne of England. I've never seen such a sour face as the expression Grandmother wore when she realized that Puritan rule was finally and irrevocably over. Little did I realize what it would mean for Matthew and me. I was so looking forward to moving into the house we had built on the property Geoffrey sold us —and being so close to you and your family. But of course the Marquess of Cressley is expected to take up residence in the old marquess's seat (how fortunate the old man passed away peacefully before Charles could snatch the title from him to bestow upon Matthew. I would have hated to benefit from the King's vengeance on such a staunch Puritan, even though Charles accused him of being one of the regicides.) Though I would still rather be in Kent, Crescent Park is lovely, I must admit, just a bit overwhelming to one not accustomed to being mistress of such a place.

Matthew seems content to run his estates (he says the new lands in Surrey and Gloucester the King granted him have great potential), watch his children grow, and see to his wool business in London, though I fear that last suffered greatly from his four-year absence. He also is expanding his talent as an artist, drawing portraits of me, the children, and anyone else who dares present his or her face at Crescent Park.

I myself am very content, having discovered that Matthew and I can have somewhat different beliefs and occasional disagreements and still love each other dearly. I do miss you, though, dear Sarah. I hope we can pay you and Geoffrey a long visit next summer, when the roads are not so clogged with mud. Gideon will be happy to see Melissa. (I think he misses her, despite his protests to the contrary). And I will be happy to spend some time in our new house that we lived in for only three short weeks.

Grandmother sends her greetings to you and your children. She is quite in awe of Matthew's lofty rank, I believe, because she scarcely says a word to either my husband or me about the "laxity" of our household and the "worldliness" of our clothing and manners. She is very good with Rachel Olivia, and I think that underneath her rigid exterior, she actually likes Matthew. He could charm the horns off the Devil himself if he set his mind to it, and he seems to have set himself the task of mellowing the dragon.

As I sit at my escritoire and look out the window at the green parkland that is now my home, I marvel at how I could have come through the last two years alive. Matthew once said that knowing me made him believe in miracles. God has given us both so many miracles—one right after another, it seems. But the good Lord has given us all the miracles we need, I hope. Matthew and I should be able to take care of the rest.

Your loving sister—

Jane

Experience the Passion and the Ecstasy

Meagan McKinney

- ☐ 16412-5 No Choice But
  Surrender $4.99

- ☐ 20301-5 My Wicked
  Enchantress $4.99

- ☐ 20521-2 When Angels Fall $4.99

- ☐ 20870-X Till Dawn Tames
  the Night $4.99

- ☐ 21230-8 Lions and Lace $4.99